A Fire Born of Exile

By Aliette de Bodard

Dominion of the Fallen
The House of Shattered Wings
The House of Binding Thorns
The House of Sundering Flames

The Universe of Xuya
The Red Scholar's Wake
A Fire Born of Exile

A Fire Born of Exile

ALIETTE DE BODARD

First published in Great Britain in 2023 by Gollancz
an imprint of The Orion Publishing Group Ltd
Carmelite House, 50 Victoria Embankment
London EC4Y 0DZ

An Hachette UK company

1 3 5 7 9 10 8 6 4 2

Copyright © Aliette de Bodard 2023

The moral right of Aliette de Bodard to be identified as
the author of this work has been asserted in accordance with
the Copyright, Designs and Patents Act of 1988.

All rights reserved. No part of this publication may be
reproduced, stored in a retrieval system, or transmitted
in any form or by any means, electronic, mechanical,
photocopying, recording, or otherwise, without the
prior permission of both the copyright owner and the
above publisher of this book.

All the characters in this book are fictitious,
and any resemblance to actual persons, living
or dead, is purely coincidental.

A CIP catalogue record for this book
is available from the British Library.

ISBN (HB) 978 1 473 22343 1
ISBN (Export Trade PB) 978 1 399 61306 4
ISBN (eBook) 978 1 473 22345 5
ISBN (audio) 978 1 409 17717 3

Typeset by Deltatype Ltd, Birkenhead, Merseyside

Printed in Great Britain by Clays Ltd, Elcograf S.p.A.

www.gollancz.co.uk

1
The Tiger Games

Minh had carefully thought out her disguise for the Tiger Games. She'd planned every detail of her physical and virtual appearance, selecting clothes with embroidery that was highly realistic, and an avatar that included fine dragons' antlers around her face and slowly whirling galaxies on her chest and back – the work was rough and detailed, clearly produced by automated routines or a new designer's brush. The bots on Minh's shoulders and wrists were middle of the range: spider-like and designed for show more than practicality, their crown of sensors glittering with jade and silver inserts, and their multiple legs beautiful and fragile, unable to really withstand any kind of exposure to vacuum. There was nothing that would signal Minh as anything other than an ordinary candidate – a scholar without much money awaiting yet another opportunity to successfully pass the imperial examinations. She'd disguised her authentication token, making it look like a student's. There was nothing that would suggest her mother was the prefect of the Scattered Pearls Belt – one of its foremost and most powerful dignitaries, her shadow following Minh everywhere she went, tainting every interaction she had.

Unfortunately, Minh and her friend *The Fruit of Heart's Sorrow* hadn't been out for more than a couple of centidays before she made her first mistake.

'One, please,' she said to a seller of steamed buns, a bot descending to circle her wrist.

The seller – an auntie who must have already been old during the Ten Thousand Flags Uprising and who had a stall in the Harmonious Dream marketplace – looked at Minh, frowning.

'What did you say?' she asked.

'One, please,' Minh said, slowly and loudly.

The seller was still frowning, looking at Minh, and at *Heart's Sorrow* next to her.

'What's the problem?' *Heart's Sorrow* asked.

He'd already strolled on further ahead into the crowds: now he blinked, making his avatar reappear next to Minh. He had the advantage of being a mindship: his body was parked in orbit around the asteroids, and he was projecting his avatar into the habitats, without having to worry about a physical layer. He'd modified his usual small likeness of his own body to depict a merchant transport, a much larger and bulkier ship, and masked his auth-token. In physical layers he was only large enough for a three-person crew: he was one of the newer, smaller generation of mindships, better suited to the transport of goods than of troops.

The seller was looking at them both with growing suspicion – and any moment now Minh was going to see it: the fear and the craven desire to please them, or rather, to please their parents through them. What had they done wrong? They'd both changed their appearance, physical and virtual; they'd taken care to work on their body language ... she asked her bots to play back the scene that had just occurred, looking for ...

Oh.

Their accents. Not only was hers pure Serpent diaspora, the one all her tutors had drilled into her, emulating the imperial court on the First Planet, it was entirely wrong for a scholar without means. What could she do? There had to be something...

A distraction, and a correction.

She pitched her voice lower. 'Sorry, I wasn't clear. Make that three buns, with pork. And overlay one for my friend here. We're meeting friends later. Bit of a busy festival?' As she spoke, she shifted the vowels and pitch of her words, moving seamlessly into something far lower class.

The seller cocked her head. She looked for a moment as though she wanted to argue with Minh, but she gave up. Not worth the trouble.

'As good as it can be, I guess. Too many people still afraid the Uprising will come back. Too many imperial soldiers – *they* don't pay market prices for street food.'

'Well, that's my first mother covered,' *Heart's Sorrow* said to Minh via their private comms channel. 'Hope she's not going to cover yours, too.'

Heart's Sorrow's first mother was the Peach Blossom Lake General, the military administrator of the Belt.

'It'd be a good distraction,' Minh said.

The mindship was joking, but he was tense, and she didn't need that to be obvious. Neither of them had, per se, permission to sneak out in disguise.

'There.' The seller handed Minh her pork buns. 'Enjoy the festival!'

'Thank you, elder aunt,' Minh said.

The bot on her wrist sent money to the seller, and then she and *Heart's Sorrow* were on their way.

'So much for our plan,' *Heart's Sorrow* said. His nervousness made him sarcastic.

Minh made a face. 'I could quote you Tôn Tử's *Military Lessons* on plans.'

They both knew them by heart – the Old Earth strategist, the one from a dead planet the scholars nevertheless insisted on teaching as though he was one of their own ancestors, as deserving of worship as they were.

Heart's Sorrow laughed, but it had an edge. 'Don't. That's dreadfully boring.'

'Boring the same way we are?' It was Minh's voice that had the edge now.

Their first mothers were a general and a prefect, Serpents so senior their origins had ceased to matter. Minh and *Heart's Sorrow* had grown up in a rarefied circle of the wealthy and influential, their paths in life determined as surely as if a fated thread had been pulling them in. Safeguarded, sheltered, privileged.

Preserved as carefully as dead things in scholars' display cabinets.

'Oh, shush,' *Heart's Sorrow* said.

He was eating his virtual pork bun: a skilful aggregation of layers that would trigger pleasant memories. Minh bit into hers. It felt like drowning, her mouth full of over-flavourful cotton, a riot of conflicting tastes from crumbly egg to the sweetness of the pork.

'Come on,' *Heart's Sorrow* said, floating further into the crowd, the sheen on his hull flashing under the lights of the habitat. 'We're going to miss the best of it!'

Minh followed him, away from the Harmonious Dream marketplace and the wide plaza, with its stalls spread under the overlay of the whole Scattered Pearls Belt – into smaller and smaller spaces, corridors crammed with people, mindships and humans both, a riot of avatars wearing shimmering fabrics in multiple layers both physical and virtual – and not just humanoid or ship ones, but kỳ lân and lions and mixtures of organic and electronic with multiple legs and elongated bodies, scales and fur, and the sheeny, oily light of deep spaces on human skin. Every few measures marked a new ambient poem or music from zither to flute, a new environment. Minh was surprised, again and again, as sight and sound and smells abruptly changed, an all-out, all-invasive feast of sounds that threatened to drown her at any moment, an utter exhilaration in every bone of her body, every pore of her skin.

It was everything she'd dreamed of. Not tame, not sterile – as vibrantly alive as the pulsing stars, and utterly uncaring of who Minh was. A person whose avatar was briny mist pushed against Minh – their touch a spray of cold water that smelled of pandanus and salt – and then they were on their way down the corridor. And then another one, with metal arms bristling with bots, and a mindship, bringing with them the fractured coldness of deep spaces – and another and another in a ceaseless dance. Minh laughed. *This* – this was freedom. This was wildness. She could dance and scream and no one would think twice or be afraid of her.

This was like finally filling her lungs after too long holding her breath.

'Come on!' *Heart's Sorrow* said.

He was ahead, so far away Minh could only see him in a tracking overlay, his position a blinking marker over the variegated crowd. Obviously he would be above everyone; his only physical footprint was the cluster of bots in the shadow of his avatar.

Ahead was a slightly larger space in front of a series of compartments: the sort of space that would usually be claimed by a middle-sized lineage. Now it was filled by a crowd in front of a huge public overlay, an enhanced-depth opening showing the Tiger Games arena. As Minh wended her way through the crowd, struggling to join *Heart's Sorrow* near the front, the view in the overlay moved, panning over the higher tiers of the arena, and Minh had a moment of nausea as she saw Mother in the prefect's private space, wearing the jade belt and tasselled hat of her rank. A blink only, and then it had moved on, showing the other dignitaries, but for that single moment it felt – overlay, perception adjustments and all – as though she stood not an arm's length away from Mother, close enough to see the disapproval on her face.

Or worse, the disappointment.

A touch, on her hand: one of *Heart's Sorrow*'s bots, nestling into the crook of her palm, the sharp, pulsing warmth of its legs steadying her. She glanced at her friend; he was beside her with absolutely no hint of anything in his posture.

'Thanks,' Minh said.

'Pff,' *Heart's Sorrow* said. 'Don't spend days preparing for this outing, and then waste it all on *her*.'

He didn't need to say who he meant. Sometimes, she envied him so much it hurt like someone twisting a fist into her belly. He seemed to have taken his own first mother's measure early on: he loved her but didn't expect her to be anything more than she was – status-obsessed, always yielding and taking the easy way, always seeking to make herself attractive to the powerful. Minh wished she had his clarity when it came to her own mother, who was sharp, navigating politics and calling in favours as easily as she breathed, extending the shadowed cloak of her protection to her intimates and subordinates. But sharpness also meant cruelty, and distance, and ...

And, sometimes, Minh felt scared that Mother just didn't love her.

The bot bit into her skin.

'Hey!'

'You're daydreaming! Look!'

On the screen, the first of the Tigers was coming in, next to their data artist. It was a huge, translucent beast with five pairs of iridescent wings, a maw large enough to swallow suns, with diamond fangs and glittering eyes – a sleek, smooth shape like an atmospheric shuttle, meant to cut through the air, the wings sharp and gorgeous weapons. It moved fast, seemingly answering the least of the data artist's commands, their fingers twitching as the Tiger moved.

Their opponent was closer to the old earth animal: a huge, faint mist that suggested stripes, and the vague idea of fire. Its data artist was a young woman with plain, unadorned brown robes that made her seem almost monk-like. She was sitting cross-legged on the arena floor – not a movement, not even a blink, as her Tiger moved to stand in front of its opponent.

'She's *good*,' *Heart's Sorrow* said, his voice filled with awe.

As the two Tigers sized each other up, the camera moved across the people seated in the arena: the non-scholar classes packed, standing, into the lower seats, the scholars in their booths, and then the higher-end dignitaries with privileged virtual booths, and the corresponding visibility and access, enabling them to watch the games from the privacy of their own homes while being seen. *Heart's Sorrow* snorted when the camera stopped, briefly, on the booth where his two mothers were: his first mother, the general, wearing her finest formal uniform with the peach blossom insignia, and his second mother, the retired enforcer, muscled and fit and looking hungrily at the fight beneath her.

Minh squeezed the bot in her hand, gently. *Heart's Sorrow* didn't answer: his attention was all on his mothers.

'This is the start of the first playoff of the day, with Black Water facing Crimson Rain. A really interesting match, with one of the opponents being brand new to the Games—'

The camera panned again, as the sound of two Tigers

clashing drifted from the arena floor. Couldn't they focus on the fight itself? Dignitaries were so boring.

And then Minh saw her.

She was sitting in one of the dignitaries' booths: one of the fancy ones with both physical and virtual access, a privacy screen half up – but as the camera panned the screen wavered, and Minh could see her clearly.

She was a woman of indeterminate age: jet-black hair gathered in a topknot and topped with a small golden crown in a butterfly shape, with the rest of the hair falling around the topknot in a cascade of blackness. Stars winked in and out of it in virtual overlay: a subtle touch. Her clothes were similarly subtle, a faint overlay of stars shimmering over a richly embroidered fabric. Her face was ... Well, there wasn't anything specific about her face, but it was the way she looked at the arena, the way she carried herself – as though the entire world was an egg that needed to be broken open to release the hatchling within. The face of someone who'd gladly set things afire with a shrug.

Minh realised she'd forgotten to breathe.

'Who's that?' she asked in private comms.

'Who's what?' *Heart's Sorrow* wrenched his attention back to the screen. 'Her? I've never seen her before.' He made a clicking noise. 'Mmm. The network says "Sương Quỳnh, the Alchemist of Streams and Hills". She's not sharing a family or lineage name.'

The Alchemist of Streams and Hills. A literary name. A scholar, then, but she was obviously not from the Scattered Pearls Belt, or Minh or Mother would know her. Next to the Alchemist was a mindship: a larger one than *Heart's Sorrow* but from an older generation, their avatar a bulky metal shape with a profusion of actuators and fins, looking cobbled together from the rejects of other mindships. *Guts of Sea*, the network said. The woman turned to *Guts of Sea*, and said something which was caught by the privacy filter. She smiled, her lips the perfect, unsmudged red of a vermilion seal, and turned back to watching the arena. Her gaze, for a moment, went upwards, and Minh was transfixed — as if the Alchemist of Streams and Hills could see her through a camera and a public overlay. As if she *knew* Minh.

A sharp pain stabbed her hand. 'Big sis! Big sis!'

She came back to the plaza where she and *Heart's Sorrow* were standing.

'What was that for?'

'Look,' *Heart's Sorrow* said.

'I don't see anything.'

'On the edges.'

There was some faint fuzzing on the edges of the overlay. And then the camera blinked — and she saw that the fuzzing wasn't transfer corruption at all, but bits and pieces of the second Tiger, the faint, undistinguished shape of mists and stripes. It had been slowly growing and expanding, and was now filling the arena.

Heart's Sorrow's voice was distant. 'The data artist has lost control of her Tiger.'

Minh watched, unable to tear her gaze away. The Tiger was still growing, officials on the lower tiers scrabbling to evacuate, while in the dignitaries' booth, the Alchemist of Streams and Hills herself sat utterly silent and composed, as if nothing could touch her — and then the mist filled the camera, a glitter of stripes in the darkness for a mere blink before it swallowed up the field of vision.

'Well, that certainly stopped the fun,' *Heart's Sorrow* said.

Minh was still staring at the camera. It showed nothing but that hint of stripes. Around her, the crowd was watching, too — speechless and tense, like a piece of metal stretched too much, in that moment before it broke.

'We should get moving,' *Heart's Sorrow* said. 'It's not going to—'

Someone screamed.

Why?

'It's here! Run!'

What?

'Run!'

The crowd was pressing against her, and there was more screaming. The tension had broken and now it was just a mass of jumbled bodies all blocking her. She couldn't breathe, or move – she was suffocated by the thickness of the crowd, a multitude of textures. There was screaming and smoke and a press of bodies around her.

'Lil bro, what—?'

Minh was being pushed right and left – she teetered, lost her footing, caught herself at the last minute. Panic. They were in the middle of a panic. Something had upset the tightly packed crowd, and suddenly they all wanted to get out. And they'd trample anyone to do that.

Breathe.

But she couldn't, not when pressed on all sides. She struggled to look up – and finally saw why the crowd was running. The Tiger was in the habitat. And not just that, but it was growing and growing, its contours expanding – and where they touched, metal bent, shrieking with the tortured sound of souls bound in the Courts of Hell.

If it touched people, it wasn't just going to be metal that died.

How—?

No. How was irrelevant. She had to get out.

'Run,' *Heart's Sorrow* said.

His bots were skittering, dancing under the crowd's feet. Minh struggled to stay upright. She could barely see him;

people had shoved straight into his space, and his body shimmered in and out of existence over a man's brocaded robes, then a woman's, then two small children's.

What was he still doing there?

'*Leave!*' she screamed at him.

'What? Am I supposed to just leave you?'

'Obviously!' Minh said, pushing her way towards the corridor she'd taken here.

The overlays were bleeding into one another with the stress on the network, the ambient music and sounds a cacophonic mixture drowned by the sound of the crowd, swelling like the motors of an atmosphere shuttle about to take off.

'One of us has to make it. Be sensible!'

'Sensible?' *Heart's Sorrow* floated, not next to her, but *over* her, as the crowd surged and pushed, a compact, bristling mass of too many people, too much noise, too many clashing overlays. 'And how am I supposed to explain to your mother I just left you?'

'I don't care!'

More screaming, a shriek of tortured metal – and a high-pitched human wail echoed by others. Something pattered over them – water from the sprinklers in the station? – but when she brushed her hand against her lips, Minh saw that it was blood. She managed, struggling, to turn her head. Behind them, the Tiger had swallowed up the whole plaza, its mist covering the now-still forms of those who hadn't pushed hard enough to escape. Some of them were too small to be adults.

How . . . ? How dare it? How dare it be there, on my turf?

Her anger was white-hot and searing, a feeling that hollowed Minh out like a lantern stretched over its light.

'Do something, demons take you!'

The small, translucent shape of *Heart's Sorrow* hovered over her chest, his hull plunging between her ribs, his turrets passing in her neck. Minh didn't feel anything; her perception filters for that overlay were off. Small mercies.

Heart's Sorrow said softly, 'I can't. I've tried. I can't recall my avatar, and I can't send an emergency signal. Comms are down. Flooded out, I think.'

Or attacked.

Minh followed the push of the crowd into the corridor, struggling. Someone brushed against her, too high to be a bot, too small to be an adult. A small girl, no more than three years old, staring at her with panic in her eyes – in that suspended moment before everything became too overwhelming and she utterly broke down.

'I can't find my mommy!'

Minh swept her up, wedging her around her hips, using her bots to provide added stability and support. Ancestors, she hadn't carried small children since her cousins had become too heavy.

'Let's go look, child,' she said.

Heart's Sorrow was now utterly focused. 'Looking her up.'

'You said the network was down.'

'Yes. I do have the cache for a lot of things. Hang on …'

A man in a dragon mask tried to push a little too close. Minh glared at him.

'You related to her?'

The man looked startled, then shook his head.

'Then move!'

And when he didn't, she sent a bot to sting his feet. He yelped, which was petty but was mildly satisfying.

The child burrowed into Minh's neck. It made her job easier, but also she was way too trusting. When they found the child's mother, she was going to have *words* with her about teaching her child to be wary of strangers, especially at a major festival.

'Sweetie, what's your name? Do you know what your mother looks like?'

A sniffle. 'I'm Nhi Nhi. Cẩm Nhi. Mommy ...' She flailed.

The noise of the crowd was getting unbearable; Minh asked her bots to set up a noise filter at weak strength. She was half expecting it not to work, with everything down in the sector, but it did, and the sound around them receded to a half-bearable level. She couldn't keep it up for long: it was exceedingly unwise to try and drown out noise while being pushed in all directions by panicking people.

A high-pitched screech, a tortured noise cut off by the filter. Nhi finally managed to send Minh an image: a small and chubby young woman alongside an auth-token. A Belt one, thank Heaven. Aha. Minh sent it on to *Heart's Sorrow*, and asked her bots to scan the crowd at the same time. She pushed back against her neighbours again. The man with the mask glared at her.

Let him.

Her bots couldn't find Nhi's mother. If the worst came to the worst, she could find her once she was back home, with the tribunal's resources, though she would never hear the end of it from her mother.

'Can't find her,' *Heart's Sorrow* said.

Tendrils of fiery mist floated their way: the air was stingingly hot, and Minh's hands were starting to burn and turn red. Nhi wailed in her arms. She could dial the pain down, but she needed the adrenaline rush. She pushed instead, into the crowd that seemed to have reached a complete stop – and then abruptly they were out of the corridor, and back in the Harmonious Dream marketplace, and Minh pushed and pushed and pushed. With the shape of *Heart's Sorrow* superimposed on her chest – it was oddly like carrying two people, the ship and the child – they were through, the crowd thinning out at last.

They were in a side street close to the market. Minh stopped to catch her breath and heard only the distant roar of the crowd.

'It's gone,' she said slowly. 'The Tiger.'

Heart's Sorrow blinked away from her chest, reappeared above a heap of abandoned steaming baskets, his bots climbing the various neighbouring stalls.

'The network is still congested, but it's easing. They say ...' He sounded dubious. 'They say there was an accident during the first match. The Tiger broke free of the arena restrictions, and the data artist's control.'

'Mother—'

'They're all safe. My mothers had already evacuated, but looks like your mother barely escaped being mauled.' He laughed, and it was not amused. 'It'll probably make for an entertaining vid.'

'Auntie ...' Nhi said, in Minh's arms.

Minh sighed. 'I know. We need to find your mother, and to get you home. Lil bro,' she started, and looked up, to see that *Heart's Sorrow* had completely frozen on top of the baskets. 'Lil bro?'

'Don't bother,' a voice said. 'He's stuck, and he's not going anywhere. Neither are you.'

There were five of them in the street, two women and three men, with barely any ornamentation to their avatars; they were *here* in the physical, unpleasantly close, the loose circle they formed around Minh and *Heart's Sorrow* tightening.

The one who had spoken – a squat, commanding woman with the wings of a phoenix – smiled, and it was fanged and unpleasant.

'Poor little rich girl, so lonely.'

'Me, or the child?' Minh asked, tightening her grip on Nhi.

An eye roll from Phoenix Wings. 'I don't care about the

child. I care about how much your mother will pay to get you back *whole*.'

She had a knife: it shone sharp and wicked, and Minh's bots very unhelpfully told her it was a vacuum blade, the kind used to cut through metal to maintain the habitats. Which meant it'd shear very neatly through skin and bone.

Shit. Shit. This is bad.

'You've got the wrong person,' Minh said.

'How dumb do you think I am?'

'I can only tell you the truth.' Minh glanced again at *Heart's Sorrow*.

'He's not going to help you,' Phoenix Wings said. 'We hacked his link to his body. All he can do is watch.' She laughed, holding the blade. 'Now come gently, will you?'

Minh was feeling distinctly ungentle, but she didn't have a vacuum blade. Or four other people with her, also armed with vacuum blades. This must be some kind of bandit gang she'd fallen afoul of, opportunists looking for a quick way to get rich. She eyed them again, forcing herself to breathe. They were a few handspans away now, their heavy, armoured bots even closer than that.

Minh said, 'I'm going to set the child down.'

Phoenix Wings laughed. 'The child can come with us. Probably not a great ransom, but she'll fetch something, one way or another.'

Which meant the bondspeople market.

'No,' Minh said. 'If you let us go, I can get you the money when I get back home.'

Nhi gripped her. 'Old Auntie...'

Minh forced herself to breathe. 'It's going to be all right.' And that made her angrier than anything else – that she had to lie to reassure a child.

Another eye roll. 'When you get home? You must really think we have no brains.'

A minute tension: she was going to signal for the attack, and Minh wasn't going to be able to meet it head-on. She set Nhi down, a fraction of a blink before Phoenix Wings actually gestured – and then her bots moved to intercept the bandits' bots, except that they were crushed in a blink, their input feeds suddenly going black in Minh's brain.

Bad bad bad, she had the time to think, before the bandits' bots leaped on her, and their combined weight pulled her down.

Minh hit the floor with a thunk, her head ringing – her avatar wavering, the dragons' antlers blinking in and out of existence as everything around her seemed to fold into throbbing pain. Someone grabbed her by her arms, hauled her up: it was one of the men, towering over her and holding her as though she was nothing but a rag doll, clasping restraints on her wrists. They bit as they closed, like ice encircling her. Minh struggled to break his hold, but her legs didn't even touch the floor and she had no purchase on him.

'*Old Auntie!*' Nhi wailed and wailed.

'Bring them,' Phoenix Wings said, and the man holding Minh threw her over his shoulder.

She was bent double like a sack of rice. Even looking at the floor required her to lift her head, which was too hard and too painful to do. She tried to raise the network, to send a signal – any kind of signal, to anyone – but the restraints were blocking her access, and everything seemed to be fuzzing over the gaping emptiness of her destroyed bots. She must have hit her head badly when she fell.

Phoenix Wings laughed. 'Looks like she's going to behave without my having to break anything. Good. We'll send a ransom demand to the tribunal once our shuttle reaches the hideout.'

Shuttle. Hideout.

They'd be going out of range of the habitats. No one was ever going to find her, because these were outsider bandits. They'd just come in for the festival, and she'd handed them an opportunity on a jade tray.

'Don't—' Minh tried to say, but her tongue felt glued to her palate. At least she'd set Nhi down. At least ...

'Kidnapping people in broad daylight is a terrible idea,' someone new said. It was a woman's voice. Not the bandit's; this was low and cultured, with the faintest suggestion of an accent – from the shipyards, maybe?

'Who under Heaven are you?' Phoenix Wings snapped.

'Someone who makes it her business to interfere in other people's business.' The voice was cool and collected. Minh tried to hold on to anything, but she felt darkness encroaching on her field of vision. She was going to pass out. Or vomit. Or both.

'Please,' she said. 'Help the child.' It was a bare whisper, physical and with no network broadcast.

And yet, when the answer came, it was said right next to her ear, softly and deliberately.

'I will.'

How—?

The woman said to Phoenix Wings, 'Put her down, and release the child. I won't ask twice.'

Phoenix Wings laughed. 'Making empty threats? She tried that, too.'

'These aren't threats. They're demands.' Matter-of-fact and cold.

Something clinked: bots' legs, pattering on the floor. One of the bandit women cursed, something fell, and there was a rapid shift in the air – then *something* happened, and Minh was falling. She flailed, bringing up her bound hands to break her fall, and *bots* caught her and gently cushioned her. The restraints opened, hitting the floor with a resounding clink – their insides gleamed with blood. Minh's blood. They must have been pumping some kind of chemicals into her. Her head felt stuffed with cotton. She tried to pull herself up, managed to stand up for a bare blink, and then fell back to her knees, vomiting all over the station's floor.

The network came back online – and as it did so, *Heart's Sorrow*'s anguished scream filled Minh's ears.

'Big sis! Are you all right?'

What does it look like? Minh tried to say, but she wasn't feeling well enough.

She was groggily aware of someone coming to sit beside her, waiting patiently until she was done: her rescuer. Minh could only catch glimpses of rich brocade. She opened her mouth, gagging on the taste of her own vomit.

'Nhi. The child.'

'We have her,' her rescuer said. 'Take your time. It's under control.'

Slowly, carefully – wincing at the pain in her neck – Minh raised her head. The bandits were lying dead or unconscious on the floor. Phoenix Wings had her own vacuum blade rammed into her chest, and the woman who had screamed was lying on the floor, nursing an arm bent at an unnatural angle. The man who'd held Minh was dead, unfamiliar bots crawling over his body; one of them came out of his throat, dragging up mucus and blood. The bandits' bots were all inert, as if someone had cut their strings. *Heart's Sorrow* was beside Nhi, whispering comforting words.

'What …? What happened?'

'I did warn them.' Her rescuer sounded distant. 'Pity they didn't listen. Those who survive will have to face the slow death.' There was a dark, vicious satisfaction in her voice that sent shivers up Minh's spine.

Minh tried to breathe. The air felt raw and painful in her lungs. Was it only a few bi-hours ago that she'd put so much thought into her dress and disguise, only a few centidays ago that she'd seen the Games start? It felt like a lifetime ago.

'Thank you,' she said – and turned to her rescuer, and stopped. 'You're ...' She paused, swallowed. 'You're the Alchemist.'

'I'm Quỳnh,' the woman sitting next to her said.

'Minh,' Minh said reflexively. 'Pleased to meet you. Not the best of circumstances.'

'Alas,' Quỳnh said.

Up close, she was even more of a presence – someone who simply drew all the attention without much trying. Her skin was dark, stippled with a light starlight tan. That great mass of hair spread around her on the floor in a pool of darkness. The golden crown atop her topknot glinted under the habitat lights.

'But ... You were in the arena,' Minh said. 'Physically. I saw you.'

'I left early.' Quỳnh's voice was cool. 'It looked like it was going to turn ugly, and why stay under those conditions?'

'I don't understand what you're doing here.'

'You sounded like you needed help,' Quỳnh said simply.

'The network was down.' Minh struggled to gather her thoughts together. 'How—?'

'Your friend managed to broadcast a message before he got frozen out.' Quỳnh gestured, and Minh suddenly noticed the mindship hovering behind her. 'It was garbled and incomplete, but *Guts of Sea* is good at deciphering.'

Guts of Sea inclined their avatar, but said nothing.

'Thanks for coming. Sorry. Not to sound ungrateful, it's just—'

'You've had a nasty shock. It's quite all right.'

'My ear. You spoke in my ear. Like you had the network.'

'I have *Guts of Sea*.' Quỳnh sounded amused. 'She helps with those little tricks.'

Guts of Sea did the mindship equivalent of glowering.

'Slipping comms between the shards of a broken network is more than a *little trick*.'

'A miracle, then.' Quỳnh's mouth turned up, in a small smile. 'Satisfied?'

'She's alive and didn't break her spine in the fall,' *Guts of Sea* said. 'And they didn't have time to harm the child either. Better than I expected.'

'How did you ...?' Minh asked.

Another smile. 'Tricks. Miracles.'

They were deflecting how exactly they'd rescued Minh – she knew it, and it should have annoyed her, but instead she just felt exhaustion and relief. They both sounded utterly in control and relaxed and having Quỳnh next to her made Minh feel perversely safe, even though they'd barely even met.

'Miracles,' she said.

Minh tried to get up, but Quỳnh put her hand on her shoulder to prevent her.

'You're pumped full of sedatives, on top of the shock. Don't move. The militia should be on its way.'

The militia.

'No!'

'It's a tribunal matter.' Quỳnh sounded puzzled. 'And your friend sent them a request as soon as he was unfrozen.'

Of course he had, if he'd panicked. And of course he wouldn't have thought that he and Minh would both have to explain being out of the family compound, in the seedier areas of the habitats – and not only almost being killed by a stray Tiger, but also how Minh had come so close to being carried away from the Belt and held for ransom by bandits.

The punishment for that was going to be horribly creative and costly.

'You don't understand,' Minh said. 'Mother is going to kill me.' And, when Quỳnh still looked puzzled, 'She's the prefect.'

'Ah. I haven't had the pleasure of meeting her yet.'

She was newly arrived, then, which explained the faint shipyard accent.

'Well, don't worry,' Minh said, more viciously than she'd intended. 'You'll have plenty of time to become acquainted.'

Contrary to Minh's expectations, when the militia showed up a centiday later, neither of their first mothers was there. Instead, it was Đình Diệu, the aide to *Heart of Sorrow*'s first mother, and Minh's stepmother San.

Minh had managed to sit down, Nhi on her knees, while *Heart's Sorrow* tried to contact Nhi's mother. Quỳnh had withdrawn a little way, clearly giving Minh some space; but she wasn't intending to leave. Not that she could, since *Heart's Sorrow* had called the militia.

Minh was singing Nhi a song from her childhood, and Nhi – who obviously had had Serpent classmates – was nodding along.

'One, two, serpent in the heavens,
Three, four, the azure cloth over us,
Five, six, official's robes,
Seven, eight, the sky afire . . .'

'Nine, ten, white birds in flight!' Nhi said triumphantly, completing the sequence of hand movements by making wings with her outstretched hand. 'Again, Old Auntie, again!'

'One, two, serpent in the heavens,
Three, four, the cloth of azure over us ...'

One minute Minh was sitting in the deserted alleyway – the next an overlay descended, all harsh and blinking lights and jarring sounds, as if she were a criminal being arrested. It ought to have thrown off her focus and co-ordination; but her throat was still burning from the vomit, her wrists covered in her own, drying blood, and she didn't have the energy to care.

'Child!' Stepmother looked positively outraged as she rushed to Minh. 'What in Heaven did you think you were doing? That's utterly unsuitable for the family.'

Well, if nothing else, Stepmother was thoroughly predictable. Minh bit down on the obvious answer.

Đình Diệu was grimmer. 'You gave us all quite a fright,' she said, running a hand through her close-cropped hair.

'How are they?' Minh asked. 'Mother and the general.'

'Better than you are,' Đình Diệu said.

Minh sighed. 'I have no regrets.'

'Oh, you're going to regret this,' Đình Diệu said.

Minh had no doubt of that.

'You look like something the scavengers dragged in.' Stepmother sniffed.

Minh winced. She held out Nhi to one of the militia people.

'Can you see her home? We know her mother's auth-token, but *Heart's Sorrow* can't raise her.'

'Of course.'

Nhi wailed. 'I don't want to leave.'

Minh hugged her. 'I know,' she said softly. 'They're scary, and your mommy told you never to mess with the militia. But they're good people.'

Well, some of them were. And most of the corrupt, power-thirsty ones wouldn't stoop to harming a toddler for no political gain.

'They'll take you home, I promise.' She hugged Nhi again. 'And then you can tell her about your adventures.'

Nhi sniffed. 'I hated the adventures.'

'Yeah,' Minh said, and winked. 'So did I.'

Nhi made a face, but let herself be handed over to the militia woman who came to pick her up.

Stepmother looked, for a moment, as though she was going to lecture Minh, but then she softened. Her daughter Vân, Minh's stepsister, wasn't much older than Nhi.

'*That* was well done,' she said.

Minh didn't say anything. There wasn't anything she wanted to say, to be honest. She and Stepmother didn't get on, and never would – not with Stepmother's insistence that Minh lacked the decorum befitting her position in the family, and her favouring of her own daughter Vân instead.

'I got the full lecture from Đình Diệu,' *Heart's Sorrow* said on the private comms channel. 'That *hurt*.'

Minh was reasonably sure her lecture was being saved for Mother.

'Lucky you. At least you're done. Mine is still in abeyance.'

'Are these dead people?' Stepmother's voice was suspicious. 'You *killed* people?'

'That was me.' Quỳnh interposed herself, smoothly, between Minh and Stepmother, *Guts of Sea* by her side. 'I apologise for any inconvenience, but these bandits were about to kidnap your stepdaughter.'

Stepmother cocked her head, suspiciously.

'And who are you?' Đình Diệu asked.

'The Alchemist of Streams and Hills. My name is Quỳnh.'

'Yes. Yes, I can see that from your display,' Stepmother said. 'Aside from that.'

'A concerned passer-by.' Quỳnh's voice was smooth.

She recounted, quickly, how she'd come to rescue Minh. She still didn't provide any details on how she and *Guts of Sea* had managed to outfight five armed bandits.

'You did that by yourself?' Đình Diệu said, eyeing the slim jewelled bots on Quỳnh's shoulder, the nacre inlays on their crowns of sensors. She looked impressed, and Heaven knew she was hard to impress: she'd fought in the Ten Thousand Flags Uprising, and at the battle of Cotton Tree Citadel.

Quỳnh shrugged. 'We've travelled. Bandits are a common occurrence outside the Numbered Planets, and they've not grown less bold since the end of the war.'

Đình Diệu cocked her head, assessing Quỳnh. Something unspoken passed between them again: Đình Diệu reporting via comms channel to her general.

'The general will want to see you both,' Đình Diệu said curtly.

Quỳnh inclined her head. 'It will be my pleasure.'

'And mine,' *Guts of Sea* said, angling her squat body to align with Quỳnh's.

Stepmother looked from Minh to Quỳnh. This was a different calculus: it took in Quỳnh's speech, the price of her clothes and the elegance of her bots.

'Where are you from?' she asked.

Quỳnh bowed. It was deep and correct to within an eyelash-width, everything Minh's tutor ever despaired she'd learn.

'The shipyards,' she said.

'You've been to court,' Stepmother said.

'It has been my privilege, but sometimes one requires solitude.' Quỳnh smiled, and there was little of joy in it. 'I wanted the streams and the hills, the hollow bamboo's pleasure. A pine, a plum tree and the moon's reflection can be their own fulfilment.'

She was mixing together literary metaphors, quoting on the fly from the poetry masters. Not just a scholar, but the kind that became a high official – the kind of dazzling talent that the ministries would fight over, the same path Mother had traced out for Minh despite her lack of enthusiasm. She was *so good*, and it was *so* effortless.

Why is she here? With that kind of talent she should be at court.

'I suppose,' Stepmother said, slowly and grudgingly, 'that you should come visit us as well. You sound like the kind of person my wife would love to meet.'

Another talented and wealthy person for Mother to obsess over, to try and win to her side for more influence and more power. Quỳnh inclined her head, but by the glint in her eyes she probably wasn't fooled.

'I would be honoured,' she said. It was exactly the same tone she'd used earlier.

Minh reached for her bots to replay Quỳnh's conversation with Đình Diệu – but no, her bots were dead, killed by the bandits. But she was sure it was the same tone. It had an edge to it, and no wonder. Stepmother had been about as subtle as a tiger in a cattle pen.

Minh felt grubby.

'I'm sorry,' she messaged towards Quỳnh on a private channel. 'You probably thought we were better than this. The adults are all status-obsessed.'

A sound, crystalline and good-natured, only for Minh's ears. It was Quỳnh's laughter.

'I've travelled. I'm not surprised. How much trouble are you and your friend in for sneaking out?'

Minh started. She hadn't expected that answer.

'I don't know yet. I've never really thanked you for the rescue.'

'You're welcome.' Quỳnh's voice was grave again. 'Tell me, Minh.'

'Yes?'

'Can I ask for a favour?'

Minh frowned. 'What kind of favour? Mother is the one you want to ask. I'm pretty she'd give you something for the rescue.'

'A gift with ... ah ... barbs? Your mother is a born politician.'

Outside the private comms channel, Quỳnh was making arrangements to come to the tribunal, and Minh was walking behind Stepmother, eyes respectfully averted – heading home, to Mother and her inevitable punishment. *Heart's Sorrow* – who had recalled his avatar straight home, leaving only the glowering Đình Diệu – was repeatedly messaging Minh, but Minh put his messages on hold until she could focus on them.

'I need somewhere,' Quỳnh said.

'Somewhere?'

'I'm new here, and I don't know much about the habitats. I'm interested in moving into a compound—' she gave Minh the address, somewhere in the inner rings, on the edge of dignitary space '—but I want to know if it's suitable.'

'Suitable for what?'

'I'm going to be here for a while,' Quỳnh said. 'And, well ...' She paused, for a while. '*Guts of Sea* is looking for a match.'

Minh stopped, so abruptly that Stepmother pushed her.

'She what?'

Whatever she associated either of them with, it wasn't marriage.

'We all reach a point in our lives when we want stability. An end to the toil and roil around us. A reckoning with our mortality,' Quỳnh's voice was edged and ironic. '*Guts of Sea* would like to settle down.'

A mindship, looking for a match. That was quite a catch. Mindships were either affiliated with the Empire, or free of their engagements. If the former, they would bring connections with high-ranking officials – if the latter, a formidable capacity for quick travel. A mindship could make or break a family's fortune, especially an official's or a merchant's.

'Does she have a family speaking for her?'

She didn't think so. *Guts of Sea* looked old, and old in a mindship meant centuries of life. It was quite likely she was the eldest of her family, and therefore the one making the decisions.

Quỳnh made a sound in private comms, like a delicate cough.

'*Guts of Sea*'s family ... didn't survive the Uprising, I'm afraid.' She put a peculiar accent on *survive*.

Ah. No wonder Guts of Sea *doesn't speak much.*

Quỳnh was desirable, but *Guts of Sea* would be a liability in a world where everyone sought to distance themselves as fast as possible from The General Who Pacified the Dragon's Tail and her rebellion.

'And you're speaking for her.'

'Yes. You can see why I want – why I *need* – to make a good impression.' There was hunger and worry in Quỳnh's voice. 'We're talking about *Guts of Sea*'s future.'

The future.

Minh thought of her own. It had been traced for her: the metropolitan examinations, a career as a scholar, a courtship with a spouse whose family connections were approved by Mother and Stepmother. It was a certainty: a comfort and a cage. But *Guts of Sea* wasn't Minh. She was from a reprobate family, and she needed a good match. And, in order to get that, to offset the taint of her family's actions, she would need to bring a lot more to the match.

'I see,' she said. 'Looking at a compound and telling you if it sends the right kind of message isn't really a great favour.'

'I know,' Quỳnh said. 'I was in the right place at the right time. I'm not asking you to return a gift of food and shelter by lending me your spouse.' She sounded amused again as she referenced an Old Earth tale. She really was a scholar: no one else would have known such an obscure metaphor. 'And I'll meet your family, one way or another.'

'You don't need me for that,' Minh said. 'Or ever did.'

'No,' Quỳnh said, inclining her head as she pointed to one bandit after another for the militia. She was wealthy, and smart, and she'd been to court. Every single dignitary would line up to seek her company.

'If that's all you want—' Minh said.

'It is.'

'Then of course, I'll be happy to have a look.'

'Perfect.' Quỳnh smiled. 'Until then.'

She left, *Guts of Sea* by her side.

Minh followed Stepmother to the shuttle that would take her back to the family's habitat. She rubbed her wrists, feeling the hardness of scabs under her fingers. Her disguise was torn and bloodied, her avatar unable to hide the damage to her clothes.

It all felt like a dream – but was she entering one, or being awoken from one ...?

2
A Lonely Grave

By the end of the Bi-Hour of the Tiger – at a time when she and her younger sister Thiên Dung were meant to be cleaning up and opening the repair shop – Hoà was still alone.

Hoà glanced at the schedule, bringing it up in overlay to see it more comfortably. At this early hour she could afford to take her eye off her customers, and it gave her a small but intense sense of satisfaction to be occupying their space.

The shop was a classic Belt compartment: a small and narrow space, the counter across it about two forearm-lengths – half the height of a person – from the door. Behind the counter was Hoà and Thiên Dung's space, clogged with tables and spare parts from bots, recycling units, vacuum protections, and a variety of larger habitat equipment. Against the wall was a series of steps leading downwards to the private quarters, and a huge series of square alcoves that looked almost like a scholar's bookshelf – except this one was full of bots. At any given time, they had hundreds of them working on low-level repair tasks that could be set on automatic, without Thiên Dung or Hoà's conscious involvement.

There was nothing out of the ordinary on the schedule.

The Tiger Games incident was still playing out, and there was speculation the tribunal might move against the data artists – or worse, the entire technologist outer ring. Most of their regulars had cancelled their pick-ups; the whole ring held its breath, waiting to see what the tribunal would decide, and who would get hurt.

Still no Thiên Dung. Hoà could have pinged her, but she had a good idea why her sister wasn't there. She paused the bots engaged in complex tasks, and went downstairs.

The privacy screen was up in Thiên Dung's room, so strong Hoà couldn't see or hear anything.

'It's me,' she said. 'Come on. I know how bad it is.'

A silence, then the screen came down.

Thiên Dung was lying on her bed. Her face was pale, her bots uncannily still, her hair – like Hoà's, barely long enough to form a topknot – sheened with sweat and dirt. She tried to smile and sit up when Hoà walked in – but her skin was flushed and she fell back against the pillow.

'You really should stop putting the privacy screen on.'

'You don't want to sleep worrying about my fever. Who's going to mind the shop if you're barely awake?'

Typical. 'You're in no state to be doing anything,' Hoà said, more bluntly than she meant. 'I want to know if we need to call for a doctor. Even if it's the middle of the night.'

That was nice – or as nice as she could be, when her imagination was filled with fears of waking up and finding Thiên Dung had died during the night, or passed some kind of no-return horizon, beyond any doctor's or apothecary's ability to help.

'We can't *afford* a doctor.'

'We can't afford your dying either.'

Hoà's remaining bots picked up the teacup from the low bedside table, and handed it to Thiên Dung. Thiên Dung didn't move at first, but then – thumb-width by thumb-width – she pulled herself up in agonising slow-motion. Hoà sat very still, trying not to move, not to immediately fuss over her. Thiên Dung would just glare at her if she tried to intervene.

'Thank you,' Thiên Dung said, holding the cup.

She wasn't sitting so much as lying a little more vertically, the cup held loosely in her lap. The tea wobbled – Hoà reached out, steadying the cup.

'I'm not *that* sick,' Thiên Dung said, giving her exactly the glare Hoà had expected. Her fingers were flecked with pin-pricks of red, as if the flush on her skin was migrating to her extremities. Hoà didn't like that.

'You're not well.'

Hoà sat down on her own bed, trying to feel less angry. Thiên Dung didn't need an elder sister lecture, but ... but how could she be so short-sighted? How could she care so little about her own health, and so much about appearances?

Thiên Dung didn't say anything.

Hoà sighed. 'Stay here. I'll mind the shop.' But she didn't move. The schedule had had one large and preoccupying line on it, one they'd put off repeatedly because Thiên Dung was unwell. 'We need to talk about *Flowers at the Gates of the Lords*.'

It was a huge job: an uncommon contract from a circle of people who usually didn't give them the time of day. It represented half of their yearly budget, and they'd defaulted twice on the deadlines already. Thiên Dung's face was pale.

'Tell them I'm ill.'

'You know we can't.'

'So?'

Thiên Dung flopped back again. The tea spilled in her lap. She tried to move a bot, gave up, and slowly put the cup back on the table.

Truth was, Hoà had made her decision when she'd come in. 'I'll fill in for you.'

'You don't know anything about fixing mindships.'

'No.' Hoà didn't know anything about their powerful clients either. The thought of having to deal with the children of dignitaries sent her in to a cold sweat. 'But do you see any other solution?'

Thiên Dung held her gaze for a while, and then lowered it. Her face was flushed, sheened with sweat.

'You know I don't. I just ... Keep your head low, do the small things first? I'll feel better in a few days, promise.'

'Of course.'

Hoà tried to keep her voice light and her smile up, as she kissed Thiên Dung — a sniff of her cheek, breathing in the stale odour of her sickness. Then she watched the privacy screen go back up, hiding her sister from sight. The fever was getting worse. She wasn't well, and she wasn't going to be well in a few days' time.

Hoà walked to Thiên Hạnh's grave.

It wasn't wise. She had a bare hour before the shop opened, and no customer due until the end of the morning — but the corridors and plazas of the ring were deserted, and the militia might be on the lookout for anything unusual. Bạch Loan — the data artist whose Tiger had gone rogue — had been arrested, along with her entire family and circle of associates. They'd be in the tribunal's jails, being interrogated, pumped full of truth drugs, physically and virtually tortured for anything they might know. And anyone who stuck out, at a time like this, ran the risk of being arrested, too.

It wasn't wise.

But she was about to set foot on a wrecked mindship with absolutely no knowledge of how to fix one. That was Thiên

Dung's area of expertise, and even the pointers Thiên Dung had sent her wouldn't be sufficient to acquire the ability in a few days. Hoà was about to mingle with the children of dignitaries who could snap their fingers and send entire militia units to disappear people, to torture them, to condemn them to the slow death. And if she displeased them ... well, she had no doubt they could get their parents involved.

Hoà was scared, and she needed comfort – and Thiên Hạnh, of all people, would understand what it meant to be doing the right thing in scary circumstances.

It was a small, pathetic grave in Crane Hill Quarter, a deserted area of the Technologists' Ring. Thiên Hạnh had died in the middle of the Ten Thousand Flags Uprising, when the entire Empire seemed aflame with civil war, and neither Hoà nor Thiên Dung had had enough money to afford her burial. There was a small shrine in an alcove, a space barely sufficient to hold offerings – and around it, in the widening circle of the plaza's walls, were ten thousand other graves, other alcoves for the forgotten. Small platforms barely sufficient to hold a kneeling person served as lifts, but few of them were ever in use at the same time.

The cemetery plaza was run-down: its network overlay was meant to be a series of rolling hills and ponds under starlight, but it was just shot through with huge holes where the relays had failed and not been repaired. It looked haphazard and broken: one moment Hoà walked under a perfectly constructed pavilion by a pond, with the song of crickets in her ears, and the next she was on the bare metal flooring of the habitat with only the distant sound of air recyclers. Right now she was in the middle of two patches of featureless darkness, because the overlays' outwards preview function had also failed. It felt as though she hung within a void that was even more terrifying than the deep spaces travelled by mindships.

Even this late in the day, there was no one here, and there would be few offerings in the alcoves. The dead slept alone, unworshipped by the living. In Hoà's dreams, Thiên Hạnh wasn't a gibbering, hungry ghost eager to feed on the guts of passers-by, or a wise and powerful ancestor extending the shade of her blessing towards her relatives. She was just sad and flickering, forever out of reach. Broken, just the way her mem-implants were. Unless Hoà was standing right by the grave, the mem-implants in her brain wouldn't even whisper in her thoughts. Thiên Hạnh had been a distinguished scholar, but she hadn't even managed to preserve her persona for her family. No accumulated wisdom for Hoà, or Thiên Dung, or anyone else left behind.

It was what it was, and nothing would change it. But it hurt all the same.

Hoà would sit down, burn some incense and offer the one wizened clementine she'd managed to save from their groceries. And she'd talk to Thiên Hạnh for a while, trying to summon again the all-encompassing comfort of her childhood, when her elder sister had been alive and everything had been peaceful and secure. It was an illusion, but one she desperately needed.

Hoà called a lift. Lines appeared around her on the floor; the platform lifted itself a fraction of a thumb-width, thin railings unfolding from the metal to encircle her. The lift waited for her command. She input the grave's co-ordinates in the navigation system, and the lift ponderously lifted off the floor, jerkily moving upwards.

There was someone at Thiên Hạnh's grave.

Who?

Hoà stared as the lift shifted from moving vertically to horizontally, floating along the alcoves. The person at Thiên Hạnh's grave didn't waver. Hoà couldn't see them clearly:

they were kneeling in front of the alcove with a light privacy screen obscuring them, and she saw only their profile, a sharp face under an elaborate topknot. A flood of crow-black hair flowed from it, in the slightly rakish style that was all the rage in the Numbered Planets. Their clothes were a vivid blue, and the expensive kind of brocade, a master's work even from a distance. Some kind of golden ornament adorned the topknot, also looking like delicate, expensive work. Who were they? No one but Hoà and Thiên Dung had brought offerings to the grave in the last ten years.

When Hoà's lift bumped into the other one, the person didn't move, but the privacy screen gently faded away – and, just as Hoà was wondering whether to start a conversation, an overlay sprang into existence. Not the broken and half-dead ones of the Crane Hill cemetery, but an expansive and detailed one: a vast swathe of star-speckled dark blue, so that Hoà stood over an intricate swirl of stars, looking down at galaxies – as if she were a mindship in the vacuum of space. It was *vast*, bearing no connection to the two cramped lifts in the physical space; the person had added some perception and interaction overlays, causing the space to be perceived as wider than it was. Any step Hoà took in overlay would be matched by a much smaller one in physical space, so she didn't fall off the lift.

There was a faint sound; she thought it was a zither at first, but then it became the familiar cadences of Serpent children's songs, the same songs Thiên Hạnh had taught her, back on *The Azure Serpent* mining rig.

The person remained kneeling for a moment: with the privacy screen down, Hoà saw that she was an utterly unfamiliar woman, the public information on her auth-token denoting her as an outsider to the Belt. She was older, and the ornament in her hair was a butterfly. She'd brought a bronze cup and five different fruits — and pristine white rice smelling of jasmine, with caramel pork. It was not a mere simulacrum; it smelled rich and strange. Her face, as she faced Thiên Hạnh's remains, was earnest and oddly vulnerable; but then she would be, wouldn't she, if she was making funeral offerings to Hoà's elder sister? A classmate of Thiên Hạnh's, or a colleague? But most of them had abandoned Thiên Hạnh after the scandal and Dã Lan's execution, as the teacher of a rebel student was herself a suspect person. Never mind that — to her dying day, Thiên Hạnh had believed in Dã Lan's innocence.

No, Thiên Hạnh wouldn't have such rich and wealthy friends any more. Those who had survived the Ten Thousand Flags Uprising — those who had become wealthy and powerful — had backstabbed and equivocated and run, and they would rather be dead than be caught in this backwater cemetery, making offerings to a disgraced and deceased woman.

Hoà waited. The other woman knew she was there, or she wouldn't have offered the courtesy of the overlay. And such a detailed one. Come to think of it, how had she done this? The network was bad in Crane Hill — that was why the overlays were not only ill maintained, but also so fragmentary. Certainly nowhere near this full set of perception and interaction filters. It should have been impossible to do something this intricate, this complex. Wind whistled in her ears, and the Serpent children sang, high-pitched and serene.

Where are you going, O white birds?
Over which rice fields, which star nurseries?
Where are you going, O white birds?

Hoà shivered. Beneath her, the stars slowly whirled, their lights wavering as though she were standing on one of the Numbered Planets, within the alien safety of an atmosphere.

Where are you going, O white birds …?

The woman finished her prayers, and straightened up, putting her incense stick into the holder. Then she turned to Hoà, and bowed as deeply as she'd bowed to Thiên Hạnh – the almost total formal obeisance, as if Hoà were a lady of the imperial court on the First Planet.

'Wait, no!' Hoà started, but the wind swept up her words and silenced them.

When the woman straightened up, she was smiling. Her auth-token was now blinking with her name: 'Sương Quỳnh, the Alchemist of Streams and Hills'. No family name, no lineage name – an outsider auth-token – and the use of the all but obsolete word 'alchemist' placed her beyond the Belt, perhaps beyond the Empire altogether.

'I'm sorry,' the woman – the Alchemist – said. 'I hadn't expected anyone to be here at her grave.'

She had a faint shipyard accent. So not altogether beyond the Empire, but close to its boundaries. But she used the *elder aunt* pronoun for Thiên Hạnh, and her bearing was pure official – that of the very high dignitaries, and her bow had been pitch-perfect, straight from those who had seen the Empress face to face.

'Alchemist.' Hoà stood there, hugging herself, very uncertain who she was talking to.

'Oh, please use big sis.'

The Alchemist bridged the gap between her and Hoà in three decisive steps. She was standing next to Hoà, smelling faintly of incense and of something else Hoà couldn't name – a mixture of sweet flowers that quivered on her tongue. Her heart beat faster, and she didn't know why.

'My name is Quỳnh,' the Alchemist said.

'Quỳnh.' Hoà tasted the name on her tongue. 'I'm—'

'Thiên Hoà. Thanh Khuê's little sister. I know.'

Quỳnh smiled again, and it transfigured her entire face. She was suddenly years younger – and she stood far too close, a warm and tantalising presence which was doing some very funny things to Hoà's heartbeat. She used Thiên Hạnh's literary name, not the intimate name Hoà had known her by. Which meant she wasn't family; she had known Thiên Hạnh as a scholar.

Hoà struggled to bring her breathing under control.

'Why? Who are you?'

Quỳnh didn't answer for a while. When she did, she gestured, and a table shimmered into existence: a metal one with the sheen of deep spaces etched into a large lotus pattern, and two cups of tea on its surface. All virtual, but with the filters they'd still smell and taste right.

Hoà didn't move.

'I want answers.'

Quỳnh laughed. It was rich, and twisted in Hoà's belly. She was ... beautiful and enticing and utterly beyond Hoà, and someone like her had no business being in Hoà's life, or Thiên Hạnh's death.

'I knew her.' She stopped smiling; her face was grave now. The bots on her shoulders were discreet, glittering in the starlight, but Hoà worked in a repair shop, and she'd have bet that they were more than ornamental. 'A long time ago.'

The sound of the children singing had faded, but Hoà hadn't forgotten.

'On board *The Azure Serpent*?'

'In a manner of speaking.' Quỳnh sighed, gestured again for Hoà to sit. 'My answers aren't going to be different if you hear them with tea. And you looked *very* upset when you arrived.'

Hoà stiffened. 'You didn't see me.'

'Just because I was kneeling at a grave doesn't mean I failed to keep an eye out.' Again, that smile that just made Hoà want to smile in return, no matter that she couldn't afford it. Someone like Quỳnh – high-flown, mysterious – represented too much trouble. 'What upset you?'

'You first,' Hoà said. 'How did you know my elder sister?'

She sat cross-legged, picking up a teacup of the finest celadon.

'We were correspondents.' Quỳnh looked haunted for a moment, but then she got herself under control. 'I ... lost touch during the war.'

'She died,' Hoà said.

'So I see. What ...? What happened?'

'She tried to save someone. It was a long time after *The Azure Serpent* was destroyed.'

Hoà kept her voice light, emotionless – because if she didn't, she was going to remember the riots, and the crowd baying for their blood, and the way Thiên Hạnh had straightened up behind the barred doors of their compartment, kissing Hoà on the cheek.

Be a good girl, will you? Watch over your younger sister.

Big sis.

There's something I have to do, Hạnh had said – and she had simply walked out towards the waiting mob, back straight, not a hair out of place on her topknot.

'I see.' Quỳnh picked up her teacup, lifted it. 'That doesn't surprise me. She believed so much in doing the right thing.'

And look where that got her.

Hoà pressed her lips together, trying to forget the sounds Thiên Hạnh had made as the mob took her – as they killed her, bot after bot torn away, slice of skin after slice of skin taken. She tried to forget the body she'd found after the mob had left: the gouged-out eyes, the torn fingernails, the broken limbs, the pieces of flesh carved out from shoulders and thighs and cheeks ...

Warmth, on her back. Hoà looked up, surprised, to see Quỳnh holding her, arms wrapped around her shoulders. She was kneeling behind Hoà – body lightly pressed against Hoà's back, a roiling warmth passing from her into Hoà, a steady, calming presence.

Quỳnh said simply, 'She died badly, didn't she? No, don't tell me how. Just let it go. Whatever it is you're remembering now – breathe. Let it go.'

Within Hoà, Thiên Hạnh's mem-implants stirred, briefly – a ghost, briefly summoned into life. She sang the same song as the children – a fragment of a verse – before dying again.

Let go.

'I wish I could,' Hoà said.

'For now,' Quỳnh said. 'There is always for now.'. Her arms tightened around Hoà's chest, Hoà leaning into the touch, tipping her head upwards to look at Quỳnh's face far above hers and then Quỳnh let go, and pulled away, leaving only a gaping emptiness, as if Hoà had grasped someone precious and let them slip away. 'You asked how I knew her. We corresponded before *The Azure Serpent*'s death.'

'You're a scholar?' Hoà turned to look at Quỳnh. She was still kneeling next to Hoà, hair spread out around her, but there was absolutely nothing of submission in that gesture. 'A wealthy one. A court official. With a shipyards accent.'

A grimace from Quỳnh. 'I spent . . . a lot of time in the shipyards. I couldn't really come back to the Numbered Planets.'

Oh. *Oh.* The most obvious explanation hadn't occurred to Hoà.

'You were exiled.'

'Nothing so harsh as that,' Quỳnh said, smoothly and easily, except the distant cast of her face bore witness to another, harsher experience altogether. 'Just . . . the vagaries of war. And then I couldn't write to your elder sister any more.'

Because Thiên Hạnh was dead.

'And now it's too late.' Hoà felt unbearably sad. 'I wish she was still there. She ...' She waved towards the grave. 'She's poor company, currently.'

'She was there when I needed her,' Quỳnh said, and it was gentle, and fraught with a meaning Hoà couldn't quite understand. Hoà had been so young, aboard *The Azure Serpent* – too young to remember anything but children's songs, and meals, and books. Not enough to differentiate people, not even all of those Thiên Hạnh had known on board, let alone her correspondents. 'Now I'm here when she needs me.'

'She doesn't,' Hoà said, more forcefully than she meant.

'But you do. Don't you?'

It was a simple question. Quỳnh looked at Hoà, one eyebrow raised, hands palms up on her knees. Offering not just fruit, not just incense, but something more.

How dare she—?

'You can't just *buy* amends—'

Whatever it was she wanted to atone for, it was none of Hoà's business. Hoà felt obscurely embarrassed. Why was she so ill at ease? No, not ill at ease. She was angry, as if she'd hoped for one thing and Quỳnh was offering another.

'Look,' she said, struggling to bring herself under control, to give voice to the logic behind her anger. 'I'm not looking for a spirit to sweep into our lives and fix all our problems.'

Quỳnh was watching her, her face unreadable. 'You're dismissing me because of my clothes?'

'No. Just saying we didn't *ask* for anything from you.'

Quỳnh hadn't moved. 'You're speaking of consent. Of not being given more help than you ask for. Ask now.' Again, her voice was gentle.

'You're—' Hoà started, stopped. 'You're the banyan and its shadow. You're a shark, a tiger, and we're just rice fish.'

Old, old metaphors for high-ranking dignitaries – for predators, and the smallest of their prey.

'I mean you no harm.'

'You'll bring us harm anyway!' Hoà thought, again, of Thiên Hạnh – of Thiên Hạnh's death. 'You asked how my elder sister died. She saved a rebel from the mob – she didn't like the rebels or The General Who Pacified the Dragon's Tail or anyone who worked for them, but she said no one should be torn apart for their affiliation. And then the mob came for her.'

'Ah.' Quỳnh's face was oddly still. 'Will you tell me one thing, then?' She held out her hand towards Hoà, palm up, without saying anything more.

It was her face, more than anything, which convinced Hoà. Offering no judgement, no blame: simply waiting. Listening.

Hoà reached out, and took her hand, feeling its warmth in hers.

'What thing?'

'Why were you so scared when you arrived here. Why today – of all days, when the militia is out in the rings, especially the outer ones, looking for dissidents to blame for the Tiger Games, did you want to visit the grave of a woman who died in disgrace, and tainted her family with rebel sympathies?'

'The Ten Thousand Flags Uprising was a long time ago,' Hoà said. 'These rebels have been dead for years.'

'*That*,' Quỳnh said, gently and delicately, 'is equivocation. If you won't answer me, just say so and I'll leave you to your offerings.'

And to the rest of your life, her body posture said, if not her words. She would leave, if she wasn't wanted – except she seemed to only think of being wanted in terms of usefulness. Such an odd, sad way of looking at the world.

Something twisted in Hoà's chest – something crushingly heavy and cold, filling her guts like ice. Pity? Except it wasn't quite that – something larger and more intimate at the same time. She wrapped her hands around the one Quỳnh was offering to her, holding her like a lifeline, as if they were both drowning and they were each other's salvation. One needing to be useful, the other needing help.

'My younger sister and I have a repair shop, and we've been struggling to keep it solvent. And ... and she's sick. She's better than I am at fixing larger things. I'm better with bots, with lots of small tasks at the same time. With organising.'

Time had slowed down, with them both in its grasp. It was just the two of them: Quỳnh's heartbeat held between her hands, their gazes meeting, the haunting in Quỳnh's dark eyes, the fear in Hoà's heart.

'She got us a contract. A very large one. A wrecked mindship that some band of rich, spoiled kids want to fix. And I ...' She plunged on, not averting her gaze from Quỳnh's. 'I have to take her place on board the ship and repair it, except I don't have any of the skills that I should have. And ...' She breathed in. 'I'm scared.'

'That you'll fail. That you'll displease them. That they'll see who you are and want you eradicated from the habitats.' Quỳnh's voice was soft, laying her deepest fears bare.

'I thought ...' Hoà laughed. 'It's nonsense.'

'Nothing is nonsense.'

'I thought that, of all people, *she* would understand.'

Quỳnh nodded, gravely. 'Of course, she would. Lil sis.'

The form of address – intimate, familiar, reassuring, alongside the heat of Quỳnh's hand in hers – was like a jolt of electricity straight into Hoà's heart.

'Yes?'

'Tell me what you need.'

Hoà laughed. It felt wild and desperate.

'I need help. Something. Anything.' She forced herself to

breathe, to think what Thiên Hạnh would have done. 'You're a scholar. You were at court. You ... must know people? Masters of Wind and Water. Ship-healers. People who would ... guide me. Work with me. Show me what I need to know.'

Quỳnh's gaze held her. 'When I was much younger,' she said, her tone light and inconsequential, as if they had been sharing tea at a poetry club, 'I found a ship. An abandoned, wrecked ruin that the Empire had judged too broken to be fixed.'

Hoà didn't speak. She didn't dare to.

'It took time, but time didn't mean much to me, not back then.' A bare upturning of the lips; a vicious and cruel amusement all turned at her younger self. 'I was naive and I meant well, and what were hours and days and months?'

'You fixed her. The ship.' The pronoun Quỳnh had used was female. 'You—'

'I did.' That same light, callous amusement – it twisted in Hoà's heart like a knife. How could anyone hate herself so much? 'You want the help of a Master of Wind and Water. I don't have the title or the renown, but I do have the experience and I can show you. Will you accept my help?'

Hoà opened her mouth, closed it.

'Yes,' she said. 'Please help me, big sis.'

Hoà wanted to say more – to bring the hand she was holding to her mouth, to gently kiss it until she found the release that emptied her chest of this feeling that was too large and too raw and too painful to be contained. She wanted to ask why Quỳnh had come to the Belt. But that was a terrible idea. Hoà and Thiên Dung had survived so far by not being noticed. And Quỳnh – wealthy, scholar, outsider, walking around like a living blade with a desperate need to cut something, anything ... Quỳnh, who so easily and casually turned her own sharp cruelty on herself ...

Quỳnh was the epitome of noticeable.

Hoà let go of Quỳnh's hand, slowly and carefully, feeling as though something was tearing inside her.

'Help me,' she said again.

Quỳnh smiled. 'Of course.' She inclined her head. Her smile was slight and ironic, as if she'd guessed Hoà's thoughts. 'I can most certainly help you.'

The mindship. *Flowers at the Gates of the Lords.* Quỳnh was going to help Hoà with *Gates*, and that was going to be it. Nothing less, but nothing more, either. Because it was obvious to anyone with eyes that Quỳnh was hurtling along some private path to some disastrous, distant conflagration. To ask more – to reach for more – would only entangle Hoà in Quỳnh's affairs, and then she'd stand out, too, the same way Thiên Hạnh had stood out. And then Hoà would go the same way as her elder sister – a twisted and broken body in a lonely and isolated grave, a sad and distant ghost, forever mournful and silent.

No. It was too great a risk.

3

Shards of the Past

In Quỳnh's dreams, she was younger.

She fell into the vacuum as *The Azure Serpent*'s airlock opened – hands bound, mouth open in a silent scream, tongue and eyes burning, skin stretching and expanding, limbs becoming round as the air in them swelled up, chest puffing to twice its size. There was nothing in her mind but the utter certainty of her death – and even her thoughts were burning and quivering, her brain shutting down from lack of oxygen. Around her, a roiling: all the rifts opened by the mindship battles, bathing her in cold, sheening light as she asphyxiated ... and one of them opened and swallowed her whole. The burning in her brain and in her mouth and eyes turned into something else, a pain that was fire and ice and the inescapable dread of something large and merciless and eternal wrapping itself around her as a distant pagoda's bell called again and again for enlightenment she'd never reach.

And the dead, *her* dead – her teacher, her mother, her husband, everyone she'd lost sliding through her fingers like grains of rice ...

Quỳnh woke up choking. Struggling again and again to

breathe, feeling nothing but her own heartbeat, louder and louder, a rising sound that had no end – bringing up her hands to her neck in slow motion, trying to navigate a weightlessness that didn't exist any more.

'Breathe,' someone said, next to her.

'I can't,' Quỳnh said.

Her tongue was burning up. She was younger, and she was dying, and there was no one to stand by her as she choked, and her death was going to last forever and ever in the abysses of deep spaces—

'Breathe!'

Bots stung her hands and feet, over and over, like ten thousand acupuncture needles. She gulped, inhaled burning air. She was shivering.

'Again. Again. Again.'

It hurt, but she did it – called slowly back into the world of the living, as she had been, back then when she woke up shivering on a cold floor with a mindship's voice speaking to her.

Quỳnh breathed out, focused on her immediate surroundings. She was in the middle of an empty space with metal floors and metal walls, its cabling laid bare at the top of the walls and the cleaning bots scuttling overhead, in and out of the small vents that served as access to the habitat's maintenance network: the huge compound she and *Guts of Sea* had rented on arriving in the Belt. *Guts of Sea* was hovering over her, glowering.

'Thank you,' Quỳnh said.

'Hm,' *Guts of Sea* said. 'Are you sure you're ready?'

Quỳnh sighed. 'I had a nightmare, that's all.'

'Yes,' *Guts of Sea* said. 'There's no room in the plan for nightmares.'

No, there wasn't. No room for nightmares, or for the past

to make her vulnerable. Quỳnh and *Guts of Sea* had hung in deep spaces for what felt like an eternity, endlessly broken and remade – honing and sharpening themselves until only one thing was left: not justice, not mercy, not fear.

Revenge.

It had been fifteen years, and her accusers had thrived. *The Azure Serpent* was dead, the people on board scattered – Quỳnh's old teacher Thanh Khuê a forgotten ghost at a forgotten grave – and Quỳnh was forever on the run, unable to settle down for long before her past caught up with her. And she'd tried – Ancestors, she'd *tried* – but all she brought trailing in her wake was death.

Because of them.

A prefect.

A general.

Time to bring them crashing down.

'The girl ...' *Guts of Sea* said, and Quỳnh knew she didn't mean Minh.

'Hoà?'

Quỳnh hadn't expected Hoà. She'd simply wanted to pay her respect to her old teacher – to reconnect, for a moment, with one of the only people who had stood by her. Thanh Khuê had fought to get Quỳnh's mother's death sentence commuted to exile, sacrificing her own reputation in the process. Now Quỳnh's mother was dead, and so was Thanh Khuê. It had made her sad, but within she was burning with that same merciless energy she'd found in deep spaces, that knowledge that time was running out.

'Yes. Hoà's not part of the plan, either.'

No, she wasn't. And yet ... And yet there was something about Hoà – a small and scared technologist, her short hair barely keeping her topknot together, her high cheekbones and her wide, soulful eyes that hid too little of what she thought

– something Quỳnh couldn't identify. A pull, as if Hoà were a sun slowly drawing her in.

'The girl doesn't mean anything.'

There was no room in the plan for friends, or love, either. Quỳnh was there to settle old debts of the past – and she owed Thanh Khuê, except Thanh Khuê was dead, and Quỳnh couldn't repay her for anything any more.

She could be kind to Hoà, in honour of her elder sister. In honour of who she'd been – Dã Lan, young and unbearably, stupidly naive, and doomed to die – before she became Quỳnh.

A moment's fleeting kindness that would mean nothing, change nothing.

'If you say so.' *Guts of Sea* didn't sound convinced, but her opinion wasn't relevant. This was Quỳnh's part of the plan, Quỳnh's life.

'I do.'

Quỳnh got up, smoothly, effortlessly disguising the quiver in her hands – too much practice at that. She got up, staring at their compound: a profoundly empty space with no overlays, no ornaments – like a page waiting for a scholar's brush. The only furniture was the small private altar she'd set up for her dead: for her mother, teacher and husband, those she'd lost in a lifetime of being a fugitive condemned to death.

'I saw that Băng Tâm wrote,' she said.

A silence, from *Guts of Sea*. She said finally, 'He did. They're settled on one of the inner rings, with *The Moon in Teacups*. They found some space on the edge of the orbital for *Moon*'s body, too. He's posing as a moderately wealthy merchant with *Moon* as his adopted niece, with a distant connection to you which someone will find if they dig – your third aunt knew *Moon*'s grandmother, and they lost touch during the Uprising. There's a vid. But ...'

Quỳnh had not watched the vid. It'd be *Moon* laughing as she played with gravity, or as she tried to make her avatar change shape – or, Heaven forbid, tried to see what she could do with the network – all with a toddler's ruthless single-mindedness.

'I know,' she said. 'You think I should be sharp.'

Guts of Sea looked uncertain. 'I think it's important.'

She didn't say what was important, and perhaps it was best, because Quỳnh wasn't sure she could have given a reply that would have made herself or her ancestors proud.

But she wanted to watch that vid. She wanted, for a moment, to smile, to feel happiness. To enjoy *Moon* – or worse, to go to that habitat and steep herself in her company, laughing alongside the child mindship.

Her child.

Guts of Sea was right: it wouldn't have been wise. She was here for her revenge, and she couldn't afford vulnerability: not just hers, but *Moon*'s. Her enemies hadn't balked at manipulating the evidence and executing an innocent woman fifteen years ago, and in the meantime they'd only become wealthier and more powerful. They had more to lose now.

It all made sense. It was reasonable. It was the best course of action, all things considered, to keep *Moon* safe, calling her *Big Auntie* rather than *Mommy*. She was here for revenge, not for happiness.

It didn't make it hurt less.

'I'll watch the vid later,' Quỳnh said.

Guts of Sea said nothing. Quỳnh could feel her friend's sadness and anger.

'How are *you*?' she asked, to deflect the conversation.

Most of the time, *Guts of Sea* was angry. She'd been raised for the service of the Empire, and during the Ten Thousand Flags Uprising, the Empire had abandoned her. She'd been wounded and broken, and her commanding officer had left her to die in deep spaces rather than take her to the shipyards to be healed. *Guts of Sea* had hung in deep spaces with no means to repair herself, with only her resentment keeping her alive – until Quỳnh found and fixed her.

Now *Guts of Sea* was healed, and out to get revenge on the entire Empire that had failed her.

'I'm well enough,' *Guts of Sea* said, in a tone that said, *Really? You're asking me that?* 'I didn't know any of them personally.'

Unlike Quỳnh. 'It's the same army who judged rescuing you wasn't worth it.'

'Too damaged.' *Guts of Sea* spat out the words. 'Yes. But the general who gave the order is long dead.'

Quỳnh wasn't sure if that made it better or worse. At least her enemies could be reached. At least she wasn't seeking to bring down a whole empire and its army – a forever unattainable goal. She'd never asked *Guts of Sea* – not in so many words – what the mindship would do when they were finished here. Perhaps because she was scared of the answer. Or perhaps because neither of them really imagined they would survive this.

'I guess.' She brought up the invitation again – the culmination of years of preparation; stared at it. 'Well, *I'm* ready,' she said – not to *Guts of Sea*, but to no one in particular – or perhaps to her younger self, who had died the moment Quỳnh tumbled into the vacuum.

They took a shuttle to the general's house: like the prefect, she was one of the few who had an entire habitat to herself. Their invitation brought an entire overlay into existence: not just an ordinary privacy screen, but something shimmering with the jade and silver of officials, a space utterly cut off from the other people on board, in which celebrated scholars read their poetry.

It was not subtle, but then General Tuyết had never been subtle.

Quỳnh rested her head against the shuttle wall, her jewelled bots immobile on her hands and shoulders – feeling the cold metal beneath the virtual mahogany wood – and thought again of burning skin, of burning thoughts.

She'd loved Tuyết, once. It shouldn't have mattered, but perhaps, on some level, it would. Perhaps her heart and soul would betray her, as Tuyết had once done.

As they approached, Đình Diệu, the old soldier who'd given Quỳnh the once-over when she boarded, shimmered into existence on the shuttle.

'The general is waiting for you,' she said.

The Peach Blossom Lake General. A title that spoke of the depth of friendship and sworn siblinghood. Such an irony.

They walked along an exquisitely decorated corridor; the alcoves displayed jade carvings, vases and a wide variety of scholars' rocks taken from the asteroids of the Belt, their colour and texture carefully chosen to resemble mountains on the First or Second Planet. There was faint, rising music – a song, or a poem set to zither, with just a suggestion of Serpent accent. Surprising, that. The general had been distancing herself from *The Azure Serpent* and its associated stigma: a mining rig with questionable loyalties during the Ten Thousand Flags Uprising was hardly the best calling card for an imperial official.

Another turn of the corridor, and they entered an overlay: a wide expanse of orchard under starlight, a mixture of cherry and peach trees, their flowers glistening. Overhead, a ballet of ships and shuttles.

It was a banquet. Tables had been set between the trees, and people, laughing, were drinking wine and raising toasts, competing with one another for the cleverest repartee. Quỳnh and *Guts of Sea* walked amid a rain of petals in a perception overlay – the coldness on her hands, the rising wind whipping her sleeves and making *Guts of Sea* teeter.

'Show-offs,' *Guts of Sea* said sharply.

Quỳnh didn't answer. She kept her eyes on the end of the overlay: the raised dais with five chairs where they waited for her. Her bots were monitoring the space, but it was just what it seemed: a banquet with few people paying attention to them. In the silence, as she approached it, she bowed: the same effortless bow she'd tendered Hoà, except this one had an edge.

'Gentlepeople,' she said.

Laughter.

'So you're the heroes.'

She raised her eyes, then. In the two furthest chairs were distant relatives. Then *Heart's Sorrow* – a callow youth who didn't really matter. And then ...

She hadn't changed, had she? The voice was a little deeper. Her avatar had been retouched to make her seem older than she really was: a matron, but not so old she was undesirable. Butterfly eyebrows arched, the mouth creased in that familiar smile – two blinks away from crystalline laughter – she was sitting down, barely moving. Quỳnh remembered how she would gracefully pick up a cup or a brush, or gently run her hands over Quỳnh's shoulder until they both shivered with desire.

'General,' Quỳnh said, slowly, carefully.

That smile became the familiar laughter. 'Call me Tuyết. I understand the family owes you a debt, younger sister.'

She'd moved effortlessly to the informal, discarding Quỳnh's formalities. She didn't seem to recognise Quỳnh at all.

It had been fifteen years, and Quỳnh's time in deep spaces had twisted and changed her, her face and body language now bearing little relation to who she had once been.

'It was merely our duty,' *Guts of Sea* said smoothly.

Tuyết laughed, again. 'A very gallant one, and we are grateful. Aren't we, lil sis?'

The last person on the dais inclined her head. She hadn't spoken: she'd been watching Quỳnh and *Guts of Sea* carefully, as if assessing a threat. She wore nondescript robes, in sharp contrast to the elaborate physical and virtual embroidery of Tuyết's clothes – a single layer of black silk, when Tuyết's robes were at least five layers of different colours, a rooster showing off its plumage. Her bots were beautiful and jewelled, like everyone else's; but unlike everyone else's, they also looked functional, and by 'functional' Quỳnh meant able to shear anything small in half in a mere blink.

'We are,' she said. 'I'm Thanh Nhăng. You can refer to me as Nhăng.'

Besides Quỳnh, *Guts of Sea* tensed, slightly. Nhăng – she used a literary name where Tuyết had used an intimate one – looked like a mild-mannered, retired scholar, with greying hair at her temples and a severe topknot that didn't have a stray hair out of place. But Quỳnh and *Guts of Sea* had both known her as an enforcer on board *The Azure Serpent*. Nhăng had arrested Quỳnh, and attended her execution.

'Elder sister,' Quỳnh said carefully, and waited, eyes downcast – her bots monitoring Nhăng for a reaction. Her heartbeat was slow, even. Unchanged. Mild interest, nothing more. They hadn't recognised her.

It ought to have satisfied her, or relieved her. Instead, she was vaguely angry, and she wasn't even sure why.

'Focus,' *Guts of Sea* said, on the private comms. 'The plan.'

The plan didn't stop at not being recognised. The plan required her to wave their bait at Tuyết ... containing the hook that would ultimately cost her the protection her status afforded her. The plan required gaining enough of Tuyết's trust, and they had only this opportunity.

'We understand you've come from the shipyards.' Nhăng

gestured, moving slightly to make space for two people: a clear invitation to join them on the dais.

Quỳnh and *Guts of Sea* moved to sit with them. Quỳnh found herself sitting between Tuyết and *Heart's Sorrow*, *Guts of Sea* next to Nhăng.

Tuyết poured Quỳnh wine, and overlay food materialised for *Guts of Sea*, the same luxurious spread in front of the human participants. It would evoke pleasant memories for the ship – though from the way *Guts of Sea* positioned herself, stiff and particularly blank-stanced, it didn't seem as though she was enjoying any of it.

'Here.' Tuyết offered Quỳnh a morsel from her own plate. 'The fish is absolutely heavenly.'

Quỳnh was taken aback as the glistening opalescent flesh was moved from the end of Tuyết's chopsticks to her own bowl. Tuyết had done this back when they were lovers, when they'd trusted each other. Only this wasn't a gesture of sharing between soulmates, but a simple mark of honour from a superior. It was different. It felt different.

'Thank you,' she said, slowly and smoothly. 'We're honoured. I've heard a lot about you in the imperial court, and I see your house is as magnificent as I was told.'

Tuyết visibly softened. 'Oh. Who told you this?'

'Minister Châu Khanh said it was a place of refinement that made one forget they were in the Belt.' Quỳnh gestured to the overlay, where the words of a poem about the moon coalesced into existence, then fell to the ground one by one – slowly transforming into Southern characters from Old Earth. 'Lý Bạch. A particularly apt choice for an evening such as this. A reminder of the impermanence of fame, and by extension, of life.'

'I'm honoured.' Tuyết was smiling, blossoming like a flower deprived of water. It was sad how little she'd changed: always angling for compliments, flattery still the key to her heart.

'It's unsubtle and gauche,' Tuyết's son, *Heart's Sorrow*, glowered. His scorn was palpable.

'Child!' Tuyết turned to him, scandalised. Some kind of subvocalised, private channel conversation took place. A telling-off.

Guts of Sea couldn't break the encryption on their private channel – certainly not without calling attention to herself – but she could and did flag the communications in overlay.

Quỳnh sipped her tea to steady herself. She watched *Guts of Sea* make polite conversation with Nhăng. Something about their journey to the Belt: light and amusing anecdotes chosen to be as innocuous as possible. These days, Nhăng was no longer an enforcer on an asteroid mining rig; she was a retired scholar who managed her wife's social calendar. But old habits die hard, and people like Nhăng would always remember suspicion.

'I apologise, elder aunt.' *Heart's Sorrow*'s voice was sullen.

Quỳnh inclined her head. 'No need.'

'Absolutely a need.' Tuyết's voice was freezing. 'Do you have children?'

She did. She did not. Quỳnh breathed in carefully, calling on her bots to start a flurry of activity designed to hide the slight shift in her vitals.

'I always wanted children,' she said, finally, truthfully. 'But alas. It wasn't to be.'

Do not think of Moon, *do* not *think of* Moon.

'Ah.' Tuyết's face twisted for a moment. 'I'm very sorry to hear that.' She placed her hand, briefly, on one of Quỳnh's bots. 'Life doesn't always take us where we want to go.'

No, indeed. It would have meant more, would have touched her more, if it wasn't Tuyết saying the words. If she ... If she'd changed more, physically or otherwise. If she didn't look exactly the same as the scared lover who'd denounced

Quỳnh to the magistrate. Because she thought that Quỳnh's ties to a rebel general – distant ties of friendship that pre-dated the Uprising and had never prompted so much as a single treasonous thought – were too dangerous. Quỳnh breathed out, carefully, purging the slightest trace of anger from her vitals. She couldn't afford to let the depth of her emotions show.

'You're still angry,' Tuyết said.

Quỳnh thought fast on her feet.

'Yes,' she said. 'Life does that.'

Besides Tuyết, Nhăng looked up at them, drawn by the sharpness of Quỳnh's tone.

'Anything the matter?' she asked.

Quỳnh had no quarrel with Nhăng – who, back on *The Azure Serpent*, had only done her duty as an enforcer, making it abundantly clear that she didn't approve of the summary justice – but of the pair, Nhăng was the more observant. The more dangerous one. Quỳnh asked her bots for a mild sedative to slow her heartbeat and tamp down her feelings. She'd feel sluggish, but at least her emotions wouldn't betray her.

Nhăng's ice-blue eyes held her, for a moment. Her mouth quirked.

'You seem familiar. Did I meet you somewhere?'

'Careful,' *Guts of Sea* subvocalised.

The reminder felt very distant, with the sedative in Quỳnh's blood.

'At court, perhaps?'

Nhăng's voice was sharp. 'I don't attend court.'

The truth. It was the only thing that would head Nhăng off.

'Honestly, you also seem very familiar to me,' Quỳnh said. Every word felt like cotton in her mouth, one step away from dissolving and completely plugging her palate and throat. 'But I've been in the shipyards and at court in the last decade, and I understand you didn't move much from the Belt?'

Nhăng's eyes held her, for what felt like an eternity. 'No,' she said curtly. 'I don't. I don't see the need to beg for attention.'

Which was interesting, given that this described her wife's weak point. Some undercurrents there. Quỳnh flagged them to her bots, to study later. Her plan didn't require Nhăng, but it might not survive interference from her either.

'Fair,' she said.

Nhăng's gaze hadn't moved. She was weighing Quỳnh, with a flicker of recognition in her eyes. Something too sharp, too perceptive. She'd recognised Quỳnh. But surely she wouldn't. Surely she couldn't.

She'd changed. No one could tell who she was any more.

At length, Nhăng's gaze moved away from her, to rest on *Guts of Sea* – with the same intensity and curiosity — before she finally looked away.

'She's worked out something,' *Guts of Sea* said, on their private channel.

But if Nhăng knew who Quỳnh was, she'd have said. She'd have had them arrested. And she hadn't. The thought that Quỳnh might have to cut and run with her revenge unfulfilled was unbearable, unacceptable.

'Something else,' Quỳnh said. 'Not our identity. We're good.'

There was no possibility Nhăng knew.

'Hmm. Fair,' *Guts of Sea* said. Nhăng was now looking at the banquet, summarily uninterested in either of them. 'She probably has some literary argument to go settle somewhere.'

Quỳnh felt relief flood her. 'Yes,' she said.

The awkward silence was broken by Tuyết.

'So, what brings you to the Belt?' she asked. 'It's a long way from the shipyards. Or the imperial court.'

Quỳnh smiled. It had teeth. 'A pressing desire to travel.

Actually ...' She paused, letting her gaze stray sideways, in a deliberate gesture of embarrassment. 'I was wondering if I could ask a favour?'

'Oh?' Tuyết's voice was non-committal.

'*Guts of Sea* and I arrived three days ago. We're a bit confused with the Belt's bureaucracy. We applied for a Belt auth-token from the prefecture, but they're telling us that it should have gone to the military administration.' She let the slightest trace of worry touch her voice. 'Without Belt auth-tokens, there's a whole host of local services we can't access, so naturally we'd like to have ours as soon as possible.'

Tuyết's face cleared. It *was* a favour. It was also a calculated one: not too large, not too inconvenient.

'It's a peculiarity of the Belt, yes. Because of the ... ah ... history.' Because the Dragon's Tail General, the spearhead of the Ten Thousand Flags Uprising, had originally come from the Belt, and the Uprising had been bloodiest in the Belt. 'We're still a military district in many ways.'

Power was flowing away from her, Quỳnh knew. Now that the Uprising was over, the Empire was moving away from military administration and back to the scholars. Tuyết was losing ground to her old ally and friend, the prefect – Minh's mother. But, obviously, Tuyết was never going to admit that.

'Ah. I wish we'd known that earlier. How long might it take to get the application processed? I'm concerned we have lost precious time.'

'Oh, leave it to me,' Tuyết said, waving a dismissive hand. 'Give me the application reference and it will be sorted out for you by tomorrow morning. Don't thank me. It's the least I can do, after you helped my child. *Heart's Sorrow* would have been permanently scarred if you hadn't dealt with those bandits.'

Heart's Sorrow was moodily eating his food, his resentment palpable.

Teenagers.

'Much obliged, nevertheless.'

'Most services are accessible to outsiders without a Belt auth-token. What local services are you trying to access?'

'Ah.' Quỳnh laughed. She sent Tuyết their application details. 'We're buying a compound.'

A pause.

'Buying?'

Tuyết's voice was flat. Quỳnh could almost follow the slow, creeping realisation as she parsed the implications of the sentence. A local auth-token was only necessary for buying outright – not for a loan or a more complicated arrangement. Meaning Quỳnh and *Guts of Sea* had money, and were willing to spend it casually on something as large as a whole compound.

If eyes could glitter with greed, Tuyết's would have been diamonds.

'I hadn't realised you intended to stay for long.'

'As I said – a pressing need to travel. To have a respite from the turmoil of the court.'

'I see.' Nhăng's voice was expressionless.

Guts of Sea's bots relayed that her heartbeat was slowing down, her skin less flushed. She was recalibrating as well, but it was different: she'd weighed Quỳnh up and realised she was nothing more than a moneyed scholar who'd come to the Belt, away from the centre of the Empire, because it was easier to have respect and influence here. Possibly because she was out of favour with the court, and unwilling to admit it. In other words, Nhăng had decided Quỳnh was harmless.

Good.

'I'm glad to hear we can count on your company for some time.' Tuyết glanced at Nhăng; a conversation passed between them on a private channel, a larger than usual stream of encrypted data highlighted in overlay. Tuyết finally added, 'We are having a gathering in five days. We would be delighted to have you in attendance.'

Excellent.

Quỳnh allowed herself a small smile, a fraction of the satisfaction she felt.

'I would be delighted.'

'As would I,' *Guts of Sea* said.

'We wonder ...' Tuyết paused, uncertain. The uncertainty didn't look feigned. 'It's presumptuous, but—'

'Go on.' Quỳnh smiled, not allowing even a fraction of it to reach her eyes.

'Would you consider composing a centrepiece poem for the occasion?'

Bait swallowed whole.

Quỳnh made a show of considering it, though in truth she didn't need to. Composing the centrepiece poem was a prestigious role. Tuyết's household would benefit from visible connections to the imperial court; Quỳnh would gain entry into this particular household, and into the larger Belt society.

It was an opportunity for further access to the compound – not just for her but for *Guts of Sea*, who could use it to sniff around the network and see deeper into its weaknesses. All good preparation for what would follow: the slow and inexorable arc of their downfall.

'It would be my pleasure.'

Later, as the shuttle took them home to their empty compound, Quỳnh listened to *Guts of Sea*'s account – the blistering opinions on the overlays and the security.

'They weren't very good. It was all for show. Did you see the trees in the overlay were fuzzing over in the distance? It wouldn't have cost them a lot more to fix that, but they didn't think it was worth it. They just wanted to impress.'

'Hmm.' Quỳnh said.

She felt exhausted and wrung out, as if she'd just survived a plunge into the vacuum, or run from the innermost rings of the Belt to the outermost.

'And just one overlay, too. You saw I could flag all their data streams? They're encrypted, but I'm not sure how well.'

'You didn't try to break them.'

'Not yet.' *Guts of Sea*'s voice was smug. 'Give me a little time, and I will.'

'How was Nhăng?'

A shrug from *Guts of Sea*. 'She was interested in where we'd come from and why, but she didn't dig very deep. I told her I was looking for a partner, but she didn't take that bait.'

'I'm not surprised.' Quỳnh tried, very hard, to forget the way Nhăng had looked at her. There was no way Nhăng could know anything. 'Too early for that one. But it doesn't matter. We have the invitation. And the request for a centrepiece poem.'

'Hmm.' *Guts of Sea*'s bots settled on Quỳnh's hands, glossy with a faint remnant of deep spaces. It was almost comforting, to remember where they'd both come from. She hadn't expected to feel this unsettled, this conflicted. 'Anyway, Nhăng is smart. Sharp, once. But going soft.' She said it as though it was an offence.

'You hate them,' Quỳnh said.

'Nhăng? No. I don't. She's upright, with a rigid honour code. I'm just surprised at her choice of wife.'

'Tuyết always had a way of making people dance to her tune.' Quỳnh laid her head against the wall of the shuttle, with that virtual overlay of wood. A good set of perception filters, but not a great one. 'I don't blame Nhăng for not seeing who her wife is.'

A silence.

'I don't hate them, but you do. Don't you?'

She wasn't sure. 'They haven't changed,' she said finally. 'Neither of them. I felt I was sitting at a banquet on *The Azure Serpent*.' A dead ship. A lover who was alive, but dead to her. 'I thought I'd feel something. Anything. But it was just ...' She saw them clearly and weighed them, and she looked at the rules they took for granted and saw only ways to hurt them with those rules. 'I'm the one who's changed.'

A silence. *Guts of Sea*'s bots rested lightly on her hands, close enough to touch her own bots.

'Yes,' *Guts of Sea* said. 'As you should.'

Destroyed and remade. Dã Lan — sweet, young, naive Dã Lan — was dead, and so was everyone else, and Quỳnh was a ghost risen from her grave, eager to feast on the entrails of the living. But for a moment, what Quỳnh had felt was beyond the deep-seated rage that Nhăng, who'd barely known Dã Lan, was the one who'd become suspicious, and not Tuyết; Tuyết, whom she'd lived with, whom she'd slept with, whom she'd laughed with, whom she'd trusted. For a moment, Quỳnh felt a profound sadness at Tuyết's limitations.

'As I should,' Quỳnh said, smoothly, lightly.

The plan was proceeding as it should. She could deal with unexpected surprises, with unexpected feelings. The net she'd woven around the Belt was a fine, lethal one, and no matter how the fish thrashed, it wouldn't change its ultimate fate.

4

Mother and Child

Mother made her wait.

She'd ordered Minh confined to her rooms – an order Stepmother enforced with glee, raising boundary filters and cutting off Minh's network accesses – but she didn't appear herself.

Of course not. She'd let Minh wait in the darkness. With her network accesses revoked, Minh felt small and naked, a child again. That she knew the games Mother was playing didn't help her to be more distant from them – not when Mother was in control of almost everything. Her bots lay in various states of disarray around the room, where Stepmother had switched them off. Minh kept reaching out for them and finding nothing, or reaching out for the network, for *Heart's Sorrow*, for Oanh's children, any of her friends. Her make-up had run and felt caked on, and she was very much sitting in the ruins of a plan gone disastrously wrong.

She hoped Nhi had got home safely. She hoped *Heart's Sorrow* wasn't confined to his body for the next five years, or whatever his mothers had thought of as punishment, though his mothers weren't as strict as Minh's. And she hoped Quỳnh wasn't in trouble with the tribunal: whatever she and her bots had done to those five bandits, it was probably not entirely legal, and Mother would have absolutely no sense of humour about that. That she'd saved Minh would make no difference. In fact, it would probably make it worse.

Quỳnh.

Quỳnh was cool and composed, a scholar to her core: everything Mother was trying to turn Minh into, everything Minh failed to be, by – inasmuch as she could tell – simply getting up in the morning. And yet she'd been friendly with Minh. Courteous, perhaps, rather than friendly, but she didn't have to be either of those things. She could have judged Minh a foolish, awkward teenager, but she'd spoken to her as an equal. She'd *asked* for Minh's opinion, sounding for all the world as though she valued it.

The experience was new, and unsettling and terrifying in the way that open space was: ten thousand paths Minh hadn't even dreamed of suddenly becoming possibilities.

Quỳnh. She really hoped Quỳnh remained there, and that *Guts of Sea* found what she wanted. Both of them deserved the best the Belt had to offer; but with Mother and *Heart's Sorrow*'s first mother in charge, they would likely get rather less than that. What Minh hoped or wanted for them was irrelevant.

Minh stared at the wall, for a while.

Focus. Breathe.

She didn't have any bots or any contact with her friends, but she didn't need them. The escapade had been risky, and by any measure inadvisable – any save one. For that brief moment in the corridor and in the plaza, she'd been anonymous and jostled, vibrating with the same excitement as the rest of the crowd. For that briefest, brightest of moments she'd been free, her thread of fate utterly unwoven from her family's – and it had been like a breath of air to someone drowning.

It had been worth it, just for that.

She must have fallen asleep, at some point, with the lights still on – woke up, thinking she should turn them off, reaching for bots that weren't there – and fell back into sleep.

When she woke up again, the lights were still on. She sent the command to dim them direct to the ambient centre anyway. It was petty, but it felt good.

She stared at her bedroom: in many ways it hadn't changed since her childhood, with overlays from her favourite vid series, *The Adventures of Lady Turtle*, with all the spaceships and their navigators arrayed on successive overlays. *The Princess Who Drowned the Sword* and Ngọc Minh had always been her favourite, and not just because they shared a first name. Minh sympathised with Ngọc Minh's dislike of insincerity. There were fewer children's toys, and more electronics and books now – and her own set-up for making food and drinks. And, in a corner of the room, a shrine to Minh's womb-mother – Second Mother, the one she'd lost in infancy and barely remembered. It held three shrivelled oranges and a burned incense stick; she'd need to renew the offerings soon, or she'd really be unfilial.

Minh's bots might be out, but she still had access to the commands for her bedroom. She got some boiling water and tea, and started brewing herself some Jade Spiral, breathing in the floral aroma, and got into the washing room – a large space with a porcelain basin and more overlays of series – where she asked the cleaning centre for something to remove her make-up. When she came out, face bare, hair flowing down her back, she felt almost relaxed.

That lasted about five blinks, until the door opened without so much as a knock.

'Child.'

Minh bowed, deep – as deep as she'd have bowed for the

Empress, a reflex that was so ingrained she couldn't even think of doing otherwise.

'Mother.'

Tinh Đức, the prefect of the Scattered Pearls Belt – its civil administrator and the highest ranking official in the asteroids and habitats – was a middle-aged woman with a bearing of steel. She'd had all the rejuv treatments afforded to the higher dignitaries: the ones that made her appear dignified and older, instead of just old and sad. The gaze she turned on Minh could have burned through layers of steel.

'So.' Her voice was cold, the same tone she must use when the accused faced her in her tribunal.

Minh cradled her tea like a lifeline.

'So.'

She didn't know how long she could cling to her defiance.

'Explain to me what you were thinking.'

Mother sat down – the chair appeared beneath her, dragged there swiftly by her bots, who barely made any noise on the floor. Around her was an overlay of darker space – shadows making her appear taller and more forbidding – and behind her was the faintest suggestion of some large, fanged animal: the giải trãi who was the symbol of justice. Minh had always thought it looked like a ridiculous horned dog, with way too many spikes on its head and snout, but the one behind Mother looked like it could, indeed, gore the guilty with its horn and devour them whole.

'You didn't have to shut off my bots,' Minh said sullenly.

So much for adult behaviour.

Mother raised an eyebrow. 'You realise the gravity of what you did?'

'The bandits? The Tiger getting loose? I couldn't have foreseen either.'

'Yes. That's the point! You couldn't name the risk, but you could see it, and you chose to do it anyway.'

'You never let me go anywhere.' Minh bit her lip. That had come out wrong.

Mother's gaze was glacial. 'And clearly, judging from your escapade, that was the right decision. Do you even realise how close you came to dying?'

Minh rubbed her wrists. 'They'd have ransomed me.'

'And so many things can go wrong during a ransom claim. As you should know.' Her face softened a fraction. 'I thought I'd taught you better than that.'

As you should know.

Everything had been laid out for her – her future planned. Mother had only deigned to see Minh when she was teaching her how to pass the examinations, how to be an official – how to be as successful as she'd been, rising from the magistrate of a ring on *The Azure Serpent* to prefect of the whole of the Scattered Pearls Belt, her name whispered in literary circles for promotion to the imperial court.

Mother said, again, 'Explain', but it was gentler this time. And, when Minh didn't speak, 'Everything was chaos during the Tiger Games. I didn't need to hear I'd almost lost you on top of that.'

Minh shouldn't have been fooled. She knew exactly what was expected of her – but for a moment, staring at Mother's face – at the elegant make-up, so expertly applied, the ceruse making her face pale and smooth, as sharply beautiful as jade and ice – she thought she saw something else. A modicum of concern. Of love. She meant well. She did want the best for Minh.

'When the crowd broke it left us in the middle of nowhere,' Minh said. 'The bandits must have been watching us for some time before that.' She thought of the interaction with the now dead Phoenix Wings, and back to the bun-seller. 'I guess my disguise wasn't as good as I thought it was.'

'You're very intelligent, but you don't pay enough attention to detail.' Mother's voice was soft. 'You disdain appearances, but when you've moved as long as I have within official circles, I can assure you they have their uses.'

Minh felt obscurely chastened – gauche and gaudy.

'Your rescuers,' Mother said.

Minh said. 'What about them?'

She ought to have known the conversation would turn to them: Mother would never let such an obvious unknown into her world-view.

'Sương Quỳnh. The Alchemist of Streams and Hills. And *Guts of Sea*.' Mother's bots climbed, unobtrusively, along her billowing sleeves, nestling in between the elaborate embroidery of crescent moons against the blue of Heaven. 'They are new to the Belt.' She pursed her lips. 'I wonder if they'll prove to be troublemakers.'

Minh started to speak, stopped. She wanted to say Quỳnh wasn't a troublemaker, but on some level she knew that Quỳnh would do as she pleased and expect the world to shape itself around her desires. It wasn't even arrogance, because Quỳnh seemed capable of achieving anything she set her mind to.

'There's no way to know.'

'Hmm.' Mother pursed her lips. 'It doesn't matter much. While they're here they'll have to behave.'

Minh looked for a subject to deflect the conversation.

'What did happen during the Tiger Games?'

'Shoddy artistry.' Mother's voice was cool. 'The Tiger burst through the arena safeguards and started burning down the station instead of its opponent.'

'That's more than shoddy artistry,' Minh said sharply. The tea was cold in her hands. She wasn't *Heart's Sorrow*, with his obsession for unpacking the truth and fixing everything, but she did have a few skills. 'Either the safeguards were faulty or it was deliberate.'

Mother smiled. It was edged and triumphant. The giải trãi in the overlay behind her shifted, its horn gleaming in the darkness of Minh's room.

See, she said, without needing to actually say it. *I'm right. You're smart.*

'Oh, I know. The data artist will talk, eventually. Or her family will. Interfering with the imperial games is an act of rebellion.'

Which meant all of them were now marked for execution. Minh opened her mouth, closed it. Opened it again, even though it was futile.

'You don't have to follow the rules so rigidly.'

'Are you telling me how to do my work?' Mother's voice was a purr. Minh could feel the tension. Her bots shifted in the darkness: no sound, just the glint of metal legs moving on the floor. Minh reached for her own, only they were still turned off. 'In defiance of all filial piety?'

Minh swallowed. 'Executing them is neither example nor courtesy. Punishment doesn't teach shame.' She referred to Khổng Tử, the First Teacher, the source of all the supposed wisdom they were taught.

Mother raised an eyebrow again. 'Parroting the classics isn't a gauge of being a good scholar.' And, more softly, 'The Ten Thousand Flags Uprising ended less than ten years ago. There are still illegal shrines to the Dragon's Tail General and her followers. We must stand strong against lawlessness. Mercy isn't one of the Five Virtues.'

To love a thing means wanting it to live. The quote from Khổng Tử came unbidden to Minh. She clamped down on it.

'We follow the rules. They're here to guard us. And we,

as the guarantors of the rule, the parents of the people – we cannot afford to be seen breaking them.'

Minh's heart sank.

Mother said, 'Attending the Tiger Games without my permission is a family matter, for which you've already been punished. That leaves the impersonation and forging of an auth-token. You know what the punishment is for that.'

Criminal laws, subsection referring to counterfeiting, article three hundred and twenty-six. A centiday in a lacerator on a high setting, and three months of comms isolation. And that was only because she hadn't chosen to impersonate an official, in which case the penalty would have been significantly higher. Minh swallowed. She didn't want to go into the lacerator; last time the cuts and bruises, physical and mental, had been so bad she hadn't been able to walk afterwards. And she could bear the loss of her bots and the network – probably – but not for three months. She'd need everything she had to help *Heart's Sorrow* repair Great-grandmother, if nothing else.

'The code also says that offenders can see their punishment reduced in exchange for monetary compensation.'

Mother's face was unreadable. 'Yes,' she said. 'You know the rates.'

And she knew those the rates were not negotiable. If anything, Mother would probably be harsher on her than on anyone else. She wanted to look good – to have her whole family above reproach. She would hurt them – even Minh, even Minh's stepsister Vân – to preserve her reputation as the irreproachable judge, the one who even went after the small offences. Minh was never sure whether to admire or hate her.

'I have the money,' she said.

'Do you? Last time I checked, you didn't.'

She'd checked and double-checked before she embarked upon this. She wasn't *totally* foolhardy. But Mother looked so certain. She knew. She always knew better. And Minh might have calculated it wrong. She might not have had the right section of the legal code in mind.

Mother smiled. 'I'll take what you have in your account and apply it to your little escapade. I'll let you know what's left over.'

Minh gritted her teeth. 'I want to know now.'

Mother's face didn't move. 'Do you? Then perhaps you shouldn't have sunk to the level of a common criminal.'

And she left, closing the door behind her and turning off the overlay.

Minh drank her tea to the dregs, tasting the bitterness of the leaves.

Minh reconnected her bots. She had to address every single one of them and then reconnect them manually – Mother's final and petty shot.

Stepmother, to her credit, had offered to help; but Minh didn't have the patience to deal with Stepmother – who on any given day hovered between enthusiastic support of Mother and trying to make Minh adhere to incomprehensible versions of decorum.

'Big sis, can I help? Mama says you got into big trouble.'

Minh's stepsister Vân, Stepmother's and Mother's five-year-old daughter, had wandered into the room.

'Shouldn't you be with your tutor?'

Vân made a face. 'She's left for the day. Can I help, please?'

Minh sighed. She loved Vân – bossy, too smart for her own good, oddly vulnerable. And envied her, too, because Mother's love for Vân seemed uncomplicated and unconditional.

'Can you help me find all my bots?'

'For sure!'

Vân pattered around the room. She only had three bots, large and sturdy constructions that would withstand being thrown and knocked about, on wheels rather than multiple legs, their sensors huge and safe behind childproof glass. They were also bright purple with sparkles, because Vân loved sparkles. She finally settled down near the tea-set – Minh had to stop herself from grabbing it and putting out of her reach – and closed her eyes, her small fists going out as her bots clambered around the room. It was clumsy – she'd get better and be able, like Minh, to control them with thought-commands – but also devastatingly cute.

While Vân mopped up the straggler bots, Minh reconnected them. When she finally had enough of them to access the outside network, she found five different messages from *Heart's Sorrow*, their length increasing and their tone also increasingly panicked. She also had a courteous message from Quỳnh, reminding Minh that they had an appointment, and signed with a small but elegant poem and her literary seal.

Minh sighed. 'I need to raise someone. Can you wait for me for a bit?'

Vân stared at her. 'Can I have a story?'

'After I've had my conversation,' Minh said. 'You can look in the rainy season chest.'

The chests were normally for storing clothes for each season, but there were no seasons on the habitats except the ones created by the Minds controlling them, so Minh used it to store her old plush toys and games, the ones from *The Azure Serpent* and the charged years that had followed the mining rig's destruction.

'Fine, but you promised,' Vân said.

'I'll remember,' Minh said, and turned on the privacy overlay.

For a moment she thought *Heart's Sorrow* wasn't going to answer her – especially unusual for a mindship, who could manage several parallel conversations on parallel threads – but then he did.

'You're back!!'

'Obviously.' Minh thought of Mother sitting in her room. 'It was not fun.'

'Yeah, I can imagine. How bad was it?'

Heart's Sorrow had materialised an avatar in the darkened overlay of the call: a streamlined version of himself, like a series of brush strokes from a calligraphy master. Minh didn't bother with hers; she just projected a version of her own seal, the literary name she'd picked for herself – Hollow Bamboo Grove, the one Mother had smiled at, as if Minh had learned a trick but not understood it.

Minh sighed. 'I don't have any money left.'

'You knew that was going to happen.'

'Yeah. Better that than the alternative.' Minh checked her accounts: they were indeed empty. Mother had been uncharacteristically swift in emptying them. Perhaps she'd thought Minh might spend the money if she had the chance. 'You?'

'A stern talking-to, and banquet duty for the next month.' *Heart's Sorrow* sounded resigned. 'It really sucks.'

'Did you talk to Thu Lâm and Thu Thảo?'

Both of their friends had declined to go on the venture. Oanh's children were sensible – entirely too sensible to be teenagers – and they'd been busy trying to get hold of advance copies of the latest *Alchemist of Black Water* ahead of the vid's official airing date.

'Yeah. If you want to see some *Black Water* ahead of time—'

'Not in the mood.' Minh sighed. 'I'll send them a message congratulating them, and they can share some other time.'

'For sure. Oh, I saw your rescuer.'

'Quỳnh?' Minh's heart missed a beat. 'How was she?'

'Busy sucking up to Mom. What else?'

Minh thought of Quỳnh, of her worry about *Guts of Sea* and *Guts of Sea*'s marriage; of the need to make a good impression. Of course she'd do anything necessary.

'In all fairness, she'd have to do that if she wanted to get anywhere in the Belt.'

'You *like* her,' *Heart's Sorrow* said.

'And that's wrong?'

'No. I can see why. But I don't have to like her, too.'

'Fair,' Minh said. 'Where are you?'

A silence, from *Heart's Sorrow*.

'You're on board again, aren't you.'

She didn't mean on board his body. She meant on board the other ship, *Flowers at the Gates of the Lords*. Minh's great-aunt and the eldest member of the family, the one whose name Mother barely spoke at home. As the younger child, Minh had been given the duty to take care of her and make sure she didn't die through neglect. Another of Mother's poisoned gifts: she and her friends had managed to do a lot of structural repairs, but of course they had no idea how to actually heal a mindship. Hence *Heart's Sorrow*'s latest and desperate idea: to hire a technologist and see what said technologist could do. They didn't expect success, but what else could they do? What they'd have needed was a Master of Wind and Water, but of course Mother would never let Minh hire one.

His voice was sullen. 'Are you reproaching me?'

Minh thought for a moment. It was his escape. Hers had been the Tiger Games. *Heart's Sorrow* projected himself on board a wrecked ship in the farthest reaches of the Belt – a ship that couldn't move under her own power, that could barely speak – and he tried, again and again, to repair damage that was far beyond fixing. Because it was something they could do, something that wasn't inherited or handed down to them.

'No,' she said finally. 'But I'm not coming today.'

A sigh from *Heart's Sorrow*. 'Fine. Fine. You know the Orca Censor is coming soon.'

'To transfer the leadership of the lineage? Yes. A day isn't going to make a difference.'

Minh felt him tense. He believed in what he was doing, that they were going to repair Second Great-Aunt, that she would be as Minh remembered her, before the battle that had wrecked her thirteen years before – laughing, her bots lifting Minh up in the air, always finding time for her regardless of when Minh called or what problem she had. He believed that Second Great-Aunt wasn't going to be declared legally incompetent by the censor – that the title of head of the lineage would remain with her, instead of passing to Minh's mother.

Minh ... Minh knew that Mother wouldn't let them attempt the repairs if there was a chance – any chance – that they would succeed. With Second Great-Aunt out of the way, Mother would become head of the lineage in name as well as in function, and be able to access the money she hadn't been able to touch so far. And much as Minh would have liked to have Second Great-Aunt back – the one in her memory, who laughed and sang and hugged her – she knew that even if they did fix her, it wouldn't be that simple. Second Great-Aunt had always quarrelled with Mother about her behaviour and the way she handled dissidents during the war. If she came back, the family would tear itself apart again.

Minh wasn't really sure what she wanted to happen.

Finally *Heart's Sorrow* said, 'You've had a terrible day.'

That was an understatement. But at least Minh was free, and she had the appointment with Quỳnh to look forward to.

'I'll be here tomorrow. I promise. Thanks.'

'Any time.' *Heart's Sorrow* said. 'Go and take care of yourself.'

*

The address Quỳnh had given Minh was a huge compound in the middle ring, in a moderately expensive part of the habitats. The compounds on either side of it were occupied, but the overlay faltered and died when Minh neared the gates. The network dropped away precipitously, leaving only the connection to her bots, and darkness ahead of her. Was this the right address? Minh double-checked, stepping forward into inky nothingness, with only the sound of her own footsteps on metal – no ambient filters either, just the bare station, with no adornment either physical or virtual. A stark reminder that a hunk of metal was all that was keeping them safe from the vacuum of space.

If anything went wrong … Minh found herself going through the steps she'd learned as a child. Locate the emergency shadow-skins: behind her, to her left. Locate the nearest airlock – she hadn't seen one in a while, which meant the nearest one was probably ahead. Prepare for moving in a vacuum, and the disorientation of not having an up or a down any more. Just as she was going through the Five Motions and the Eight Orientations, the gates loomed out of the darkness: three steps of carved stone leading up to the pillars of the entrance. It looked like something straight out of the vid dramas that Thu Lâm and Thu Thảo enjoyed so much, the ones that Minh didn't care for because no one seemed to have any common sense.

Beyond the gate was a courtyard between the various sub-compartments of the building, a vast expanse of beaten earth that turned into the starry sky, and then into an ink-black sea with the faintest hint of creatures that might have been carp or dragons. There was a faint hint of music, a song that was almost familiar but not quite – her bots couldn't pick up enough of the harmonics to figure out what it was.

Quỳnh was waiting for her at the other end of the courtyard, her sleeves billowing in an overlay wind. She was alone; *Guts of Sea* didn't seem to be around.

'Child,' she said, inclining her head. 'Glad to see you. Thank you for coming.' She wore layered robes: white, then blue, then a darker blue that touched just the sleeves and hems, and in overlay was only the faintest suggestion of mountains, like a master's painting. 'Will you have some tea?'

They sat down in a pavilion within the courtyard, where Quỳnh's bots brought out a translucent celadon teapot and matching teacups, the porcelain thin as eggshell and shot through with cracks. When Minh touched them, shadows moved in overlay, the faintest suggestions of a galaxy's stars slowly moving across the sky. The tea tasted of grass and sweet flowers, like the apricot ones of New Year's Eve. Exquisite and tasteful – like everything of Quỳnh's.

'How is the aftermath?' Quỳnh asked.

Minh laughed. She couldn't help it. 'Painful, but nothing unexpected.'

'Mm.' Quỳnh poured more tea. 'I've seen your mother on vids. She looks fierce.'

Fierce didn't quite seem to cover it.

'I guess.' Minh stared at her cup, and then at the rest of the courtyard. 'Is this the compound you were thinking of buying?'

'Yes,' Quỳnh said. Her face was smooth, elegant: just the right amount of ceruse to highlight the arch of her eyebrows, her skin shimmering with golden highlights in overlay. Her eyes, unadorned, were piercing and sharp. 'We're renting it at the moment. Trying to get a feel for it. It's not much right now – I just threw the overlays together – but ultimately I'd hope to get in physical furniture as well as more elegant virtual designs. Professional work.'

'Professional work?'

Minh held her cup, turning around to see the courtyard. The overlay shifted from beaten earth to stars to water, slowly and gracefully, mesmerising in its delicacy. The perception filters on the pavilions were good enough that she could feel the warmth of the parquet, the cold smoothness of the lacquer on the pillars and table. The physical space underneath them was perhaps a tenth of the size of the virtual, but the overlay was stretching it effortlessly, making it seem like a vaster expanse. There were no gaps, no blurry parts, nothing that stood out. And Quỳnh looked like a scholar, the perfect image of everything Minh's tutors exalted – everything Mother wanted her to be – all effortless, and Minh knew, in her heart of hearts, that she was never, in any lifetime, going to be that person.

Minh laughed. Her bots, on her shoulders and back, felt small and inadequate in the face of such painstaking perfection. Bitterness welled up, inescapable.

'Why do you need me at all?'

Quỳnh stared at her, not moving from her cross-legged position on the other side of the table. Her bots were at a complete standstill.

'What do you mean?'

'You know exactly what I mean, elder aunt. This is *perfect*. You're *perfect*. Why under Heaven would you need me at all, unless you want something from my mother I can't understand yet? You don't need me to judge the suitability of a compound. You don't need me!'

She was up, dishevelled and unable to control the tone of her voice, her bots scattering around her. She saw herself in Quỳnh's cool eyes, out of control and wild and utterly, vividly inappropriate. Always falling short. Always failing – and she braced herself for a sharp rebuke.

Instead, there was silence. That gentle, unidentifiable background music swelling up, becoming the familiar sound of a lullaby from her childhood – a Serpent lullaby Mother no longer sang to her, because it wasn't politically suitable to be a visible Serpent.

'I see.' Quỳnh's voice was gentle. 'Your mother casts a large shadow, doesn't she.' She used the word that referred both to legacy and to protection and influence.

Minh bit her lip. She felt suspended – on the edge of turning tail, of running.

'Do you know why I asked you here?' Quỳnh said. 'You, and not your mother?'

Minh looked down. She didn't trust herself to speak.

'When you were about to be carried off-Belt, to some uncertain fate – to ransom, to mutilation – all you thought about was making sure I helped Nhi.'

Minh opened her mouth, closed it.

'Do you know what your mother is famous for?'

'The Serpent Rebellion,' Minh said bitterly.

For Dã Lan and everything that had followed: implacably purging anyone who might have rebellious thoughts, no matter how close they were to her. Quỳnh would not know, but Mother had talked about denouncing Second Great-Aunt to the Empire for having rebel sympathies. All that had stopped her was Second Great-Aunt's wreck, rendering her mute and immobile before Mother could level the charge against her.

'Would your mother have helped Nhi?'

The Iron Judge, they called her. The Implacable One. They compared her to Judge Bao, the Old Earth magistrate who was said never to smile. Mother was harsh but ultimately fair. Ultimately, she held to rules and codes, rigidly: an unmoving reassurance in a fluid world.

'I don't know,' Minh said.

Quỳnh's gaze – dark, deep, a black hole which threatened to swallow Minh whole – held hers.

'Don't you? Truly?'

Minh stared back at her. She could uphold filial piety, or speak the truth.

'No,' she said, and the words burned.

Mother would have thought of herself first — because she was the magistrate. Because there would be chaos if she was captured by bandits, and because it was important to uphold the laws of the Empire.

'A truth befitting a gentleperson. Nothing inaccurate in words.' Quỳnh's voice was sharp and ironic. It was almost a direct quote from the First Teacher. 'If I wanted your mother, do you not think she would come here? Eagerly beseeching me for the favour of the imperial court? I'm not here for that.'

'I ...' Minh called her bots back, trying to steady the fast beating of her heart. She envied Quỳnh's coolness, her steady vitals. 'I don't know what you see in me!'

'Kindness. Mercy. Humaneness. Qualities that do you credit and that you did not inherit.' Quỳnh rose in a sweep of blue robes, never taking her eyes off Minh. 'The true mark of a scholar. Will you walk with me? I want to show you the rest of the compound.'

Her bots trailed towards Minh: an invitation.

Kindness. Mercy. Humaneness.

Minh didn't possess those virtues. She knew she didn't. And yet ... And yet, Quỳnh hadn't moved. And the utter certainty with which she'd uttered those words was in her stance, in her gaze — and it made Minh feel larger and somehow seen more clearly than she saw herself. She took a deep, shaking breath, sent her bots to meet Quỳnh's.

'Yes. I will.'

Outside the courtyard, the compound was much smaller. Quỳnh took Minh through a series of small bare metal rooms, each of them only slightly larger than a compartment in the middle rings. They ended up in the room furthest away from the gates, a simple rectangle that was perhaps ten forearm-lengths across. It held a bed that was little more than a mat spread on the metal floor, and a bedside table that was a roughly hewn metal box, on which was a small, featureless screen with old-fashioned calligraphy that was clearly an ancestral altar. More metal boxes in a corner: it seemed they were containers for personal belongings. The bedside table held a horseshoe teacup in delicate celadon, with a carved pattern of waves; it was the only thing in there that wasn't devoid of personality.

Quỳnh caught Minh's gaze, and smiled.

'As I said, I haven't had much time to settle yet.'

'Where is *Guts of Sea*'s space?'

Mindships didn't need physical space for their bodies, but when they lived on station, like *Heart's Sorrow* or *Guts of Sea*, they required space to conduct their lives.

'*Guts of Sea* hasn't had time either.'

There was something in Quỳnh's voice Minh couldn't quite identify, a tightness. It made her uncomfortable: a vulnerability that shouldn't have belonged with someone such as Quỳnh. She cast about for a change of subject.

'*Heart's Sorrow* said you visited his first mother.'

'Yes.' Quỳnh picked up the teacup, stared at it thoughtfully, a bot on the back of her hand shining in the overhead light. 'The Belt isn't the imperial court. The circle of people with influence is much smaller, and I can't afford to ignore them. General Tuyết has invited me to compose a centrepiece poem.'

Of course she did.

'You're going to need her favour if you want to match *Guts of Sea*,' Minh said. 'Her banquets will host everyone who's anyone.'

'Mmm.' Quỳnh said. 'Including you?'

Minh shrugged. 'They're old friends, Mother and her. They go back to *The Azure Serpent*. But you know this already, I assume.'

Quỳnh inclined her head. '"The snake and the horse may look at odds but they will work together, if there is a planet they think worth conquering."'

'That's ...' Minh looked up, sharply. The author was Xuân Trúc, a scholar turned rebel general. 'I wouldn't quote *that*.'

'Because of who it is?' Quỳnh laughed. 'Ah yes, this isn't the court. People still remember the taint of the Uprising.'

The Belt had been its hotbed.

'We're still under military rule.'

'Yes. The court has forgiven,' Quỳnh said. 'Well ... not forgiven so much as chosen to forget. It came and went, and they can afford to be magnanimous because it didn't touch them.' She smiled, and it had teeth. 'Do you want to see the rest of the rooms?'

It was a short visit. The compound comprised more bare rooms without either physical or virtual adornment: worn and pitted metal plates hastily smoothed to appear new, exposed pipes and wiring at the seam between walls and ceiling, and a few empty alcoves here and there that only emphasised how far this was from a living space. There were ten or so of these, spreading on the three sides of the courtyard away from the gates. They finally stopped in the largest room, on the opposite side of the courtyard from the gates.

'I'm thinking this could become the banquet room,' Quỳnh said.

Minh looked at it, desperately struggling to say something smart.

'With more tables, obviously. And something central for the dais, instead of placing it at the end. I thought a large longevity character that would slowly grow to encompass the whole room.'

Minh closed her eyes, visualising the room. Quỳnh's voice was soothing, reminding her of earlier times. She thought of the banquets she'd attended with no joy, of the succession of rich overlays, of poets' masterworks – the spread of tables, the click of bots bringing tea and wine and food, the gleam of porcelain with the artistry of virtual decoration moving at the same time as the cup was lifted to the lips.

'The room isn't very much longer than it is large. You'd have to have a differently shaped overlay for that. It would work, but a lot of people find it disorientating. There's only so much perception filters can do. People are more comfortable when it's just a scaling, an expansion or a shrinking of existing space.'

Quỳnh smiled, and sunlike warmth flooded Minh, a tight, unfamiliar feeling.

'Indeed. Perhaps I could—' she moved her hands, her bots flowing to her, and a sketch appeared in overlay— 'place tables here, and dais here. Still in the centre of the room.' The furniture appeared like ghosts, in ink-black strokes like those of a calligraphy master. 'What do you think?'

Minh stared at it. 'I don't know. It could work. It wouldn't be standard.'

'You assume I don't want to stand out. Sometimes a little distinction requires a little risk.' She left the overlay on, thoughtfully moving tables. 'I assume you're preparing for the examinations.'

Minh laughed. She couldn't help it. 'I already sat them – I'm awaiting the results.' Awaiting with nebulous fear, which she buried as deeply as she could. 'Mother has high hopes.'

'And you?'

'I don't know. I think I can pass. Just not the way she wants.'

What Mother wanted for Minh was a bright success, a prestigious mentor, a prestigious posting: a blazing trail of a career leading Minh to the imperial court. Minh already knew she wouldn't be the first of the candidates; she wasn't remarkable or distinctive, the way Quỳnh was. Just getting by, the way she'd always done, bearing the disappointment in Mother's face, in her tutors' faces. She could do that, in exchange for safety.

'Ah.' Quỳnh said nothing for a while. She was busy modifying the dais in her virtual overlay, tweaking it so that the chairs were slightly more spread out, though to do that she also had to widen the overall virtual space. 'Mothers can be difficult.'

'Yours?' Minh asked.

'Mine has been dead for a few years, sadly. I never ... I never really got a chance to talk to her.' Again, that odd tone, carefully emotionless, a taut piece of cloth over a vacuum. Sadness.

Minh's gut twisted. 'I'm sorry.'

Quỳnh's laughter was edged. 'You're a kind child.'

She said it almost as though ... as though it was unexpected. Of course it would be, given Minh's mother. Was there anything she hadn't touched?

'I'm sure you have a bright future ahead of you.'

The one Mother had traced for her – the thread that led from examination to posting to marriage and beyond. Predictable and safe. Comforting. Minh deflected.

'The hope of all parents.'

'Indeed.'

'Was your mother proud of you? Sorry. If you'd rather not speak about her ...'

'No.' Quỳnh looked at her, as if turning over some thoughts in her head. At length she said, 'Mother never really got a chance to see what I turned out to be. Sometimes I think it's for the best. There have been ... hard years.'

'Ah.' Minh started to say she was sorry again, but it was trite and by now meaningless. She felt the weight of her bots all over her clothing. 'It's so hard to tell. What our dead would have thought, whether they'd have been proud.' She thought of her own mother – not Mother, but Second Mother, the one who'd borne Minh. The lesser spouse in the marriage, who'd died too early of a sickness that couldn't be cured. 'We'd so like to believe it, and yet we can't really know.'

'No,' Quỳnh said. Another of those silences. 'They take up so much space, don't they? The dead.'

Of course. The altar.

'Sometimes,' Minh said.

They sat together companionably, staring at the room.

Minh looked at the overlay again, at the translucent furniture and the twist that made the room larger in virtual than in physical. Beneath it all, she saw metal and wires, rivets and filtration exhausts, bot alcoves – and a shadow, right where the room appeared to dip and narrow. Not, not a shadow. Yellow. A distinctive shade of yellow.

'Wait,' she said.

Quỳnh's face froze. 'What is it?'

'Behind the dais, to the right. Can you turn it off? The virtual? I think ...'

Minh's bots were already scuttling across the floor, making for that patch of oddly shaped shadow near the corner. Quỳnh turned the overlay off – Minh had the dizzying feeling of local topology twisting itself out of shape, distances and orientations suddenly vastly compressed. Her first bots, still following instructions given before the overlay disappeared, hit the wall; the following ones slowed down and only gently bumped into it.

There was a hole, but that wasn't what had caught her eye. The yellow was a sharp point, a mere triangle poking through the hole, but she would have known that colour anywhere. She'd grown up near the tribunal.

'That's a finger bone,' Minh said, in fascinated horror. 'Wait ...' Her bots' sensors and the network kept telling her she was mistaken: that the hole was small and there wasn't space for the rest of the finger. Her bots pulled at it, couldn't move it. 'The network says there's nothing there.'

'I see it.' Quỳnh's voice was grim. Her gaze raked the wall from top to bottom. 'The network is wrong.' She did something with her hands, something too fast for Minh to see it – a sound like metal tearing, and everything around them shivering for a mere blink. 'There. It's gone now.'

'What ...?'

'A privacy filter. A very strong one. I'm not sure even accredited government officials would be able to breach it, unless they noticed it. And it was made not to be noticed in the first place.' Her voice was slow and thoughtful again; her bots travelled down her extended hand, towards the wall.

It wasn't a hole. It was a *room*, a whole space that had been sealed off and hidden away. It was a metal partition; she couldn't see anything behind it and neither could her bots. But she could guess, couldn't she?

A hand, on her shoulder: Quỳnh's touch, cool and steady.

'Help me?' she asked. 'It's riveted shut.'

'Help. Yes. Of course.'

Minh sent the commands to her bots, watched them march across the wall, painstakingly undoing bolts and rivets that had been welded shut. Too slow, too tortuous – she kneeled and started helping them, her fingers tearing away at old, rusted metal.

Quỳnh's hand, on her shoulder again.

'Don't,' she said gently. 'You'll just break your nails and your skin. Let them.'

Minh watched the bots. Watched the rivets coming out one by one, the wires being snipped, the old, fragile metal being bent. Watched the bots' sensors finally coming online as the first of them crept into that large, hidden alcove.

'Bones,' she said, softly, slowly. 'It's full of bones.'

There were so many of them, trembling in the light projected by the bot. As its crown of sensors swivelled, it caught on fingers and arms and femurs, and the hollowness of eye sockets, everything yellowed, a rich brown, like leather being tanned.

'There's more than one corpse there.' More than two or three, and all piled together in disarray, like the discarded scraps of a child's game. 'There's—'

'Fifteen or sixteen, I would say,' Quỳnh said, her hand still on Minh's shoulder, steadying her. 'And they're quite old. Perhaps seven or eight years.'

Minh took a deep, trembling breath. 'I'm all right.' She swallowed, feeling bile in her throat. 'I'm sorry, but we have to call the tribunal.'

Quỳnh smiled, and it was oddly satisfied. 'I wasn't here seven or eight years ago. I appreciate you're worrying about what might happen to me, but this discovery is hardly going to touch me.'

'I think … I think you probably should find another compound if you want to throw a banquet.' Minh was on the verge of laughing – because she badly needed to lose control, and it seemed safer than any of the other options. She kept it bottled up, but it cost her. 'Mother will take care of this.'

Quỳnh's voice was smooth and reassuring. 'Of course. I have absolute trust she will.'

5

The Affairs of Mindships

Hoà was packing a box of equipment to go to *Flowers at the Gates*. Thiên Dung had been watching her through the vid-link on her bots, but she'd grown dizzier and dizzier, visibly struggling to follow what was going on until Hoà cut off her feed, sternly reminding her she should be in bed. Thiên Dung, not to be deterred, was now making suggestions through text-chat, which Hoà was steadily ignoring. The only thing Hoà was interested in was how in Heaven she was supposed to get to the mindship, because all Thiên Dung's employers had given her was a docking address and a dodgy-looking chat channel that looked like a set-up for kidnapping or murder. It was probably neither – rich kids *were* bored, and generally had as many scruples as a scorpion, but this was a lot of effort to go to when they could just grab Hoà or Thiên Dung from the shop with few consequences. But the lack of detail made Hoà anxious, and the last thing she needed was more anxiety.

A chime at the door made her look up. They did have a few customers due to pick up their orders. Hoà had left them all in boxes keyed to their auth-tokens, but since she was there, she might as well...

'Coming,' she said, and found herself staring at Quỳnh. 'Oh. Oh.'

Quỳnh was wearing a simple grey-blue robe with a matching sash, and a fur-edged grey cape over it. Both physical and overlay were the same: extremely simple, almost homespun, the clothes of an outer ring bots-handler rather than a scholar. Her face was bare of make-up: just her eyebrows, expertly shaped to mimic moth's wings. She smelled of cedar and jasmine flowers and she bent towards Hoà – Hoà thought, for a bare moment that it was to kiss her – but she simply sniffed Hoà's cheeks, the way Hoà's aunts used to do back on *The Azure Serpent*.

Hoà felt obscurely disappointed, and angry at herself for being disappointed.

'Big sis. I didn't expect you so soon.'

Quỳnh laughed. It was crystalline.

'That's on me. I wasn't exactly very clear, was I, on when I'd come?' Her eyes took in the shop, the tools spread out on the table. 'If it's a bad time—?'

'No, no, not at all.' Hoà felt herself colouring. 'Hang on. I'll get you some tea.'

Her bots, which had been packing the tools, hastily rearranged themselves to find teacups and tea.

'There's no need …' Quỳnh actually looked flustered and embarrassed, and much younger. Much more vulnerable. She was close to Hoà – too close, the heat of her body a palpable thing.

Don't go there. That's such a terrible idea.

'Sit,' Hoà said, surprised by her own boldness. 'I'll find you some snacks.'

They didn't have steamed buns any more, but they had leftover fried rolls, which Hoà hastily had her bots re-fry so they didn't seem too shabby. She mixed the sauce herself, scrambling to open the lime.

'Here,' Quỳnh said.

She laid her hands on Hoà's own hands, gently guiding them to split the fruit apart. Hoà felt something twisting and rising within her again.

'Sit,' she said again, putting the bowl of dipping sauce between them, with its load of shrivelled salad and mint leaves. Most of them were half-black. 'I know it's not the fare you're used to.'

She was absolutely not going to apologise for not being able to afford the freshest vat-grown vegetables, but still, she felt obscurely ashamed.

Quỳnh smiled. 'I grew up on it.'

She sipped the tea, the perfectly formed leaves, the aroma of jasmine that was too smooth to come from planet-side. It tasted exactly like a Jade Spiral tea should, with barely any variance for harvest or shaping: the fare of the outer rings.

'You did?' Hoà stared at her, but she looked utterly sincere. 'You can't ...'

Quỳnh's laughter was mesmerising, transfiguring her. 'Scholars don't grow fully formed from a bed of perfect earth and wealthy tutors. Sometimes the examinations do work as they should.'

As a system to give everyone – even the less wealthy, the less privileged – a chance to join the government.

'Not here.' Hoà wasn't even bitter about it; she knew it was the way the world worked, not the way it was described in Thiên Hạnh's old stories.

Quỳnh gracefully dipped a fried roll wrapped in salad and mint into the dipping sauce.

'No. The Belt is small and insular, isn't it? It's funny. I had this exact conversation with someone else recently.' She didn't say who, and Hoà didn't probe. 'How is your younger sister?'

'I'm sorry?'

'You said she was sick.'

'I didn't think you'd remember.' Of course she would. Of course she had bots, even if she didn't remember herself. 'I'm sorry.'

'You apologise much too quickly for too many things.' It wasn't said as a reproach, more as though it made her sad.

Hoà coloured again. 'She's fine. Recovering.'

She wasn't sure if Thiên Dung really was fine, but it was simpler to not start a conversation where Quỳnh might end up paying for a doctor. Thiên Dung was messaging Hoà non-stop. Hoà paused, briefly, to say she was busy with someone – she didn't say a customer because it wasn't quite true, but it was in the service of customers, wasn't it? She finished her fried roll, enjoying the crunch of it, the way the dipping sauce, acid and sweet and salty, filled her mouth, a memory of how Thiên Hạnh – and their dead parents before Thiên Hạnh – had mixed it.

'You know I'm not going to offer you anything you don't ask for.' Quỳnh's gaze was piercing. Too perceptive.

Hoà felt as though she was burning inside, a heat that rose to her cheeks and entire face. The only thing that came to her was the truth.

'No. I don't. Not yet. I barely know you.'

'Fair.'

They stared at each other for a while, over blackened salad leaves and twice-fried rolls. Quỳnh's lips were tinged purple, a thin, elegant line. Would they feel cold, like the vacuum of space?

'The mindship,' Hoà said finally, because she couldn't trust herself with anything else.

'Yes.' Quỳnh's gaze was sharp. 'Tell me about the ship.'

'Her name is *Flowers at the Gates of the Lords*. There was some kind of ... accident, thirteen years ago. I haven't inquired because it's outside the scope of the work.'

'Wise.' Quỳnh nodded. She appeared to be mulling on something, but didn't speak.

Thirteen years before had been the height of the Ten Thousand Flags Uprising. Hoà's 'accident' was most likely to be divided loyalties, or a battle, or both.

'As I said … a bunch of rich kids want to fix it, and they hired us to help. They're all young.' Hoà hadn't set foot on the ship, but she'd seen them when Thiên Dung had negotiated the contract: five or six of them, including the mindship, all painfully naive and sheltered. 'Babies.'

'You feel sorry for them.'

'No. I feel scared. Fixing a mindship is the job of a Master of Wind and Water. I'm a small-time fixer of machinery and devices. They're young enough to expect results, and spoiled enough to be explosively unhappy when they don't get them. And a mindship is such a huge undertaking I'm not even sure Thiên Dung could do it. But with Thiên Dung sick, it's on me.' She laughed. 'And my total lack of expertise.'

Quỳnh watched her, for a while. At last she said, and she sounded surprised, 'You're not bitter.'

Why would I be? Because most people are? That isn't how I work.

'Of course not. I know where my skills stop. And my prerogatives. But—' Hoà bit her lip '—we need the money. We need to survive. I need to make sure I seem competent and proficient. So what can you teach me, and how fast?'

Quỳnh laughed. Hoà could have listened to that sound all day; could watch the way it transformed her, made her younger, more vulnerable, yet genuinely happy, instead of looking as though she was searching for a way to hurt someone, anyone – including herself – all the time.

'I'll show you the basics, but you're right that it takes time. How long are you working for?'

'Today? Three to five hours. And later this week as well.'

'Mmm. Mmm.' Quỳnh's bots came alive while Quỳnh's face stilled. Finally, she extended a hand, with a bot perching on the end of it, its crown of sensors glinting in the light. Unlike the rest of her clothes, it was modern and elegant. 'If I may?'

'May what?'

'Will you agree to take some of my bots with you, and a comms-link? That way I can guide you on board. I can't be there the entire time, but I can at least advise for a few centi-days, should you need me. And my bots know some of the routines for fixing mindships.'

Hoà stared at the bots, and back at Quỳnh. It was ... It made sense. Of course it made sense. It was just ... She struggled to voice something. Sharing bots was a thing when on board a mindship, but between people it felt ... like an offer of intimacy which was both attractive and frightening. But it was the only way she'd appear even remotely competent. She reached out: the bot climbed from Quỳnh's hand to hers, and as its legs touched her palm, a dozen pinpricks of steel – Quỳnh's request to open a comms-link – flashed on her overlay. She accepted it, feeling as though she'd just thrown herself into the vacuum without a shadow-suit.

'There,' Quỳnh said. 'Now let's talk about mindships.'

'She's an older mindship,' Quỳnh said. 'Smaller, less refined, and not designed for multiple failures.'

She'd called up an overlay with a comprehensive privacy filter. Hoà had watched her warily, like someone who knew all the conjurer's tricks and was looking to see exactly how that one had been achieved. She was smart and careful, like someone who had been betrayed too many times by life. And yet not bitter. It made Quỳnh feel a pang of something she couldn't quite name, something twisting in her heart.

It wasn't much of an overlay: a dark sky above and below, and that same flock of white birds whirling in the air, singing a mournful lullaby from *The Azure Serpent*, from Quỳnh's childhood. Somehow it felt fitting for Hoà, and for the memory of who Quỳnh had been.

She opened her hands, and between them was a model of a mindship. She'd taken one from the same generation as *Flowers at the Gates of the Lords*. As she talked, her hands moved, and various parts came into sharp relief. Hoà watched her, utterly entranced by every word.

'Everything small can be fixed, just like you would fix a bot.'

She made schematics briefly flicker into existence.

'You have these?' Hoà asked. 'They look private.'

It would certainly have made things easier to have the schematics.

'Not for the whole ship, no. They're classified, if they exist at all. This is from a comparable ship. The layout remains the same, and the smaller parts have schematics. I can share these with you, and my bots will be used to processing them.'

Hoà scrunched her face, considering a problem.

'Changing cables. Refitting connectors. Making sure it all flows properly, I can do all that.' She stopped, then, and looked straight at Quỳnh with an intensity that would bore through metal. 'How do I do this without killing her?'

Quỳnh hadn't expected that; it came out of nowhere, like Hoà's remark on her own expertise, with no trace of self-deprecation or self-hatred, a simple question cutting through all the clutter to what Hoà judged the heart of the matter. The heart of the matter, because she was right: ultimately a ship was a living person. Hoà's words jolted her, made her remember what mattered: being uncomfortable and gloriously alive, much like Đình Sơn had made her feel when he'd looked at her with his entire heart in his eyes.

Hoà's voice cut through her reminiscences.

'You think so very little of me, don't you?'

Quỳnh, startled, looked at Hoà. 'What do you mean?'

'Before. When you said I wasn't bitter. And now. Both times, you were surprised. As if I gave you more than you were expecting. As if you'd already dismissed me.'

She was breathing hard – Quỳnh's bots could track it, but beneath it all her heartbeat was level, her skin dark. There was no fear. Minh had been absolutely terrified when she'd confronted Quỳnh, bracing herself for some tongue-lashing or cutting remarks – and no wonder, with Prefect Đức as her mother – but Hoà appeared to believe, deep down, that she was safe with Quỳnh. It was new and unsettling. Quỳnh hadn't come to the Belt to reassure anyone.

She said finally, 'No. I'd forgotten.'

'Forgotten?'

Of course she'd forgotten. She'd had to. She'd had to focus on the things that mattered to her. She'd had to be filled with anger and bitterness, else she'd never be able to sustain such a prolonged effort to avenge herself. And yet ... And yet Hoà reminded her that, beyond all the betrayals and backstabbings, and grievances that begged for ten-thousandfold reparations, there could be absolute clarity, the kind that cut through every attempt to lie or obfuscate.

'What it means to see things clearly.'

Hoà opened her mouth, closed it. 'It's not an insult, is it?'

'No.' Quỳnh moved then, pressing her hands around Hoà's. She felt Hoà's flesh on hers, held between her palms, the overlay interpreting it as a gentle touch, like the wings of a bird taking flight. Hoà's breath hitched – Quỳnh found hers caught and couldn't seem to get it back. 'You know who you are, and who other people are. You know what you can and cannot do, and you work to change what you're unhappy with.'

'That's hardly extraordinary.'

'It's rarer than you realise.' Quỳnh withdrew her hands, and opened them up again on the model of the ship, her bots clustering under her robes. 'People get caught up in so many things. So many feelings.' A choice she'd made. A choice she didn't regret. 'And before they realise it, it's too late.'

'Is it too late for you, then?' Hoà's voice was challenging.

'For what?'

'You tell me.'

And for a moment, the words came to her lips. For a moment she thought of Đình Sơn, and of *Moon* – for a moment only, everything bubbling up, all the secrets, all the plans, begging to be shared, to be abandoned.

And then she remembered Đình Sơn had died because of who she was – of the heaviness of a secret he couldn't keep, and couldn't live with.

'Someday, perhaps.' Quỳnh shook her head, and looked down at the ship. 'Someday.'

'I see.'

Hoà tried to pretend the dismissal didn't hurt her. Quỳnh wanted to sweep her up and kiss her, drinking her in until everything was forgotten – but that wasn't what she was here for. Overhead, the birds wheeled, singing that distant lullaby from a time neither of them could lay claim to. A time before Dã Lan died, before Thanh Khuê and Mother and Đình Sơn. A time when she'd still thought *Moon* would call her 'Mommy'.

A time that was forever gone.

Quỳnh said, in the silence, 'Most of the things you do outside the heartroom won't affect her. Or rather, she'll be able to bear them.'

'That's not the same thing,' Hoà said sharply.

'No, it's not.'

'Can she hear me? Feel something?'

Quỳnh tried to think of an answer that would be acceptable to Hoà, and couldn't find any.

'When you fixed your mindship, what did you do?' Hoà stared at her. 'You didn't much care.'

'*She* didn't much care, and neither did I.' Quỳnh made her voice light and ironic. It wasn't hard to feel the distance that separated her from Dã Lan, from the hopes she'd had, the belief that it was all a mistake, that she had a chance to fix things, to go back. Such naive, sickening foolishness. And *Guts of Sea* was no longer a small, shivering mindship, begging for someone – for anyone – to save her. They'd both changed for the better, for the stronger. 'But mindships always speak, if you care to hear them. Even when immobile and voiceless ... you are standing in their bodies. You have to learn to listen. You are right – you're trying to fix a living person, and that does change things.

'Look.' Quỳnh opened her hands, and the ghostly ship between them spread out, became rooms that rose all around them, with the underlying structure shimmering. 'Here. Cables. Vents. Tubes. Connectors. You can't tell where they'll be, exactly, but this should give you an idea.' She sent them to Hoà. 'And that's quite enough, I think, for a first lesson.'

Hoà was still looking at it all.

'Can you wait for a bit?'

'Of course.' Quỳnh bowed, her face smooth and unperturbed, her emotions and memories under perfect control once more. 'Just leave the overlay when you're done. I'll be in the shop.'

Quỳnh came back to the shop to find a call from *Guts of Sea* waiting for her. She put up a privacy screen to take it – nothing as fancy as the one she'd put together for Hoà, a thing of necessity rather than concern. The entire workshop became distant, as if behind a pane of frosted glass, and *Guts of Sea*'s avatar coalesced into view.

'You have news,' Quỳnh said.

'Yes.' *Guts of Sea* tilted her boxy shape in a pattern of trepidation.

'Good news?'

'Mmm,' *Guts of Sea* said. 'I've made some inroads with the scholars.'

'Ah.' Quỳnh was busy ostensibly courting the powerful. As her companion, *Guts of Sea* was expected to meet the less important scholars, which suited them both: there was a wealth of relationships, favours and secrets in the literary circles. 'And ... ?'

'You were right,' *Guts of Sea* said. 'Many of them don't like Prefect Đức.'

The contrary would have been surprising, given Đức's arrogance and high-handedness.

'Anything we can use?'

'Mmm. There are a handful of scholars with specific grudges against what seem to be specific injustices. Prefect Đức likes to paint herself as harsh but fair, but ...'

But, in reality, as they both knew, she was always the first and seldom the second. But Đức had always been good, even as a magistrate, at *seeming* virtuous. Quỳnh remembered, as Dã Lan, how Đức had seemed so compassionate, so reasonable. How she'd made it seem she could make the accusations against Dã Lan go away, if Dã Lan would only explain. How the tea had tasted, grassy and smooth, as Dã Lan had spoken, opening up under Đức's gentle gaze. And later, Đức's face, ordering the guards to drag Dã Lan away for further interrogation since she had admitted to sedition from her own mouth. And later, the cell, the taste of Dã Lan's blood on her torn lips, the shreds of clothes on her body, the marks of the lacerator oozing into the merciless metal. And later still, the airlock, and the descent into darkness that had choked the breath out of her.

'Can you ask around? Discreetly.'

Guts of Sea snorted. 'Easily. There's a couple who own a printing house, Vĩnh Trinh and Mạt Lỵ. And some ships. *Sharpening Needles into Steel*, *The Shadow's Child* – she has a scholar associate. They specialise in consultation for the tribunal but bear no love for the prefect.'

'Any one of these will do.' Quỳnh thought, for a while. 'Especially the ones likely to be in close proximity to Minh.'

'The printing house, then. Vĩnh Trinh. Mạt Lỵ.' *Guts of Sea* said the names, slowly and deliberately, in a soft purr like a tiger's. 'Perfect.'

Quỳnh nodded. 'You'll want a backup.'

'I'll handle it.' *Guts of Sea*'s voice was curt. 'We're not looking for anything right now, are we?'

'No. No hurry yet. Just ... a willingness to share Đức's dirty little secrets with an eager audience.'

Minh, the tribunal, the military officials. It was the makings of a quiet little rumour war to destabilise Đức until the final blow. Minh, especially, was Đức's weakest point: the daughter she hoped to control, the daughter Quỳnh was going to make sure she'd lose her grip on. And the best part was that it would all be caused by Đức's own faults and failings.

Đức was smart. It would take a lot more than this to bring her down. But Quỳnh was smart as well.

'You're with her, aren't you?' *Guts of Sea* asked. 'The girl. To help her with her mindship.' She disapproved.

Quỳnh hesitated. Then, softly, 'That ship is *Flowers at the Gates*.'

Đức's own aunt, the ship that was the nominal head of Đức's lineage but incapable of handling its day-to-day affairs – the one whose absence meant Đức controlled the lineage and its wealth.

Soft laughter, from *Guts of the Sea*. 'Don't try and tell me that's why you're helping her.'

Quỳnh thought, for a while. It was true that it was in her own interests to help Hoà with the ship, because if *Flowers at the Gates* woke up and Đức lost her hold on the lineage, it would weaken her.

'No,' she said finally. 'The ship isn't part of the plan. She's too badly damaged, and there are too many variables. Her being fixed is not something we can rely on.'

And that was a lie. The truth was that Hoà wasn't part of the plan, and shouldn't be. What Quỳnh was doing – the help she was giving, the odd and disquieting pleasure she took in Hoà's presence – was a gift to Hoà. A debt paid to her old teacher. A chance to build rather than destroy, for a handful of moments. She'd help, and then move on, with Hoà none the wiser.

When Hoà came out of the overlay, she felt the weight of Quỳnh's two bots: sleeker and sharper than hers, riding on her shoulders with an unfamiliar mass, subtly and disturbingly wrong. She couldn't quite address them, either; she felt as though she was sending them commands through a pane of glass, and with a significant lag. It was odd and unsettling. She could obviously park them when she wasn't on the ship, but all the same, it felt as though she was sharing something special when she and Quỳnh had absolutely nothing special going on.

Thiên Dung's messages had tapered off. Hoà checked on her. There was no privacy screen up, and Thiên Dung was asleep, having propped herself up with pillows so she was essentially sitting, pale and with drool on her lip. From time to time, a cough racked her body.

It didn't seem to be getting better. Hoà tried not to worry

about it, but it had been ten days now, and she *was* worried. They might have to call in the doctor after all.

Quỳn was leaning against the counter and making small conversation with Aunt Vy, one of the shop's customers, who specialised in logistics and owned a number of fully registered shuttles, and an equal number of not entirely legal ones. Quỳnh's bots – sharp, elegant, glittering – clustered on her shoulders, accentuating the contrast with Aunt Vy, whose bots were mismatched and repaired over and over. Her clothes were a little too brash, a little too perfect: an aggressive statement that everything was fine, because the alternative – admitting or showing in any way that it was not – was an unthinkable loss of face.

But Quỳnh appeared completely absorbed in what Aunt Vy was saying.

'Really?' she said.

'Yes,' Aunt Vy said. 'The phoenix-class bots don't look like much, but the parts are extraordinary. Almost like they threw together every scrap from a higher-end manufacture.'

'Hm.' Quỳnh fingered one of her own bots. 'What are you using them for, elder aunt?'

Aunt Vy grinned. 'I've got one whole one.' She pointed to one of the sleeker bots, the one on her wrist. 'The other ones I took apart.'

'It does make sense.' Quỳnh nodded, and pointed to her own bots. 'These aren't worth much, to be honest. They're just for show.'

'That they are. You really should get better ones. You've got the money, haven't you?'

'Mmm.' Quỳnh pinched her hands, picking up a bot by the body. 'I do. But sometimes appearances matter more than capability.'

'It's a sad, sad world.'

Quỳnh smiled. 'In so many ways, yes.'

Aunt Vy cocked her head, in case Quỳnh was making fun of her. But she wasn't. Hoà could tell she wasn't. She was genuinely fascinated by Aunt Vy and by what the older woman was saying, when every social rule would have encouraged Quỳnh – the high-flown scholar, the superior intellect – to ignore her. It was upending everything Hoà had believed about Quỳnh.

Hoà cleared her throat.

'Oh, child!' Aunt Vy smiled at her. 'Came to pick up my repair.'

'For sure.' Hoà gestured to the box. 'It's keyed to your auth-token.'

She looked at Aunt Vy's face, with its usual distrust for anything issued by the authorities – and who could blame her? The military had just arrested entire clusters of people around her house, probably including many of her family members.

'Never mind. I'll open it for you.' She sent her bots to do that, while she took care of Quỳnh.

'Thank you for the lesson,' Hoà said. 'We're done, aren't we?'

'Why are you asking?'

'Are you still here out of politeness? In order not to appear as though you're dismissing me?'

Quỳnh looked surprised again.

'Thank you!' Aunt Vy waved the package with her repaired holo-display. 'I've paid.'

Hoà waited for the payment to clear before she nodded.

'Yes, I have it. Goodbye, Auntie.'

'Goodbye, child!'

Aunt Vy looked at Quỳnh a little uncertainly; Quỳnh had used a respectful pronoun to address her, and she therefore wasn't sure who should bow to whom. Quỳnh saved her the trouble by bowing deeply to her.

'Delighted to meet you, elder aunt.' Again it sounded utterly sincere, not like mere politeness. 'I hope we meet again.'

Hoà waited until Aunt Vy was gone, but Quỳnh still hadn't moved.

'You don't *have* to talk to her.'

'No.' Quỳnh raised an eyebrow. 'Do you think I shouldn't?'

Hoà was uncomfortable, and that made her aggressive.

'I just don't understand. You're a scholar, you must be the talk of the rings in every habitat. You most certainly didn't have to give her consideration.'

Quỳnh's voice was low and ironic as she threw Hoà's words back in her face.

'Do you think so little of me?'

Hoà forced herself to breathe. 'I just feel you could afford to behave differently.'

'You mean worse.' Quỳnh's voice was sharp. 'Just because scholars never give the people below them any time doesn't mean they're unworthy.' She was angry now.

Hoà had misjudged Quỳnh. She was sharp and looking for someone to hurt – and would probably be cruel to her enemies. But she was also free of the prejudices that plagued so many scholars – more than that, she listened to people and empathised with them. She took time to centre them, and it didn't matter how important they were. It was ... unsettling, as if a black hole had suddenly spouted a viable orbit for a space station.

'I'm sorry,' Hoà said. 'I shouldn't have said that.'

A silence. Then, 'I'm not angry at you for that. I'm angry because too many people have taught you that's entirely acceptable behaviour, or at the very least normalised behaviour.'

Hoà's treacherous heart fluttered in her chest. She knew the scholars weren't better than them, but the scholars believed, absolutely, in their own superiority. Not one of them would have said that – and certainly not sincerely and absolutely believed it.

'You're still here,' she said, struggling to breathe through a mess of feelings.

Quỳnh's bots were now clustered by the box Hoà had been packing prior to Quỳnh.

'You're going to the ship?'

'Yes?' Hoà said.

'Do you want a lift?'

'Why are you offering?'

She tamped down the panic – the very idea of her and Quỳnh standing close to each other, Hoà visible and vulnerable at the same time, without the protection of anonymity.

A pause. She had the distinct impression Quỳnh was going to say something and had changed her mind.

'Because I'm curious.'

And that sounded like the truth. So she'd been going to offer Hoà a poor excuse – a lie – and had changed her mind. Hoà had never been the kind of person to let subtleties hang in the air.

'Thank you for the honesty.'

Quỳnh's face was a study in conflicted feelings, beneath a veneer of calm – but Hoà's bots were perceptive, and their sensors could track the minute movements of Quỳnh's face beneath the make-up. They had to be, because it was the difference between survival and death. And she was not naive. Obviously Quỳnh didn't tell her everything.

'Look,' she said, gently and carefully, 'You knew big sis.' She ought to have used Thiên Hạnh's posthumous name, to ward off ill luck, but in truth using it felt like acknowledging Thiên Hạnh was dead, and never coming back. 'I don't know why you're here. I don't want to know. You're helping me. Just keep it that way?'

'Honest?'

'Tell me the truth,' Hoà said. 'What bits of it you can tell me. I can't work with lies.'

Quỳnh's mouth quirked up. 'Clarity.' She looked distantly amused. The two bots she'd lent Hoà weighed heavily on her shoulders. 'All right. As you wish. You haven't answered my question.'

No, she hadn't, had she. And ... truth was, she wanted to accept the lift, but she couldn't show up on a job accompanied by Quỳnh. Quite aside from the panic the very notion induced – how visible would she be, in the wake of a force of nature such as Quỳnh? – there were eminently practical reasons.

'I can't,' she said. 'You know I could also ask Aunt Vy for a shuttle, but I didn't. The kids expect me to take a particular shuttle, and they won't understand if I show up in another. Besides, I don't want to be dependent on you. Not in that.'

Hoà got an amused glance from Quỳnh. 'As you wish,' she said again, looking at Hoà, and Hoà felt, for a moment, as though she was filled with starlight and ready to burst.

6
Remains of the Past

The magistrate who interviewed Quỳnh was not Đức, but one of her flunkies, Bảo Toàn, seemingly cut from the same mould as Đức: he was preoccupied with projecting a virtue and unshakable righteousness that was likely all illusion. But Quỳnh was being unfair. Perhaps Magistrate Toàn was made of better stuff than his superior.

At the moment, Bảo Toàn was standing by the opening in the wall, watching as the tribunal's bots cleared away the remains of the bodies. Eighteen of them: Quỳnh had counted them prior to Minh's arrival. She had not, of course, selected this compound on a whim or solely because of its situation. She had expected the bodies, and enough time with Minh had enabled her bots to calibrate Minh's reaction times, and to gauge how overt she could be about directing Minh to the finger bone poking through the opening – the same one that had helped Quỳnh find the cache earlier.

Quỳnh had expected to find it, but she'd been through enough planning to know expectations rarely dictated reality. It was good to know that they'd been clumsy enough to leave it there.

'When did you arrive in the Belt, again?' Bảo Toàn asked. He was old, beefy and squinting as though his eyesight needed adjusting – which was for show, as the civil service would have fixed it early on in his tenure. His bots were all different, elaborate works of art ranging from metal that sheened all colours to sky-blue, translucent celadon.

Quỳnh smiled, slow and dazzling. 'Seven days ago.'

Bảo Toàn's gaze went from her to the bones. With no overlays, the militia just had to look for physical evidence. There wasn't much – the bones had been scoured clean and left there – but who knew: there might be some unexpected and welcome trail to tie them to a murderer. It didn't much matter. Quỳnh had enough evidence for Bảo Toàn anyway.

'And you've never been to the Belt before.'

'No.' Quỳnh said. It was the truth.

'I'm given to understand it was the prefect's daughter who found the bodies.'

'Yes. She was here to help me with a private matter,' Quỳnh said. There was no private matter: she'd needed Minh there to find the bodies and call the tribunal. She'd needed Minh to bear witness for her – Minh's trust in Quỳnh's character and Minh's friendship with her were her shields. 'Is she all right? That was probably a nasty shock.'

Bảo Toàn pursed his lips. He said finally, 'Her mother is seeing to her. I've interviewed her. She'll recover, but it was a surprise, indeed.'

He relaxed a little, a minute shift of his eyes and face caught by Quỳnh's bots. She was a fraction more respectable because of Minh.

Excellent.

'Thank you,' Quỳnh said. 'I was worried about her.'

That last was a lie, coming out so smoothly Bảo Toàn couldn't spot it. Quỳnh didn't care about Minh: she was Đức's daughter and Đức's pride. She was a decent person, but Quỳnh was acutely aware that she might have to hurt Minh at some point, in order to hurt Đức. She wasn't going to get attached.

'She'll be all right.' Bảo Toàn looked at Quỳnh for a moment. 'You don't look very shocked.'

'I've seen bodies before,' Quỳnh said. 'During the Uprising.'

'Oh. A soldier?'

Quỳnh shook her head. 'I was in the shipyards.'

The shipyards had been the scene of fierce battles between the rebels and the Empire, but that wasn't how Quỳnh had become inured to bodies – it was that long, endless descent into darkness after she'd been cast adrift, that stretched-out time while she and *Guts of Sea* tried to fix each other, to keep each other living in the midst of deep spaces. And then later, seeing her husband's body and knowing it was her past that had killed him.

Bảo Toàn sighed. 'And I take it you didn't notice anything odd with the compound?'

Quỳnh laughed, slowly, pitching it to be a scholar's cultured, gentle amusement.

'It was convenient. A little cheaper than it ought to have been, but I assumed that was because it hadn't been occupied for so long.' She dropped the bait casually into the conversation, waiting to see if he would go for it.

'Wait. This was empty when you moved in?'

'Oh, for a long time.' Quỳnh smiled again, and then deliberately stopped. 'You mean there was an issue with it?'

By Bảo Toàn's face, he was wondering, too. The man was used to controlling his expressions, but not the minutest of changes, the ones Quỳnh's and *Guts of Seas'* bots could track. General Tuyết and her wife had been more skilful. It was somehow deeply unsatisfying.

'I'm happy to forward the documents that were given to

me,' Quỳnh said, 'though I assume you will also have the relevant information.'

He would, but he would have to request it from the military administration, and obviously Tuyết and Prefect Đức didn't get on. And one other thing that Quỳnh knew and he didn't: Tuyết had a connection to the man who had once owned the house.

'I'd be grateful if you did,' Bảo Toàn said.

'Done,' Quỳnh said. 'One thing ...'

'Yes?'

Quỳnh looked away, as if she were ashamed. 'I used some of my scholar contacts to get the information. Not all of it is ... in the registers.'

'Ah.' Bảo Toàn looked at her, sharply. 'And why should I trust your information, rather than the registers'?

Quỳnh made a dismissive gesture with her hands, subtly accentuated by the movement of the bots wrapped around her fingers.

'You don't have to,' she said. 'But it's reliably sourced. You can follow up on it if you want. It doesn't matter to me.'

Another lie. But all the information was true, and he could verify it easily enough. And if Tuyết's administration made the mistake of sending something that didn't match what Bảo Toàn now had ... well, then, she'd have less work to do to set Tuyết and Đức at each other's throats.

She watched Bảo Toàn leave, thoughtfully looking at the militia bots still collecting bones. The entire reception room was now an extension of the tribunal. Quỳnh watched the bots for a while, and then called up the privacy screens again. They would be gone soon enough, with so little evidence to pick over. What mattered was the age of the bones, and their genetic signature, as damning and as unique as an auth-token. Only one owner would align with the time period of death of these eighteen bodies, and the genetics would be easily traced to courtesans and entertainers who had gone missing. And they, in turn, would easily be traced back to Scholar Gia Kiệt, the dignitary who had once owned this compound. It would be a straightforward case.

And a rewarding one for Đức – and for Quỳnh, if she could help the tribunal establish the link between Gia Kiệt and the general who had been his lover at the time. The general who had quite likely either condoned or covered up the murders.

That would require more work. Tuyết was flighty, but she had never been sloppy. And yet ... it was a challenge. Bảo Toàn – well-meaning, transparent, *honest* – had been such an obscure disappointment. Too easy to manipulate, like a bone that cracked under the slightest pressure.

Quỳnh looked at the time. Good, Bảo Toàn hadn't overstayed his welcome. She had a letter to write to the court on the First Planet: the other half of her plan to bring down two of the Empire's respected officials.

In the Belt, she was sowing chaos: using Tuyết's past transgressions against her to exacerbate the rivalry between her and Prefect Đức, with the goal of finally having Đức move against Tuyết – which would take Tuyết down and leave Đức to deal with. To do this, Quỳnh was counting on the chaos to demonstrate that Đức had strayed from her role and authority. In a context where the Empire was trying to rebuild itself after the Ten Thousand Flags Uprising, a prefect who wasn't able to keep order was vulnerable.

But in order to pull this off, Quỳnh needed court influence: the Empress was the one who could remove the prefect, and she needed people who had influence in order to do that. She and *Guts of Sea* were leaning on allies at court – Minister Giai Khanh and Academy Chancellor Hàn Lâm Bình, two ambitious newcomers who had the ear of the Grand Secretariat and the

Censorate, and some deeply held prejudices against Serpents.

It was to these ministers she now wrote: a continuation of her earlier letter, detailing the fallout of the Tiger Games incident and Minh's endangerment, and the way Prefect Đức's ruthless handling of it was causing unrest in the technologist quarters. And in a sly coda, she alluded to the eighteen skeletons, hinting that the prefect had not known of their existence, or who was really the owner of the compound.

There. Perfect. Just the right mixture of truths, stopping just short of sedition: facts that, when linked together, showed Đức was slipping.

This single letter wouldn't induce Giai Khanh and Hàn Lâm Bình to move against Đức — the darling of the court, the one who kept the heavenly order in the Belt. But it would make them wonder if such a thing was feasible, and that was all Quỳnh needed for the time being.

She sent it off, and stared at the opening in the wall. *Guts of Sea* was currently trying to track down a particular merchant who had access to the general's compound, and hadn't reported back. Which meant Quỳnh had time for something that *Guts of Sea* would not approve of. Not exactly disapprove of, but not encourage, either. She thought that Quỳnh should be strong — that she needed to focus on revenge, on carrying out the plan.

Guts of Sea could think like that. She spoke very little of her family, and Quỳnh hadn't dug deeper; there was a well of pain and neglect there. But what *Guts of Sea* could do, Quỳnh couldn't.

She called Băng Tâm.

He picked up immediately. 'Elder aunt. It's good to hear from you.' Băng Tâm wore his disguise well: ornate merchant's robes with far too much embroidery for a scholar's austere tastes, enough virtual overlays with details of unfolding flowers and shimmering stars – a reminder of his wealth, and a way for prospective partners to judge how much he was worth. 'This is encrypted, but—'

'*Auntie!*' *Moon*'s avatar leaped into Băng Tâm's arms, wriggling and throwing off golden squiggles in overlay. 'Look what I can do now!' More golden squiggles – *Moon* tilted in concentration, and they joined together to form a lopsided animal shape. 'I can do a whole cat!'

'That's lovely.' Quỳnh smiled. 'Do you like the compound?'

'Mmmmf,' *Moon* snorted. 'It's small. And the gravity is weird.'

'How so?'

'Nothing does what it should.' *Moon* sounded outraged that on-habitat gravity was failing to conform to her desires. 'I liked it better in the shipyards.'

Băng Tâm said gently, 'We had to leave the shipyards.'

'Yes, I know, Big Auntie,' *Moon* said.

Quỳnh's breath hitched. It was necessary – their cover couldn't depend on a toddler keeping a secret. *Moon* had to be lied to, for her own good, for everyone's own good. Quỳnh had already lost Đình Sơn to her past; she wasn't going to lose Đình Sơn's daughter – *her* daughter – to it as well.

It was necessary.

Which didn't make it hurt any less.

'Do you want to show your auntie something else?' Băng Tâm said.

Moon laughed. 'Yes. Look, Auntie, I can spin all the way now!'

Her avatar disappeared, reappearing in another layer of overlay, and then another, spinning all the while. She was laughing, and the sound caught in Quỳnh's chest – an unfamiliar, hollow feeling like floating. *Happiness*, she thought, and she'd almost forgotten how it felt.

'That's good,' she said. 'Show me again.'

Moon laughed. 'Yes!'

After a while of watching her spin – Quỳnh was entranced, not just by the ease of movements between layers, but by the very sound of *Moon*'s laughter, who didn't have a care in the world – Băng Tâm finally said, 'I think your auntie has other places she needs to be. And we need to take a day trip to your body, see how you're growing.'

'Oh.' *Moon* looked crestfallen, her nose tilting downwards.

Quỳnh said, her heart in her throat, 'I'll see you soon. I promise.'

'You're the best, Auntie!'

Moon blew a series of virtual kisses and cuddles at her, before Băng Tâm cut the comms.

Quỳnh leaned against the metal wall of the compound, and felt something painful well up inside her. She stared, for a while, at the remnants of the reception room, and burst into tears – great big sobs welling out of her for no good reason, a series of heavings that seemed to have no end, wave after wave of intense sadness wringing her entire body. When it finally stopped, she breathed in, shaking and drained.

She leaned against the wall, fighting the fatigue. It felt as though she'd crossed the entire habitats from inner to outer rings and back again. And yet ...

It had been worth it, to talk to *Moon*. To remember who would survive her and her work. And yet she'd lost so much – *Moon* had lost so much – and she wasn't sure they would get any of it back.

She needed someone to talk to, and she couldn't talk to *Guts of Sea*.

But she could call Hoà. She could get that feeling again, the one she'd had whenever she and Hoà were together: an odd, familiar feeling in her throat as if she were breathing pure unfiltered, unrecycled air – something that made her want to spread her arms and spin, weightless, in another universe where she was a wholly different person.

She could talk to Hoà.

Hoà wasn't kidnapped or murdered; at the dock number that her employers had given to her, a sleek and discreet shuttle was waiting for her. By the looks of it, it belonged to a mindship, which was confirmed when she scanned her auth-token at the boarding airlock, and a voice came over the comms.

'You're not Thiên Dung,' a male voice said, with the accents of the scholar class and the private compounds.

'No, I'm her older sister. Thiên Hoà. Thiên Dung is ill, so I'm filling in for her.'

'Ah.' A silence. 'All right, then. Come on board.'

Another silence as Hoà settled in. The shuttle was bare, with no overlay: just a sheer metal box with benches on either side, the space narrowing down near the nose. It didn't have portholes, but viewing overlays did spring up on either side when Hoà sat down, keeping her hands carefully folded and her bots utterly still. Magnetic clamps sprang up to grip her box. She looked up; bots were clustered on the ceiling, a series of eyes observing her. That didn't surprise or unsettle her: it was to be expected, and in any case she could hardly be *more* unsettled than she currently was, still frantically processing all of Quỳnh's lesson, not to mention Quỳnh herself.

'Is she all right?' the voice asked.

'I'm sorry?' Hoà asked. The pronoun used was 'child', which seemed odd if applied to Quỳnh. 'My younger sister?'

She carefully avoided referring to the mindship, because she had no idea how they'd prefer to be called, and nothing they'd said so far was helpful.

'Yes,' the voice said patiently.

'I'm sure she'll be fine.'

'That doesn't sound like a resounding vote of confidence.'

There was wry reproach in the ship's voice, and that wasn't what she needed right now, not on top of everything else. She didn't need her employer getting upset with her.

'I'm sorry, I shouldn't have said that.'

Please, don't get more upset. Please.

A silence, then the voice said, 'I'm not sure we're starting this the right way. My name is *The Fruit of Heart's Sorrow*. Everyone refers to me as *Heart's Sorrow*. You can address me as *younger brother*. I'm pretty sure I'm younger than you.'

Hoà opened her mouth to protest, shut it. That was going to be a terminally unhelpful move.

'Yes,' she said, shifting to a more familiar register. 'Of course.'

'We hired you for the job, not for servility.' A hint of amusement in the ship's voice as the shuttle went through the field of smaller asteroids and rock debris that orbited the Belt. 'Almost there.'

Almost there.

Hoà touched Quỳnh's bots on her shoulders, and wished she had even a fraction of Quỳnh's effortless self-assurance. Routines, she'd said. Hoà tried to remember everything: all the rest of it, all the schematics that had flashed in front of her eyes. She tried to hold that single moment when she'd stood in the middle of a ghostly mindship and breathed it all in, trying to make sense of it the way she made sense of small devices – what went where and why, and what she needed to fix to make it flow again. She touched the bots again, and felt as though Quỳnh was besides her, hand on her shoulder, ready to carry her through anything.

She could call Quỳnh, but that was too risky – not on the shuttle, with the mindship watching her. And ... And, if she was honest, she didn't want to. Not unless she absolutely had to. She would get through this on her own terms, with Quỳnh's help – not as one of Quỳnh's water-dancing puppets.

The shuttle changed direction and slowed down. On the overlays of the outside view, the field of asteroids was replaced by an approach vector, slowly shifting around to match the orbit's velocity. Then a clunk, and a silence – and the hiss of an extending airlock, even as part of the metal walls opened along an almost invisible seam on the bench opposite Hoà, into an absolute darkness like the vacuum of space.

'Welcome on board,' *Heart's Sorrow* said.

Hoà took a deep, shaking breath, and got up to do her job.

There was a small, dark corridor: as Hoà walked, the lights blinked on, and overlays flickered in and out of existence. It felt like the Crane Hills quarter cemetery: once it must have been very beautiful, but now only fragments were left – songs, landscapes merging into one another, and areas of absolute darkness where the transitions failed.

There were voices, talking in what appeared to be a heated argument. Hoà followed them through multiple changes of broken overlays, into what must have been a communal area. It was an octagonal room with a pond – a physical one, sheared in half by a huge, molten wound that ran through the entire room.

'Ah, elder sister.'

There were four people inside the room: *Heart's Sorrow*, whose avatar was a small, sleek mindship, and the other three present physically, wearing shadow-skins with their helmets off. 'These are my friends. Nguyệt Minh, Thu Lâm and Thu Thảo.'

Of course she knew who they were: Minh was Prefect Đức's daughter, and the other two were the daughters of Hồng

Oanh, one of the wealthiest merchants of the Belt. Minh was scowling like someone who'd got up and found there was the wrong kind of noodle soup for breakfast, and by the looks of it, she had been one of the people engaged in the argument. By the pitch of *Heart's Sorrow*'s avatar, he'd been one of the others. Oanh's daughters just looked uncertain about who they should support. Hoà would have said they didn't look like the kids of the most powerful people in the Belt — just like four sullen teenagers having a fight — but there was something in their stance: a near-total relaxation and absence of fear. These were people who had gone through life without a day's hardship.

'I apologise for interrupting,' she said.

She laid her bag on the floor: all the tools she'd packed in anticipation of being on the ship, as well some rice cakes and a water bottle.

'It was nothing to concern you,' Minh said, somewhat drily.

She was seventeen or eighteen — her age wasn't part of the information she publicly displayed alongside her auth-token — with an oval-shaped face, an impeccable topknot with elegant silver pins holding it in place, and an elaborate overlay over the shadow-skin, a weave of sea-waves and cloud patterns. Her bots were impeccable and expensive, the patterns on their shells matching her clothes. Rich people's toys.

'Big sis! That's *rude*,' *Heart's Sorrow* said. And, with an apologetic stance towards Hoà, 'I'm sorry. It's been a trying couple of days.'

Hoà inclined her head. Minh was right: their quarrel really was none of her concern, but there was something almost adorable about *Heart's Sorrow*.

'What is it you want me to do?' she asked. 'Specifically.'

Heart's Sorrow looked as though he were about to speak, and changed his mind. He'd probably been going to say 'fix the ship' without any specifics. It was Thu Lâm, the eldest of the merchant Oanh's daughters, who made a gesture, calling up a map. They were near the rear end of the ship, and there was a lopsided circle around their position.

'This is where we have air.' She pointed to one of the alcoves around the room. 'You'll find a shadow-suit here.' Locations blinked as she spoke. 'We think the heartroom is here.' She was using *elder sister* for Hoà, matching *Heart's Sorrow*'s choice of pronouns without any visible resentment.

'Think?' Hoà asked.

Heart's Sorrow made the mindship equivalent of sucking in a breath – a slow spin of his entire avatar.

'She's a warship, and she's damaged.'

'Weapons?' Hoà asked.

'Security systems. Except they don't recognise anyone.' Black dots blinked on the map. 'Don't go beyond these points. I mean it.'

'How are you planning to deal with that area if I don't go there?' Hoà said. Surely the riskiest jobs would be hers.

'We'll find a way to deactivate them.' *Heart's Sorrow*'s voice was firm. 'Minh?'

Minh detached herself from the wall she was leaning on, looking as though she wanted to spit out something particularly sour.

'Yeah,' she said. 'I guess.'

Hoà fingered the bots. Nothing about this was quite what she had expected: the only familiar thing was Minh's contempt. Their casual familiarity was one thing, their concern for her well-being another. She guessed it'd be hard to find another person willing to help them. Still ... something about this was wrong, and she wasn't sure what.

'I don't understand what you want me to do.'

'Today? Have a look,' *Heart's Sorrow* said. 'I'm sending you what we've done. Just ... look around her and try to tell us what you'd do.'

What she'd do. What Thiên Dung would do, what Quỳnh would do. What a real Master of Wind and Water would do, not a jumped-up repairer with a stranger's bots and an hour's worth of hastily delivered expertise.

'All right,' Hoà said, with a confidence she didn't feel. 'I'll have a look.'

It was silent, out there, but not dark. After Hoà had put on the shadow-skin and exited through one of the side airlocks, lights came on – small, fist-sized ones, likely emergency ones that had survived the ship's breaking. She turned on her glider and the map overlay, and headed towards the centre, where Thu Lâm had said the heartroom was.

Hoà sent her bots parallel to the glider, in the corridors she wasn't exploring; bit by bit, they compiled a map of the ship that she could see growing in real time. She kept Quỳnh's bots with her, but she passed the basic patterns of cabling and plugging they provided to her own bots, so they could map as many items of relevance as they went around the ship. She also asked, cautiously, the furthermost bots to check the black spots on Thu Lâm's map. She wasn't sure how observant Thu Lâm was, and she'd need to know what self-defence mechanisms they were facing. Rich kids could afford to avoid problems; Hoà and Thiên Dung's work was going to involve facing them head-on. At some point in the near future, they were going to have to negotiate past the self-defence if they wanted to help this ship.

Then Hoà left her bots to their own devices, and just opened her eyes, taking in the ship.

Gutted corridors, empty cabins, sheared bulkheads. Metal twisted and dulled, with none of the sheen of living mindships, that particular quality of light that always made Hoà feel they were one step away from diving into deep spaces – and one step away from *The Azure Serpent* and distant, fraught memories of her own childhood. This was just ... She wanted to say just a *thing*, but as the glider turned into a larger room and her light played over the remnants of paintings – apricot sprigs, plum-tree branches laden with snow, elaborate calligraphy that flowed like water, from at least three different hands, and she caught a low thrumming that made the walls vibrate – Hoà remembered again that this wasn't a thing. This was a person, who had been hurt and had possibly lost all hope of getting well ever again.

She stopped the glider, paused by one of the walls, body in a prone position. Her hand brushed the apricot sprigs; they were at a child's height and looked to be in a child's hand. There was no signature.

'Grandmother,' she said. 'I'm here to help you.'

Nothing, in answer. Obviously it wouldn't be as simple as having an epiphany while she stood in the middle of a broken, damaged metal section. But under Hoà's fingers was the slow and distant heartbeat; in overlay the map was coming to life, section by section, and over her shoulders were Quỳnh's bots. Hoà called up Quỳnh's schematics, stared at them for a while. Then she lined up the file *Heart's Sorrow* had sent her against the map she'd just drawn: fragmentary repairs that radiated from the central hub, the one where they had light and air. They didn't have much idea of what they were doing – which was good, because Hoà only had marginally better ideas.

She fingered Quỳnh's bots. She could call Quỳnh. She wanted to call Quỳnh – to feel once more that she might be challenged and afraid, but that she was now and always utterly safe. But this would not help her now.

What would she do, if this was a water-filter or an ice-cooler, and the client had already tried to fix it?

Hoà thought for a while. Then she sent Quỳnh's bots forward, with a flick of her fingers.

'Check the repairs,' she said. 'Tell me how good they are.'

Quỳnh's bots left, and Hoà felt bereft without knowing why.

Hoà's alarm blared in her head: a non-critical one. Two of her bots had hit the defence system. No, wait – they weren't the only ones, but they were the only ones getting shot at. It wasn't worrying, per se – the bots had a fallback routine, and she'd set their priorities to survival rather than information – but it was weirdly asymmetric. Thu Lâm's map had shown them in a rough circle that seemed equidistant around a central location: the one Thu Lâm had thought was the heartroom. That made sense. But why were only a fraction of the defences active?

She was about to ping *Heart's Sorrow* when Quỳnh's bots sent her feedback on the repairs – and she stopped.

Hoà knew nothing about mindships, but she knew a lot about repairs. And while these were extensive and amateurish – a client trying their best with a welder and a lack of other professional tools, nothing really unusual – there was something else going on. To Hoà's untrained eyes, it looked like a second set of repairs. To Quỳnh's bots, it looked like many of them would snap given half a chance. They were impressive, but something was wrong every single time: a connector plugged into the opposite polarity; a cable that was a little too fragile; a spot of welding that wouldn't withstand the pressure of the vacuum for long.

Shoddy repairs? But surely even very rich and very spoiled kids would know you just didn't plug things the wrong way around or leave fracture points in a weld. And it looked as though their work was layered on top of the existing repairs – which meant someone else who'd had access to the wreck.

Or one of her employers.

Did she want to bring this up with them? Not yet, not until she got a better picture of what was going on.

'Forward,' she said to the bots who weren't under fire. The other ones were mapping response times and firepower of *Flowers at the Gates'* automatic responses. Hoà didn't really know what to compare these to.

The other bots – a cluster of five, in a wide circle around the area – were converging towards a single point. A grand, deserted room with a steady burn pattern fracturing its walls and floor – the pattern of koi fish and galaxies barely visible under the charring. And beyond ... an intact door.

That was the last thing Hoà saw, because *something* took out her bots with pinpoint precision. They winked out one after the one, dragging Hoà's consciousness into darkness.

Disengage.

She had to disengage from being plugged into them, but there were too many and she couldn't—

She came to, breathing hard – hand still on the apricot flower sprig on the wall.

'Are you all right?'

Heart's Sorrow winked into existence near her. His avatar, hovering over the floor of the room Hoà was in, seemed much larger than he had on the shuttle – as if he was dragging some of his physical body with him.

'What?'

'Your heartbeat went haywire,' *Heart's Sorrow* said patiently.

'Oh, that's right. You're not paying me to get killed.' Hoà was tired and full of adrenaline and her capacity for diplomacy had gone elsewhere – and even as she said it she knew it was a mistake, because no one spoke this flippantly to the son of the Peach Blossom Lake General and got away with it. 'I'm so sorry. Please, forgive my disrespect.'

A sigh from *Heart's Sorrow*. 'I feel like I wasn't clear before.

If I want respect, I can hang out with First Mother's sycophants. What happened?'

Hoà looked at him. He sounded utterly sincere, the tilting of his avatar relaxed, his voice carrying nothing but mild exasperation.

'You're not supposed to act like this.'

'Like a normal person?' His bots were catching up with his avatar, clustering in his shadow, their magnetic legs clinging to the faded patterns of the floor. 'I get it. Our parents have power. You think we're spoiled kids. And maybe we are. But this isn't going to work if you panic every time you think you're offending me.'

Hoà forced herself to breathe. Where she lived – where his first mother ruled – offending the powerful was a fast way to get thrown in jail and never seen again.

'All right,' she said.

Try to look at it like a repair job. Try to not feel afraid. Try not to get noticed.

But he was right: it couldn't work on those terms.

'Tell me the rules, then.'

Heart's Sorrow tilted his avatar sideways. Disbelief.

'Really?'

'You're my employer,' Hoà said stubbornly.

'How about you tell me what would make you comfortable?'

Hoà's mind went blank. *You can't ask me that*, she wanted to say, but it wasn't what she wanted to hear, and she knew saying it wouldn't make the situation any better.

'It's a repair job,' she said finally, because she didn't have anything left in the emptiness of her thoughts.

A silence.

Heart's Sorrow said, 'As team members, then. We're all trying to do the same thing. Which includes being safe, and being flustered if not safe. All of us.' His voice was firm. 'Now, what happened?'

Rules. Boundaries. Hoà could deal with that.

'Good news,' she said. 'I found the heartroom. Bad news – my bots are gone.'

For a moment, she felt his anger around her – the way he was going to lash out at her for disobeying her orders – and then he spun, and it was all gone.

'Show me.'

Hoà sent him clips of her bots' progress, in the blink before they were destroyed.

'Uh.' *Heart's Sorrow* said. 'That's *very* powerful.'

'Yes. Any idea what it is?'

'Before my time,' *Heart's Sorrow* said. 'Some kind of war weaponry. She did fight in the Ten Thousand Flags Uprising.'

And presumably got wounded there.

'Mmm,' Hoà said, trying to focus on the problem at hand. 'Can you look in to disarming the systems?'

Someone pinged Hoà, completely disrupting her focus. It was Quỳnh – there was no subject, but the question was obvious. She didn't have any spare space for Quỳnh right now.

'Give me a moment,' Hoà sent back, and Quỳnh simply acknowledged the message.

Good.

Heart's Sorrow was still talking. Hoà pinged her bots to get the tenth of a centiday of conversation she had missed. He'd just said he would ask Minh.

'*Flowers at the Gates* is her great-aunt, after all.'

'I'll leave you to deal with Minh,' Hoà said softly. Minh was in a bad mood, either temporarily or permanently, but either way, she didn't want to find out. 'I'm done here for today. Can you take me back to the docks?'

She needed to call Quỳnh, to tell her what had happened

– so much less than she'd hoped for, and yet so much more than she'd thought she was capable of. She needed to run what she'd seen past her – she wanted to hear her opinion, and the thought of talking to Quỳnh was a fluttering in Hoà's stomach.

Heart's Sorrow's happiness was a palpable thing. He felt they'd set a good relationship, which was nonsense. The power differential remained, and wasn't going to change because he was kind.

'Of course.'

Hoà took some time to answer Quỳnh. When she finally did, she was on the docks, in what looked to be one of the furthest bays.

'A moment,' she said, and threw up a privacy screen.

It was an audiovisual call only, with no perception overlays. Quỳnh thought Hoà looked paler than usual, and carefully composed: her round face, bare of make-up, framed by a few stray hairs from her topknot, the steel hairpins glinting in the light of the docks. Quỳnh's bots still hung on her shoulders, but—

'Did you send your bots away?' Quỳnh asked, sharply.

Hoà winced. Quỳnh had asked so sharply, and she'd worsened Hoà's unease – now that she thought about it, her careful composure was nothing more than a paper-thin mask.

'I'm sorry.' Quỳnh thought about what she could do to make Hoà feel safer. 'Do you want to talk about it, or would you rather I left you alone?'

Hoà's mouth opened and closed. Something came back into her eyes – a mixture of shock and anger and sadness that Quỳnh wasn't too sure how to dissect.

'No,' she said firmly. 'You're not leaving me alone, big sis.' The emphasis was on the *you*.

'As you wish,' Quỳnh said, taken aback. 'I wanted to know

how it had gone, on the ship. Did you manage to do what you wanted?'

Hoà didn't speak for a long while. At length, she said, 'Figuring out the ship was fine. Your bots helped a lot, and so did the lesson. It does feel like a repair job – something I can do, or fake doing, until Thiên Dung is better. Thank you.' Her voice was tight.

'But . . . ?' Quỳnh asked, unpacking the unsaid sentence.

'Can I ask you a question?'

'Of course,' Quỳnh said.

This wasn't going at all as she'd envisioned. Hoà herself was soft-spoken and anxious, always worried that she'd do the wrong thing. But Hoà in her element – a repair job, she'd said – was almost intimidating.

'Does anybody have particular cause to hate the prefect's family?'

What?

Quỳnh had to pause, parsing the question.

'I don't understand,' she said.

Hoà's eyes, wide and luminous, held her – and for a moment she seemed to see through her, not to Quỳnh but to Dã Lan, and everything else. Quỳnh felt her heart in her throat, ten thousand butterflies fluttering within her, a feeling of emptiness she couldn't seem to shake off.

'I imagine a lot of the Belt doesn't like the prefect, currently,' she said, forcing her voice to remain calm. 'She did arrest a lot of people in the Technologists' Ring.'

'Mmm. No.' Hoà shook her head. 'It's less recent than that.'

'Why?' It had felt like a direct question to expose her, but Hoà sounded utterly sincere, and surely that wasn't the sort of thing she would preoccupy herself with at all.

Hoà sighed. 'Someone has been sabotaging the repairs.'

Quỳnh started to ask if Hoà was sure, but that was the wrong question.

'How do you know?'

'It's small and subtle. And I don't see who would be doing this. I don't know much about mindships, but I imagine repairing all that damage—' she made a sweeping gesture and Quỳnh received files that her bots started processing for highlights— 'would take a lot of time.'

'Hmm.' Quỳnh paused, because her bots were flagging something just outside the residence. 'Give me a moment. Something serious has come up.'

She dropped the privacy screen, putting the call on hold, and opened the doors of the compound.

There was a young woman walking past – a food-seller, pushing a cart with grilled skewers of meat, calling out to the neighbourhood to come and eat, both physically and through the network. But that wasn't the issue. Quỳnh's bots had flagged the man following her. They'd assumed he was skulking around trying to sneak into the compound, but Quỳnh saw the way he lurked, and the way he stared at the food-seller, and she knew this wasn't about the compound.

She walked, slowly and deliberately, to the food-seller.

'One skewer, please.' And, as she sent the bot on her fingertip to pay for it, she also sent a message in overlay. 'There is a man following you. Do you know him?'

The skewer-seller looked at Quỳnh as if shocked, and then at the image Quỳnh had sent along. She shook her head, mutely. She looked scared.

'Thought so,' Quỳnh sent along. Outwardly, she'd paid for the skewer and was waiting for it to finish charring. 'I can call the militia. I can have a word with him. Or do something else with him. Or I can walk you home. But that last is unlikely to solve the problem, long term.'

The food-seller swallowed. 'Not the militia. I can't afford—'

'Mmm,' Quỳnh said. 'Then a word with him?'

A moment's hesitation, then a mute nod.

'I can most certainly do that.' She turned her attention to *Guts of Sea*. 'Big sis? I need help to deactivate some bots.'

A sigh, from *Guts of Sea*. 'All right,' she said grudgingly.

She didn't really approve of Quỳnh doing that – doing anything that might get them noticed. But she had given up arguing.

Quỳnh walked back, as if going to the compound – turned, halfway there, her bots scuttling, lightning-fast, towards the man. Before he'd even registered what was happening he was flat on the floor, his wrists pinned to the metal, and all his bots were deactivated. He stared up at Quỳnh as she kneeled by his side, looking at him.

'You know,' she said conversationally, 'I have your auth-token. And a rather good relationship with the Peach Blossom Lake General. And if I can deactivate your bots and do this . . .' She gestured, and her bots tightened their grip on the man's left wrist, applying enough pressure to bruise. His lips were white. 'Then there are so many other things I can do, aren't I? And so many other things the militia would be glad to do, when they catch you. They don't really like your kind.'

The man made a sound.

'Ssssh.' Quỳnh made her bots tighten their grip again. Bone cracked; the man struggled not to scream. 'I suggest you go home. And stop following her. Or anyone else. Or I'll know.' She smiled, keeping it as light and as innocuous as possible, keeping her voice utterly level and matter-of-fact. 'It won't just be your wrist I break. And it won't be fast, either. Do we have an understanding?'

The man stared at her. For a moment defiance warred with hatred and fear. Quỳnh met his gaze, levelly. She had no fear left, and so very little to keep her in check, and he would see that. Finally he swallowed.

'Yes,' he said.

'Good.' Quỳnh got up, her bots withdrawing. 'I'm glad we had this little chat.'

She watched him scuttle away, and then walked back to the food-seller.

'Thank you,' the food-seller said. 'But why ...?'

Quỳnh withdrew her skewer from the bowl.

'It doesn't really matter. Be careful out there, younger aunt.'

'Yes, of course. Let me—'

Quỳnh made a dismissive gesture. 'No.' The firmness in her voice made the food-seller stop. 'I was glad to help.'

As she walked back to the compound, Hoà said, in her ears, 'She's right, though. Why?' She sounded even more out of composure than before.

Quỳnh realised she'd forgotten to cut Hoà off.

'Because I could,' she said with a shrug. 'Who else was going to step up?'

Hoà made a sound Quỳnh couldn't interpret.

'I see. Well, thank you. For stepping up.'

Quỳnh fought the chasm that opened in her stomach. She wanted to say she hadn't done it for Hoà's thanks, but it would have hurt Hoà.

'You're welcome. Let me go back to your question about the ship,' she said, throwing the privacy screen up again.

She opened the files Hoà had previously sent, glanced at them – sent more processing patterns to her bots, refining them dynamically based on the results they were sending her.

Flowers at the Gates was old, and very damaged. Every image Quỳnh had seen suggested an older ship than *Guts of Sea*, and the damage was extensive: it looked as though she'd been caught in a hail of weaponry, including heavy-duty vacuum cutters and lasers.

'You're right,' Quỳnh said. 'Your friends did a good job patching the structural damage on *Flowers at the Gates* – bar the sabotage. But the issue is fixing the Mind itself. The heartroom and the surrounding circuits were heavily affected when *Flowers at the Gate* was wounded. Getting her awake is going to take a long time. *Guts of Sea* was far less damaged than this, and the damage never touched her heartroom.'

'And how long did it take you to fix her?'

Quỳnh thought of time slowing and twisting until it had lost all meaning – sheen trembling on floors, walls that seemed to melt and flow into one another.

'Big sis? Big sis!' A voice insistently pulling her back, but not like the sting of *Guts of Seas*' bots, or of the syringes her bots knew to stab into her forearms if she started slipping. 'Big sis?'

'I ...' Quỳnh pulled herself together with an effort. 'Yes. Sorry. Bad memories.'

Hoà looked at her again – and again Quỳnh felt transparent, the varnish of the Alchemist and her years at court stripped away until she was young once more, her heart beating a frantic rhythm in her chest.

'I'm sorry,' Hoà said. 'I didn't know the memories were unpleasant.' A pause. 'Are you sure you want to do this?'

Quỳnh was as sure of it as she was of her revenge – as utterly convinced as she was that time was running out, and that she'd tear them down and bring down on them the justice of Heaven first – as utterly sure as she was that she would not survive this.

'Yes.'

'Why?'

'Why?' Quỳnh hadn't expected the question.

'You told me you wanted to help me for Thiên Hạnh's sake. And I said yes because I didn't want to probe too much. But now what I'm asking you touches the prefect – brings up questions of seditious activities – and you haven't even blinked.'

'You're scared.'

Hoà stared at her. 'Yes. Obviously. Who wouldn't be?'

'And you want my advice?'

'No. I want the truth.'

'Yes,' Quỳnh said. 'No lies except by omission.'

She wasn't sure what she was trying to do – why she had said, sharp and cutting and cynical, the most hurtful thing she could think of.

Hoà merely stared at her. 'No. I'm not the stone or the water you'll use to wear your blade to a needle. Find someone else. Or stop it altogether.'

It was a jolt. No one had spoken to Quỳnh that way in years, not even *Guts of Sea*. She stood stock-still, trying to process all of it.

How dare she. How dare she look at me and not see what I could do to her, if I chose? How ...?

A touch, on her shoulder. It was Hoà: she'd changed the call from audio to perceptual, and her hand rested on Quỳnh's shoulder – moving a fraction higher, towards Quỳnh's face, resting on Quỳnh's lips, a touch the perception layers rendered as a bare thread of warmth with hardly any pressure to it. Hoà's gaze was level, utterly fearless, with that same faith she'd had before that Quỳnh wouldn't lash out, wouldn't hurt her – absurd, when Quỳnh was out to hurt so many people.

But only those who deserved it.

Only them.

Quỳnh took Hoà's hand, moved it away from her lips – held on to it for a bare blink more, squeezing it lightly, that same warmth travelling up her arm, something she shouldn't seek, that she couldn't afford. Love was loss and vulnerability, and she had time for neither.

'You're right,' she said. 'I shouldn't have said that.'

Hoà inclined her head. She looked even more exhausted – the aftermath of running a physical and emotional race. Quỳnh wanted to hug her, but didn't. She couldn't allow this to go any further. Instead, she said, 'Prefect Đức has got enemies, but the only reason I can think of for harming *Flowers at the Gates* is personal.'

'Someone who hates her?'

Quỳnh pursed her lips. She'd considered harming *Flowers at the Gates*, but the truth was that Đức despised her great-aunt and couldn't wait for her to die, so why give her that satisfaction? And she'd already made the decision to help Hoà: to give her what she needed in this matter, rather to use this as a chip in her revenge plans. This was a kindness untouched by everything else.

'The reverse. Whoever sabotages *Flowers at the Gates* will be doing the prefect a favour.'

'I don't understand.'

'*Flowers at the Gates* is the current lineage head. The next one would be the prefect, but for that ...'

'Oh.' Hoà's face went through a particular twist, a sharpening that made her seem older. 'If she dies, the prefect gets the family wealth. Oh. Thank you. That helps.'

Quỳnh hesitated, for a moment. She shouldn't get more involved. She shouldn't seek to be closer to Hoà. But she had that feeling in her belly again, like ten thousand birds trapped within – as though she could be herself with Hoà after so long putting on so many masks.

'Do you want me to make inquiries?'

Hoà thought about it, for a while. She never made decisions

lightly: another thing that drew Quỳnh to her – that mixture of fretting and sharp, uncompromising practicality.

'I'm not getting involved in their affairs,' she said finally. 'If—'

'Yes?'

'If I ask you something, can you answer it? Without omissions.'

'I'll tell you if I can't,' Quỳnh said finally.

'How much danger do you think I'm in?'

Ah.

'Because you've been hired to fix something someone else has been sabotaging?' Quỳnh thought, for a while, on how to phrase this in a way that wouldn't make Hoà more anxious. But she had promised the truth without omissions. 'I don't know. If I were you, I would be very careful, and do my best not to be alone in dark places. Sabotage isn't murder, but—'

'But it may lead to it. Understood.' Hoà's face was hard again. 'Then can you look in to it? So I know what I'm getting into.'

'Can I ask you a question?'

Hoà looked surprised. 'Yes, of course.'

'Some would say the best course of action is to leave. Those who can afford it. They're paying you a lot, aren't they?'

Hoà's face was a curious thing – working her way through what Quỳnh was saying, frowning, unsure whether to be offended.

'Yes,' she said finally. 'And I appreciate your concern, but it's not yet at the point where I'd bail out.'

They stared at each other for a while. Hoà's gaze was defiant, the shoulders on which Quỳnh's bots rested utterly immobile. Quỳnh wasn't sure what was in her own gaze – admiration, worry, awareness that Hoà had no idea what she was getting into? But she couldn't offer Hoà charity; that would never fix anything, and Hoà had already made her feelings clear about it. And neither could she reveal who she was or why the prefect was dangerous. She simply reached for Hoà's hand again, held it.

'Of course,' she said, fighting back an unfamiliar wave of guilt. 'I'll make inquiries.'

7

A Banquet and a Poisoning

Minh was trying to get her topknot to co-operate – with an ever-increasing number of bots deployed to catch her stray hairs – when the door opened. She looked up, and saw Mother, just as the overlay of the room darkened. Her heart sank.

'Mother.'

'Child.'

Mother sat on the side of the bed, watching Minh's bots. There was no giải trãi this time, no beast to swallow Minh whole – just the darkness pooling on the floor, and the faintest suggestion of a banyan tree behind her, making Mother cast a much larger shadow than she ought to.

'That hairstyle doesn't suit you,' she said.

'Mother!'

Mother's face didn't move. 'You know tonight is important.'

One banquet out of so many other banquets, but time was running out for Minh.

'There is still time,' Minh said mildly.

'The best mentors are already making their choices,' Mother said.

Her bots climbed on Minh's shoulders, gently pushing

Minh's bots out of the way – started fiddling with Minh's hair, straightening it into a perfect topknot.

'Are you afraid no one will want me when the examinations results come out?' Minh sounded more aggressive than she'd thought; she wasn't sure if she was afraid of Mother's disappointment or simply expecting it, like the solar storms and the cycle of day and night over the habitats.

'I've raised you since you were a child,' Mother said. 'I know you. You're smart, but you fall apart under pressure.'

Do I? I could never measure up. I will never measure up.

Minh struggled with the disappointment, the hurt, of being seen so clearly, and so clearly found wanting. But there was another voice within her – Quỳnh's voice – that whispered, *Mothers are hard*. Not just hard to navigate, but as hard as titanium, as harsh as the laws of gravity.

Needlessly hard. And she knew that, didn't she?

'I only want what's best for you.' Mother's voice was soft. Her bots had finished pulling at Minh's hair, reshaping it into something more suitable: the austere topknot that was the mark of a student. 'Now, what about your dress?'

Minh bristled. 'I'm not changing my dress.'

It was a peach áo dài with embroidered peach blossom flowers, and in overlay the branches and flowers moved as if in an invisible wind, as the flowers blossomed, shedding petals on the floor – moving as if Minh's gestures were giving them life.

Mother's gaze was full of pity.

'You know no mentor will consider you like this.'

'Why would they not?'

'This is ...' Mother rose, the shadow of her overlay moving to cover Minh's. 'You want to give the best impression, don't you? Many of the Belt's foremost scholars will be there. Your friend Quỳnh will be there.'

As if Quỳnh would care what Minh wore.

'You don't like her,' Minh said sharply.

'I have no opinion on Quỳnh.' Mother's voice was altogether too smooth. 'I dislike that her compound seems to be a place of pollution and a major headache for poor Uncle Toàn's tribunal.' She paused, eyeing Minh's dress again, like a predator pondering the best way to catch prey. 'Something blue, I think. Like the cloth of Heaven.'

'I don't want blue!' Minh said.

'Now, be reasonable.' Mother's voice was hard. 'You know I don't love you when you're being unreasonable. And you want to be loved, don't you?'

Minh could say no. She absolutely could. She had before. Mother would get upset and storm out, and not talk to her for the next five days – Minh could already feel the dread of that roiling in her stomach. She could say no, and everything that followed would be her fault. Or she could say yes, and Mother would smile and hug her, and there would be that warmth in her stomach: that sense of being seen, of being valued. Of being a good girl.

Minh so desperately wanted to be a good girl.

'Something with a pattern on it,' she said, trying to find some compromise which would give her a little freedom.

'Waves,' Mother said firmly, and her bots threw out a cobalt áo dài with an abstract pattern of waves that rippled in overlay. 'You love the sea and it goes so well with your complexion.'

And the way she said it made it absolutely true. Minh loved the sea, and surely it was better not to make a fuss. Surely it was better to keep Mother happy, because then Minh would get to be happy, too.

'Fine,' Minh said, trying to ignore the growing emptiness within her, which seemed to swallow every emotion. 'That blue is fine.'

*

From the moment their shuttle entered the general's compound, Minh felt on display, with only the familiar weight of her bots on her wrists, shoulders and back for comfort. The áo dài Mother had chosen felt slightly too tight, the overlay of waves not moving as it should when Minh moved. Mother, of course, was perfectly composed, immaculately dressed in robes that prominently displayed her badge of official rank, the tiger shifting subtly every half-centiday or so.

'This is so fun! Look, big sis, they've put lanterns up.'

Vân was riding on Minh's shoulders, excitedly pointing at the entrance corridor as the whole family disembarked.

'Behave, child,' Stepmother said, but without much heart.

'And look at all those alcoves!'

The banquet room was a re-creation of some strategist's private rooms: a crane-feather fan was lying negligently in the antechamber, and sky lanterns in trapeze shapes were hovering all over the reception room. On the distant walls were alcoves displaying various weapons, including a selection from Old Earth – swords, crossbows, Quan Vũ's hooked halberd – and more modern weapons – vacuum blades, ion-guns, soft darts. Others held a random assortment of scenes; a series of lanterns floating upwards; a monk with short hair and an arrow poking out of his head; an underground boat ride with two emperors; a river with iron stakes.

Oh, of course: Grand Prince Hưng Đạo and Khổng Minh, two strategists from Old Earth. A blatant statement from General Tuyết on the traditions she drew from, verging on the blasphemous, since she wasn't connected to either of them.

The reception's tables were set on an overlay of green, rolling hills, with a river running on either side, and silver streams of rice fish turning and wheeling with excitement as soon as a guest approached the riverbank. There were scholars, planetary merchants, wealthy hydroponics estate owners ... all the dignitaries of the Belt the elite prefect effortlessly courted and kept in check. They drank the finest rice wines, not from the vats but from the Numbered Planets. The food, piled high on the polished wood of the tables, was the best of what the station had to offer: Eight Treasure Rice – each grain a small sliver of perfect colour; crêpe rolls as translucent as the finest porcelain; dumplings wrapped in elaborate shapes and steamed until the vegetable filling looked as though it was going to burst through the wrapping; pineapple duck and stuffed crab claws; seared scallops with scallions; longevity noodles with eels ...

Vân was positively vibrating with excitement – she was sending her bots towards the walls, presumably to check if they could climb on the alcoves. Minh swung her down from her shoulders.

'Lil sis! You know you're going to get into trouble.'

Vân made a face. 'I know, but come on! Don't you want to know if they're overlay ...?'

Minh sighed. She sent her own bots' feedback to Vân.

'Here,' she said. 'These are physical.'

'Wow.' Vân looked at the sword. 'That must be ancient. Wonder if they got it from the First Planet?'

In spite of herself, Minh smiled. Vân's enthusiasm was infectious. Unlike Minh, she was just there to be indulged – a child whose poetry would be smiled at, whose scraps of scholarship would be praised – and Minh ought to have been bitter about it, but in truth she was happy. It was *very* hard to be bitter at Vân.

'Child!' It was Stepmother, frowning and clearly addressing Minh.

'I'm coming,' Minh said. 'Vân wanted—'

'Leave Vân.' Stepmother's voice was stern. 'You're a bad example to her.'

'She's a child.'

'Yes.' Stepmother's face was perfect, her robes a rich overlay of dragons and pearls and clouds, the clouds slowly growing to take over the entire cloth before rain burst from them. Every thumb-width of her was the consummate scholar, the lesser spouse supporting Mother in all her endeavours. 'This is an important reception for your mother. You know this.'

Because I'm being put on display?

Minh bit back the words before they could come out. 'She told me.'

Stepmother made a face. 'Your behaviour affects this entire family, and you think it's just a joke.'

Minh couldn't help it. 'Is this because I'm not your daughter?'

Vân was busying herself with the sword, trying to escape the adult anger.

'Of course not,' Stepmother said, in a way that failed to be convincing. 'You should have been taken in hand earlier. Your *mother*—' and it was clear she meant Minh's Second Mother, the one who'd carried her in her womb— 'was too indulgent, and Đức has indulged you in turn.'

If that was indulgence, Minh didn't want to see the rest of it.

'Let's go,' she said.

'See?' Stepmother said. 'One day your mother is going to realise your insolence and you'll pay dearly for it.'

Minh ignored the venom, or tried to, as she walked towards the back of the room.

Quỳnh was already on the dais, kneeling in front of a giant piece of paper and chatting with Tuyết. Behind her was *Guts of Sea*, the mindship friend Minh had already met. As they all approached, Quỳnh made a series of sweeping gestures, her sleeves billowing in the invisible wind of the room, the brush in her hand flowing over the paper, back and forth – words forming in its wake one after the other, in the calligraphy of a master. As she did so, she spoke the poem that she was writing – and the words appeared in the overlay, hovering over the lanterns.

> 'Tiles clattering like sparrows in the Eagle Garden,
> Red thread, yellow chrysanthemums, and blood lingering in the roiling water.
> How scalding her tea feels, bringing oblivion,
> How loudly the pagoda's bell calls for the boat to cast off its moorings.'

Quỳnh lifted her brush, smiling. Servants rushed to take the paper, hanging it on either side of the dais.

And then Minh and her family were on the dais, too, bowing.

'This is a masterful poem you have gifted us, lil sis,' Mother said to General Tuyết and Scholar Nhăng. And, to Quỳnh, 'I have heard so much about you, master. I'm glad to see all of it is true.' She used the form of address reserved for scholars who held an official post.

Quỳnh smiled. 'You're too kind. I'm not worthy of such an address.' She looked at Minh and gracefully nodded at her. 'It is a pleasure to see you here, child.'

'Thank you.' Minh swallowed. She was finding it hard to breathe and wasn't sure why.

'I hope you've recovered from our last meeting? I worried.'

Mother glowered. She was no longer the centre of attention, and hated it.

'You're the Alchemist of Streams and Hills.'

'I have that pleasure,' Quỳnh said.

'Your poem is a masterpiece. You do the general great honour. You could easily find patronage elsewhere than in the

Belt.' Tuyết smiled. Nhăng, less susceptible to flattery, made a tight face, lips narrowing. Mother's words were dangerously close to an insult, implying the general wasn't good enough for Quỳnh.

Minh said to Quỳnh, via the private channel, 'It is a really good poem.'

Quỳnh's laughter echoed in her ears. 'I'm glad you think so.'

The poem *was* a masterpiece: referring to other work by two of the great, timeless poets from the Starless Wanderers – and bringing in imagery from at least three classics. And something else that Minh couldn't quite place but was sure she'd heard somewhere.

'Hey, big sis,' *Heart's Sorrow* said to Minh on a private channel. 'Don't take this the wrong way, but you look terrible. Are you all right?'

'No,' Minh said sullenly.

Mother was introducing Vân to Tuyết, with a beaming Stepmother behind her. Mother was *smiling*, relaxed and proud – the same expression she'd had when Minh put on the waves dress, but that Minh saw so seldom.

'I feel like a bird at the butcher's shop. You?'

Heart's Sorrow shrugged, angling his body to catch the light from the poem.

'Watching Mom trying to seduce everyone. At least Ma is more sensible.'

Nhăng wasn't looking at Minh's family but at the rest of the gathering, scowling at them as if she suspected them of something untoward, like an uncouth memorial to the throne or a mediocre poem.

'Come,' Mother said, her bots climbing Minh's shoulders once more. 'There are people you should meet.'

Behind her, Stepmother and Vân were being guided to their

table – one at the head of the room, just below the dais.

Minh couldn't have said no even if she'd tried to. *Heart's Sorrow* sent her a sympathetic wave through the network, but as the son of the hostesses he had to remain on the dais and pay some attention to what was going on. Like Minh, his mothers had put him on display, expecting him to perform his part.

'This is my daughter,' Mother said. 'Child, this is Scholar Vĩnh Trinh and their partner Mạt Ly. Trinh is one of the foremost poets of the Belt, and Ly has her own printing house.'

The scholars rose from their table, and bowed. Vĩnh Trinh was a forbidding, elderly non-binary individual with an androgynous appearance, their topknot – like Quỳnh's – leaving part of their hair flowing down their back. Mạt Ly had her hair cut very short, almost short enough to be a monk. Unusually for a scholar, her bots were unadorned and utilitarian, and she had what looked like ten thousand different ones, on her shoulders and arms and in every fold of her very wide robes.

'Very glad to meet you, child. Have you eaten yet?'

Mother said, 'Minh passed her examinations and is awaiting the results. She's an utterly brilliant scholar, if disorganised.'

'Mother!' Minh ought to have been used to it by then, but it still hurt.

'She's going to need firm guidance to navigate politics. You know how it is,' Mother said, putting a hand on Minh's shoulder, ignoring the way her daughter flinched. 'Too smart to pay attention to small details.'

'Details aren't always necessary,' Vĩnh Trinh said, smiling. It had teeth, and suddenly Minh had the dizzying revelation that they didn't like Mother. But surely everyone liked Mother – she was always the centre of attention in the room, always smiling and drawing everyone's gaze, always connected to everyone and everything. 'What do you want to do with your life, child?'

They were looking at Minh, not at Mother. Minh, pinned beneath their gaze, saw her chance, and fought back panic. This was her moment – except that she didn't really have an answer.

'I've not really thought about it—' she could feel Mother gathering herself up to cut her off, and nausea filled her— 'but I want to make a difference.'

'To Empire politics?' Mạt Lỵ looked interested. As if what Minh had said was important. It made her feel ... exposed, as though it was all wrong. 'That's an unusual answer. What difference?'

Minh's answer came bubbling out of a hard, private place within her.

'Kindness.'

'Kinder laws?' Vĩnh Trinh looked at her for a while.

Minh swallowed. 'Yes.'

Mother snapped, 'That's an utterly ridiculous concept. Please forgive my daughter for her naivety, she doesn't know better.'

Vĩnh Trinh laughed, the bots on their wrists uncoiling and linking to the ones on their elbows and hand to form a long, translucent chain.

'A lot of us scholars could benefit from kindness, and forgiveness for our work.'

And they were looking at Mother for a moment: a quick glance that Minh caught, but Mother – too busy scrutinising Minh for more fault – didn't.

What do they mean?

'The law is the law,' Mother said. 'It was not made to tolerate exceptions, and this child should know better.'

'Of course. Your Excellency would be most familiar with this,' Mạt Lỵ said, softly and smoothly.

She was still looking at Minh, who didn't feel safe enough

to message them and ask what they'd meant by this exchange. What did Mother need to be forgiven for? Intransigence? Minh chafed at it, but she knew full well that leniency was a favour, not something one had any right to. Mother was always unfalteringly fair.

Vĩnh Trinh flipped their hand up, showing Minh a translucent seal: a personal comms channel.

'Here,' they said. 'If you think it would be useful.'

It was as good as saying they'd mentor Minh, if Minh asked.

'It might,' Mother said smoothly, and bowed to the scholars, gently steering Minh away from their table before she even had the time to react. 'Now let's see the others.'

'They looked perfectly fine,' Minh said.

'They're both newly risen. Their families aren't influential. You can do much better,' Mother said, pursing her lips.

'Then why did you even introduce me?'

'Because I knew you would say the wrong thing at the first interview,' Mother said, shaking her head. 'Kindness. You're too soft.' She snorted. 'Find something better. That might work for jumped-up peasants from the hydroponics farms, but the wealthier families won't have a taste for naivety. Let's go.'

Afterwards, Minh didn't really remember the whirlwind of introductions that followed. An endless series of faces painted with ceruse, of diplomatic frowns, of pitying gazes – of questions probing how good a scholar she was, angling to see if she knew the origin of a quote, if she could use the classics to make her arguments, if she knew how to behave in the face of various slights and challenges – again and again, until the words burned in her throat and nausea threatened to swallow her whole. All the while, Mother was with her, her bots on Minh's shoulders, explaining how good Minh was, how bright a future she had if only someone would straighten her out, until Minh's world reduced to that pinpoint of bots' legs through the thin layer of silk, stabbing into her skin – to Mother's words stabbing into her brain ...

'Child?' Mother's stern voice. 'Child?'

'What?'

'You're not listening.'

Minh stared at Mother – at the ceruse so white and sharp that it seared her eyes, at the thin, blood-red lines of her lips, pursed in disappointment – and something primal and unstoppable welled up from the pit of her stomach.

'I'm sorry. I need some air.'

Before Mother could draw herself up to voice her outrage, Minh pushed past her and left the banquet room, brushing Mother's bots off her shoulders and throwing up the strongest privacy screen the compound would allow her.

Outside, it was quieter. The din of the banquet was muffled – though Minh could hear the scuttling sound of Mother's bots returning to her. She'd be along any moment now; Minh needed to keep moving to stay beyond her reach.

She moved unsteadily into narrow, windowless corridors. The overlay here was purely cosmetic, as if she'd crossed a line and entered a backstage area. Faint traceries of light under the metal, and narrow corridors.

'Are you all right?' a voice asked.

It was Quỳnh, on a private comms channel.

'You're still at the banquet.' Minh stopped in the middle of a wider room – a glorified cupboard with blinking lights, and maintenance bots pooling on the seam between the walls and the ceiling – and tried to breathe.

'It's hard to leave a banquet when one is the centrepiece poet.' Quỳnh seemed amused.

Minh leaned against a wall; the bots that had been clustering on it fled as if scalded or scared. It did not make her feel better.

'I needed a moment,' she said.

'A break from being a sacrificial offering?' Quỳnh's voice was ironic.

Breathe in, breathe out.

'From being *herded*,' Minh said. 'You asked me about my future. *This* is my future. I don't have one.'

Hard mothers. Harsh mothers.

'I'm sorry,' Quỳnh said. 'I'd offer to be your sponsor if that would make things easier, but I don't think your mother likes me very much.'

Minh's heart skipped a beat. She'd offered. There was no way under Heaven that Minh was going to be able to accept, but she'd offered. She'd valued Minh enough to offer.

'Mother doesn't like anyone,' she said bitterly. 'Not unless they're important.' Scholars Vĩnh Trinh and Mặt Ly swam back into the morass of her thoughts. 'And some people don't like her.'

'Don't they?' Quỳnh's voice was toneless. 'Well, as I said … mothers can be hard. And your mother does have a reputation for being harsh but fair.'

Harsh but fair – but if she'd always been fair, what would she have done that required forgiveness?

'No,' Minh said. 'I don't think that's quite it. But thank you for the reassurance. I'll see you later?'

'Of course.' Quỳnh sent a textual bow via the channel. 'I'll be delighted.'

Minh thought of the seal Vĩnh Trinh had shared with her, and stared at it.

A lot of us scholars could benefit from kindness, and forgiveness for our work.

She was going to find out what Mother had done.

Hoà woke to a message from her bots: they had finished parsing the footage of the ship. Thiên Dung, who had reviewed it, had added her annotations – but Thiên Dung was now asleep, tossing and turning in the grip of that fever that never seemed to go away. Hoà had a quick look at her fingers: the pinpricks of red were more prominent, and they'd taken on a blueish tinge. Hoà might have to pull elder sister privilege and call a doctor, regardless of Thiên Dung's wishes on the matter, and their dwindling finances.

Hoà needed rest. She dismissed the message and closed her eyes again, trying to sleep. But she couldn't seem to: she was worrying about Thiên Dung and the ship – and Quỳnh, and what she'd agreed to. What would she do if one of her clients was sabotaging the ship? How were they going to take the news when they hadn't even paid? What if Thiên Dung got sicker and sicker?

She tossed and turned, closing her eyes and trying very firmly to tell herself to sleep, but it was futile.

Fine.

She got up, throwing up a privacy screen so she didn't disturb Thiên Dung's rest, and pulled up the annotations.

Thiên Dung had a few more ideas than Hoà: she thought the damage was extensive, but that there was very little point in focusing on small gains. What mattered was checking the heartroom, because it was likely the ship had gone into shock following the shearing wounds, and that damage needed to be dealt with first. Which meant getting past the defences. She'd made notes on the blast patterns from the bots' last transmissions before *Flowers at the Gates* took them out, and was suggesting a way for the bots to weave their way through.

Easy for her to say. Hoà sighed. She supposed she could ask the community aunties for the faster kind of bots, but they would be expensive. If she told *Heart's Sorrow* …

Wait.

She stared again at the footage Thiên Dung had annotated.

'Run it against known weapons,' she said to her bots, distributing the comparison checks among all of them and sending some to the shop's common bots as well. There were too many weapons, and so many had been used during the course of the Ten Thousand Flags Uprising.

The answer, when it finally came, was unequivocal: butterfly lasers.

But that wasn't right. The response time was wrong. At the time *Flowers at the Gates* had been shot down, the fastest response time for butterfly lasers was thirteen hundred blinks. The response time Hoà was seeing was less than five hundred blinks. That was well outside the range of what was possible thirteen years before, even with advanced military-grade weapons. And even now it was fast ... Hoà didn't have access to the latest military weapons, but she did know someone who did.

She started pinging Quỳnh, but then she stopped, because something else caught her eye in the images her bots had managed to capture before the defence system wiped them out. The image was half-formed and half-corrupted – the compression algorithms hadn't had time to finish their work before the bots crashed – so what she got was the cache, hastily transmitted in a reflex arc with the last slivers of online time. Fortunately, however, the compression was hierarchical: she had an overall fuzzy image, with the areas of interest more sharply delineated. She zoomed into the information-rich parts of the image, holding her breath as she did.

There.

That was where the lasers were, those glints in the seam between wall and ceiling. Except ...

She zoomed in again. The image blurred – she didn't have *that* much information in there. She did, however, have several bots, and she could stack their images on top of one another and make another attempt at deblurring ...

Yes.

That butterfly laser wasn't thirteen years old. In fact – lopsided, ill put together, gleaming with the sheen of the mindship's inner corridors – it was brand new, and it had been put together by bots. By the ship's bots. Except that installing butterfly lasers wasn't a simple reflex task; it would require conscious volition. It would require focus. It would require purpose. It would require awareness in the long term.

And that meant...

Hoà stopped, then. She wanted to shake Thiên Dung awake, to talk to her about what she'd uncovered. To make it real. But she was a repairer, and while her knowledge of mindships as a whole was superficial, she could absolutely characterise devices.

'You're *awake*,' she said, to the frozen images in the overlay. Not just wounded and trapped in the heartroom, not just shooting people and bots through automated defences, but conscious enough to direct bots to put something this complex together.

Awake.

And someone was trying very, very hard to make sure *Flowers at the Gates* wasn't repaired. If they found out the ship wasn't just dormant, but conscious and in the process of repairing herself, it was very likely they wouldn't stop at mere sabotage.

How do you kill a mindship?

By getting access to the heartroom, and it isn't that hard, is it?

Given a little time, Hoà could probably go around the heart-rooom – and if she could, so could the saboteur.

She needed to— No, she couldn't warn *Heart's Sorrow*, because any of them could be the saboteur, and she had no idea if it was him, or the scowling Minh, or the too-helpful children of Oanh. She needed to warn *someone*. She...

The inevitability of what needed to be done settled on her like a mantle of vacuum – cold and unforgiving, stealing the breath in her lungs.

She needed to warn *Flowers at the Gates*.

Hoà got all the way to the ship before the adrenaline wore off, and she realised how bad an idea this had been.

Fear for *Flowers at the Gates* had driven her to the docking bay, where she'd managed, through Auntie Vy, to find a not entirely legal shuttle, and to ride, silent, all the way to the ship. All the way to the common area where she'd first met Minh and Oanh's children. It felt as if they'd just stepped out, their shadow-skins hastily stuffed in a drawer still protruding from one of the walls, their half-eaten dumplings and half-drunk tea still in plates and cups.

It was dark and desolate, with that peculiar feeling of loneliness, that same fear as a filled cemetery – that everything around her was dead. Hoà retrieved her water bottle from the bag on her shoulder and took a swig, trying to feel more at ease.

What had I been thinking? That I was going to swoop in like an upright magistrate and save Flowers at the Gates?

She only had a handful of bots left, plus the ones she'd borrowed from Auntie Vy, that she didn't have much of a feel for yet.

What had I been thinking?

Well, she'd come this far and it had been costly enough. She might as well go all the way.

In that same deathly silence, Hoà put on her shadow-skin, and went through the airlock, towards the place where her bots had died. The mindship would be putting together further defences, but that would take time. For the moment, the configuration was exactly the one she'd seen earlier. At least, she hoped so. She still sent her bots ahead, cautiously – and stopped well ahead of the plaza in front of the heartroom. Her heart was beating against her ribs, so fast it was almost painful, and she had a faint metallic taste in her mouth. Fear. *Flowers at the Gates* had sheared through her bots in less than a heartbeat – if she wanted to, she could take Hoà out, too.

'I know you can hear me,' she said, in the midst of the silence, broadcasting on all the frequencies used by mindships.

Nothing. A faint scuttling? Bots. There had to be bots on the ship, though she hadn't seen them yet. Something that was building the lasers and adapting the defences. Trying to safeguard the heartroom from further damage.

'Someone is trying to kill you,' Hoà said. 'And I don't know who, but maybe you do. And maybe that's why you have the lasers. You ...' She took a deep, shaking breath. 'You can defend yourself against them.' And, against the silence of her comms, she played on a public overlay every single one of the small sabotage acts she'd seen. 'I don't know what they're going to do. I ...' She swallowed. It still tasted metallic. 'I can help you, but I know I haven't given you any reason to trust me.'

Silence. The last before the lasers fired on her? Or was there no response because she'd been wrong, and *Flowers at the Gates* was too severely wounded, still dormant and utterly unaware of anything outside the heartroom? Nothing, because there was nothing.

A scuttling, on her right. Hoà turned her head, and saw the flow of bots coming out of the seam of the ceiling, a long thin line of corroded metal, half-blind sensors and half-intact legs. There were so many of them, mindlessly making for her as if to swallow her whole. So many.

She fought down her body's instinct to run.

No.

She'd come all this way and possibly it had been a bad idea, but she couldn't turn back now. She sent, slowly and carefully, one of her own bots to meet them.

Flowers at the Gates' bots batted it away. Inside, the bots stopped in the middle of the floor, and a space shimmered into view: a trembling spherical overlay that included perception filters. The invitation was clear. Hoà's heart was now syncopating wildly in her chest, the metallic taste strong enough to overwhelm everything.

Do I want to do this? Do I . . . ?

Oh, that was silly. *Flowers at the Gates* wanted to be fixed. Hoà supposed this could be an elaborate way to kill her, but she was still out of range of the lasers, and why go to all this trouble?

Shaking, struggling to breathe, Hoà glided into the overlay.

She didn't get words — instead, she was hit by a wave of jumbled feelings and sensations: the silent arc of ships' weapons systems in space; the cold of the vacuum; Prefect Đức's face, and Nguyệt Minh's face; the sound of feet running in corridors, the feeling of them touching floors one after the other; a brief jolt of warmth — and the rising tone of voices getting angrier and angrier . . . Then it broke off, and the bots withdrew, leaving Hoà panting on the floor.

'The prefect? *She's* the one sabotaging you? Through Minh?'

Hoà struggled to make sense of it. Her mouth felt stuffed with cotton.

The bots were still on the floor. They hadn't moved.

'I am so fixing your voice centres,' Hoà said. Words came sluggishly. She . . .

Wait.

She wasn't well.

Her vision was wobbling, the bots dancing and stretching. The metallic taste was now unbearable; it seemed to have taken over her entire face, and she was having trouble staying awake. She'd had that taste in her throat since she'd drunk the water.

Not just unwell.

'Poison,' she said, struggling to speak, and the bots seemed to waver and nod.

Of course.

Whoever was sabotaging *Flowers at the Gates* would want to stop Hoà, too. She'd have laughed. A few days before she'd been worrying about whether she'd fool her employers about her ability to do large-scale repairs on *Flowers at the Gates*. Now it appeared she'd done her job too well, and the saboteur wanted her out of the way, too.

She was in space. She was in the middle of nowhere. In the middle of the night. She could …

The shuttle.

She needed to get back to the shuttle.

Hoà took a deep breath, inhaling air that tasted of molten metal, and started up her glider, going back towards the shuttle. Everything was warping and twisting out of shape – the corridors not in the places she'd expect, walls coming up at odd intervals and hitting her hands and face …

No, not the walls coming up.

She just couldn't control her glider well enough to avoid them. Her heartbeat was in her ears, fragile and syncopated, and it felt as though at any moment it was going to shudder and stop – or tear her chest apart. Corridors. More corridors. She couldn't breathe any more. A moment of clarity bubbled up, surfacing like a mindship tearing through the fabric of space. She was never going to manage two airlocks like this – the one to get back to the common area, and the one to get into the shuttle. But her bots could perform some simple tasks for her.

'Get the shuttle to the airlock,' she said, sending all of them off – just keeping Quỳnh's bots with her, a comforting weight on her shoulders. Her glider hit something again, hard enough to send her flying upwards in the low gravity.

Wall. The wall with the apricot flowers.

Or at least she thought so, because it was all so hazy, and it took an effort to stay conscious.

If Hoà fell unconscious, she'd die. No one would check in on her until it was far too late. Hoà had to keep her eyes open. She had to keep moving – she clenched her hands on the glider, trying to hang on to it. Every muscle wanted to spasm and let go.

Forearm-length after forearm-length, agonising – her hands kept under tight, shaking control, the glider weaving sharply to avoid hitting the walls of corridors. Ahead, the airlock … Staring at the map overlay was an effort, and she gave up. Everything hurt.

After what felt like an eternity, she hit another wall, hard enough that her hands opened in shock. She tried to get them back under control, but they wouldn't answer her. The airlock dilated open, and Hoà's bots came out of the darkness, pushing the glider towards her.

You can do this.

You can—

Within her, distant and sad, was Thiên Hạnh, the ever-silent mem-implants shuddering into life. Her elder sister was watching her as Hoà slid in and out of darkness.

Be a good girl, will you? Watch over your younger sister.

Too late, Hoà thought, fighting the urge to laugh.

Thiên Hạnh wavered and was lost, as Hoà's hands closed on the glider one final time. She moved forward in shudders, struggling to swallow. The airlock closed, and there was a hiss that became more and more pronounced as air cycled in. Hoà huddled on the floor, hands clenched on her glider, as the shuttle detached itself from the airlock and went back to the docks on autopilot. Aunt Vy was going to be livid, but then there wasn't much that she could do, was there? It was going to be too late by the time Hoà made it back to the docks. At least she was clear of *Flowers at the Gates* now. At least she didn't have to worry about the saboteur.

She wasn't going to make it. She should have expected it.

Too late. Too . . .

On her shoulder, that unfamiliar, reassuring weight: the weight of Quỳnh's bots.

Quỳnh.

Hoà didn't even think. She was past that entirely. She sent the message to Quỳnh, an absurdly small and improbable request. Quỳnh was busy; she likely would never see it in time.

Big sis. Help me.

Big sis.

And then there was only darkness, and the fading memory of Thiên Hạnh's presence.

8

Clarity

Hoà woke up gasping. Her throat was raw; when she tried to move, she scattered dormant bots all over the bed—

Bed?

She was in a bed, and it wasn't hers.

Where . . . ?

'You gave us quite a fright,' Quỳnh said.

She was leaning against the doorway of the room, with an unfamiliar mindship next to her, their avatar tilted in scowling disapproval.

'Where . . . ?' Hoà tried to speak, but her throat seemed to have sealed up.

'Gently,' Quỳnh said. 'You're in my compound.'

The room was bare. Not bare like *Flowers at the Gates*, but utterly devoid of any ornament or overlay, showing the guts of the habitat: the dull metal, covered with the crisscrossing of bots' legs, of station life; the cables threaded through the walls, the numerous trapdoors and bots laid visible. It felt very much like seeing the underbelly of some water-dancing puppet show – surprisingly intricate but verging on seedy. There was a metal box next to the bed, with a tray holding a reddish-brown teapot and two teacups of translucent porcelain – and more metal boxes piled up against the corner furthest away from Quỳnh. It must have been a spare room.

'You're lucky I wasn't far away,' the mindship said.

'This is my friend,' Quỳnh said. '*Guts of Sea*. She brought you here. Discreetly.'

Hoà breathed a sigh of a relief. It hurt. An emergency landing by a mindship was the worst sort of gossip; it'd spread faster than an air leak.

'Thank you,' she said.

Quỳnh said, 'What do you want me to do with the shuttle?'

'The shuttle?' Hoà asked.

'Yes,' Quỳnh said. 'The one you were on. I presume Aunt Vy needs it for her own trade, but I don't know how much you want me to tell her.'

Hoà's head hurt. 'I . . . You can tell her. And yes. You should return the shuttle. Thank you.'

Quỳnh looked genuinely surprised. 'That's only natural.' Of course she'd think so, but so few people did. Quỳnh said, slowly and softly, 'You're free to leave at any time, of course. I don't mean to keep you where you shouldn't be. I just felt you'd be safer somewhere no one expected you to be. Given what happened.'

What happened. The water bottle. The metallic taste in my mouth.

Hoà's voice scraped in her throat. 'The poison—'

'Oh, we got that out.'

Quỳnh crossed the threshold and came to kneel by Hoà's side. Her bots slid out of her sleeves, glittering in the light. She was suddenly far too close for comfort, her presence a palpable weight. If Hoà bent down, she'd be able to touch Quỳnh's face – to run her fingers on those sharp cheekbones, on those lips that were unusually bare of make-up.

'What ...? What happened?'

'I could return the question,' Quỳnh said. '*Guts of Sea* and I picked you up from the shuttle, and brought you here. I have your water bottle, by the way. When you want to look at the evidence.'

The evidence. Someone had tried to poison me.

'What was it? The poison.'

'Nothing too elaborate.' Quỳnh's face was hard.

'Cinnabar Clouds,' *Guts of Sea* said.

The name meant nothing to her.

'It's a poison from the shipyards,' Quỳnh said.

The shipyards.

'I don't understand ...'

'The antidote is hard to come by here. Fortunately, I always have some on me.'

Hoà tried to think. Everything scattered and skidded within her brain.

'You ... you saved—'

'You need to rest,' Quỳnh said. 'Surely you don't need me to say it, but you almost died.'

'It's not relevant.'

Quỳnh's face went through a series of interesting contortions. She said finally, 'It is to me.'

A silence. The words spread within it, like a pebble thrown into a pond, a widening circle that seemed to catch the entire room. Hoà opened her mouth, closed it.

'I see,' she said, and it felt small and inadequate. 'I see.'

And, before she could think, she took Quỳnh's face in her own and kissed her, gently and lightly.

She tasted of jasmine rice and cedarwood. When Hoà breathed in, she felt as though she'd swallowed cold, carved jade, something that caught her own heartbeat and magnified it in her throat. Quỳnh pulled away – and for a panicked moment

Hoà thought she was going to walk away, but then she leaned forward and kissed Hoà back, their tongues mingling together. Hoà's chest felt full of birds, clamouring to be released. Then Quỳnh withdrew again, laying a finger on Hoà's lips.

'You need to rest,' she said, but there was a smile that hadn't been there before. 'We can take this up afterwards.'

This. Whatever this was. Whatever it meant.

'We need to talk about the ship,' Hoà said.

Quỳnh laughed. It lit up her entire face and made her seem decades younger.

'I broke a kiss with you so you can get some rest, and you think a technical conversation is going to be more attractive? Rest, lil sis.'

And she left, closing the door behind her and *Guts of Sea*.

Hoà rested. Or tried to.

She drifted in and out of the boundary of consciousness, tasting the coldness of Quỳnh's lips on her own.

She'd ... Ancestors ... she'd kissed her. She'd kissed her and it had felt good, like something finally blossoming.

You need to rest.

She didn't want to rest. She wanted to—

In her dreams she saw the ships – *Flowers at the Gates of the Lords* and *Guts of Sea*. They were dancing, or talking, flowing past each other gracefully against the vast background of a nebula, the clouds of stardust shimmering around them. And then it moved further away, and she saw that Quỳnh held them both in the palms of her hands, and held them out to Hoà, smiling.

'Are we going to talk about it?' *Guts of Sea* said.

'About what? The poisoning?'

Quỳnh lay against the door of the room where Hoà slept,

feeling the weight of hard metal against her back. She had bots in the room, monitoring Hoà's vitals – not that she thought anyone was going to try and poison Hoà again, but she hadn't thought anyone would try and poison Hoà in the first place.

And with her own water bottle, too, which raised a number of questions about how it could have happened. Hoà didn't seem like the kind of person who'd leave the bottle where anyone could get to it.

'You know I'm not talking about the poisoning,' *Guts of Sea* said. 'Out of all the people you could pick, you go for the one who's inextricably linked to our targets.'

'Surely that's a good thing.'

Quỳnh ran a finger over her lips, finding them warm and supple – still wet from the kiss, as if Hoà were still next to her. She felt odd. Vulnerable in a way she hadn't been in a long time. And the worst was that she wanted more of it.

Guts of Sea sighed. She said nothing. Quỳnh could feel anger radiating off her.

Quỳnh said, finally, 'I don't know why you're staying with me, if you disapprove so much.'

A silence, from *Guts of Sea*. 'Because I'm more than your friend,' she said. 'Because we both want to bring down the empire that hurt us.'

'But you don't need me. You could do all this without me.'

Another silence. *Guts of Sea* said finally, 'I'd have died, if you hadn't fixed me.'

'So would I,' Quỳnh said sharply.

It hadn't been charity or kindness that had led her to repair *Guts of Sea*, but a primal need to survive in deep spaces.

'Yes. We saved each other. We spent months together in deep spaces. There's a thread between us. Duyên.' *Guts of Sea* used the word for a fated bond, the ones between intimates.

Between lovers. 'We're united in purpose, and in sisterhood. Seeking not to be born on the same day, in the same month or in the same year, but hoping to die on the same day, in the same month and in the same year.' She was loosely quoting from the Oath of the Peach Garden, an Old Earth text about sworn brotherhood.

Ah. So that was what it was. Fear, and jealousy, and the worry she'd lose Quỳnh to Hoà.

'So you care,' Quỳnh said.

A silence, from *Guts of Sea*. Then, with unexpected vulnerability, 'Of course I do.'

Quỳnh said finally, 'I haven't forgotten what we promised each other. Nor my revenge. But I can't be you.'

'Me?'

'To you, it's like ascension to immortality. Like – something you dedicate your entire waking life to. I ... I don't have your willpower. I'll break, if I do that. I need other things to keep me in focus.'

Guts of Sea glowered. 'So you're saying Hoà is a distraction?'

'Yes,' Quỳnh said.

Guts of Sea's voice was very quiet. 'I saw that kiss. That was not a distraction.'

'What would you call it, then?'

'Falling in love.'

'And what if I am?'

'Love is an emotion with a future. A sharing of life. What future do we have?'

Quỳnh touched her lips again. There was no room in the plan for a future. And yet ... And yet ...

Chimes echoed in the empty room. Someone at the gates.

'Who ...?'

Quỳnh called up the bots at the entrance, and saw Prefect Đức, waiting for them on the stairs of the compound.

'Elder aunt?' Đức said, looking unerringly at the bots. 'Alchemist? I'd like a word with you, if I may.'

They sat in the courtyard of the compound, a measure away from the open wall where eighteen dead bodies had been hidden. Quỳnh's bots brought tea, which she poured for Đức – all too aware of the irony. The last time she'd drunk tea with Đức, Quỳnh had been tricked into confessing her 'crimes' – nothing more than her friendship with Xuân Trúc, an insufficiently loyal scholar turned rebel general – and been arrested for them.

'I wasn't expecting you,' Quỳnh said.

She raised her cup – a smooth celadon one, the glaze shining in the light – to stare at the tea within.

Đức had changed, unlike the general. She'd been young, and at least had a semblance of compassion; now she was all sternness, her topknot perfectly straight and every hairpin a glittering mass of entwined silver, kỳ lân and giải trãi, their horns tangling with one another into a single sharp point. Her face was a perfect oval of ceruse, her lips the vermilion of imperial seals, her eyebrows two impeccable arches – cheek bones of jade, ice-white skin, the paragon of beauty according to the classics, except it was the kind of beauty that cut like a knife, with no pliancy or kindness to it.

Between her and General Tuyết, Đức was most definitely the more dangerous of the two. And now she was in Quỳnh's home – not just that, which Quỳnh had planned for, but not two measures away from a sleeping and exhausted Hoà, which Quỳnh had most definitely not planned for. She did not want Hoà to come to Đức's notice, which was why she'd asked *Guts of Sea* to throw a privacy screen over her room – the kind of subtle hiding that would take work to spot.

'I was curious.' Đức sipped at her tea, looking around her

– weighing everything and subtly indicating she found it lacking. 'Since you seem to be in such good company with my elder daughter.'

Ah. Going for the throat, then.

Quỳnh was made of sterner stuff than Đức suspected.

'Indeed.' Quỳnh inclined her head. 'I met her in tense circumstances, and thought it would be more appropriate to see her outside of such stresses.'

'Mm.' Đức pursed her lips. 'I see.' Her hand moved towards the militia's tracings, marking where the bodies had been found. 'It hardly seems finding eighteen bodies would be less stressful.'

Quỳnh weighed what she could say that wouldn't be a lie, since Đức's bots, negligently clustered on the table, were obviously scanning Quỳnh's vitals and the least of her gestures, which meant Quỳnh couldn't calm herself with a sedative. Not without making Đức immediately suspicious.

'I hope she's recovered,' she said finally. 'It put a distinct crimp over what should have been a pleasant tea.'

'You mean much like the one we're having today?' Đức's voice was sharp.

'I'm not sure what you mean,' Quỳnh said, though she suspected Đức thought something was off with Quỳnh. Which was ... not unexpected, but a little more frightening than Quỳnh had thought it would be. Twenty years before such a conversation had led to the lacerator, the taste of blood, the death sentence so casually passed.

She was older and stronger now. She could take on Đức.

'Don't you?' Đức's voice was soft. 'Let's talk about you, then. The Alchemist of Streams and Hills. It's an interesting name.'

Unorthodox and brash. Quỳnh had selected it deliberately.

'Because there haven't been alchemists at court for a while?'

'Don't play coy with me. You come from the shipyards, don't you?'

'I've lived there a long time.' Quỳnh was busy sorting out possible answers – which bits and pieces of truth she could afford to give up.

'And you're wealthy.'

'I have that good fortune.'

'Why are you here, then?'

'Why?'

'This is the Belt.' Đức set her drained cup on the table. Only a single drop glimmered on the celadon, like a frozen tear. 'We are outside the Numbered Planets. No one comes here from the imperial court unless they have something to hide. Or a mission. Which one is it, Alchemist?'

Quỳnh had both, and she could admit to neither. She said finally, 'I've come here on behalf of another, who had unfinished business before she passed away. I feel beholden to her.'

'And were eighteen dead bodies hidden in a wall part of this business?'

She couldn't dodge that one, but she had to try.

'I don't understand why you leap to that conclusion.'

Đức laughed. 'Again – don't play coy, elder aunt. The bodies were well hidden. That you found them seems a little more than coincidence.'

'Your daughter found them.'

Đức's perfect eyebrows arched. 'Minh is naive and disinclined to pay attention to details.'

Quỳnh shouldn't have felt sorry for Minh. She had other pressing business, like keeping Đức from arresting her and torturing her again, and keeping Hoà safe, but she felt a pang of sympathy nevertheless. Đức's pained contempt for her own daughter was worse than outright hatred.

'Nevertheless, Minh was the one who noticed the finger bone from the alcove. I merely helped.'

'Did you?'

Đức's gaze held her. Her bots were all around the table now, surrounding Quỳnh in a circle of glimmering steel. The kỳ lân and giải trãi – the horned beasts symbolising peace and justice – had turned darker and sharper; Đức had seized control of the overlays in the compound. She wouldn't find the one hiding Hoà, not yet: *Guts of Sea* knew how to avoid imperial detection. But she was close. Too close.

Which meant a distraction, and Đức had just handed Quỳnh the perfect one. Would she rise to the bait?

Quỳnh said finally, 'Your daughter is a bright, smart, compassionate woman who does you credit. You underestimate her.'

The overlay around them darkened further, throwing Đức into sharp relief, as if she were an immortal in a halo of light.

'Oh, is that it? Are you trying that play?'

It took an effort for Quỳnh to remain still. Đức had pulled herself upright and when she'd last done that, the overlay darkening in the same fashion in her small office aboard *The Azure Serpent*, she'd called for the guards to take Dã Lan away – and it had ended with that long slow descent into suspended time, that dying by finger-lengths as the universe tore her apart.

'A play,' Quỳnh said flatly.

Đức laughed. 'You want to be her mentor. You want to *guide* her.'

'Why would I want to do such a thing?'

Quỳnh didn't want to be Minh's mentor. She wanted to set Minh and Đức at odds. If Minh publicly denounced her own mother, Prefect Đức – an official incapable of controlling the filial piety of her own daughter – would suffer a massive loss of face and authority, both in the Belt and at court. It might even be the impetus the minister and the academy chancellor needed to move against Đức on the First Planet.

'*Alchemist*. You're out of favour with the imperial court.'

Quỳnh said, slowly, carefully, 'I'm not part of the empress's inner circle. But—'

'Oh, no buts. The surest path back to power is mentoring a promising graduate.'

Quỳnh clamped down on the natural reply that Đức had just disparaged Minh. It would just make Đức angrier – and she was already angry, and she'd always used the law as a weapon against others. She could have Quỳnh arrested and tortured again, and once again Quỳnh would be imprisoned and alone, with no one to help her. This was a fine line to walk.

'Your daughter has many qualities. And a future that you no doubt envision casting a large shadow.' An office high enough to protect others, like a cloak drawn around relatives, students and dependents. 'Her mentor would indeed bask in her success.'

Đức watched, for a while. Her gaze was burning – the animals on her hairpins unfolding in overlay, ghostly shapes growing larger and larger. Then she laughed.

'I'm the one who has the final say in Minh's mentorship and career. Her own mother.'

'Of course.' Quỳnh inclined her head.

'I would advise you to stay out of trouble. And living in a house where eighteen people have died is plenty of trouble already. I'm watching you, *Alchemist*.'

'Of course.'

Đức picked up her cup, drained the last drop from it, and set it back on the table. The kỳ lân and giải trãi swirled around her for a moment more, and then vanished, but the tension in the air didn't disappear.

'I'm glad we had this conversation. Until I see you again, elder aunt. Though for your own sake, I hope I don't.'

And she left, taking her bots with her.

Quỳnh watched her leave the compound. She remained seated, making sure that Đức was truly gone. Darkness was rising across the overlay – the glimmer of deep spaces, the memory of choking with every limb swelling up. She kept it at bay – or she tried to.

Gone. Đức was gone. Quỳnh had fended her off – except that she knew who Quỳnh was, and Quỳnh's pretence of being a social climber might not hold so well the next time.

Gone. She was gone.

Quỳnh rose, stilling her trembling hands – walked back through the compound, trailed by her bots, through empty room after empty room, until she reached the invisible privacy screen she'd asked *Guts of Sea* to put together. Her heartbeat was a painful spike in her ears – and pain hovered, kept at bay only by sheer willpower.

'It's me,' she said. 'She's gone.'

The overlay slowly vanished, and the door coalesced into existence once more, materialising out of what seemed an empty wall – just as Hoà's vitals appeared once more in Quỳnh's field of perception.

'How did it go?' *Guts of Sea* said, from inside the room, and then stopped. 'Lil sis!'

Quỳnh tried to say 'good', but the thing welling up inside her – the fear and the roiling and her own heartbeat, and the tension of keeping them at bay in front of Đức – suddenly seemed to burst, and she fell to her knees, struggling for air that wouldn't come, tongue and eyeballs and nostrils on fire.

'Big sis!' Hoà's voice, a scream coming from very far away.

I'm all right, Quỳnh tried to say. *I'm all right*, but the lie wouldn't come out of her mouth, and she lost control of the rest of her body and flopped on the floor face first.

Hoà had seen plenty of frightening things – Thiên Hạnh's death, the riots on board the habitats, the destruction of *The Azure Serpent*. Amid all these, Quỳnh's fall ranked as terrifying. One moment she was standing in the doorway, vaguely staring towards Hoà and *Guts of Sea* – the next she raised her hands to her neck as though she were choking on something, *Guts of Sea* screamed 'Lil sis' in a heartbreaking tone of utter loss, and Quỳnh was on her knees and then lying on the floor, convulsing.

Hoà's bots were all offline – she turned them on, but *Guts of Sea* got there first, her bots swarming over Quỳnh as the ship screamed 'Breathe!' again and again. Quỳnh spasmed, mouth wide open, jerking back and forth as if she'd touched a live wire, except that the only sound that came from her lips was a small, wordless mewling as if she'd lost all air within her lungs.

'Breathe!'

Quỳnh's face contorted in pain, and something just broke within Hoà.

She gave up trying to gather her scattered bots, and simply walked towards the two of them on the threshold.

'She can't breathe,' she said. 'Screaming at her isn't making it better.'

Guts of Sea whirled to face her. The ship seemed larger and darker, expanding as though she was growing to her full size – nothing cute or faded in it, a sense of coiled power and a presence that would gladly blast Hoà to cinders.

'We've been through this before. I know what I'm doing.' And, to Quỳnh, 'Breathe!'

Hoà clenched her fists, and did not move.

'Just because it's always worked that way doesn't mean you have to keep on doing it.'

'You dare?'

For a moment Hoà thought the ship was going to just swallow her whole. *Guts of Sea* had bots, and the control of enough perception layers that she could make Hoà feel the flesh was being stripped from her and molten metal poured onto her bones, or any of ten thousand horrors. But then she seemed to give an expansive shrug.

'Take care of her, then. If you're so keen.' Her bots withdrew, leaving glistening needle-marks on Quỳnh's flesh. 'The antidote should have run its course. Tell Quỳnh I've gone to talk to the scholars.'

And then she was gone, avatar blinked out of existence – before Hoà could ask about the antidote or the bots, or whatever any of this meant.

Hoà stared at Quỳnh – who was now lying on the floor, the last of the convulsions leaving her. Her normally dark skin was ghastly pale, with the translucency of the jade that was her namesake – except nothing living was supposed to have that hue.

Quỳnh's eyes opened, met hers.

'Lil sis?'

Hoà grimaced. 'Yeah. Just you and me. Can you get up?'

She kneeled, sliding a shoulder under Quỳnh's armpit, her bots coming to help her support the weight.

'Where is—'

'*Guts of Sea?*'

No lies. Even if Hoà had been inclined to them in the first place.

'I told her to stop yelling at you.'

'It's—'

'Necessary?' Hoà shook her head, with cold, absolute

certainty. 'Whatever she's injecting is. Shocking you into fighting for your life when you're in that state is needlessly hurtful.'

'I ...' Quỳnh opened her mouth, closed it. Hoà could guess what she'd been about to say: that she deserved to be hurt.

'No,' Hoà said quite firmly. 'Nobody deserves to be hurt. Come on.' She rose, wobbling, Quỳnh rising with her – trembling, her muscles turned to jelly. She had her bots, but they weren't really enough to compensate for Hoà's weakness. 'Let's get you to the bed.'

A sound that felt like a hacking up of lungs. Quỳnh's mangled laughter.

'There's ... only ... one.'

'One bed?' An eye roll. 'You can have it.' And then what Quỳnh had said hit her. 'You mean in the entire compound.' She looked again – at the bare walls, the lack of ornaments and overlay – and saw what she hadn't seen before: the small squat altar with a handful of names on the metal box closest to the bed. An ancestral altar, for worship. She felt her stomach twist. 'This is your room.'

Quỳnh said nothing. Hoà suddenly felt there was nothing she could say that wouldn't sound like a reproach. She focused on putting one foot in front of the other – on clenching muscles that felt as though they were going to melt at any moment.

'I had an accident,' Quỳnh said softly, as they walked. 'It left sequels. My bots and *Guts of Sea* inject me with something to open up the small and medium airways.'

'Mmm,' Hoà said. The same accident that had left her fixing *Guts of Sea*. 'In space,' she said flatly. 'You fell into space without a shadow-skin.'

'Something like that, yes.' Quỳnh's voice was distant.

Her eyes were rolling in their orbits, but she managed to shrug off Hoà's shoulder and half-fall, half-sit on the bed. Hoà sat down by her side, back against the bare metal of the room, and thought for a while.

An accident. Quỳnh was a scholar who'd quite obviously never done any manual work, so she wouldn't have had much opportunity to go out in the vacuum. If she'd been in space without a shadow-skin, it likely meant the whole section of the habitat she was in had blown up. And she'd survived, somehow. She and *Guts of Sea*.

Hoà turned to stare at Quỳnh. Quỳnh stared back, eyes still unfocused. Composing herself. Getting her breath back. She looked much younger, much more vulnerable, her hair dishevelled and hairpins scattered all over the bed. Not just younger, but ... there was something haunting about her, something that reached into Hoà's chest and kept twisting.

An accident. It all sounded like a little more than that. And now Hoà had to know, one way or another.

After a while, Quỳnh shifted. She stared at Hoà, cocking her head.

'Lil sis?' she said.

'Still here.'

Laughter, but this time it didn't sound like that of a dying woman.

'What a fine pair we make.'

Poison and the sequels of an accident. Hoà reached out, took Quỳnh's hand in her own. Quỳnh tightened it around hers – raising it, gently, to her lips and kissing it.

'Does it happen often?'

'Only when I'm tired and stressed.' Quỳnh sighed, leaning her head against the wall. 'Which is most days.'

'An accident.' Hoà left the words to hang in the air. She stared at Quỳnh and felt again that faint flicker of something within her – as if Thiên Hạnh were trying to speak. But Thiên Hạnh's mem-implants didn't work, had never worked except at the grave. 'The way I had an accident on board *Flowers at the Gates*?'

A hesitation.

'Yes,' Quỳnh said.

She raised Hoà's hand to her lips again – and this time slid the fingers between her lips, gently teasing them with her tongue. Desire rose, slow and trembling, in Hoà's belly.

'She's awake,' Hoà said. '*Flowers at the Gates*. She told me the poisoning was ... family.'

Though it had been confused and angry, and Hoà still wasn't sure what the ship had meant at all.

Quỳnh paused and said, 'I'm not surprised.'

'Someone tried to kill you, and you survived.'

'Yes. It was a long time ago.' More kisses – a slowly tightening tide of desire that was swallowing everything. 'But I've not forgotten.'

'Why are you here?' Hoà said.

'There was a plan.' Quỳnh sounded amused. 'It didn't involve you. I'd rather it continues not to involve you. But it also didn't foresee you. Or what you made me feel.'

Hoà's breath caught in her throat. She pulled her hand away – rose, slowly and painstakingly, to stand before Quỳnh for a bare moment, before Quỳnh grabbed her by both wrists and drew her to sit on her lap with her legs spread on either side of Quỳnh's hips. They were now close enough to kiss.

'What I made you feel.' Hoà bent and kissed Quỳnh, pressing her lips against Quỳnh's and feeling the warmth and pliancy of her lips. 'What you made me feel.' It was a bare whisper, shared between them like a breath.

Quỳnh smiled. She didn't let go of Hoà's wrists – but her bots went up, into Hoà's hair, slowly drawing down each strand, hairpins scattering on the floor, a series of downward strokes that sent goosebumps to Hoà's head, a tingling heat that made her feel as though she were floating, a flock of birds within her throat and chest.

Hoà freed her hands with a twist of her wrists. She took off her tunic, and – with a little more difficulty – her trousers, the blackness of them pooling up on the floor. The air from the ducts was slightly cold; Hoà shivered, feeling exposed. But then Quỳnh made a gesture, and perception filters descended, cutting off the feeling from the filtration and recyling system.

Hoà stroked Quỳnh's chest, watching Quỳnh's breathing come in faster and faster, the flush climb from her cheeks into her entire face. They kissed again, this time more frantically. Hoà moved back and forth on Quỳnh's legs, her bots sliding Quỳnh's embroidered tunic from her shoulders.

A soft touch, between Hoà's legs – Quỳnh's bots, descending from her hair and gently stroking the inside of her thighs, again and again. Hoà pushed, her bots pushing with her until Quỳnh sprawled on the bed, lips slightly parted, eyes glazed. Hoà gently pulled the áo dài's trousers away, and the underwear, until Quỳnh lay gloriously naked beneath her, a spread of dark skin shining like ten thousand stars.

'Lil sis.' Quỳnh's voice was a hiss as Hoà slid two fingers inside her and hooked them inside, stroking her again and again, feeling Quỳnh's breath hitch every time – and Quỳnh's bots were drawing circles between Hoà's legs now, and Hoà could hardly breathe as the entire room seemed to contract and pulse.

With a shaking moan, Quỳnh came, hardening and pulsing under Hoà's touch – but her bots didn't stop, still stroking Hoà. The thing in Hoà's chest and belly grew and grew and tightened, unbearable – again and again, Hoà moaning and struggling to breathe – the circles growing smaller and smaller, the touches stronger and stronger, until every single one of them sent white-hot desire into Hoà's lower belly. Until she threw her head back, shaking with each rising wave that travelled through her, with each tightening circle she couldn't escape from, with each shuddering breath that brought no release – again and again, and Hoà screamed as pure bliss finally arced through her like an electric shock, leaving her wrung out but utterly sated.

9

The Past Like a Poison

Hoà woke up, and found Quỳnh gone. She panicked, before she realised that Quỳnh's bots were still in the room, carrying a teapot carved with lotus patterns. A plate of dumplings was on the bedside table, a clear invitation.

Hoà wasn't hungry – her throat still felt raw – but she was suffused with a peculiar, unfamiliar sense of serenity she'd not had with any of her previous flings. She got up, wincing at the way her legs protested, summoned her bots to her wrists and shoulders, and went looking for Quỳnh.

She'd assumed the rest of the compound would be like Quỳnh: grandiloquent, dramatic, with a sharp sense of fashion, and a gift for saying the best or the worst thing at any given time. Instead, what she got was … empty rooms. Not just empty in the sense of no furniture – though they were – but no overlay, no adornments, nothing but the bare, exposed bones of the station. The room Hoà was in wasn't bare, as she'd thought; it was, in fact, the most ornate of them all, and that wasn't saying much. It was like standing in the middle of a desert and walking into a patch of scorched earth – and Hoà, walking through empty room after empty room, felt only a profound sadness. This was the home of someone who'd not settled down, who'd never bothered to or needed to.

There was a plan. It didn't involve you.

Hoà reached up, touching Quỳnh's bots on her shoulder, the cold and unyielding touch of metal.

'Big sis,' she whispered, and blinked away furious tears.

The last room opened on a courtyard, and a privacy screen that displayed the militia seal, the giải trãi spinning in the middle of the empty compound. It looked like someone had dug a hole in the wall to Hoà's right, and then the privacy screen had been thrown on top of it.

Quỳnh was in the courtyard pavilion, arms resting on the railing. As Hoà walked up to her, the overlay Quỳnh was seeing shimmered into existence around her: a wide expanse of stars with the oily sheen of deep spaces threaded beneath them. Quỳnh said nothing, merely shifted to leave Hoà some space. Hoà took it, not knowing what to say that wouldn't break the easy comfort of standing side by side, feeling the heat of Quỳnh's body next to hers.

She wanted it to last forever, and she knew that it could not.

'About yesterday,' Hoà said finally.

Quỳnh turned, to look at her. Her face, bare of make-up, looked young – lined and odd, until Hoà realised that she merely looked vulnerable, exposed in a way that she hadn't been before. Something rose in Hoà's thoughts, a bare whisper of a voice, a ghost turning back on the way down into Hell.

'Yes,' she said, and smiled – and bent to kiss Hoà, slowly and gently and with the delicacy of someone afraid she'd shatter a piece of jade.

Hoà breathed it in – all of it, that fragile understanding and happiness.

'I'm not sure we should have done that,' she said finally. 'But I don't regret it.'

'Good.' Quỳnh smiled. Her bots clustered in the unbound mass of her hair. She wasn't looking at Hoà. 'We do need to talk, though. About what I didn't tell you.'

But Hoà was looking at her — and the whispers in Hoà's mind became Thiên Hạnh's voice, the inert mem-implants jolting into a brief, faint life, forming a name.

'Dã Lan.'

Quỳnh jerked as if stung. Then she smiled, and it was bitter.

'I forgot. You have your sister's implants.'

'They ... they don't work properly.' Hoà could barely feel Thiên Hạnh now: the ghost in her mind was turning away again, leaving only the void of her absence. 'Most days she's simply not there. Like a ghost in my thoughts, distant and silent.'

'I had guessed.' Quỳnh's voice was gentle. She reached out and hugged Hoà, as if she'd never let anyone or anything harm her. 'It must be hard.'

It was hard, but Hoà kept forgetting that it was — because that was the only way to survive.

'But yes. She's right.'

Dã Lan was dead. She'd been executed for sedition against the Empire — but Quỳnh had said, hadn't she, that someone had tried to kill her and she'd survived.

'You found the mindship. That's how you survived your execution.'

'If it can be called survival. Yes.'

'You ...' Hoà settled for the first thing that came to mind. 'You've changed.' Which wasn't the most perceptive of comments: anyone would change, in those circumstances. 'I'm sorry. That was thoughtless.'

Quỳnh's hands were wrapped around hers, her bots lightly resting on Hoà's wrists.

'Don't ever apologise for what's not your fault or your responsibility. I have changed. In many ways, Dã Lan is dead.'

And empty, like those rooms?

Hoà didn't dare to say the words. She said, instead – not daring to move her hands from Quỳnh's, 'Why are you here? You said there was a plan. To rehabilitate yourself?' But Hoà wasn't that naive. The dead – especially the seditious dead, in habitats still controlled by the military lest their population rebel again – couldn't be rehabilitated. 'No. That's not it, is it?'

A quirk of the lips that wasn't a smile, from Quỳnh.

'You were too young at the time.' She sighed. 'The people who wronged me have thrived. They've risen, become scholar-officials in this society. And it's time for the banyan that casts the largest shadow to be shown for what it is – dead, rotten wood.'

'They ...'

Most of the Serpents hadn't thrived, except for ... Hoà tamped down the panic that flowered in her gut.

Don't assume – that is the way to disaster.

'The prefect,' she said. 'The general. Others?'

'I should say that's plenty.' Quỳnh almost sounded like she was laughing, except it was such a serious, deadly matter. Sedition. Her face went grave again. 'As I said – the plan didn't involve you. And it shouldn't.'

Hoà said slowly, 'The ship ...' Because of course it would be in Quỳnh's interests if *Flowers at the Gates* was fixed.

Quỳnh shook her head. 'I'm helping you with the ship because you asked me for my help. That's all there is to it.'

Hoà stared at Quỳnh's face, and saw only wary sincerity within it.

'Help.'

'Yes. Help.' And—' Her hands were very still around Hoà's own— 'I can understand if you'd rather not, in the light of who I am, of what I bring.'

'If I would rather not what?'

Quỳnh bent, slowly and carefully, hands running through Hoà's hair, untangling mussed and dark strands – her fingers gently resting on Hoà's scalp, sending a tingle through Hoà's hair, her bots gently pressing on Hoà's wrists, their touch delicate and quivering. Hoà turned her face up, and kissed her – because she wanted to, because it felt good, breathing in all of her and feeling seen and valued.

'This,' Quỳnh whispered, and her breath was a warmth that filled Hoà to bursting.

Hoà said, 'I can't help you. And ... they scare me stiff.' She breathed.

'I know. And one of them tried to poison you, didn't they?'

'Using my water bottle?' Hoà had had some time to think it through.

'Yes. You left it in the common area, didn't you? With all of the younger children.'

She had. It could have been *Heart's Sorrow* – it could have been any of them – but she suddenly thought of Minh's scowling face, and her heart missed a beat.

'Yes. I'm still not walking out on that job.'

Laughter, from Quỳnh. 'Of course not. Just as I'm not walking out on my plans.'

Hoà could have asked. But if she did, it would implicate her further than she already was. She wouldn't be able to deny much of anything. If she asked ... she was afraid of what she'd find out.

Hoà said, 'I have to help her. She's alive and she's desperately trying to repair herself. It's not fair that she should be under attack.'

'Fairness. Of course.' Quỳnh's voice was grave. She withdrew her hands from Hoà's, but her bots remained on Hoà's wrists, small pinpricks on Hoà's skin – and of course Hoà still had

Quỳnh's bots on her shoulders, as if Quỳnh herself were still holding her. 'I will help you, with the ship. And we will not talk about my revenge, or involve you in it, because it would be unfair of me to involve you. What I'm planning to do is mine and mine only. My revenge is none of your business, and nothing you should get caught in. But ... if we see each other ...'

There was a risk Hoà would be caught up in it all anyway. She breathed, trying to sort through it all – trying to think past the rising tide of too many feelings within her: fleeting contentment; fear; the faint voice of Thiên Hạnh; the memory of how she'd died; of how she'd been *noticed*, how she'd stood out, how she'd taken sides.

'I ...' she said, trying to get words through the obstruction in her throat. 'I know this.'

'You do. Good. Lil sis – what do you want?'

Hoà stared at her. Saw Quỳnh, as clearly as she'd seen her at Thiên Hạnh's grave. Standing very still and ready to walk away from her own happiness, with the same readiness she had to set the habitats afire; saw her chat with Aunt Vy as an equal; help a skewer-seller with no expectation of anything.

Why?

Because I could. Who else was going to step up?

Something shifted within Hoà, as if she had been dancing on the edge of a chasm and had finally plunged in.

'I want you,' she said slowly, through a mouth that felt full of shards. 'I'm willing to take the risk of association.'

It made it sound distant and impersonal. Like people preparing to break the law together instead of dating each other.

Quỳnh exhaled, sharply. 'If the plan goes wrong, you won't be implicated.' Her voice was grim.

'Please don't commit suicide on my behalf.'

Quỳnh laughed, but it had an edge to it. 'I'll simply say you were not aware.'

'They'll ...' Hoà started, stopped.

'They'll try to wring it out of me?' Quỳnh's hands rested gently, on Hoà's shoulders. She squeezed, the bots on Hoà's wrists squeezing as well, until Hoà felt wrapped in something large and comforting. 'I've been in the lacerator before. And I fell, living, into space and deep spaces.' A smile that was a rictus, and an oily sheen in the whites of her eyes. 'There is no pain that will work.' It wasn't a boast: just a quiet certainty.

Hoà said finally, 'But it will work on me.'

A silence.

Quỳnh said finally, 'They will likely not question you if I admit my guilt. If it goes wrong. It's not meant to go wrong. But I cannot guarantee your safety, because it would be a lie.'

'And we said no lies.'

Hoà moved towards Quỳnh, pressing herself against her – head resting on Quỳnh's chest, listening to Quỳnh's steady heartbeat. She felt scared and small, but it was worth it for that other feeling: the growing exhilaration in her chest, the happiness of being by Quỳnh's side, listening to her breath.

'I know,' she said finally. Bending Quỳnh's face towards her, she kissed her again, long and deep until nothing of fear remained. 'I'll take the risk.'

Minh no longer had the seal they had given her, but Scholar Vĩnh Trinh was easy enough to find. As Mother had said, they were one of the foremost poets of the Belt, and their compartment was overflowing with visitors and bots, everyone seeking a centrepiece poem for a banquet, a birthday, a death anniversary or some other important occasion. Everyone was waiting in a large antechamber, where people mingled with ease. Minh – who had taken the opportunity to slightly alter her appearance, just to be sure – found herself a spot against one of the walls, and pulled up a semi-translucent privacy screen which masked her from everyone else.

She barely had to wait before someone pinged her on the comms. An invitation from Vĩnh Trinh, with a faint tinge of surprise to it — and a thread leading her from the antechamber towards the empty space at the back. As she walked the thread shone and an overlay opened around her: a path that made the variegated crowd fade into nothingness, with the faint sound of rushing water that soon became a pond — and then she was in another space altogether.

It was a library. Tables held piles of books, bound in the old way, with thread across the spine. Minh caught a glimpse of the titles: compendiums of everything from star maps and guidebooks of the Numbered Planets to mathematics and alchemy, and poetry collections, from the Belt and further afield. Pages fluttered in an invisible wind.

'Beautiful, isn't it?'

Minh started. Mạt Lý had appeared out of nowhere, sleeves billowing in the wind, her bots glinting everywhere on her clothes. By her side was Vĩnh Trinh, their face a careful mask.

'Elder aunt,' Minh said. 'Elder pibling.'

'You honour us with your visit,' Mạt Lý said.

Vĩnh Trinh cocked their head. 'I'm surprised to see you here.'

Minh swallowed. 'You did give me your seal.'

'Which you didn't present — I presume because your mother kept it.'

Mother. Yes.

Minh swallowed. 'She doesn't know I'm here.'

'Ah.' Mạt Lý's long stare made even Minh's bots scatter. 'Come.'

They walked deeper into the library — there was a rhythmic sound like the pounding of a mortar, which climbed into Minh's body until her very bones seemed to vibrate. Paper fluttered between the tables – there were alcoves with rolled-up scrolls, and sleeker pads. It was a physical space, Minh belatedly realised – the only overlay was the path that had brought her there.

Printing press.

Mother had said Mạt Ly owned a printing press.

'Are these the books you print?'

Mạt Ly smiled. 'Some of them.'

The library – or the warehouse, Minh wasn't sure which – was huge: it must have taken up a quarter of a ring. Realising she'd never seen it before was a little odd, like finding a spot for tea and dumplings in an area of the habitats she'd crossed every day of her life. Their footsteps echoed under the cavernous ceiling. Minh looked up, and saw ten thousand lanterns floating above them – they were overlay, but the overall effect was impressive.

Finally they reached a larger, circular space in what seemed to be the centre of the warehouse, an engraved metal medallion of a lotus with a pearl.

Vĩnh Trinh leaned against one of the stacks of books, watching Minh.

'That's the heart of the warehouse. No one should be listening in, here.'

Minh pursed her lips. 'Who would be listening?'

Mạt Ly's gaze was full of pity. 'Do you really not know?'

On some level, she did. Minh clenched her hands.

'I'm here because of her. Of Mother. Because of what you said.' She watched them both, the way their gazes turned towards each other. 'And you're not surprised by this, are you? Despite what you said earlier.'

It was Mạt Ly who spoke. 'Somewhat.' Her smile was wry; she picked up a handful of her bots and scratched their backs as if they were pets. 'We were not expecting to see you. But once you came, there could only be one reason why.'

Minh glared at them. 'I'm tired,' she said. 'I'm not here to play games. Or solve cryptic riddles. Or hear poems. I don't have the time or the energy.'

Mạt Lỵ laughed. It was a sound that echoed under the rafters, a thing with metallic undertones that made her bots tremble.

'You're here because of your mother. Because of your great-aunt.'

'My great-aunt. The ship?' Minh glared at them again. 'What do you know?'

Bad enough that *Heart's Sorrow* was bringing total strangers on board – that girl Hoà, rifling through the ship's innards with too much familiarity and a gaze that saw too far and too much – but now scholars?

'You know she and your mother fell out?'

Minh picked up a book from a table. The collected sayings of some scholar she was unfamiliar with, bound with thread that felt as though it would fall apart with a mere breath.

'I know Mother would have arrested her. For the good of the Empire. But that's what she's always done, hasn't she? Harsh but fair.'

She let the words hang in the air, deliberately. Daring them to contradict her.

It was Vĩnh Trinh who spoke, the bots in their hair shining in the dim light of the library.

'Harsh,' they said.

'But not fair,' Mạt Lỵ said. 'You know this.'

Minh thought of the money Mother had taken, the games she'd played. The seal so expertly vanished. That blue dress Minh had worn, the thought of which still made her sick with something she couldn't articulate. A fear rose, deep in the heart of her – a vertiginous dizzying thing opening in her belly like the largest of black holes – that everything Mother had told her had been a carefully calculated lie. A story for children. For *her* child – of a perfect childhood, a necessary harshness to keep them all safe, to maintain the law.

'No,' she said. 'I don't. I really don't. I shouldn't be here. I really ...'

She wanted to run, to throw up, to leave while there was still time. And yet something kept her rooted there.

They both watched her, immobile in the centre of the pattern on the floor. Bots flowed to surround them, Vĩnh Trinh's avatar unchanging, Mạt Lỵ's flowing and reshaping itself – dragon antlers, lion's mane, galaxies whirling on her hands. Watching. Waiting.

Minh should leave – she even turned to run away – and then, unbidden, Quỳnh's face swam up. Quỳnh, who'd thought Minh was worthy enough to invite her to her house – who'd offered to be Minh's sponsor. What would she think of a girl who walked away from the truth, no matter how painful it was?

Minh said nothing, merely waited, staring at the book in her hands, as if it could disgorge the truths she wanted.

Vĩnh Trinh made a gesture, and something happened in the centre of the pattern. A seal faded, becoming a shimmering set of files. When Minh still didn't move, Mạt Lỵ sent it to her.

It was a list of names, dates and places. It was long, and with no annotations. The first name was someone called Dã Lan on board *The Azure Serpent*, and then it kept expanding, the dates coming faster and faster together during the civil war. Minh's bots, sifting through the information, plotted graphs, but even without them Minh already knew that they would match Mother's postings. Then the frequency decreased in the Scattered Pearls Belt, but there was still a name every fourteen days or so.

'What are these?' Minh asked. But on some level she already knew. 'Cases.'

Her voice was flat. Dã Lan was the case that had made Mother: the uncompromising decision she'd made to jettison a young scholar with rebel sympathies, rather than let the rot spread across the space station.

'Harsh but not fair.' Mạt Lý's voice was a whisper. 'You have what you wanted, do you not?'

She had files the very thought of which scared her, and fear made her bold. Or aggressive; she wasn't sure which.

'Why?'

A silence, during which all she could hear was the distant rustle of paper. Mạt Lý broke it.

'We're scholars,' she said. 'Seekers of the truth. Keepers of the truth.'

'Those who don't see the world as it is are doomed to be destroyed.' Vĩnh Trinh's voice and face were harsh. 'Your mother holds sway over the entire Belt. It is prudent and needful to understand what kind of person we're dealing with.'

'She . . .' Minh opened her mouth to say Mother wasn't like that, and couldn't find any words in the emptiness that threatened to swallow her whole. 'Thank you,' she said instead. 'I appreciate your trust, and I'll read what you've given me.'

They were watching her as she left, bowing. Vĩnh Trinh's face was harsh, Mạt Lý's distant – but what seared her to the bone was the pity in their gazes, as if they already knew what she'd find if she looked.

Minh went to see Second Great-Aunt.

She could have asked *Heart's Sorrow* for a lift, but she couldn't face the explanations she'd have to give him. She could either lie to him – which she refused to do to a friend – or tell him the truth, and have to withstand his pity, or worse, his sympathy. She wanted — she *needed* — to be alone. To know where she stood, what she had. And she most certainly would not get that privacy at home. Home was a safe place — and she realised as she thought this that she was nauseous, and everything was trembling and whirling in her head.

Safe.

Safe for whom?

So, instead, Minh hired a shuttle from the docks, and used her bots to pilot it to *Flowers at the Gates*.

The common room where they hung out was deserted, with the tea they'd been drinking still in the cups, and the overlays *Heart's Sorrow* had displayed to Hoà still everywhere. Minh wasn't in the mood for thinking about Hoà. She hadn't really thought it through when *Heart's Sorrow* had mentioned hiring an expert to help with the ship, but now she couldn't face the thought of an interloper on board — someone who was neither family nor friend, with no loyalty, and no knowledge of the stakes or of the meaning. One by one, she dismissed the overlays, and sent her bots to sweep the table until no trace of Hoà's presence — or of her disturbingly perceptive gaze — remained. Then she sat down, cradling the file the scholars had given her.

Names. Dates. Places.

Around her was the ship. Her great-aunt. If she closed her eyes, she'd remember her as she had been, pulsing with life, the now dead metal walls brimming with flowers and shimmering overlays. Not the flickering monstrosities of abrupt transitions and dead spaces, but a graceful merging of curtains of light, of flower petals gently lifted by the wings — of children's songs that Minh, laughing, had sung over and over again as Great-Aunt's bots made her fly for a moment, a mere few blinks that had felt like ten thousand years.

There was a network, weak and patched too many times,

but still in working shape. Minh put together a few anonymising filters, and – still unsteady and shaking – started to look up names, starting with the most recent.

They didn't have much in common: they ranged from bots-handlers and technologists to scholars, from foreigners to the Belt to people who had lived there for generations. What had happened to them was all over the place, too, ranging from short lacerator terms to exile or execution. Minh exhaled, forcing herself to breathe. Nothing wrong, really. Just random data put together to make her afraid; the scholars playing some obscure power games for their own satisfaction. Why had she been stupid enough to believe them? All their theatre, all their mysteries, as if they were passing on information that could send them to the lacerator or worse, and she'd fallen for it.

So naive, Mother would have said. *How can you be my daughter and still fail to see people for who they are? You're so lucky I'm here by your side.*

Wait.

Wait.

The last one was Bạch Loan, the data artist arrested for the Tiger Games incident and condemned to the slow death. But accidental destruction of property, even on a large scale, was only exile, wasn't it?

And Mỹ Thuần, who had stolen some rice to feed her aged mother. She'd been condemned to exile, but that sentence should have been reduced on account of her elderly relative.

Minh brought up name after name, stared at them all. Everywhere the same: the penalty seemed plausible for the offence, but it was always harsh. And ...

She brought up the data again, stared at it.

'Look up penalties for their offences. And the timelines,' she said to her bots – and waited, with bated breath, for the results.

For the older ones, it was difficult to find out what had happened exactly. Dã Lan, for instance, who'd died on *The Azure Serpent* for seditious talk, her entire family exterminated: all the records were gone, or under imperial seals that Minh didn't have. But the more recent ones were public access, which meant that the entire transcripts of the trial were available.

And for all of them, it was the same pattern: a punishment that looked plausible from a distance, but far outstripped what the penal code recommended for the offence. It wasn't that visible, because the magistrate and the tribunal had so much latitude in what they chose. And for all of them ... yes, they'd all confessed to their crimes, not knowing it would make it worse.

But surely ...

The final results blinked across Minh's screen, and she tightened her hands around the files, because they were exactly what she had expected, and exactly what she hadn't wanted: all of them had been interviewed by the magistrate or the prefect – and all of the magistrate's interviews had likely included the prefect, because that was how Mother worked. She liked to take the pulse of common crime, she said. To talk to people and find out what moved them, to exercise her prerogative of judgement.

She was ...

Minh stared at the data, daring it to lie. But it couldn't. Not unless she made it.

Mother was convincing people to confess to her, and using their confessions to give them harsher punishments. And not just once, or twice. Or a long time ago. So many times, and over so many years, that it wasn't a matter of error. She was doing it because she ... because ...

Minh struggled to breathe, but she couldn't back away from the truth just because she didn't like it.

Mother was doing it because she *enjoyed* it. Because it was the same kind of game as with the dress and Vĩnh Trinh's seal: of holding out something – the promise of comprehension, of mercy – and then snatching it away.

Harsh but fair, Mother had always said. Doing what was necessary.

But that ...

That wasn't necessary.

That was just *cruel*.

10

Encirclement

Quỳnh and Hoà had tea before Hoà left.

Hoà sat slumped against one of the pillars of the pavilion, looking as if sheer strength of will was the only thing keeping her upright, her bots loosely clinging to her clothing.

'Tell me about the prefect,' she said.

Quỳnh thought of Prefect Đức pouring her tea, the soft, sweet smell of grass, the brutality that had followed. Her hands clenched.

'Which one? The niece of *Flowers at the Gates*? Or the one former magistrate of *The Azure Serpent*?'

Hoà's gaze was clear-eyed and dry. 'Which one do you want to talk about?' And, gently reaching out, she squeezed Quỳnh's hand. 'You don't have to if you don't want to.'

Hoà made Quỳnh feel at home – made her feel, for the first time, that there was space for her. That there was somewhere that included the two of them, which didn't need to be more than a moment in time: the smell of the dumplings they were sharing, the soft touch of Hoà's bots on Quỳnh's skin, the awareness of her own bots tangled in Hoà's long, flowing hair,

Hoà's clear gaze – which saw everything about Quỳnh and yet still chose to care.

Still *dared* to care.

Guts of Sea cared, but *Guts of Sea* was venom and spite and revenge, and it wasn't the same. In Hoà's world, there was so little space for hatred, for payback. But it wasn't naivety, either. It wasn't innocence: Hoà had lost that a long time ago, with Thiên Hạnh's death, and it was clear enough, though Hoà wouldn't discuss it, that it had been traumatic, that she'd witnessed too much. Hoà had seen the worst of what the world had to offer, and yet still chose to be upright. To stand, unmoving, in the centre of a universe that had wounded her again and again – and choose to be kind.

Quỳnh couldn't imagine how much strength that would take. She knew she didn't have it, and never would. And it made her – not envious, not angry – but somehow reassured that Hoà had it. That there was still, somewhere, light and goodness in this world, and love.

Love for Quỳnh.

Quỳnh wanted to cry, but she couldn't afford to any more.

She took a deep breath, stared at the tea. Her hands scarcely trembled any more, and she had control over her bots again.

'The magistrate promised safety, if only I would tell her what had happened. She poured me tea and sympathised with me. And then, without a moment's regret, she sent me to the lacerator. She needed to be harsh, you see. To convince the Empire she had everything under control. That she was worthy of her post.'

It was Hoà's hands which trembled; her gaze which turned dark.

'And the general?'

That's not relevant to you or the ship, Quỳnh wanted to say, but Hoà had asked. She needed to trust Hoà – to trust her words.

'General Tuyết was...' She focused, not on her hands, but on Hoà's hand wrapped around hers, on the touch of Hoà's skin. 'She was my fiancée. She was the one who denounced me for having rebel sympathies. I'd written a letter to a scholar, years before, who later became a rebel officer. The general thought it was too much of a liability, and she was scared for her own life.' A silence. 'My mother wasted away after I ... fell off *The Azure Serpent*. They said she died of hunger. I think she didn't see any point in living, with me gone.'

'I'm sorry.'

A silence.

Hoà said finally, 'Big sis never really told me much about Dã Lan. About you. Just that there had been a terrible injustice, and that she'd failed.'

Quỳnh forced herself to breathe. 'She wouldn't have told you. She was exiled. Haven't you ever wondered why you live apart from the Serpent diaspora? You arrived in the Belt a year before the mining rig was lost.'

'You can't know that,' Hoà said sharply. 'You were—' She stopped.

'Dead? I can still put a timeline together.' Quỳnh laughed. It felt rusted and painful, and more wounding than she'd thought it would. 'I'm sorry. I've forgotten how to be fit company.'

'It's all right.' Hoà's voice was gentle. There was no judgement in it. Fear and distant worries for herself – but even that seemed to be a poor second to Hoà's worries about *Flowers at the Gates*. 'This isn't going to work out if you feel you need to put on a performance for my benefit.'

'Performance?'

'Isn't that what you do, most of the time?' Hoà's gaze was uncomfortably sharp. 'Play the part that will make your enemies fall?'

She saw too much, and too little.

'Yes.'

Hoà said simply, 'No lies, remember?' And the naked hope in her eyes *hurt*.

She was so eminently vulnerable – someone like Đức would swallow her whole and break her bone by bone, and in that moment Quỳnh knew she would do anything rather than let that happen.

Everything, save renounce her revenge.

'No,' Quỳnh said finally, and bent down to kiss Hoà, drinking in the sharp sweet taste of her lips. Hoà kissed her back, and she thought she was going to break then and there, with no regrets whatsoever.

When Hoà broke away, they stared at each other for a while. Quỳnh struggled, for a bare moment, to breathe and remember who she was – what she wanted.

She said, 'Prefect Đức hasn't changed all that much. Manipulative, greedy for power, no scruples. Destroying lives left and right for the thrill of it, and calling it righteousness.'

The moment of closeness between her and Hoà had passed – and yet, while it lasted, it had felt so good. She felt a visceral wrenching, the loss of something precious.

'And the general?'

'Flighty, vain, inconstant.'

Hoà's face didn't move, but her bots quivered.

'I'm sorry,' she said. 'You loved her.'

Quỳnh tried to shrug, and stopped, because they'd told no lies.

'Once. It shouldn't hurt that much.'

'Of course it does.' Hoà's face looked oddly twisted, as if she was going to cry at any moment. She leaned against the pillar; it flickered in overlay, showing the bare metal underneath the lacquered virtual surface with playful dragons. She waited, but Quỳnh couldn't find any words to fill the silence. 'The ship. *Flowers at the Gates* was a rebel sympathiser. Or at any rate, was altogether too critical of imperial policy. A liability for someone like the prefect.'

Of course, she's done her homework.

'Yes.'

'Would she say she's still one?'

Quỳnh thought about it, for a while.

'I'm not sure,' she said. 'The war is over.'

'But the military still handles the Belt, because they're still worried we'll rebel.' A laugh, swiftly extinguished. 'Like they did with *The Azure Serpent*.'

'Miners. Technologists,' Quỳnh said. 'These aren't people invested in maintaining the Empire. These are the people facing its worst harms.'

'Mm. Not quite,' Hoà said. 'You forget the shipbuilders at the shipyards, the outer moons folk and all the other ethnic minorities. The Empire isn't kind to those on its borders.'

Or to anyone who doesn't conform.

'Lil sis ...'

Hoà laughed. 'Yes, I know. Sedition. Who's going to tell the prefect?'

She was utterly magnificent, and something twisted in Quỳnh's chest.

'Of course I won't,' she said.

A sharp look, and a host of unasked questions in Hoà's eyes.

'So you're not sure?'

'About *that* motivation? No.' Quỳnh went on, carefully, 'But you're thinking politics?'

'Because that's all she cares about, isn't it?'

What Đức cared about was power, in all its forms. Including at home. Quỳnh felt a pang of pity – swiftly extinguished – for Minh.

'You forgot greed.'

'Money?' Hoà stared at Quỳnh. 'Oh. It's been thirteen years, hasn't it, since the wreck? *Flowers at the Gates* is about to be declared unfit.' A pause, while she accessed the network. 'She's head of the lineage, isn't she? She holds not just the wealth and the voting privileges that go with it, but also the fire and incense portion of the wealth.'

'Yes. It's not insignificant.'

The fire and incense portion was dedicated to ancestral cults, but for a family like Đức's, it would be a staggering amount of currency: physical and virtual space owned either in perpetuity or as part of a lease from the imperial family.

Hoà looked distinctly annoyed. 'So if we fix her – if she's able to verbalise her thoughts to other people ... if we prove beyond a shadow of a doubt that she's not broken past function or repair ...'

'Then she'll remain head of the lineage.'

'And Prefect Đức gets nothing. That's a very good motive for murder, isn't it? No, wait.' Hoà shook her head. 'She'd just send someone to arrest me. It's easier than trying to poison me on board the ship. Just find a charge and sweep me up, like she's done with so many people. Why the poisoning? It's so convoluted.'

'You seem remarkably collected for someone who's almost died.'

A brief flash of irritation from Hoà. 'I'm scared to death, obviously. Who wouldn't be? But I'm not letting that get in my way.'

Quỳnh spared a flash of pity for anyone who did get in Hoà's way, because they would likely never understand what had hit them. She was all incandescence and sharpness – not for herself, but for the sake of what she felt was right. It was intoxicating and terrifying – and yet utterly and comfortingly right.

'I love you,' Quỳnh said.

Hoà froze, hand in mid-air. She exhaled. Quỳnh got there first.

'I'm not expecting an answer to that if you'd rather not.'

'I don't know yet,' Hoà said finally. 'Perhaps I could. Perhaps.'

And she was right, wasn't she? What future did they have, outside this little bubble of frozen time where they shared everything with each other? Quỳnh bit her lip hard enough to draw blood.

'So you're not liking the prefect, then?'

'Hmm. I don't know,' Hoà said. 'You said it had to be one of my employers.'

'Your bottle was poisoned. Surely that would be easiest to do while it was on the ship.'

'I leave it lying around in the shop.' Hoà's voice was thoughtful. 'And most people in the community know I take it on site visits. So much as I don't like my employers—' it seemed to be one person in particular she was thinking of— 'I'm not sure that's the evidence you think it is. Can you forward me the chemical analysis?'

'Of course.'

A silence, while Hoà scanned it.

'I don't know,' she said finally. 'There's not a whole lot of other motives around, or anyone who benefits as much as the prefect does. But ... but nothing tallies with what you've told me of her. She wouldn't pick such a risky plan, to start with.' She stopped, then. Her eyes widened.

'What?'

'The symptoms,' Hoà said. 'In the report. The common poisoning ones – the low dosage ones. Dizziness. Fever. Flushed skin with pinpricks of red on the fingers and toes.'

'I don't understand.'

'That's exactly what Thiên Dung has.'

'But Thiên Dung didn't visit the ship. And ...' Quỳnh shook her head. 'She ...'

Hoà's face was hard. 'She'd be dead by now. But she's not, is she? Not yet.' She rose, abruptly. 'I'm sorry, I have to go. Can you give me that antidote?'

Quỳnh fished in her sleeves, and found the carved bottle that she always carried with her, a habit she'd taken up when living in the shipyards.

'Here. Do you want me to come?'

A pause, and then a shaking of Hoà's head. 'No. This is my mess to sort out. But thank you.' A quick peck on the lips, something that sent a thrill into Quỳnh's bones. 'I'll be back.'

And then she was gone, and all Quỳnh had left was the sweetness on her lips, and the memory of her touch.

Quỳnh sat down in the empty bedroom, by the altar to her dead, and tried not to think of Hoà.

It was hard. *Guts of Sea* was right: she wasn't meant to care. She wasn't meant to worry – not just about Hoà, but about Thiên Dung – or to wonder how on earth Thiên Dung had been poisoned.

She should be worrying about Tuyết, and Đức – and Đức's uncomfortable suspicions about her that struck a little too close to home. She made some tea – not the one she'd made for Hoà, the soft and grassy one of their childhoods aboard *The Azure Serpent*, but the sharp one from the shipyards, the one she'd drunk after seeing Đình Sơn's unrecognisable body in the compartment they'd furnished, surrounded by the jade and metal pieces they'd painstakingly selected to build a life together. It tasted astringent, almost bitter, because of its long brewing.

Her bots had put together the usual compendium of morning

news: which scholars were allied with each other; the latest rumours in the Empire. There was strong talk a censor was going to visit, to finalise the transfer of the habitats from military to civil rule. The scholars were aligning themselves to seem either the most righteous or the most detached from this. Everyone's avatar suddenly included either quotations about continued loyalty to one's betrothed, a transparent comparison to fidelity to one's emperor, or very studied references to hollow bamboos, wild orchids and other poetic metaphors for scholars who were away from the court either by choice or by force.

There was an answer to her letter to Minister Giai Khanh and Academy Chancellor Hàn Lâm Bình: a cautiously worded letter of thanks for passing on information vital to the harmony of the Empire, and an equally cautious promise that if Đức did indeed lose her grip on the order within the habitat, they would move to depose her.

Good. That part was proceeding as planned.

Ah.

Minh had visited Vĩnh Trinh and Mạt Ly, and had left in something of a shock. Quỳnh felt a twinge of pity. She could imagine what Hoà would say about Minh — that Minh hadn't chosen the circumstances she found herself in. But Minh was also the eldest child of Đức — her heir, and the person Đức loved most, if Đức was even capable of love. She'd know the truth about her mother, and it would devastate her — and her turning against her mother would make Đức's position more uncomfortable. But Đức wasn't the priority there.

There.

It was a small sidebar in the scholar world's news, but *Guts of Sea* had already flagged it for her, with a note that said: 'When you've finished flirting, call me.'

It was a report that the tribunal had arrested Scholar Gia

Kiệt on suspicion of murder. There wasn't a lot of sympathy: Gia Kiệt had been moderately wealthy, from the wrong background altogether – a merchant's son – and hadn't taken the time to court those who'd shelter him in the scholarly world. He'd relied too much on his position as Tuyết's lover, but she wasn't going to save him. Tuyết wasn't going to advocate on anyone's behalf, especially not someone with Gia Kiệt's track record. Quỳnh had investigated him thoroughly. Enough brothels and entertainment houses remembered him, and enough ledgers held transactions that could be traced to him. In addition to being thoroughly repulsive – the skeletons had presented clear evidence of excruciatingly painful deaths – Gia Kiệt was not smart, and his past had just caught up with him.

Now, all that remained was for him to take Tuyết down with him.

Which meant Quỳnh gaining access to him.

And that meant through a non-legal route, because Đức was already suspicious of her.

Quỳnh wasn't sure she wanted to talk to *Guts of Sea*. Thinking of the ship made her think of the bots' needles, and Hoà's anger, and Hoà herself, and everything *Guts of Sea* manifestly didn't approve of. But what other choice did she have?

The ship picked up her call immediately. The overlay wasn't her avatar, but the inside of her – the room where Quỳnh had lain, shaking and shivering as everything tore itself apart, with only *Guts of Sea*'s voice anchoring her to reality. The walls still showed the traces of Quỳnh's repairs, like broken celadon shards glued together, except the joinery wasn't gold but sheening, pulsing metal that still felt infused with their shared anger.

'Big sis,' *Guts of Sea* said.

Quỳnh braced herself for a biting remark, but all *Guts of Sea* said was, 'You got my message?'

'Yes,' Quỳnh said. 'Do you have access to Gia Kiệt?'

Guts of Sea's tilt was thoughtful – harder to read from an overlay inside the ship than with an avatar.

'Access to a magistrate's jail? That's a bold move.'

Quỳnh wasn't sure why the game suddenly irritated her.

'You don't approve?'

'Not of everything,' *Guts of Sea* said smoothly. 'As you well know.'

That was, at least, familiar if not comfortable territory.

'I'm not talking about Hoà.'

'I didn't think you were.' *Guts of Sea* sighed. 'I just hope you see it before it's too late.'

'See what? She *knows*.'

'Does she?' *Guts of Sea* said, slowly, softly, 'About Đình Sơn?'

'Why would I tell her?'

'Oh, lil sis. You know how dangerous our past is. How fragile everything is around us. Do you think it's fair, what you're doing to her?'

'It's nothing she didn't agree to,' Quỳnh said – too fast, too smoothly.

Does Hoà really know the truth – all of the truth? There is so much unsaid between us.

How fragile is everything around us. How everything could turn to loss in the smallest of moments. How happiness was ... not fleeting, but reserved for other people. People who hadn't endured, who hadn't done the things Quỳnh had or planned to do. People who deserved blessings from Heaven.

'Tell me about the jail.' Quỳnh could feel *Guts of Sea*'s satisfaction. Her friend knew her argument had landed.

'It's old, ill secured, and its network has a physical interface that can be accessed by some service ducts.'

'Surely someone has hacked it by now?'

'The security on the network itself is rather good,' *Guts of Sea* said. 'But nothing is impossible.' Bots scurried on the floor of her overlay, started tasks that Quỳnh could see scroll: various stages of planning. 'Do you want that interview?'

Quỳnh didn't hesitate. 'Of course.'

Quỳnh deliberated for a while, but in the end she went for full immersion. In this conversation she would need to be free with her movements, and a simple call with a flat overlay wasn't going to work.

She sat cross-legged in the bedroom, and gradually the single table with her ancestral altar, the bed she and Hoà had slept in, the four chests of personal things she so seldom opened – it all faded away, replaced by the pitted floor of the prison hallway. Each cell was little more than a rectangular box, with enough space to stand and turn, and not much else – and the overlay and perception filters within, which prisoners had no control over, could make it feel much smaller or much larger. All the cells were stacked on top of one another, the stacks aligned in row after row that felt like a series of buildings on the First Planet – except that instead of compartments and housing space, they held hundreds of prisoners.

Quỳnh focused, and the scene shifted again as *Guts of Sea*'s bots guided her: now she was inside a cell, her bots skittering on the floor. The overlay was metal with a faint sheen, like deep spaces, and it was currently vast, like some underground cavern, with the profoundly alien sound of dripping water, as if something were leaking within the stations' water reserves, a prelude to an absolute disaster.

Not that it mattered to the man in the cell, because he could hardly see any of it in his current state.

He was lying on the floor, bleeding, skin sloughing off in flakes, the blood seeping onto the floor. He'd been through several rounds in the lacerator, the telltale patterned wounds raw on his exposed back, and one of his arms flopped at an angle that didn't look good.

It would smell of rank mustiness and of blood, of urine, of sweat, of despair. Not to anyone outside – the perception filters would make sure of that – but to Gia Kiệt. Quỳnh's bots skittered on the floor, the sound of their legs echoing under the vast cavern, and into the careful emptiness of Quỳnh's mind. She'd been there, once. She'd been lying in her own filth and facing nothing but the certainty of her own prolonged agony at Đức's hands.

Fifteen years.

A lifetime.

It wasn't her, any more. It really wasn't. He was a sadist and a murderer, and she had a job to do.

Quỳnh closed her eyes for a moment.

'Scholar Gia Kiệt.' She pitched her voice carefully: the accents of the court, the accents of power on the First Planet – the utter certainty and arrogance of those whose futures had never hung in the balance.

There was no answer. Perhaps she'd have to jolt him into consciousness ... but just as she mentally went through the methods she could use if she wasn't physically present, Gia Kiệt stirred.

'Who ...?' His voice was a whisper through split lips, with the rasping of damaged vocal cords.

'Think of me as a friend.'

Quỳnh used the word with its court connotations: the one just shy of mentor and teacher, the person who would support a young scholar in return for their future support.

Gia Kiệt pulled himself up. It was a slow, painstaking rise that made Quỳnh wince inwardly; she had to work to remain still, to keep the neutral, forbidding expression on her face.

Avatar space made it easier, but someone like Gia Kiệt – a serial predator – would likely catch the smallest and most subtle of signs. Not that she felt in danger – she could break him in half, with or without her bots – but she couldn't afford to have him work out what was going on.

Finally Gia Kiệt managed to sit – shaking, shivering, his skin covered in layers of grime.

'Who are you, and what do you want?'

Despite his wounds, he was attempting to gather himself. Quỳnh would have been impressed if she hadn't examined the skeletons of his victims.

'Let me tell you how it goes,' she said, slowly, softly. 'You claim your innocence, or your guilt, and it doesn't really make a difference to the tribunal. Perhaps you've even seen the prefect. Perhaps she's promised you something. Freedom, in exchange for a full confession.'

A minute movement of Gia Kiệt's eyes.

Aha.

Đức was – at least in this regard – predictable.

'She won't keep her word,' Quỳnh said.

'You seem very well informed,' Gia Kiệt said.

A fit of coughing that bent him double. *Fluid in his lungs*, Quỳnh's bots said. He might not live long. Which would have been a good thing – he deserved all of it – only she still needed him. And, if he realised how poor his health was, he would clam up. She couldn't use the future as leverage if he didn't have one.

'I've witnessed it first-hand,' Quỳnh said.

A sly look from Gia Kiệt. 'Ah. A magistrate. From another district?'

If only.

'A friend.'

'Mmm. What do you want?'

'To help you,' Quỳnh said.

He stared at her – dissecting her, trying to find vulnerabilities. She wasn't about to let him see any.

'Help me?' He coughed again. Quỳnh's bots, augmented by *Guts of Sea*'s own bots, started charting his breathing. 'To escape this cell? I notice you're not here physically.'

'You're sharp,' Quỳnh said.

'You make it sound like that's a problem.'

'No. I should think a smart man like you would understand the predicament he's in. And I can offer escape.'

'How? And don't try and sell me an easier death. I'm not here to die.'

Gia Kiệt was dying already – he just didn't know it yet. That was the irony.

'Everyone is here to die.' In her mind, she was younger, and she was being dragged out of the cell, Nhăng directing the guards, Magistrate Đức distant and preoccupied, everything already played out. That was the worst: that she had represented nothing of interest. 'But you might just survive.'

She could easily offer him advice to make it quicker – shared all the things she'd wished she'd known when she was young, when it had all been hopeless. He had no bots, but the prison did – the guards, the maintenance ducts – and *Guts of Sea* could shear through them all as through wet rice paper. But he wanted to live. Beaten down, lacerated, betrayed – he still wanted to live.

If only Dã Lan had been like him.

A laugh. 'Lying to me? That's not the greatest of starts, elder aunt.'

Sharp. Too sharp. She'd thought he wasn't smart, but she didn't have a good enough hold on what moved him. She'd studied Đức extensively – Đức was dangerous but predictable. This ... This was a hungry, desperate man, and she remembered being that way, but not well enough, because Dã Lan had been soft and naive and altogether unsuited to survival – no wonder she'd tumbled into deep spaces and vanished from life altogether. Quỳnh didn't regret her – except when Hoà looked at her, outraged and sad on her behalf, and she suddenly remembered what it had been like.

'I can tell you how to get Prefect Đức to pardon you.'

That got his attention.

'Really?' He was shivering and shaking, watching her, naked in more ways than one – no finery, no clothing, no bots. 'You just said I couldn't trust her.'

'Yes,' Quỳnh said. 'Which is why this doesn't rely on her.'

A minute shift in his posture, a small blinking of his eyes. She had him now, but he was still wary.

'What do you want me to do?'

'You killed eighteen people. And I know who sheltered you.'

'You're either well informed, or mistaken.'

Quỳnh smiled, and it had teeth. 'Shall I tell whose idea the trick wall was? Whose soldiers protected you while you toured the courtesan houses?'

He blanched. 'How ... ?'

'I have my sources.' The archives had a long memory, and *Guts of Sea* had extensively researched this. 'And you were her lover, weren't you?'

She couldn't even imagine what Tuyết had seen in him. Perhaps he'd had more presence, years ago, than this slick, oily miasma – like the man who'd stalked the skewer-seller; had had the easy power Tuyết had always been drawn to.

'You hate that. Interesting. So you're here against the Peach Blossom Lake General, are you?'

Quỳnh was losing control. She was too nice. Being with Hoà had addled her brains. She ought to ... She ought to force him to his knees, to have him show some respect. Except if she did that, he would fear her but not trust her, and she needed his trust.

No, she didn't need his trust. She needed him to trust what she was offering, which was different.

'You're still protecting her?'

'What would I gain by denouncing her?'

Revenge ... but interestingly he didn't seem to be moved by that consideration at all.

'Prefect Đức and General Tuyết have been at odds for years. Đức wouldn't care about you, if you gave her the means to take Tuyết down.'

A head, cocked. Consideration. A modicum of wary listening. Better. She could do this. She could overcome whatever softness Hoà had brought out in her.

'Not caring sounds a lot like quietly getting rid of me. She would need me as a material witness, but my statement would do, wouldn't it? Much more convenient to have a dead body than a live one, isn't it?'

'Not if you denounce Tuyết publicly.'

A pause. He stared at her. 'That's what you want? To record me?'

'Yes,' Quỳnh said simply. 'With enough remorse—' he didn't feel remorse, he never would, but he likely could fake it well enough '—it should make for a pretty narrative.'

She could see his mind working, behind the ruin of his face. He reached up, drew a blood-streaked hand across his skin.

'All the habitats would know.'

'Yes. They dislike scholars, but they dislike the general even more. She's been in charge for such a long time. The idea that she turned a blind eye to your crimes – worse, that she helped you with them – will enrage them. And if anything happened to you, they would suspect foul play from either Đức – the ruling class protecting their own – or from Tuyết's partisans.'

Đức was canny; she wouldn't want a riot on her turf.

'And you want the general?'

Quỳnh weighed the cost of being honest, and couldn't find any disadvantage.

'Yes. I want her to fall.'

He was looking at her, the same way Magistrate Đức had once looked at her, and she felt small and dissected – as if he knew everything of her and found everything lacking, painfully naive. But what he said was, 'So you're not much better than her, are you?'

'Than ...?'

'The prefect.'

It was sharp, and wounding, and altogether unwelcome. She wasn't Đức. She was bringing Đức down. She was delivering heavenly justice. Quỳnh breathed, slowly, carefully – had her bots release a light sedative in her blood.

'I'm the person who's offering you a chance to live. Will you take it?'

Gia Kiệt watched her. The overlay of the jail flickered around her, everything turning constricting and suffocating. The sedative took the edge off it, but the disquiet, the fear, the anxiety – it was all behind a pane of glass, waiting to ambush her when it wore off.

'I don't have all day.' Quỳnh dragged the words out slowly, regretfully – tamping down the panicked beating of her heart. She didn't have many choices, and she'd invested so much in this avenue already. With Đức suspicious, she might not have a second chance. 'If you'd rather rot in your agony, then I'll leave you to it.'

That same hollow, dry laughter.

'I recognise what you want, but it doesn't matter, does it? I'll do it, and you'll have your blood.'

Afterwards, Quỳnh turned everything off, and stared at the darkness. The sedative was wearing off, and she was sitting in the emptiness of her own compound. Her bots were compiling the recording from Gia Kiệt before they sent it on to a contact – a scholar who specialised in the ugliest gossip. From there, it would disseminate to the entire network. And Gia Kiệt would request and get an interview with Đức.

She wrote a letter to her allies at court, keeping the wording careful, hidden beneath elaborate literary allusions:

Prefect Đức will arrest General Tuyết in connection with an affair her tribunal failed to close years ago. There are allegations she's been needlessly cruel in her judgements, leading to widespread unrest and anger in the Belt. Her daughter is being unfilial. The prefect will soon lose her grip on order on the habitats as she is losing it within her family. If that happens, then it would be right and proper for the Empress's favour to pass from such a weak official.

Minister Giai Khanh and Academy Chancellor Hàn Lâm Bình would understand the message: it was time.

She sent to *Guts of Sea*, 'Everything is going according to plan.'

An acknowledgement from her friend. 'Good. Get some rest. You're going to need it. Things will come to a head soon.'

Very soon. Đức would move against Tuyết. And the entire ugliness Quỳnh had been spreading – the unrest, eighteen skeletons, Minh's turning against her mother – was going to blossom the colour of blood. And Giai Khanh and Hàn Lâm

Bình would move against Đức at court. Speaking of which, she was going to need to give Minh another nudge.

Quỳnh wasn't sure what would happen, or what it would lead to, but it meant bad things, for either or both of them. She was halfway there. She'd have her revenge. Everything was going according to plan.

So you're not much better than her, are you?

She'd given a sadist and a murderer a reprieve so she could achieve a higher goal. And while she had no regrets, she knew what Hoà would think. She knew how Hoà would ... not exactly judge, because Hoà didn't really judge. But she knew Hoà would see it, and that she always chose compassion.

And it wasn't that Quỳnh judged herself – she was doing what was necessary. But she'd known the cost when she started; she'd always known she didn't deserve happiness, and wouldn't achieve it. She'd always known that being driven by hatred and grief and revenge was unsuitable and unacceptable – that her parents and her entire ancestral line were watching her from the afterlife, and withholding their blessings. She should have been focusing on *Moon* and *Moon*'s happiness – except, of course, that *Moon*'s best chance at happiness lay in not being Dã Lan's daughter.

She stared at her altar, at the names there. Mother. Teacher. Husband. All she cared about, extinguished because they'd been too close to her.

Quỳnh laid a finger on her own lips, the same way Hoà had – except this was a pale imitation, a faded reflection of happiness, like a fragment of asteroid to a blinding star.

So many people, in fact, had a better chance at happiness if they didn't enter Quỳnh's orbit.

How fragile is everything around us.

You'll have your blood.

She was doing the right thing, but she already knew the

price for it. She already knew there would be no reward for her – nothing but blood and tears and the pain of her enemies would be her only comfort.

She knew that sooner or later, she would lose Hoà, because she didn't deserve, and had never deserved, Hoà.

11

Clarity, Power and Justice

Hoà ran.

It was pointless, rationally – it wasn't as though Thiên Dung would get worse if she walked.

She sent a single message to Thiên Dung through the network: 'Don't move. Be careful.' She'd have called, but she couldn't run as fast while calling, and she didn't think she could really tell Thiên Dung she was being poisoned via message. Too many explanations required.

When – out of breath, preceded by the skitters of the few bots she had left – Hoà arrived home to their compartment, she found Thiên Dung downstairs, waiting for her behind the counter.

'Big sis?'

Hoà took a deep, shaking breath. 'I need you to listen. Carefully. And not to ask questions. Please. I promise you can ask all the questions you want afterwards.'

'Fine. But you'll still get all the questions at the end, and you'd better be able to answer them.' Thiên Dung breathed, slow and hard; at least she didn't seem like she was going to choke any more.

Good.

She listened. By the end of it, she was sitting on the single chair beside the counter, her bots thronging around her like a court. She raised a hand to her mouth, a bot trembling on her hands.

'Poison.' Her voice was flat. 'Cinnabar Clouds. From the shipyards. And you were poisoned, too?'

'My water bottle,' Hoà said. 'On board the ship.'

'That's ...' Thiên Dung closed her eyes. 'All right – what's the antidote?'

'Here.' Hoà put down the carved bottle Quỳnh had given her.

Thiên Dung stared at it, suspiciously. 'This isn't yours.'

'No,' Hoà said. 'But I really think—'

'No, I think this is relevant. Where did you get it? You said you were poisoned with a high enough dose to knock you out, but you're fine now. Which means you were cured. Which means you went somewhere.'

'And ...?'

'And I need to know how many liabilities we're dealing with.'

'She's not going to talk.' Hoà thought of Quỳnh's touch on her hair, and felt herself turn beetroot red. 'I doubt it'd be in her interest to.'

Thiên Dung stared at her sister, and then she sighed. 'The Alchemist, is it? The one who came here?'

'Is it that bad?'

Thiên Dung sighed again. Her bots heaved. 'People like her – they mean well, but they distort everything they touch. They bring upheaval in their wake, and the kind of trouble that just gets you noticed.' She paused. 'But that's really besides the point. We should be focusing on the problem at hand.'

'Which is taking the antidote?'

'Mmm.' Thiên Dung weighed the bottle in her hand, curiously. 'At some point, yes. But the problem at hand is actually ... how were we both poisoned?'

'It was the ship.'

'But I never saw the ship,' Thiên Dung said. 'Only *Heart's Sorrow*.'

'And the others?' Hoà crouched, trying to breathe. 'All right, let's try this another way. I'm all for having this conversation, but I want you to take those pills first.'

'That's hardly going to—'

'Help? Yes it is. You're distracting me. I know you're not going to die right now, but I could use some reassurance.'

'Fair.' Thiên Dung took three pills from the bottle, and downed them in one go. 'Happy?'

'I don't know. How did you get that job?'

'The usual way. A client walked into the shop and asked for a repair job. Except the client was a mindship who wanted to fix another mindship.'

'And that's it?'

'No, there was somebody else with him.' Thiên Dung thought for a while. 'A girl. Teenager? Barely old enough to be a scholar herself, but she had the bearing of someone raised that way.'

Hoà put a picture of the others on the ship – scavenged from the memory banks of one of her surviving bots – on an overlay.

'Yes.' Thiên Dung pointed to a scowling Minh. 'She looked about as happy, too, come to think of it. I don't know what her problem was.'

'I don't know either,' Hoà said. 'But ...' She hesitated. 'One of them did it, you realise?'

'*Heart's Sorrow*? Why would he try to poison someone he'd hired?'

'Perhaps he wasn't expecting them to succeed.'

'Really?' Thiên Dung snorted. 'For a start, he wouldn't do it before I'd even started the job. And also, he's observant and entirely too nice, but he's a poor liar. That project of fixing the ship was clearly his, and he wanted it to succeed. Desperately. I'm not going to inquire why.'

Because he'd wanted something he'd made himself, something that didn't come from his general mother. Hoà shook her head at the unwelcome thought. She didn't need sympathy for *Heart's Sorrow*.

'I'll take your word for it.'

'You're better with repair jobs than with people.' Thiên Dung's tone was fond.

Hoà wasn't so sure, and she certainly wasn't in a very charitable frame of mind. She still felt weak and her throat was raw, and Thiên Dung probably didn't feel much better.

'And what did you think of Minh?'

'Mmm.' Thiên Dung said nothing. 'I'm not sure we need to go in to what I think of Minh. Rather, how did we both get poisoned? Because I don't leave a water bottle or a cup lying around the shop. Not without bots watching it.'

'Food?'

'No,' Thiên Dung said. 'And you overlooked something.'

'No,' Hoà said. 'I haven't. To have your symptoms, you'd have needed a regular infusion of poison. Except they never came back to the shop. And there's nothing that would have remained around that long. Food gets thrown away, so does water.'

'Do Cinnabar Clouds need to be ingested?' Thiên Dung pulled up the poison sheet, stared at it – a technologist dissecting a problem. Hoà wanted to scream at her that she'd almost died, stopped herself with an effort – forced the feeling away until she could deal with it. 'I see an injection would work, but would have killed me faster.'

'Not helping,' Hoà said curtly.

'I can tell. I know you're putting in a lot of effort to be that composed. Honestly, if you want to vent at me and it would make you feel better, go ahead.'

Hoà gave it some thought. 'No,' she said finally. 'It wouldn't be fair. But thank you.'

'Any time,' Thiên Dung said with a shrug. 'So the poison? Ingestion?'

'Yes,' Hoà said. 'Could it be clinging to your hands from something you've touched.'

'Mmm. I wash my hands.'

Thiên Dung didn't protest too much. They both knew she wasn't consistent about doing it.

'Other clients?' Thiên Dung looked, curiously, at the deserted shop. 'Or something we use regularly?'

Hoà tried to remember how Thiên Dung had fallen sick, what she'd been doing. Working on some smaller projects that were overdue prior to the Tiger Games, and just … growing weaker until she couldn't seem to breathe properly any more.

'Do you remember what you were working on?'

'Old Linh's tea storage box?' Thiên Dung bit her lower lip. 'Maybe?'

Hoà pulled up the archives. They didn't include work hours: just who had paid for what.

'That was a fairly large job, and you handed it to her just a couple of days before falling sick. Let's look. Can you do it? I don't have enough bots.'

'I noticed.' Thiên Dung's voice was dry. 'We'll get some more.'

When we get paid. The words hung unsaid in the air.

She could have asked Quỳnh, and Quỳnh would have given

them to her without a second thought – but she wasn't here to be *helped* by Quỳnh, Heaven forbid.

'The box,' Hoà said firmly.

Thiên Dung sent her bots to drag it to the table. Above them was Hoà's overlay, blinking: the picture of Minh and Oanh's children and *Heart's Sorrow*, like a series of unanswered questions. The ship was Minh's great-aunt. Minh hadn't seemed to like Hoà, but ...

But she was the prefect's daughter, and they all knew what the prefect was like.

Hoà's bots, Thiên Dung's bots and Quỳnh's bots mingled for a moment – a few blinks, with data being exchanged on ephemeral links – before Thiên Dung and Hoà looked at each other. Thiên Dung was still pale with exertion, her breath unsteady and her temperature above average. Hoà fought the urge to tell her to sit down, because Thiên Dung was probably about to tell her the same thing.

'No,' Hoà said, a fraction of a blink before Thiên Dung did. 'Was there anything else?'

With the help of their bots, they took a look at everything in the alcoves, every piece of tech they hadn't handed back to a client – even at the alcoves themselves. Everything was clean. No trace of poison.

That didn't make sense. How in Heaven had Thiên Dung been poisoned? Hoà called up the recordings of that room aboard the ship, the one where everyone had hung out. She'd left her bag behind, unguarded, so all she had to look at was a centiday or so, those moments prior to putting on the shadow-skin and going aboard the ship. Nothing of interest. A ballet of movements: Oanh's children, Minh scowling, *Heart's Sorrow* being overly courteous and helpful. No significant movement she could see near her bag, and yet ...

Yet her bottle had been tampered with, and she was sure

it had happened there. She'd always had the bag with her afterwards, including in the shop – because she'd been too preoccupied by the repairs to let it out of her sight.

'You're sure you never went to the ship?' Hoà asked.

'I think I'd remember!' Thiên Dung tried to laugh, gave up as her breath seized up.

'Lil sis!'

Thiên Dung raised a hand. 'I have it under control. Mmm.'

'I don't know that we have anything under control.'

They had the antidote now, but Hoà wasn't going to stop trying to fix *Flowers at the Gates*, which meant their poisoner would try again. Using the same means – which they hadn't managed to find – or some other approach which they might not be able to counter at all.

'We should sleep,' Thiên Dung said. 'You've had a day, I've had a day. And everything will seem better in the morning.'

Or we'll be dead.

Hoà sighed. 'Let's make some tea first, shall we?'

'For sure. I'll be upstairs.'

Alone in the shop, Hoà watched as Thiên Dung's and Quỳnh's bots cleaned up, all the tech being stuffed back into the alcoves, ready for customers. Everything gleamed. Hoà called up the footage again, stared at it. Nothing.

She turned off the lights, and headed upstairs to meet Thiên Dung, leaving Quỳnh's bots to finish cleaning.

Her sister had fallen asleep by the tea tray, her breathing slow and still laboured. The two cups lay untouched. Her bots waited for Hoà in the darkness, with a simple message from Thiên Dung: 'Don't think I can stay up any longer, but you should have some. Pretend I'm awake, and I'll catch up.'

Hoà's heart shivered and broke.

'Oh, lil sis.'

She sat down, wrapping the blanket around Thiên Dung,

bringing up a faint overlay of the night sky above them. She brought the cup to her lips, inhaling the soft floral fragrance of the tea ...

Wait.

The two cups didn't quite look the same. The tea in Thiên Dung's was slightly different. Hoà had her bots run a comparison: yes, it was cloudier by a fraction, unaccounted for by the tea itself or the minute differences in the ceramic. She picked up Thiên Dung's cup, sniffed it. It wasn't just floral: it had that faint metallic aftertaste, like her water bottle. Thiên Dung probably wouldn't have noticed, but she, exhausted, hadn't drunk from her cup. Thank Heaven. Thiên Dung was fine.

But how?

Hoà pinged Thiên Dung's bots, asking for access. They pinged back with full privileges, giving her the recording of the bedroom, which was utterly uninteresting: Thiên Dung's bots set water to boil and dragged out the tea leaves — and ...

There.

At the very beginning, when there were just two cups on the table, in the moment before Thiên Dung settled down — a sliver of smooth, fast movement, a blur of *something*.

'Look for that in the other footage,' Hoà subvocalised. And sat, alone in the darkness, while the bots ran their analysis.

There was that same blur in the room, moving across the walls. Only one thing could move that fast and evade all detection: a bot. Not any bot, but one with official network privileges — belonging to the tribunal, or the prefect's household.

Minh's bots.

One in the shop, one on board the ship. No — not just one, because it would have taken more than one to sabotage the ship's repairs. But the one in their shop was probably just one, because more would have been noticeable. More would have been impossible to hide.

Which meant she was only dealing with one poisoner and killer bot, rather than a swarm of them.

Great.

Hoà desperately wanted to call Quỳnh – because Quỳnh would surely know what to do. But it was late, and she was afraid that Thiên Dung was right: Quỳnh wasn't discreet enough. And what could Quỳnh do, really? It was just her and the dark, and whatever was trying to kill them both.

It was a bot, which meant it was fast. It was small – but its routines would be limited, and its intelligence circumscribed. In particular, it would be avoiding people, but it wouldn't be expecting anyone who knew exactly what they were looking for.

What commands had it been given? Poison the food? Or the drinks? Probably whatever it could. It'd be smart enough to recognise and look for anything unguarded. But not smart enough to recognise that Thiên Dung had been replaced by Hoà – since it was still Thiên Dung's food it was trying to poison. Which meant it hadn't been updated. Which meant it wasn't in contact with whoever had left it there.

Good. It had no idea they were on to it and the poison it was using.

And the other thing was – if it was one bot, it meant it was blind. If it was upstairs trying to see if Thiên Dung could be poisoned, it certainly wouldn't be able to keep an eye out downstairs.

Hoà focused. Quỳnh's bots were downstairs, still cleaning up. She sent them into the kitchen to unspool lengths of razor-sharp wire, the kind that would cut through human flesh with a single sweep. Then she recalled them into the shop, as if nothing in particular had happened. She'd used a series of instructions on a high-privacy channel, and made it look as though she'd requested more video footage.

Hoà shook Thiên Dung awake.

'Mmmmf?' Thiên Dung said, eyes still blurry with sleep.

'I'm going to make some fried noodles,' she said, even as her hands made another kind of gesture, the old Serpent one for 'careful, hold'.

Thiên Dung's eyes fluttered. She gave no sign she'd seen Hoà move.

'Sounds nice,' she said, and fell back asleep.

Hoà sent Quỳnh's bots ahead into the kitchen, positioning them near the stove. She watched warily as she came down – she'd carefully placed the wires so she could navigate past them, but it was still nerve-racking to have to avoid them in a way that felt natural. By the time she made it to the stove, she was winded with the effort of holding herself still.

A further two of her depleted stock of bots went into the cupboard to look for plates. She made a show of cooking the fried noodles under the watchful eyes of her bots, and then served them in two matching bowls – and left the kitchen muttering to herself, as if she were looking for something she'd forgotten, recalling all her bots to her. One of them brushed against the wire – *no no no*. Hoà sent it swerving away, almost into the next piece of wire.

Focus. She needed to focus.

Halfway to the door, another bot skidded on the floor, a little too close to a piece of wire. Hoà sent it a fraction to the right – breathing hard – focusing on keeping the other bots elsewhere. She wasn't sure how long she could hold her mental picture of where she'd placed the wire. She'd just made sure it surrounded the table with the bowls as thoroughly and as finely as possible, but now she needed to make it seem as though it wasn't there at all, and a mistake would be so easy, and so costly.

Almost there.

Almost there.

The last of her bots made it to her. Hoà let out her breath, and rose, shaking – pretending to be going to the alcoves. She had to trust the bot wasn't watching her heartbeat, or at least that it wasn't smart enough to know what to make of its elevated rate. It might know she was afraid and be concerned about the significance of that fear. Most bots wouldn't, but if it was one of the prefect's high-end ones ...

Hoà waited, heart in her throat.

Silence. Nothing. The bait had been too obvious. She should have known.

She could wait a moment longer. A few more anxious breaths that felt they were burning her throat. She could—

There was a sound, in the kitchen, a silken thing – a soft patter like the shortest of rains – and then nothing. Had it worked? She couldn't be sure.

Hoà walked to the door, and turned on the lights again – and there it was, a thumb-width away from the bowls, legs half-sheared away, innards glistening in the light. A bot with the seal of the prefect's house – a hastily repurposed one, judging from the lack of official identification and the haphazard re-painting of its body from vermilion to grey.

The prefect's house. The tribunal. The machinery of the Empire.

This wasn't what she'd signed up for when she agreed to take Thiên Dung's place. This—

No. No panic. Not now.

She sent Quỳnh's bots to respool the wires, and her other bots to dismantle the remaining legs of the lone prefect's bot.

She walked to it and turned it off; it was an easy enough task now that it couldn't evade her.

Then she sat down, breathing hard, to see what it could tell her.

'So, I gather it was an eventful night,' Thiên Dung said, when she woke up.

Hoà had been up early: she was sitting in the kitchen area downstairs, in the midst of an overlay of a pavilion with a pond, her bots and Quỳnh's in a tight circle around her bot. She was staring at the wreckage of the poisoner bot.

'You saw my messages.'

Hoà had sent messages to Thiên Dung, but she'd also received one. It had been there for a while. It was from Quỳnh, and it simply asked: 'Do you need help?'

She didn't know what answer she could give to that.

'Yes. They weren't always very clear.' Thiên Dung poured herself some tea, and swallowed three of the pills from Quỳnh's bottle. 'A bot?'

'Several. Some on board *Flowers at the Gates*. I'm not sure what damage they can do.'

'Other than poisoning?' Thiên Dung stared at the bot. 'That's—'

'A prefect's bot. Yes. But it's not from the tribunal.'

'No, of course not. The tribunal would have raided us and closed us down. Poisoning means someone who can't afford to be caught.'

'Mm.' Hoà stared at the bot. 'It's not Minh.'

Thiên Dung said nothing for a while. At length, she set aside the teacup.

'You suspected Minh, and now you feel you've been unfair.'

'Minh was unpleasant,' Hoà said. 'That's not a reason to suspect her.'

'To be fair,' Thiên Dung said, 'when you're the one being poisoned, people being unpleasant to you do shoot to the top of the list of possible poisoners. So if it's not Minh, who is it?'

Hoà stared at the bot for a while. 'The only one who benefits from the ship being declared unfit is the prefect.'

'But we know it's not her.'

'Yes,' Hoà said slowly, and said it all the same. 'It's not her. But she has a wife. And of course, anything that benefits the prefect would also benefit her wife.'

San. Minh's stepmother. She'd seen her in vids, in holos, by the prefect's side, always perfectly manicured and stern, unsmiling, except when her own child was running towards her.

Thiên Dung cocked her head, watching her. 'You don't know what to do with this information.'

'No,' Hoà said. 'It ... It means nothing. I've never met her. I've seen pictures. Holos. At official functions. In the news reels. But ...' It meant nothing. It felt unreal. Untrue.

'You feel she should hate us to want to harm us?' Thiên Dung shrugged. 'She won't. Her kind barely even know we exist.'

'I guess,' Hoà said.

'What are we going to do?'

Hoà touched the bot, feeling the sensors under her fingers. She remembered how it had felt to struggle to breathe – the rawness in her throat. She remembered Thiên Dung's breath hitching, the pallor of her face. She thought of the ship, and of the bots flooding a deserted corridor, trying to speak of the prefect and of Minh – *Flowers at the Gate*, the same ship that the prefect's wife would cheerfully kill because she meant nothing. She just stood in the way.

A cold, icy certainty rose in her.

'You are not going to do anything, but I am.'

And, before she could change her mind, she sent Quỳnh a curt, 'I know who's doing it, and I need your help to stop them.'

12

Confrontations

When Quỳnh walked into the shop, Thiên Dung – who had been arguing with Hoà – looked up.

'Oh,' she said. 'It's you. Please talk some sense into her.'

Quỳnh's face underwent a number of expressions. 'I can leave, if you'd rather.'

'No,' Hoà said. 'Please stay.'

They looked at each other. Hoà's face was burning.

'What kind of sense am I meant to put into you?' Quỳnh asked.

Hoà gave up.

'Thiên Dung knows about us,' she said. And, on a private comms channel, 'She doesn't know you're Dã Lan, and I'm not going to tell her.'

'I figured.' Quỳnh's voice was wry. She wore scholars' clothes – not a rich overlay, a subdued one that remined Hoà of her elder sister. Privately, she said to Hoà, 'Because it would distract her?'

'Because you don't want people to know.'

A pause. 'She's your sister. I wouldn't mind.'

The casual trust, more than anything, gave Hoà pause – it

was wholly undeserved and gave her the feeling of dancing on the edge of a chasm.

'I appreciate it,' she said, colouring. 'Really. But I don't think it's a good time.'

Thiên Dung's bots made tea and the small, crescent-shaped dumplings of Hoà's childhood, as Hoà and Quỳnh sat facing each other. For a moment Hoà remembered another time, when she was much smaller and listening to her elder sister and Dã Lan chatting about the merits of scholars. For a moment she felt such nostalgia for their lost home that she thought she was going to burst.

Thiên Dung pulled up a chair and sat, stone-faced, next to them, as Quỳnh's privacy overlay spread to cover the shop: that vast deserted plain with the white birds flying overhead.

'Don't even think of keeping me out of this one,' Thiên Dung said.

Quỳnh's voice was mild. 'You're one of the victims. You're owed restitution.'

Or revenge, Hoà thought. She was trying to focus on something.

'You've been to the prefect's house.'

'I haven't.' Quỳnh's voice was mild. 'But I've seen her more than once. You haven't told me what the problem is, exactly.'

Hoà sighed. 'It's the prefect's wife who's poisoning us.'

A silence. 'Minh's stepmother?'

Hoà described, as shortly as she could, what had happened, and then opened up the overlay to reveal the broken bot.

'She never came to the workshop,' Thiên Dung said.

'Did Minh come to the shop?'

A pause, from Thiên Dung. 'Yes. Once, with *Heart's Sorrow*. Hoà was out on an errand at the time and didn't see her. You think ...?'

Quỳnh stared at the bot, for a moment. 'I think she used

Minh as an unwitting carrier both times. It would be an easy enough matter to hide the bots in Minh's dress.'

'Surely Minh is smarter ...' Hoà said.

She saw Thiên Dung shake her head, that old amusement with a trace of pity. *You're too charitable to the people you don't like.* But it wasn't charity: it was fairness.

Quỳnh said softly, 'Minh has been worried about so many other things. It would be easy enough to sneak a bot or two past her.'

Hoà didn't dare ask what things, because she could guess. And she knew if she asked, Quỳnh would tell her exactly what she was doing and why. Then Hoà would have to walk away, or help her – and she was scared of making that choice.

'What do you want?' Quỳnh asked.

Thiên Dung scowled. Her bots, which were on the floor next to her, drew closer to one another.

'Justice.'

Quỳnh's smile was dark and biting. 'In this place?'

'I can hear the words you're not saying.' Thiên Dung crossed her arms over her chest. 'You mean for us.'

'I mean for everyone. The Belt isn't covered by the blue cloth of Heaven's fairness. It's altogether darker.'

It was so matter-of-fact it tore at Hoà's heart. Quỳnh really didn't believe in anything any more. Not in fairness, not in justice, not in happy endings. And Hoà knew why, but still ... Still, it hurt, as if some bright star had been forever dimmed.

Hoà said, 'I want the ship to be made whole. Which means stopping San.'

'You're meant to say you want to survive first, you know,' Quỳnh said. It was low and affectionate.

'She's always been very bad at that,' Thiên Dung said.

'I want San stopped, but—'

'But she's the prefect's wife.' Quỳnh poured herself tea,

offered some to Thiên Dung – who took it with a cautious nod. She was obviously still deciding if she liked Quỳnh.

Hoà said, 'Do you think the prefect approves of what she's doing?'

'Probably not,' Quỳnh said. 'But she won't stop her. If the ship never gets fixed, the transfer of lineage head goes ahead, and Đức gets access to all the wealth and power she's coveted in the personal sphere.' Her tone was dripping with sarcasm. Thiên Dung's face was a mask of horror.

'You can't—'

'Sedition?' Quỳnh sighed, her voice softening a fraction. The bots in her hair gleamed. 'We're past that, you realise. Your elder sister has evidence of an attempted double murder implicating the prefect's wife.'

'If it becomes public—'

'The scandal will be of epic proportions,' Quỳnh said. 'As prefect, she's doubly responsible for keeping order in her household. As the head of it, and as a magistrate.'

Hoà thought of it – of being *exposed* as a witness to an attempted murder and as the intended victim of another; of the torrent of questions and interrogations.

'No,' she said. 'I can't ...'

Quỳnh said, slowly and gently, 'There is work we can do in the dark. Rendering her harmless.'

'Poisoning her as she poisoned us?' Thiên Dung's voice was a challenge.

'Would that be fair?'

'No.' The words came out of Hoà's mouth before she could stop them. 'We're not doing that. That's not the way. We're not turning into murderers and poisoners, not even for justice.'

Quỳnh's gaze held her – grey, the colour of a mining ring turned to debris and cinders, of the darkness of the space the general and the prefect had cast her into. Then she sighed, and it was wistful and sad, as if something had passed out of her reach.

'Very well,' she said. 'Some other way, then. Harm doesn't have to be physical or real.'

'You mean threats.'

'I mean blackmail.' Quỳnh put her hands on the table, a bot coming down her arm to encircle her wrist. 'We won't cause a scandal, but San has absolutely no reason to believe that.'

'A scandal with her wife?' Hoà started, and then said, 'No. With the censor. The one coming for the transfer of lineage. She can't afford the scandal and neither can the prefect.'

'No, she can't. Her position is fragile. The Empire is thankful for her maintaining order, but Censor Tang Thuyền — the one who is coming — has no fondness for Serpents. Or corrupt officials.'

'Would she demote the prefect?'

Quỳnh's voice was bitter. 'Not unless the situation was dire and Prefect Đức lost control, or was widely discredited. Or both. The Empire will always choose the preservation of order and stability. Even if that means sacrificing some righteousness.'

Of course, Quỳnh would have more than enough reason to be bitter.

Hoà stared at her bots — the ones she'd lost felt like missing limbs, and she felt vulnerable without them.

Blackmail.

'No,' she said. 'We're not doing that, either.'

Quỳnh raised an eyebrow. 'Are you afraid of being noticed by her?'

'Rightly so,' Thiên Dung said. 'She's the prefect's *wife*. You might move with the powerful and the wealthy and the cultured, but we're just technologists they'd be quite happy to purge. She could swat us and not even remember she'd done it.'

Something was rising within Hoà, a mixture of fear and anxiety and a hard, desperate certainty.

'No,' she said again. 'I'm afraid, and that won't make me a good blackmailer. San will be on the lookout for any weaknesses if we try. But, more importantly ...' She sighed, again. 'It isn't right. I'm not a blackmailer, and neither should you be.' She addressed this last to Thiên Dung, who was glowering at Quỳnh in a very petulant manner that made her seem years younger.

'And how do you suggest we stop her? By asking nicely?' Thiên Dung sounded as though she was ready to march into the prefect's compound and ask in a decidedly not nice manner. Her bots were clustered together in an aggressive configuration. Hoà knew the signs: Thiên Dung was exhausted, angry, and ready to do anything to put an end to it all, even if it wasn't the smartest or best thing.

Hoà was just ... scared. Scared of losing the ship, scared of losing Quỳnh – and most of all, scared of losing herself. Not her life, but her self-respect. The values she stood by, the honesty she tried to keep to.

She said, 'If the ship is fixed, then she's got no motive to continue poisoning us.'

'I disagree.' Quỳnh's face was grave for once – her hand resting lightly on Hoà's own, a jolt of unexpected warmth. 'Revenge is a powerful thing.'

As she should know. But San wasn't Quỳnh. Poison was a coward's weapon, not an elaborate scheme like whatever Quỳnh had in mind. San didn't want to be caught. Quỳnh ... Hoà was well aware that Quỳnh *expected* to be caught, and had to complete her revenge first. And ... Hoà didn't want to think what that meant for the tentative thing they had together.

'Not if San knows she can't get away with it.'

'So how do you exactly intend to achieve this miracle?'

Hoà said simply, 'Everything changes if the ship knows.' She'd have told the prefect, too, but the idea of informing the woman who'd caused Quỳnh's collapse that her own wife was attempting murder terrified Hoà to her bones. 'She'll remain head of the lineage, and as such will be responsible for San's behaviour.'

'So you're throwing herself on her mercy and hoping she'll protect you?' Thiên Dung's face was eloquent in its fury.

'I'd be asking for protection in exchange for services rendered,' Hoà said. 'Why does that make you so angry?'

'Because we've never been beholden to them. To any of them. Why would you start now?'

Hoà stared at Quỳnh – who simply squeezed her hand, her gaze open and curious. Not judging. Just watching. It gave Hoà the courage to say, 'Sometimes you need the shadow of someone's grace.'

'I don't agree,' Thiên Dung said.

Hoà said finally, 'I can ask only for myself. I'd ... I'd prefer it if you were protected, too, but I can't force you.' The thought that Thiên Dung might be poisoned was a leaden weight in her belly. And, to Quỳnh: 'Can you keep me safe until the ship is fixed?'

'Absolutely,' Quỳnh said. There was no hesitation. 'How long are we talking about?'

Hoà thought. 'I don't know,' she said finally. 'All we need is for the ship to be aware and able to defend herself, and she's already partly awake. That's not the same as fixing the motors, or even the initial job you took on. It should be easier.'

Thiên Dung looked from Quỳnh to Hoà, and sniffed.

'When is the censor coming?'

Quỳnh's eyes went distant for a moment, the privacy screen wavering – the birds becoming a fraction less defined.

'The tribunal has planned for a welcoming ceremony in four days.'

'Four days. That's not a lot, but it's doable if I come with you.'

'I thought you didn't agree,' Hoà said, puzzled.

'I don't.' Thiên Dung glared at Hoà. 'I'm not happy, and I'm not asking for any ship's protection. But you obviously need someone watching your back. Several someones. And also, I have the expertise to fix the ship, and neither of you do.' Another glare.

'Thank you,' Hoà said.

'Don't mention it.' Thiên Dung said to Quỳnh, 'I'll have more of that antidote, if you have it.'

Quỳnh looked amused, but her voice was grave and courteous. 'I'd advise waiting a few days before actually going anywhere.'

'Duly noted.' Thiên Dung's voice was brisk. 'And no thank you.'

She and Quỳnh stared at each other for a while, and Hoà thought she could see the sparks flying between them. The last thing she needed was for them to be at each other's throats.

'Can you please make an effort to get on?'

Thiên Dung raised an eyebrow. 'Duly noted,' she said, and it sounded like she was laughing.

'Good,' Hoà said. 'Now let's go and fix a ship.'

Minh had no idea how much time had passed on board *Flowers at the Gates*. The light didn't change, and her bots had scattered across the deserted room.

Mother was fair. Mother was just. She was harsh, which was exactly what the Empire needed, in the years after the Ten Thousand Flags Uprising.

Only ...

Only there was nothing of fairness in this, at all.

'Big sis!'

It was *Heart's Sorrow*, her friend shimmering into existence in the middle of the ruined floor. His bots' legs clicked on the floor: he was here, then, or as physically present as he could hope to be.

'I thought I'd find you here,' *Heart's Sorrow* said.

Minh laughed. 'Really? I was never very enthusiastic about fixing her.'

Heart's Sorrow's image wavered. She'd wounded him. And done it so easily; he was earnest and kind. He said, after a silence, 'Is this really the time?'

'I don't know,' Minh said. 'You tell me.'

'You have everyone worried sick,' *Heart's Sorrow* said. 'Oanh's twins are bickering about search parties. 'Your mother—'

'I don't want to hear about my mother,' Minh snapped.

He leaned sideways, staring at her. 'I was actually going to say that your mother *doesn't* sound very worried. She's too busy preparing for the Orca Censor's visit. Her ship is touching down in the Belt in two days' time, and your mother is preparing a grand reception. She hasn't realised you're gone. She's worried because Censor Tang Thuyên isn't really her friend, and she's got a reputation when it comes to officials she doesn't like.'

Serpents. And corrupt officials. And Mother was certainly the first, and Minh couldn't be certain she wasn't the second. She inhaled, slowly, sharply. Was this good? She didn't have to worry about confronting Mother. But Mother didn't care, either.

'I'm sure she'll be fine. And she'll worry about me, eventually. When she needs someone to display to the Orca Censor.'

A silence, then a ghostly squeeze from *Heart's Sorrow* on Minh's shoulders.

'Is this about her? I thought it was about the ship.'

'Maybe it is about the ship.'

Minh was still thinking of the data flowing between her fingers: of the revelations within; of the litany of injustices she could barely begin to comprehend. How could she respond to this?

A silence. A touch on both of her shoulders: his bots, gently resting on her skin, their coldness spreading from the sharp point of contact to the rest of her shoulder blades. The overlay became fuzzy and slightly out of focus, as if wrapping her in some cocoon away from the rest of the world.

'Why are you here, big sis? Just ... don't snap at me because you think keeping me at bay is easier.'

'Why are *you* here?'

'I'm here because I was worried about you,' *Heart's Sorrow* said. 'Don't worry about the twins. I've got them handled.'

Minh heard what he wasn't saying. 'Your mother—'

'Yes. I wanted to find you before either of our mothers did. Or Quỳnh.'

Quỳnh. Minh thought of that extended hand at the party, the casual empathy.

'Is Quỳnh worried?'

A snort from *Heart's Sorrow*. 'Worried? Quỳnh doesn't really worry about anyone.'

'She did,' Minh said. 'About me.'

A slow, cautious exhalation. He was upset and angry, and trying not to show it.

'I really don't want to talk about this.'

'Don't you?'

'It's not the right time.'

'Well, I don't want to talk about why I'm here,' Minh said. 'So how about you tell me what you mean?'

'I mean that you've been hanging out with Quỳnh far too

much and with far too little caution. How do you even know you can trust her?'

'You mean unlike my mother? The one who's been sitting on *years* of miscarriages of justice and cruelty, and pretends to be fair?'

A silence, like the one after a gut punch.

'I mean that no matter what your mother has done or not done, you can't just trust a stranger with everything! Is Quỳnh the one who told you this about your mother?'

'What if she is?'

'I told you! She comes out of nowhere, conveniently rescues you and inveigles herself into your favour, and everyone's favour, and every single person around me is acting like it's totally natural. Except your mother, and I never thought I would ever agree with your mother!'

Quỳnh had seen her. Not as the prefect's daughter, but as someone struggling to get out of her shadow – an uncertain, angry, perceptive teenager.

'She's not the issue. And she's not the one who *told* me this, as you put it. I got the information from someone else.'

'Who?'

'Scholars.' Minh opened her mouth to tell him who – surely they told each other everything and had no secrets – and then she realised that the thought of his reaction made her sick. 'Does it matter? All the information is there.'

'You can make information say whatever you want.' He sounded concerned again, in a way that just made her angry. He just made her feel like an unreasonable child pitching a temper tantrum – as if what she'd seen and learned was a meaningless attempt at manipulation from Quỳnh, or some elaborate plot by the scholars. Everything dissected for motive rather than for meaning.

'Not this information,' Minh said. 'Not this much of it. Just go. I'll make my own way back.'

'I'm not leaving you alone in the dark on this ship.'

Heart's Sorrow was spinning again, a sign of distress. Concerned about her, only nothing he said was coming out right, everything just making her angrier and angrier.

I'm not a child any more – how dare he treat me like one? How dare Mother treat me like one?

'I'm *fine*.'

'You don't sound fine,' *Heart's Sorrow* said. 'And don't claim you intend to fix the ship this late at night.'

Minh stared at the ship around her – at the wreck of her great-aunt surrounding them both: the gouged-out walls, the silence, the nonexistent bots. A corpse in almost every way, except that she felt safe there, in a way she didn't elsewhere – as if she still remembered being held, being comforted, back before the accident. She opened her mouth to say they couldn't fix her – to wound him deliberately, to make him turn away, to be her mother's daughter.

But then he spoke. 'What ... ?'

He shared what he'd just received: a shuttle heading their way, its sheen-pattern unfamiliar, not *Heart's Sorrow* or any of the transports Minh habitually used. And on board ...

It was Hoà, the useless technologist – the one who'd managed to get her bots destroyed on the way to finding the heartroom. With her was her younger sister, whom Minh had met once. And ...

Minh's blood ran cold, because the third person on board – leaning against the bulwark, cool and composed and utterly unexpected – was Quỳnh.

13

Reparations

Quỳnh wasn't altogether surprised to see Minh and *Heart's Sorrow* waiting for them when they arrived at the spaceship. She'd hoped to be able to tighten her protection around Hoà without having to deal with either of them, but she knew the value of wishful thinking.

Once the initial presentations had been made, it looked like they'd formed battle lines: *Heart's Sorrow* and Minh on one side; Hoà and Thiên Dung on the other. Quỳnh hesitated, but remained in the centre, watching Hoà warily.

'Explain again.'

Minh sounded annoyed and terse. She was dishevelled and looked like she hadn't slept in hours, which meant that *Guts of Sea* had done her work and she'd found out about her mother's pattern of sentencing. What she'd do with it ... well, hopefully it would be enough for her to take a position, but maybe she'd need another nudge before that happened. Looking at Minh's drawn face, Quỳnh felt, again, that twinge of regret that things had to be that way. But she couldn't afford that. She was out to hurt. There were so many ways she could hurt

Đức, and she'd need them all before she was done, in order to trigger Đức's downfall.

'How many times do we have to say "poisoning"?'

Thiên Dung, in many ways, was the polar opposite of Hoà. It didn't really seem to matter to her who her counterparts were, or what power their parents might wield. She just hit them with all she had. No, that wasn't fair. Hoà had the same disregard for consequences or social class – if the cause was just. She was just far more soft-spoken.

'No one is poisoning anyone.' Minh glared at them. She kept glancing uncertainly at Quỳnh, as if not sure what to make of her presence, but she hadn't dared ask so far.

'Bots have been doing it,' Thiên Dung snapped. Her own bots were on her shoulders, their legs tight, underlining her angry posture. 'Now, can Hoà and I fix the ship, please?'

'There's only two of you, and one of you lost half her bots finding the heartroom.' Minh's voice was wounding. 'I'm not sure you're fixing anything.'

'I'm going to need a little more context.' *Heart's Sorrow* hadn't been watching Minh or Hoà, but Quỳnh, and his look was decidedly unfriendly. 'I understand both you and your sister got poisoned ...' His voice softened when he mentioned Hoà. He liked her. Interesting. Quỳnh filed that away with all the other information she wasn't quite sure how to use yet. 'And you said bots are doing it, but you sound like you definitely know who is behind it.'

Thiên Dung stopped, then. She looked at Hoà – who hadn't said a word, but had been trying to melt back into the wall. Hoà looked at Quỳnh, who would have laughed, in other circumstances, but this was utterly serious. She was going to have to navigate it carefully if she wanted to keep both her revenge and her relationship with Hoà intact.

'That's not entirely relevant to the issue at hand.'

'I'm going to need to know why you're here.' *Heart's Sorrow*'s voice was blunt, his bots clustering around him and Minh in a clearly defensive manner. He was concerned about her involvement. Afraid of her. Interesting. He'd barely seen her or what she was capable of.

'I'm here as Hoà's friend,' Quỳnh said.

'Not for Minh's sake?' *Heart's Sorrow*'s voice was dry.

'Do you want me to lie?' Quỳnh asked.

'I think you lie as easily as you breathe,' *Heart's Sorrow* said.

'You have your bots,' Quỳnh said. 'You can check if I'm lying.'

A silence, so tense she could have cut it with a knife, while *Heart's Sorrow* spun and spun, glaring at her.

It was Hoà who broke it.

'We don't want to fix the entire ship,' she said. 'We just want to make sure she's conscious and able to defend herself before the Orca Censor arrives.'

Minh stared at her, and then back at Quỳnh. Her face went pale, bleached of all colour. Quỳnh knew what she was thinking: she had her mother's transgressions fresh in her mind, so would naturally think of her mother as the guilty party. Quỳnh weighed the consequences in a fraction of a second, running hypotheses through her own bots: what would they gain, if they denounced Minh's stepmother? Not necessarily a lot. There would be explanations and disbelief, and in the short time frame they had before the Orca Censor arrived, finding whoever was responsible wouldn't change much of anything. Minh's mother, on the other hand, made a handy and believable culprit. And...

Well, it wouldn't hurt if Đức's house was in a fraction more disarray, would it?

She sent to Thiên Dung and Hoà, 'Let me handle this', and said, 'You understand now.'

Minh's face was white, her gaze distant. She was messaging *Heart's Sorrow*, who was getting angrier and angrier and trying not to show it – but Quỳnh could read it in the curve of his avatar, in his increasingly fast tilting and swerving.

Heart's Sorrow said, 'You have no proof.'

'I'm not here for proof,' Quỳnh said, which was perfectly true.

Hoà said, '*Flowers at the Gates* is *alive*, and someone is trying to kill her. Can we stop arguing for a moment and care about the right things?'

Quỳnh felt an upswelling of pride and warmth that threatened to burst through her chest. She could have kissed Hoà then and there, except Hoà would never have forgiven her for making their relationship public.

Heart's Sorrow looked at Hoà, for a while. Thinking. He was going to give more leeway ...

'How do you know Quỳnh?'

Hoà breathed fast and hard, as if she'd just been shoved into deep spaces.

Oh no you don't.

Quỳnh said, smoothly and fast, 'I'm an old friend of the family.' Which was perfectly true.

'Is that so?' *Heart's Sorrow* asked, but he was looking at Hoà, not Quỳnh.

Hoà nodded, mutely. She was blushing furiously, and Quỳnh could see *Heart's Sorrow* weighing them, weighing their reactions to each other. He was smart – and much more observant than Minh, much less encumbered by self-hatred and years of abuse, much better trained. One of his mothers, after all, had been an enforcer whose life depended on noticing small discrepancies and details.

So much for hiding themselves.

Why couldn't he have taken after Tuyết? Although that would have made it much harder to deal with him at all.

Perhaps she was being too harsh. They were kids, and they didn't know what their parents had done. They'd benefited from it all, and she knew her plans would likely hurt them in some fashion. She couldn't afford to think of either of them as anything more than adversaries or bargaining chips.

'Hmmm,' *Heart's Sorrow* said. 'Fine. I agree fixing *Flowers at the Gates* should be the priority. How do you propose we go about it?'

Minh still hadn't spoken. She looked as though she'd had a set of nasty shocks, her bots slack on her shoulders and back, and Quỳnh saw pity in Hoà's eyes when she looked at her. She wanted to say Hoà was too soft, but it was more that she worried that Hoà's care for everyone but herself would wear her down to the bone.

Hoà opened her hands, and between them shimmered an overlay of the bot she'd taken apart.

'There are probably a lot of these on board. You need to make sure they're disabled.'

'They're doing the poisoning?' *Heart's Sorrow* asked.

'And other things,' Hoà said. 'Sabotage.' Her voice was hard. And, more gently, to Minh, 'It's a lot to take in, I know. It shocked me, too.'

'I don't need …' Minh started, and then stopped, fists clenched, breathing hard. 'I'm sorry. It's been a trying few hours. I need some space.'

And she sat down, a privacy screen shimmering into view around her.

Heart's Sorrow did the mindship equivalent of blushing, the patches of colour on his avatar flickering.

'I'm sorry,' he said. 'She'll come around. She does love her great-aunt, but—'

'But she's been out of Minh's life for a long time, and it's a lot to realise she might suddenly be healed?' Hoà's voice was sharp. Why had Quỳnh thought she was soft? That was as unforgiving as a paring-knife wound.

Heart's Sorrow said nothing. He didn't need to.

'What else?' he asked instead, to Hoà.

Thiên Dung said, 'Heartroom access. Which means convincing the ship not to kill us first.'

'How long is this going to take?'

Thiên Dung hesitated. 'Big sis—'

Hoà said, 'It would be best if we remained on board for the three days. We can take shifts.'

Quỳnh said, 'I can look for the bots.' And, to *Heart's Sorrow*, with an ironic bow from elder to younger, 'Your bots can help, too, since you don't trust me.'

'Oh, I definitely don't,' *Heart's Sorrow* said. 'But I'll trust Hoà that in this specific case, you'll do what you promised to do.'

Hoà blushed furiously. 'I can't—'

'That's a lot, isn't it?' *Heart's Sorrow*'s voice was soft and compassionate. 'Promises made on behalf of other people you may not know as well as you think you do.'

How dare he?

He was Tuyết's son – the son of the woman who had ruined Quỳnh's life – and he spoke so blithely, so wisely, of things he knew nothing about.

Quỳnh opened her mouth, but Hoà said, 'It's my life, not yours.' And then she seemed to realise what she said, and panicked. 'Sorry, I really shouldn't ...'

A sigh from *Heart's Sorrow*. 'We've been over this before. No apologies for honesty.'

Now he pities me? From his eighteen years of soft, rich life, he lectures me as if I were a naive child?

Quỳnh opened her mouth, but Hoà got there first.

'Please don't,' she messaged Quỳnh. 'I really don't want this to centre on me.' The words were fast, unsteady. She was scared. Of course. Too much limelight.

'As you wish,' Quỳnh said on the same private channel.

Heart's Sorrow gave a satisfied sigh, as if some private suspicion had been confirmed. Quỳnh made a note to keep an eye on him. He was too perceptive, and too volatile, and not in ways she could take advantage of.

'I'm going to hunt for bots,' Quỳnh said, reconfiguring her own bots to recognise either the appearance or the signature of the offending bots. She pinged *Guts of Sea*.

'Yes?' *Guts of Sea* asked.

'I need some help.'

'Mmmm?' *Guts of Sea* sounded distracted

'I need to filter out bots with known owners, and disable or kill all the other ones.'

A silence.

Guts of Sea said finally, 'You're on the ship, aren't you? *Flowers at the Gates*.'

'Yes.'

'With Hoà?'

'Yes.' Quỳnh didn't elaborate, because she knew whatever she said would result in a castigation for straying too far from their revenge, from the goal *Guts of Sea* held above all other goals. 'Minh is here, too. She got a series of very nasty shocks about her mother and is busy processing them. That part of the plan is working perfectly.'

'Mmm,' *Guts of Sea* said. 'I know what you're doing.'

Quỳnh said nothing.

'You understand that you'll bring Hoà nothing but trouble.'

Guts of Sea sounded sad. 'I just hope it finishes before anything bad happens to her.'

Quỳnh looked at Hoà – who was now talking with Thiên Dung and *Heart's Sorrow*, making animated gestures as she demonstrated something. She'd drawn a map of the ship in public overlay, and was busy pointing things on it. She was in her element – alive, flushed with excitement, smiling and laughing and looking absolutely stunning. It squeezed at Quỳnh's heart.

Quỳnh thought of carrying her, pale and barely breathing – of the same bots that had poisoned her lurking in the pipes and in the corridors of the broken ship, invisible and deadly. Of Minh and *Heart's Sorrow* and all the attention Hoà had wanted to avoid – steadily coming to the attention of the powerful, a world of appearances that would crush Hoà to dust and never even pause to regret. After all, who would miss a mere technologist?

'Nothing is going to happen,' Quỳnh said, with more confidence than she felt. 'Because I have this under control.'

Guts of Sea said nothing more. She didn't need to.

'Here,' she said. 'The algorithmic update you wanted for the bots. Be careful with the filter, or you'll take out everything around you.'

'Thank you,' Quỳnh said.

'Be careful, lil sis? This is unexpected.'

'You're too cautious.'

'It's my job.' *Guts of Sea* huffed. 'Don't get killed before we can pull it off. Oh, and, regarding the prefect—'

'Yes?'

'She's throwing a party to welcome the Orca Censor in three days' time. Everyone who's anyone in the Belt is invited, and that includes us. And the general.'

'Perfect.' Quỳnh smiled.

That part of the plan was proceeding as expected. Đức could

have arrested Tuyết then and there, but of course she wasn't going to do that – not if she could humiliate the general in front of an imperial censor and all the dignitaries of the Belt.

Of course Đức would wait – and it would make Tuyết's fall all the sweeter.

While Quỳnh was hunting killer bots, Hoà, Thiên Dung and *Heart's Sorrow* went into the wreck of the ship, Hoà and Thiên Dung with shadow-skins and gliders, and *Heart's Sorrow* merely materialising elsewhere on the wreck. He looked upset, and Hoà wasn't going to address that, but it was an uncomfortable thing to witness.

Thiên Dung, muttering darkly to herself, went straight for the room where Hoà had seen the flow of *Flowers at the Gates*' bots. She kneeled in the middle of what had been the overlay, unpacking the very large box she'd brought with her – glaring at *Heart's Sorrow* as though challenging him to disturb her.

Hoà said, 'It's not safe.'

Thiên Dung shrugged, pointing to three of Quỳnh's bots on the wall above them.

'It will be.'

'I wasn't talking about these bots.' Hoà stabilised her glider, trying to forget how it had felt to fight to breathe. '*Flowers at the Gates* has some, too.'

'Mmm. If they show up, we'll deal with it then.' Thiên Dung eyed a series of instruments. 'How comfortable are you getting closer to that door?'

Hoà eyed the door. It was dark and massive, and the last time she'd seen it from up close, butterfly lasers had taken out her bots.

'Not very, in person. Are you paying for my replacement bots?'

'We're paying,' *Heart's Sorrow* said decisively.

That didn't really make Hoà feel better.

'All right,' she said cautiously.

She eyed Quỳnh's bots on the wall. At least no one was going to try and sabotage things again.

She said aloud, 'We're just here to help you. We know someone has been tampering with your repairs, and we want to make sure you're safe.'

She nudged her bots forward, towards the door. The heart-room: the place where the ship lived and died. She held her breath, clinging to her glider, as the bots neared the door. Shaking camera views – any moment now the ship was going to protest. Instead, what she got was simply the door, closed tight – and a sense of something large and barely contained inside.

'Lil sis,' she said to Thiên Dung.

'What is it?'

'Can you feel it?'

'No.' Thiên Dung picked up a screwdriver and a vacuum blade, cursed at the tangle of wires that came with them. 'What am I meant to feel?'

There was ... a presence. One that made the room heavier than it should have been. Not an overlay, but something that suffused everything and made it sharper.

'The ship,' Hoà whispered.

And in answer, on a private comms channel, she simply received images – blurred and indecipherable – and fragments of sound, like voices run through an aggressive filter.

'She's in there,' Hoà said. 'She's waiting for us. She ...' It wasn't that hard to interpret. 'She doesn't want us to open the door.'

'She wouldn't.' *Heart's Sorrow*'s voice was quiet. 'You only show trusted people into your heartroom. She's got no reason to trust us. Minh, possibly …'

But Minh was still thinking. Or sulking. Or crying. Hoà wasn't sure which. It was obvious Minh was under a tremendous amount of stress, and equally obvious that their being on the ship – and whatever Quỳnh had said – had just made it worse. But for all that … Minh didn't like her, and likely never would. It was the usual contempt of the scholar class for the technologists. That they were both Serpent wouldn't really matter.

Hoà tried to recall Quỳnh's lesson.

'We don't need access right now.'

'No,' Thiên Dung said. 'We just need to help her shore up her defences. She's recovering all by herself.' She used a series of pronouns that didn't make it clear whether she was addressing the ship or them.

Hoà decided to make it explicit.

'Do we have your permission?'

More inchoate, fragmented images from the ship. A sense of … frustration.

'She doesn't think it's going to be enough,' Hoà said.

'We're not going to be able to do more without access to the heartroom,' Thiên Dung said, confirming Hoà's suspicions.

Another series of pulses. One of Hoà's bots skidded on the floor, dragged towards the door until it ran smack into it.

'You want the bots in? Or me?'

The entire door seemed to shudder and split, irising open – except that the opening was too small for anything but a line of bots. Well, that was clear. Hoà shivered. She breathed in, shaking – trying to steady herself – and sent a single bot through the opening.

Inside was a jumbled, inchoate darkness at first, then an unfolding of space. The bots sensors caught the ship's heartroom only through bits and pieces: a mass of writhing cables; the clicking of other bots' legs on the floor; a sound, rising up, a distant thing that sounded like a pulse and then became a steady heartbeat, seizing the bot and resonating through its entire body. Hoà leaned on the wall – and felt the heartbeat there, too, almost like a phantom pain.

Thiên Dung, who was seeing all of this through their shared connection, said, 'She's awake.' Her voice was almost reverent. 'Putting herself back together.'

Labels came on to the bot's image as Thiên Dung rattled off a series of technical explanations, too fast for Hoà to follow.

Heart's Sorrow was gently pinging her. Asking for access. Hoà hesitated, then granted it to him. A long silence, then he said, 'I didn't think it was so bad.' There was awe and guilt in his voice, and something else.

'Are you worried she can't be fixed?' Hoà asked.

Heart's Sorrow said nothing for a while. Then, 'I don't know. I don't know.'

Neither did Hoà, but she felt the ship all around her – in a way that she hadn't before, and that heartbeat was in her hands and in her bots. She sent another one into the heart-room – half-expecting it to be sheared in two, bracing herself against the shock of losing it. But instead, there was just more of that silence. Waiting. *Flowers at the Gates* was waiting.

'Here.' Thiên Dung was labelling part after part, repairs that needed to be dealt with. 'This connector needs to be replaced. This needs to be rewired, and this as well. And this.'

It was going almost too fast for Hoà – Quỳnh's lessons seemed so far away – but then she remembered Quỳnh's touch steadying her, and as she stared at everything Thiên Dung was labelling, the shape of the repairs suddenly started making sense to her.

'Here.' She pointed to a patch of darkness further in the room, on the edge of some steps. 'This is completely blocked.'

Thiên Dung made an appreciative noise in the back of her throat.

'True. Anywhere else?' She sounded grudgingly impressed.

'Here,' Hoà said.

Her first bot had scuttled deeper into the room, and still the ship allowed it through. Still the ship watched her – a disquieting thing, like the tiger that had ripped through the habitats in the wake of the Tiger Games; the attention of something huge and unpleasant. No, that wasn't it. She was like *Heart's Sorrow*. She wasn't huge or inhuman, or even incomprehensible. She was damaged and worried – a saboteur had been blocking her repairs – and the ship was unsure who she could trust.

'We'll fix you,' Hoà said. 'Enough that you can defend yourself.'

A slow shift, a growing warmth. A missing beat from the huge heart that seemed to have hers in tow.

'There,' Thiên Dung said, pushing away, back towards her box on the floor. 'Now we wait.'

Hoà thought about withdrawing her bots from the heart-room, but no, it wasn't fair to leave *Flowers at the Gates* in the darkness.

Something flared in Hoà's field of view: she realised it was Minh, who was wearing the last of the shadow-suits and was silently moving towards them. *Heart's Sorrow*'s entire attention had moved to her; something was going on between them, on a channel neither Hoà nor Thiên Dung was privy to.

'She's not much fun, is she?' Thiên Dung asked, on a private channel of their own.

Hoà made a face. 'She's not been very forthcoming. Or generous.'

'How much trouble is she going to be?' Thiên Dung pursed her lips.

Hoà tamped down the sheer panic at the thought of what Minh's mother could do to her or to Thiên Dung — sweep them up the same way she'd rounded up the technologists after the Tiger Games.

'So long as nothing happens to her, I think we're fine.'

'Mmm.' Thiên Dung made a sound that seemed a lot like *rich kids*. 'I hope not.'

'We'll be fine,' Hoà said, just as Minh halted, still quite far from the door.

'I'm sorry,' Minh said. 'I wasn't very pleasant to either of you.'

'I'm sorry?' Hoà asked.

Rueful laughter from Minh, but it had an edge. Her bots were clinging to the wall by her side, in a cautious configuration.

'You're trying to help my great-aunt. I'm grateful. It's just ... been a lot to think about lately.'

'That's fine,' Hoà said, though it wasn't fine, really. She wasn't sure what to make of Minh. And what had Quỳnh been up to with her? 'We're just waiting for—'

'We've reconnected the emergency and self-defence pathways from the heartroom to the rest of the ship,' Thiên Dung said sharply. 'Your great-aunt should be in a better position to deal with the sabotage attempts now.'

'And the poisonings?' Minh's voice was just as sharp.

The only thing that came to Hoà was the truth.

'Your great-aunt won't let these continue, once she's back.'

A silence. Minh was watching her. Weighing her. It was not ... not just disconcerting, but panic-inducing, because it felt as though she was seeing Hoà as a person, not just as someone who repaired the ship.

'I see,' she said finally. 'Thank you.'

And she moved back, wedging herself against a wall and waited.

Hoà wasn't sure whether she'd given any of the right answers. Thiên Dung didn't really seem to care; Hoà could feel her exasperated amusement through the channel. She shut it down, and remained where she was, one hand on the wall, feeling the ship's heartbeat in the gloves of her suit.

A ping on a private channel.

'Are you quite recovered?' *Heart's Sorrow* asked. He'd thrown together a hasty overlay that reminded her faintly of station space, and isolated both of them.

'I'm sorry?' Hoà asked.

'After the poisoning,' *Heart's Sorrow* said.

Oh, Ancestors help me. He's trying to be sociable again.

'I'm fine,' Hoà said curtly. 'Thank you for inquiring.'

He sighed, his avatar blinking in and out of existence. 'We've been over this before.'

The thought of what he could do – of what his *mother* could do – if either were so minded, was like a naked blade in Hoà's thoughts.

'Yes,' she said. 'We have.'

'Will you at least tell me what happened?'

Hoà considered not telling him. 'It was my water bottle. Cinnabar Clouds.'

A sharp intake of breath, the avatar sheening red: Anger. 'That's lethal.'

'Yes. Fortunately Quỳnh had the antidote.'

'Quỳnh.' His voice was low, and thoughtful. A judgement there. Something he'd noted. She felt sick to her stomach. She didn't need his attention.

'You don't like her,' Hoà said.

A slow gyration: indifference. 'No. I'd offer you my advice, but I don't think you'd take it, would you?'

No, she didn't want it. She *really, really* didn't.

'If you're here to judge, I don't think this is the place.'

'No.' *Heart's Sorrow* picked his words carefully. 'You know she's not who she pretends to be.'

Dã Lan. The fear in Quỳnh's voice when she'd spoken of Đức, the sorrow and anger at Tuyết. None of this was his fault, but ... but that he still dared to try and impugn her.

'Many people aren't what they pretend to be.' Hoà barely kept the biting edge from her voice. 'I don't understand what you're trying to do.'

'I'm going to find out.' *Heart's Sorrow* stopped then. 'She's been ... talking to a friend.'

'Minh?' Hoà asked.

'Yes,' *Heart's Sorrow* said. 'Why do you think she's in this state?'

'I can tell you're worried about her,' Hoà said slowly, carefully – backing down in the face of his anger and the consequences it was likely to have for her. 'But you can understand I would care less about her than you do.'

Laughter. It wasn't amused, but it wasn't aggressive either. Just ... jaded in a way that it shouldn't have been for someone so young.

'No. And I don't expect you to. But I'm not going to be the only one who looks in to her.'

Hoà's blood chilled. 'You're bringing your mother into it? Is that what you're doing? Threatening me?'

'We seem to keep talking past each other. I'm not here to threaten you! I just want to make sure ...' He spun and spun around in frustration. 'I just want everyone to be all right.'

A child's wish, an impossible thing. Too many wounds, too much death.

'Then what is it that you're trying to tell me?'

'You know who Minh's mother is. She's going to take an interest. When she does, do you trust Quỳnh to keep you safe?'

More than anything, it was the concern in his voice – something he didn't have the right to – that felt almost unnatural. The children of the wealthy didn't worry about people like her. *No one* worried about people like her. It didn't make her feel safer. It made her *seen* – and being seen was dangerous.

'She said she would,' Hoà said.

His voice was pitying. 'And you believed her?'

'Are you accusing her of lying?'

'Not yet. But no one is going to protect you against the prefect, except perhaps the Orca Censor, and will the Orca Censor really take your side?'

Of course she wouldn't. No official would. Hoà was Serpent, and a technologist, making her an outcast in more ways than one.

'Quỳnh will protect me,' she said again.

She trusted Quỳnh – she did – but he was right: the prefect was all-powerful and officials always won out.

Hoà watched Minh, watched *Heart's Sorrow*. She'd known the danger. She'd known it when she'd chosen to come back and do the right thing. When she'd chosen to be with Quỳnh. And yet...

'Stop being opaque,' Hoà said.

'You want me to be blunt? You should leave.'

'With the ship still in danger?'

'Lil sis, it's not the ship who's in danger. It's you.'

'That's not ...' Hoà opened her mouth to speak, and found only the taste of poison on her tongue. 'That's not because of Quỳnh.'

'Quỳnh will make it worse. Quỳnh is trouble.'

'Because you're going to find out who she is?'

A silence. 'You know, don't you?'

Hoà exhaled slowly. 'It's not my secret to tell.' Daring him to do what his kind always did: take and take and never give any thought to what they broke.

Hoà even longer silence, his avatar watching her unblinkingly.

'No, it's not, is it? I respect that. But you understand that I cannot let Quỳnh rampage through our lives without intervening.'

'She's not ...' Hoà opened her mouth to protest at his description, closed it again. She'd chosen not to ask Quỳnh about what she was doing, and she couldn't make any promises on Quỳnh's behalf. It made her faintly dirty and dishonest – especially with *Flowers at the Gates*' heartbeat still pulsing under her fingers.

'I'm going to find out who she is and what she wants,' *Heart's Sorrow* said. 'And so are our mothers. And when I do ... I really, really hope that you're not there any more.'

'Because we're *friends*?' She spat the words in his face, fighting the rising wave of panic.

'Because I would hope we can be, yes.' His voice was serious. 'But I don't think that's likely to happen if you remain in Quỳnh's orbit. And I don't think it's the right place for you. You're a kind person, lil sis.'

'You know nothing.'

Hoà was choking on her panic. He was seeing her, taking in the whole of her, and there was nowhere she could run from his scrutiny.

'I know you're not *her*. I know you came back to help *Flowers at the Gates*. I know Minh was unpleasant to you and you still try to be fair. I know you're terrified right now.'

She was. *Of him*. Of what he could do. Of what the prefect and the general could do.

'Leave me alone. Please. Leave me alone. Now.'

Every word tasted acrid, like tainted oxygen – air that filled lungs but didn't actually provide anything to survive on.

'As you wish.'

Heart's Sorrow didn't know anything. He couldn't know anything. But if he dug into it – if the prefect did – and if Quỳnh was arrested ... then what? Quỳnh had promised Hoà protection, among many other things, but she'd also said she'd keep Hoà out of her revenge – and here was Hoà, standing in the middle of a ship with the daughter and son of Quỳnh's greatest enemies, one of whom was volatile and hurt, and the other suspicious of Quỳnh and sure enough of himself to warn Hoà away from her.

It hadn't been meant to go wrong that fast.

Thiên Dung's voice swam out of the morass of her thoughts, cutting through Hoà's panic.

'Big sis? Elder uncle? We're done here, but we need to talk.'

14
Grief

Something had changed, in the ship. When Hoà came back to the plaza in front of the heartroom – fingers clasping her glider tightly – all of her bots' feedback came flooding in. She hadn't even realised she'd muted them; she'd been so tense, she'd been trying to avoid other distractions.

Thiên Dung was staring at her. Or glaring at her, rather.

'Are you done?' she asked.

Minh was behind her. Even with the transparent cloth of the shadow-suit, her face was unreadable, but she was standing very still, staring at the heartroom's door. It was closed now, the hole sealed, Hoà's bots standing next to it. Pushed out. And...

There was something around them, hanging over them in the vacuum. That same sense of presence Hoà had felt – the vast heartbeat that had coursed through the charred walls, except now it was everywhere around them. Except... Hoà caught the movement, at the edge of her field of vision. Bots, scuttling out. Things that glinted and moved. New defences.

'You're awake,' she said softly.

Something pulsed in response, the entire space around them

contracting as if a giant hand had closed over them all and briefly squeezed.

'She is,' Quỳnh said.

She'd come up silently from the corridor behind them, her shadow-suit overlaid with an avatar so that she seemed to float within the vacuum wearing her normal clothes: the spread-out peach brocade, with the slowly shifting fish, and the sharp planes of her face. Around her was a cloud of bots, slowly spreading out in a loose circle, limning her body-shape within sharp metal facets.

'That's quite an entrance,' *Heart's Sorrow* said, drily.

Quỳnh bowed.

Hoà said, privately, to Quỳnh, 'Please tone it down.'

'Is it distressing you?' Quỳnh's voice was sharp.

'Yes,' Hoà said. 'I don't want to talk about it right now.'

She was still fighting the aftermath of her panic when *Heart's Sorrow* had ... she wasn't even sure what he'd done. Talked some sense into her? Threatened her? Simply talked?

'All right,' Quỳnh said. 'Of course.' A brief, ghostly squeeze through their shared interface, a touch from afar that made Hoà's body feel light and absurdly fragile. 'What do you need?'

'To be in charge,' Hoà said. 'Will you follow my cues?'

'Yes,' Quỳnh said, and Hoà wanted to hug or kiss her or both, because it would cost Quỳnh and could damage the plans which Hoà didn't know. Hoà didn't want to know. Or did she?

There was silence now. No, not silence, because Hoà could feel the ship. The ship's heartbeat, filtering through her gloves. She could see the bots scuttling, glints of moving metal – and feel the presence standing next to her, suffusing her. Holding her.

'How long?' she asked Thiên Dung.

'Until what?' Thiên Dung asked. 'Until she's got enough defences? Until she can speak?'

'Both,' Minh said, slowly, carefully. She sounded like she'd been crying.

Hoà asked, 'What about the other bots? The saboteurs?'

'There are no foreign bots remaining on the ship.'

Quỳnh opened her hands, and it was like a magic trick, because Hoà was sure they'd been empty before, and now they held a small cloud of bot fragments. A lot of bot fragments, contained in the perfect expanding sphere that Quỳnh held between her fingers.

'That's a lot of bots,' *Heart's Sorrow* said. 'How did they get there?'

'At a guess?' Quỳnh's voice was sharp. 'On Minh's shuttle.'

Minh's unhappiness was palpable. Hoà bit her tongue not to point out what they knew. Minh's mother was the prefect – but her being a horrible person who had wronged Dã Lan beyond belief didn't change the fact that she loved Minh and Minh loved her back – but it felt unfair to let Minh believe that her mother was behind all this.

'I see.' Minh's voice was stiff. 'And what do you expect to do about this?'

'That rather depends on Thiên Dung's answer,' Quỳnh said, inclining her head. 'And on Hoà.'

Everyone turned to look at Hoà. Which was what she'd asked for, but not what she'd expected. All that combined attention was a palpable weight constricting her: the thought of Quỳnh watching her and judging her reaction; of *Heart's Sorrow* and Minh waiting for her input, resentful of being upstaged by a mere technologist; of the ship, inchoate and speechless, trusting her with no good reason ...

It was terrifying.

'Lil sis?' Hoà asked Thiên Dung.

'Mmm.' Thiên Dung frowned. 'Another half a day, I think,

until she's able to put together reasonable defences. You've shared the sabotage locations?'

'Yes,' Hoà said.

'That will help.'

Thiên Dung closed the box of tools, unclamped it from the floor and held it close to her chest. Her bots flowed back to her. Her voice was thoughtful. In the overlay, everything she'd labelled as needing to be fixed was still blinking, a record of how far they'd come.

'For speaking? I don't know. That's a more delicate thing. She needs to *heal*.'

'And we can't—' Minh's voice was hesitant.

'No. That's like brain surgery on a live, conscious human. Not even a Master of Wind and Water would attempt that kind of repair. And ...' Thiên Dung hesitated. 'She won't let them. Except maybe Hoà.'

'She doesn't trust me?' Minh's voice was taut.

The presence of the ship shifted, became heavier.

'No,' *Heart's Sorrow* said softly. 'You're family. She doesn't want you to see her like this, because she's so far from who she was. She's upset.' He spun, frowning. 'No. She's *hurt*. No one of her blood should see her so diminished.'

'Ashamed,' Hoà said finally.

Minh was crying, slowly, softly. Hoà fought the urge to comfort her. It would serve no one's interests. *Heart's Sorrow* had moved closer to her, bots gently resting on Minh's hands and back.

A squeeze, on Hoà's shoulders: Quỳnh.

'You can be sad, too,' she said on the private channel. 'It's all right.'

'You hate them all, don't you?' Hoà asked.

A silence. Quỳnh said finally, 'No. They're not the ones who hurt me. But ...' She was quiet for a while. 'But I might have to hurt them.'

She sounded sad but resolute, and Hoà didn't quite know what to make of that. Was it fair? Was it just, given that Minh's and *Heart's Sorrow*'s parents would readily obliterate Quỳnh if they ever found out who she was?

'I don't want to know any more,' she said.

'Fair,' Quỳnh said.

Hoà said, aloud, to everyone, 'So we need to keep a watch for another half a day?'

'Mmm.' Thiên Dung said. 'It'd be safer.'

'I'll do it,' Quỳnh said.

Heart's Sorrow glared at her. 'No.'

'Do you see another solution?' Quỳnh's tone was ironic.

'Big sis!' Hoà said sharply, and realised she'd said it over the public channel and not the private one – and felt the sting of *Heart's Sorrow*'s judgement like a rebuke. He knew, and he didn't approve. He'd do everything in his power to bring Quỳnh down, and Hoà would just be collateral damage, the way technologists always were. She fought the urge to apologise, felt Quỳnh steadying her. Quỳnh's touch suddenly felt too close, too intimate, an association that was too threatening and too unsafe – and she disengaged, breathing hard.

Quỳnh said nothing. Which just made it worse.

Hoà said slowly, struggling to control herself, 'You don't trust Quỳnh. And Quỳnh doesn't trust you, either.' She hesitated. 'Would you trust us? Thiên Dung and me?'

A slow, considering spin from *Heart's Sorrow*.

'I'm not sure,' he said finally.

Hoà, ever the peacemaker, the diplomat, the one causing the least upset, knew how to do this.

'Then bots from each of us? All of us? With publicly shared instructions given to them and the date of the last alterations publicly displayed. And a shared private network between them, with no other external access. No tampering possible.'

'Access permission to each of us?' *Heart's Sorrow* sounded dubious.

Thiên Dung said, 'You know it's the only way. And it's only a few bots. We're not asking for privileged access, or access to *your* heartroom.'

A flinch, from him. He was on edge, which made Hoà nervous, because nervous wealthy kids tended to take it out on other, easier victims.

'I suppose it's acceptable,' *Heart's Sorrow* said. 'Only for half a day.'

'Make it a day.' Minh's voice was shaking. 'We're not having her die on our watch, lil bro.'

Heart's Sorrow made a sound that Hoà couldn't quite interpret, halfway between exasperation and fondness.

'If we want.' It sounded like nothing so much as *we need to talk*.

'Let's do this,' Hoà said – before she lost her nerve.

It was quick and almost perfunctory: bots were placed in the centre, each of them opening up privileged access to one another, then some uninterested haggling over the very simple instructions. *Heart's Sorrow* kept looking at Hoà, and Minh was obviously still upset. Quỳnh was serene, calling forward two bots that looked a little different from her own, a little less sharp and a little more cobbled-together. When questioned, she simply said that they would be more effective.

'Hmmm,' *Heart's Sorrow* said.

Was he going to challenge her again? Hoà held her breath, but he said nothing more.

It was Minh who spoke after the bots had scattered.

'The Orca Censor arrives in two days' time.'

'I know,' *Heart's Sorrow* said.

'How ready are we?'

Quỳnh looked at Hoà, but said nothing. Hoà knew she wanted to say something, to volunteer. That unthinking generosity extended again, even if it cost her part of her revenge.

'No,' Hoà said on the private channel. 'It's not our responsibility.'

If Minh and *Heart's Sorrow* wanted to blow open the entire network of beliefs that held Minh's family together, they'd do it alone.

Quỳnh shrugged. 'As you wish.'

But Hoà knew it wouldn't stop there – not for any of them.

Afterwards, she let Quỳnh take her and Thiên Dung home. Thiên Dung was silent, biting her lower lip.

She finally said, as the shuttle neared the docks, 'Are you going to explain what's going on?'

Quỳnh sighed. 'Family politics.' She'd taken off the shadow-suit, and there was just the avatar left, but her voice sounded exhausted. 'Hoà is right to not want to get involved.'

'With the Serpent scholars? The darlings of the Empire's elite in the habitats?' Thiên Dung made a face. 'I totally agree with my elder sister. For once.'

'Behave,' Hoà said sharply.

Thiên Dung nudged her in the ribs. 'When did I ever?' She laughed, but it was tense. 'It's big, isn't it?'

Quỳnh's voice was firm, her bots utterly steady on her hands. 'It's not going to touch you. I made a promise to Hoà, and that promise includes you. Whatever *Heart's Sorrow* and Minh end up doing, it's my business, and their families' business.' She held Hoà's hand, squeezed it.

Hoà wanted to believe her, so badly. But she still had *Heart's Sorrow*'s voice echoing in her head, and the memory of it was choking her.

At the door of the workshop, Hoà and Quỳnh were left alone. Thiên Dung had mysteriously disappeared, though Hoà knew she would ask questions later.

'Do you want to come up?' Hoà asked. 'For a tea?'

Quỳnh hesitated. Then, 'Yes. Of course.'

She sat on the bed by Hoà's side, still holding Hoà's hand as if she couldn't quite believe that Hoà was there. Hoà raised a privacy screen, out of sheer habit and to reassure Quỳnh – not because she believed Thiên Dung was listening in. Her sister wasn't that type. Quỳnh's overlay was flickering in and out of existence; beneath, she looked exhausted, rings under her eyes and her skin as pale as that of a corpse. Her bots, always sleek and elegant, barely clung to her shoulders.

Hoà hadn't realised how bad it was.

'You really shouldn't,' she said.

'Shouldn't what?' Quỳnh asked. 'Help you? You don't like it?'

Hoà flushed. 'Being in the cross hairs?'

'I saw you pull away,' Quỳnh said. 'It's too much, isn't it? Are you doing it for the sake of the ship?'

'I have to.' It wasn't even a question. 'But . . .'

But she was scared. But she was coming to the attention of Minh and *Heart's Sorrow*, and it wasn't because of *Flowers at the Gate*, but because of Quỳnh.

She said, instead of words that would only hurt them both, 'You drive yourself too hard. You can't do everything. Whatever it is that you're doing.'

'You're not asking.' Quỳnh's voice was . . . wistful.

'I can't. I don't want to know. We've been over this.'

'I know.' Quỳnh bent, and – still holding Hoà's hands in hers – kissed Hoà, slowly biting her lower lip and then moving upwards, both her lips on Hoà's, a stinging pain followed by the warmth of her skin on Hoà's. Her breath mingled with

Hoà's, robbing Hoà of speech. It felt so good, like everything Hoà had ever wanted or dreamed of. And yet ...

And yet.

Hoà kissed Quỳnh back, breathing in all of her: the steady presence, the utter confidence in Hoà, that thoughtless generosity — no, it wasn't generosity, was it? Quỳnh was all too ready to sacrifice her own happiness, whether for the sake of her revenge or for Hoà's own sake, or for others' sake. Did she value herself so little? When had that started?

'You're worth more than that,' Hoà said, pulling away but keeping her hands wrapped in Quỳnh's own, and her bots on Quỳnh's upper arms.

'More than what?'

'Revenge.'

'Are you trying to dissuade me?'

'No! No. I just ...' Hoà struggled for words. 'I wish you thought about yourself more.'

'I can't.' Quỳnh's voice was dark. 'Not any more.' She said, finally, 'There is ... I have a child. A mindship.'

Hoà stared at her, feeling it all open up within her own chest like a flowering of knives, cutting her breath into sharp, bloodied ribbons. The punishment for major crime was visited on the descendance of criminals. The child of Dã Lan — a dead, executed rebel — would be marked for death as surely as her mother had been. The child of Dã Lan would have no future.

'Where are they?' she asked. 'With their father?'

'Her father is dead.' Quỳnh's voice dipped a fraction.

'I'm sorry,' Hoà said. 'Did you ...? Do you love him?'

'Very much.' Quỳnh's face softened. 'I ran away, to the edge of the Empire. In the shipyards, where they count everything differently. His name was Đình Sơn.'

'I'm sorry,' Hoà said again. Her bots stroked Quỳnh's arm, soothing, gentle.

'Our child is safe.' Quỳnh's voice was taut, neutral – pain carefully tamped down. Hoà tried to breathe and found only sharpness in her lungs. 'And she doesn't know who her mother is.'

'Until you're done with your revenge?'

Bitter, sharp laughter from Quỳnh. 'Until the suns swallow up the Numbered Planets. Revenge is retribution, but not justice. Dã Lan will always be a convicted rebel.'

'You could appeal—' Hoà opened her mouth, closed it.

'To whom? The Orca Censor? Who would she believe?' Quỳnh shook her head. 'No. There is no forgiveness for rebels. No forgetting. The extinction of the nine generations is still the only punishment. Do you know how Đình Sơn died?'

'Was it because of you?' Hoà asked. Because, of course, there was no other answer.

'Because of Dã Lan. Because of Đức. Because he wanted to shield me from the Empire's justice, from which there is no shield or defence. The taint of rebellion will not wash away, not even after ten thousand years. And for me, there is nothing left but revenge. It's the only thing I can reach for. The only difference I can make.'

Hoà looked for words, found only emptiness.

'I don't know what to say.'

'I'm not asking you to say anything.' Quỳnh smiled, and for the first time she sounded happy, and it was fragile and heartbreaking. 'It's enough that I have this. That it brings me joy in the present. That I hope it brings you joy, too.'

Did it? Hoà tasted ashes in her mouth. Did it bring her joy, or was it just ... grief? Was it just a dark orbit she was being pulled into, wild and self-destructive and, above all, as noticeable as a star going supernova? She'd seen it when Quỳnh had entered her life, and perhaps she should have listened to it more carefully.

She remembered her panic when *Heart's Sorrow* had talked to her – the way his attention had turned to her throughout.

It wasn't Quỳnh now.

It was *her*. She was as noticeable as Quỳnh.

Hoà forced herself to smile.

'Do you have pictures of them? Of Đình Sơn and your child?'

'Oh,' Quỳnh said. 'I can do better than that. Do you want to meet her?'

Hoà's heart somersaulted in her chest, torn between being moved at the trust put in her, and ashamed of her growing doubts.

'Of course,' she half-lied. 'I'd be delighted.'

'Can I talk to you?' Minh asked.

Hoà, Thiên Dung and Quỳnh had gone, and it was just her and *Heart's Sorrow* in the common room.

'Of course,' *Heart's Sorrow* said.

His posture was mildly curious. She'd half-expected a rebuke, but he seemed relaxed, as if their earlier fight hadn't happened – which was more disquieting than she'd thought it would be.

'I was wrong,' Minh said.

Heart's Sorrow spun, questioning.

'There's something off about Quỳnh.'

Not the dark suspicions *Heart's Sorrow* seemed to harbour, but ... Minh thought of the casual way Quỳnh had pulled out the bots, the way she'd steadfastly refused to provide any explanations. The interactions between her and Hoà – and even the more straightforward Hoà had refused to explain anything. A careful game of mạt chược tiles, held close the edge of the table.

'They know something they're not telling us,' she added.

It hurt. She'd *liked* Quỳnh, and the idea that Quỳnh might

be like all the others — the sycophants trying to get at her mother through her — was a stab like a vacuum-blade through the belly.

'And you want to find out what it is?'

'I want to find out who Quỳnh is.'

Minh pinged the twins — Oanh's children — on her comms. A fraction of a second later, Thu Lâm showed up, rubbing at her eyes. Thu Thảo appeared as well: she was awake, holding a calligraphy brush and frowning.

'I was trying to write a poem,' she said, reproachfully. 'Oh. Wow.' Her avatar turned to look at the ship, slowly and carefully. 'What *did* you do?'

'Fixed her,' Minh said. 'Some of her.' She explained, tersely.

'Uh.' Thu Lâm was rummaging around, finally coming up with a cup of tea, her bots dragging a plate with some sesame and peanut candy. 'And now you want to find out more about Quỳnh? Shouldn't we be worrying more about the poisonings?'

'They've stopped for now,' *Heart's Sorrow* said.

'Yes, but ...' Thu Lâm sipped at her tea. 'Someone who was motivated enough to do that is hardly going to let a few bots stop them.'

'It's your mother, isn't it?' Thu Thảo — always blunt — asked.

'They never said so in so many words.'

'Did they need to?' Thu Thảo's voice was almost pitying.

Minh bit down on a scream. *I know it's Mother, I don't want to deal with this. I don't understand what's going on, or what game is being played. I just want things to make sense.*

She breathed out. As she did, *Heart's Sorrow* said, 'How about you look into it?'

'Us?' Thu Thảo looked sceptical. 'I mean, I can tinker with a few things, and big sis here can write poems ...'

Thu Lâm hefted her calligraphy brush as if it were a weapon, her bots flowing from the floor to her call.

'I can do a lot more than write.' She chewed on the words, her avatar billowing in an invisible wind, a few forearm-lengths over the tiled surface of the common room. 'But fine ... we can do that. We'll let you know. What are you going to do?'

Breathe in, breathe out.

Minh tried to steady herself in a world that didn't seem to make sense any more.

'We're going to follow Quỳnh and find out what her game is.'

15

Futures

Quỳnh wasn't really sure why she'd offered to introduce Hoà to *Moon*.

No, that wasn't quite true. On some level she knew exactly why she'd done it: because she'd seen the way Hoà stepped away from her, the fear in Hoà's eyes. Because she could see it happening again – her secrets causing a rift in the relationship. She remembered Đình Sơn's dishevelled face after learning who she was, his painstaking reassurances that it changed nothing, all the obvious ways in which it did. And the inevitable ending, his fatigue and stress and distraction causing the accident that had killed him, out there in the vacuum, the body in their compartment while she tried not to crumple under the weight of grief.

Love was as fragile as eggshells: held close, it would eventually break past all repair. She ought to know that. She ought to remember that, and not search for that warmth she could hold close to her chest. But it was such an unfamiliar, exhilarating warmth – and it promised all the unfolding of a future she'd lost long ago, and so she'd offered, and Hoà had said yes.

They took one of the private shuttles to the Outer Rings,

Quỳnh drawing on *Guts of Sea*'s bots to obscure their identity and their passage. She knew that it was only a matter of time until *Guts of Sea* realised what was happening, but right now her friend's processing threads were all busy, trying to find a weakness in Đức that they could lean on after the prefect had taken out Tuyết for them.

She felt as though she was choking and she wasn't sure why, as if she were on the verge of being thrown into space again. Hoà held her hand, taut, her whole being as rigid as a ship tearing through space. No comfort to be found there: it felt as though they were heading to a funeral and not a family reunion.

'Tell me about him,' Hoà said. 'Đình Sơn.'

Quỳnh tried to gather a coherent thought from the desert of her mind.

'He was sweet.' She thought of his hands on her shoulders, of his crooked smile – of the way the world had seemed to hold its breath, folding itself around them like the cloth of Heaven. 'He liked to tinker with things, to make sense of the world. He wanted us to build a ship.'

'*Moon*?'

'No, a ship that would be ours and the Empire's, something that people would remember. A bigger project. We just ... I thought we didn't have time, so I asked for *Moon* instead.'

A silence. Hoà squeezed her hand.

'Do you love *Moon* less?'

'Of course not.' Quỳnh laughed, and it tasted like ashes. 'I just wish she were mine, that I didn't have to pretend.'

Hoà's gaze was clear, compassionate. 'Yes,' she said. 'I can see that. She couldn't well lie about her parentage at that age, could she? For her own good. And yet ...'

'And yet.'

They were off the shuttle now, going into the sparsely

populated section of the Outer Rings – not the areas where they'd parked technologists or the less desirable, just areas that were isolated and all but abandoned.

Hoà breathed in, slowly and carefully – straightened up, squaring her shoulders, the stress gone from her.

'I wish,' she said darkly, and with obvious anger, 'that you would think more about your own good, big sis.'

'I—'

'No lies,' Hoà said.

'Then I don't have an answer.'

Hoà smiled, and it was a little sad, a little worried, a little fond.

'I know,' she said, and kissed Quỳnh gently, her bots softly pressing against the skin of Quỳnh's lower arms. It felt fragile and undeserved. 'But you're going to need one if you want this to survive.'

'I ...' Quỳnh opened her mouth again, closed it. 'I don't have one.'

It felt like something stretching between them, some tether about to snap.

The compound Băng Tâm had found was large and isolated, but Băng Tâm had decorated it with a riot of colours, swathes of scrolls with elegant calligraphy, paintings of starscapes, of mountains and rivers and of the large temples on the First Planet, clinging to the side of spires and skyscrapers like boughs to a tree. He was sitting cross-legged near a table, watching *Moon* drawing. *Moon*'s bots were weaving three separate trails of colour on the paper, a twining design that looked so different and so much more structured than Quỳnh had last seen from her. She had changed so much.

Moon stopped when they came in, frowned. The three bots went clattering sideways.

'Big Auntie!'

The name felt like a stab in her chest.

'Child,' she said, trying to hide her upset, and failing.

Hoà squeezed her hand gently. 'It's all right,' she said, in private.

'It's not,' Quỳnh replied. And just admitting it *hurt*. She wasn't doing it for *Moon*, but for what *Moon* could have had, in a different world. 'But thank you.'

'How long are you going to keep hurting yourself?' Hoà asked, and Quỳnh didn't have a good answer to that, either.

'Elder aunt.' Băng Tâm was more guarded as he rose, staring at Hoà. 'I hadn't been expecting you.' His gaze moved from Hoà to Quỳnh – and he smiled, unexpected. 'Ah. A visitor?' He sounded *glad*, which felt wrong. He'd certainly not felt that way about Quỳnh's revenge.

'My name is Hoà,' Hoà said. *Moon* was spinning, her avatar changing and then shifting again to the small ship. Her bots had gathered themselves under her, legs clattering in a not entirely coordinated display. 'I'm ... a special friend.'

'You're Big Auntie's Special Someone?'

Moon leaped towards Quỳnh, careless – and Quỳnh caught her avatar in her arms, the weight relayed by the perception filters. It felt as though she was holding something between a ship and a baby, heavy and metallic and trying to burrow into her chest. She wanted to hold that weight forever – wanted time to freeze and be only this: Hoà by her side, her child in her arms.

She wanted miracles, at a time when the Empire had scoured them all out of existence.

'She is,' she said.

'Oh?'

Moon turned in Quỳnh's arms – Quỳnh held her a moment more before *Moon* shot off towards Hoà. Hoà opened her arms with an ease Quỳnh envied her – no hint of the earlier fear or doubt – and folded them around *Moon*, as if she'd done it all her life.

'You're warm,' Hoà said. 'Is that something you chose for your avatar?'

'Oh.' *Moon* giggled. 'My motors are warm so my avatar is, too.' She pulsed, thoughtfully. 'I think. Anyway. You're fun!'

'I'm glad to hear that,' Hoà said. 'Do you want to show me what you were drawing?'

'For sure!' *Moon* beamed, her pleasure filling the room. 'Come on, Big Auntie, you, too!'

Quỳnh followed them both, trying to jolt herself into the present moment. She was thinking about the ship – about *Flowers at the Gates* – about Minh and *Heart's Sorrow*, and what might happen if they investigated her. She was thinking about the Orca Censor's welcome party and Đức's inevitable moves. Too many unknowns, too much risk. She was thinking of Hoà, and whether their relationship had any chance of surviving. Of whether *she* had, or deserved, any chance of surviving.

'You're not paying attention!' *Moon* said.

'Oh. Sorry.' Quỳnh kneeled by the table, staring at the pattern on the drawing. 'It's very good.'

Moon made a face. 'You always say that.'

Hoà nudged Quỳnh in the private channel.

'That's not how you praise a child. Watch me.'

She turned back to *Moon* – who still hadn't left her arms and was snuggling with obvious pleasure. 'I really like that bit. Where the gold meets the blue. Are you proud of it?'

'Mmm.' *Moon* made a face.

'Which bit do you like?'

One of *Moon*'s bots rested on the top of the drawing.

'Here. Look. All the colours mix together. It looks like space.'

'Like space?' Hoà asked.

'Yes!' *Moon* said. 'It's cold and hot and I can feel the pulse of the stars on my hull.'

'Ah. A problem I don't have,' Hoà said, deadpan. 'But you can show me.'

'Yes, look!'

Hoà nudged Quỳnh in private. 'That's your cue, you know.'

'I was watching you,' Quỳnh said.

Hoà made a face only Quỳnh could see, but didn't say the obvious. *Do you not know what to do with your own child?*

Quỳnh hesitated. 'How do you know this?'

Hoà laughed. 'I raised Thiên Dung. And there are children in the neighbourhood. Auntie Linh's, for instance. Vy's daughters.'

Quỳnh kneeled by the drawing. *Moon* vanished from Hoà's arms – she was there one moment, and the next she was tucked under Quỳnh's arm, making small contented noises.

'I want cuddles, Big Auntie.'

'Of course.' Quỳnh looked at the drawing again, at the pattern slowly coalescing through the mixes of colours. 'Space,' she said. 'It's a really nice drawing of it. The colours are very pretty. Do you prefer it out there in space, or here?'

'I don't know.' *Moon* sounded startled. 'It's nice here because you're here.'

'You've got your uncle.'

'Hmmmf,' *Moon* said. 'He's not very *nice*, you know.'

Băng Tâm looked as though he was making a very dignified and deliberate effort to not laugh.

'Shall we get some tea? You can do another drawing for your aunties.'

'Oh yes! With blue and red and gold!' *Moon* wriggled off Quỳnh again and went to tinker with her bots.

Băng Tâm gestured towards the other low table, the one not

covered in drawing paper. Bots were already putting together the tray, teapot and teacups, and the aroma of jasmine was filling the room.

Quỳnh wasn't sure she could bear to taste anything, at the moment. Everything felt too taut, too fragile — as if a wrong word, a wrong sentence would utterly jeopardise ... she wasn't sure what exactly. All she knew was the fear lodged in her throat, so strong it seemed to radiate into the metal of her bots: the fear she'd lose something infinitely precious.

Which was ridiculous. She'd already lost everything, not once but twice, and she'd never been so close to making her enemies pay for it all. She'd made the best choice for herself, and above all for *Moon*: remove herself entirely. Become the sharp, wounding edge of revenge. There was so little space in her life for anything else.

Then why haven't I made the best choice for Hoà?

The thought hurt. She set it aside, tried to focus on the tea that she had no intention of drinking.

'She's a delightful child,' Hoà was saying to Băng Tâm.

'And a handful.' Băng Tâm sighed. 'It's not always easy for any of us.'

'I imagine not,' Hoà said, and there was that same clarity in her gaze — the same dry-eyed compassion. 'Big sis isn't easy to be friends with.'

Băng Tâm stared at Quỳnh, for a while. 'How much does she know?' he asked, via a private channel.

'She knows who I am and who *Moon* is. Not the details of our plan.'

'Ah. Yes. Makes sense.'

His voice was ... pitying. She didn't want pity. She didn't want any reminder of the mess she was making of her life. She'd made her choices. She would not make other ones.

Someone pinged her: *Guts of Sea*. She didn't want to talk

to *Guts of Sea* right now. She tamped it down, turning off the display for those messages.

Hoà squeezed her hand again. 'You're wandering.' A silence. 'It's difficult?'

Quỳnh opened her mouth to lie, and remembered she'd promised she wouldn't.

'More than I thought it would be. But ... *Moon* matters to me.'

'She's lovely,' Hoà said. 'And ...' She hesitated. 'It's hard,' she finally said. 'I can see that. She makes you wonder if you made the right choices.'

'Don't,' Quỳnh said. 'Please.' She was watching *Moon* reconfigure her bots, the mindship slowly listing in thoughtfulness. 'I'm ... I'm trying to share something with you. It's hard.'

'Yes.' Hoà's gaze was distant, and Quỳnh wasn't sure whether she could bear it. 'I know. Thank you. It means a lot to me.'

Quỳnh wanted to kiss her. To hold her as she'd held *Moon* and stand there forever, without having to worry about anything. But Băng Tâm was there, and so was *Moon*. And so she said nothing, merely tried to hold on to Hoà for as long as she could.

Something seized her – her entire field of vision fading away, *Moon* and Hoà receding into insignificance in the background.

No, no. Not now.

She was doing fine, she wasn't going back into the nightmares of choking again. She couldn't be doing that now, or ever. She—

Words flashed across her field of vision.

'Lil sis, read my messages now.'

It was *Guts of Sea*. She'd hacked Quỳnh's interface.

'Big sis, are you all right?' Hoà said. 'Are you all right? I think she's gone.' Hoà's touch felt very far away, Hoà's panic an abstract thing. 'Big sis! Big sis!'

Quỳnh came back to the compartment, tasting blood on her tongue.

How dare she. How dare she hack me?

'Leave me alone,' she growled.

'No,' *Guts of Sea* said. 'You're being enough of an absolute idiot already.' Her voice overlaid Hoà's voice, and *Moon*'s. 'Look outside. See what you brought here.'

And then she was falling away from the compartment again, except that it wasn't just darkness, but an image taking up the whole of the room: the tea house facing the compartment, where *Heart's Sorrow* and Minh sat at a table, watching.

They'd followed her. Of course. Quỳnh could still feel the blood in her mouth.

'See?' *Guts of Sea*'s voice was sharp and angry. 'Now tell me it was worth it.'

Quỳnh took a deep, shuddering breath. She ought to have known that happiness wasn't for her. That love was fragile and doomed. That she'd already chosen between love and revenge, and she couldn't have both.

The edges of her field of vision were blurring. Breathing hurt, more and more, and she was growing cold again. The beginnings of another episode. *No.* She couldn't afford that, not now.

'We need to discuss this later,' she said, to *Guts of Sea*.

Her friend still looked as though she wanted to pick a fight. Quỳnh imagined it wasn't *Guts of Sea* there, but someone else – the prefect, the general – and said, simply, with all the authority and nastiness she could imbue in her voice, 'Later.'

Focus. Focus.

'Big sis?' Hoà was looking worried, ready to send her bots to Quỳnh at a moment's notice. Of course, she would have access to Quỳnh's vitals, and the attack would be obvious.

No lies, they'd said. Ice-cold clarity descended on Quỳnh

– she let it settle over her, turning everything sharp and clear and wounding.

She could say true words, but they didn't have to be the whole of the truth. For Hoà's sake. That was all that mattered.

'I need you to head home,' she said.

'Why?' Hoà frowned. 'Are you well?'

'No worse than most of the time,' Quỳnh said, slowly and smoothly. 'But I need you to head home because I need to be alone to deal with something.'

'Something?'

Quỳnh still felt the tightness in her chest, the way everything wobbled and threatened to leave her, jellied and limp, on the floor. Words, usually coming to her so easily – the scholar's tools that she wielded when nothing else was left – were fraught and difficult. Her best and most brutal weapon was gone: she couldn't act or lie. She could only obfuscate and be herself. Breaking the spirit rather than the letter of the promise she'd made to Hoà.

'Someone is coming to see *Moon*,' she said. 'And I'd rather you weren't here when they arrive.'

Hoà's face was set. 'Does this have to do with your revenge? I thought you weren't going to involve her.'

'It does, and I wish,' Quỳnh said bitterly. 'But someone's found out about *Moon*'s existence, and they're likely to try and use her as leverage against me.'

Ten thousand questions crowded on to Hoà's small, honest face. She finally said, 'Are you in danger? You and *Moon*?'

Quỳnh watched *Moon* fly, giggling, through the reception room with Băng Tâm chasing her, *Moon* spinning new overlays in her wake, pieces of starlight and nebulas that shone briefly on the floor.

'No,' she said, and it was the truth. Because it was just the children, and she knew how to handle them. 'But if you stay here, I'll have to worry about you. And I can't afford that. And I don't think you want to stand out in this particular conversation, either.'

'The prefect?' Hoà asked. 'The Orca Censor?' Her face was raw fear.

Quỳnh said carefully, 'I'd rather not say. You did say you didn't want to be involved with any of this. Suffice to say it's someone who can make enough of a fuss.'

Hoà looked afraid: the tension in her body; the rising heartbeat; the way her bots dangled on her shoulders, a little more crooked and a little more unsteady.

'Are you sure?' she asked.

'That I can deal with this without you?' Quỳnh said. 'Absolutely. Can I ask you to leave via the back door?'

She hesitated about offering *Guts of Sea*'s escort, but no, Hoà would take it badly and *Guts of Sea* was too angry.

Hoà made a huffing sound. 'Only if you let me know you're all right.'

'Always.'

Quỳnh moved, to catch Hoà's face between her fingers. There was a gaping hole in her stomach at the thought that she might not be able to protect Hoà for much longer. She ran a hand over Hoà's cheek, slowly and carefully, ending with a slow, increasing pressure on her lips – feeling them tighten beneath her touch – then inserting the tip of one finger, gently, into Hoà's mouth. Hoà sucked on it, sending a thrill of desire down Quỳnh's bones. It felt like a stolen kiss, moments before a battle. It took an effort of will to keep the encroaching darkness at bay – to stand apart from her plunge in deep spaces, from the memories clogging up her lungs and throat. She was going to have to face Minh and *Heart's Sorrow* with nothing but willpower and stubbornness, and pretend that everything was fine. That she could breathe normally. That she wasn't five blinks from total collapse.

'I'll see you. It's a promise,' Quỳnh said.

She asked her bots to inject her with the antidote to the constriction attacks. It was usually best saved for the worst of them, because the injections had to be spaced out enough for it to work, but this would take off some of the edge. This would give her some space.

Quỳnh was going to pay for it later, when the attack did hit.

Hoà withdrew her lips. Her face was unreadable: too many strong emotions battling for control of it.

'Promise,' she said.

Hoà held her position a fraction of a moment longer before she turned to hug *Moon* goodbye, and Quỳnh felt as if something between them was tearing itself apart.

16

Filial Piety

Minh hadn't been sure what to expect, but seeing Quỳnh and Hoà walking hand in hand like a pair of anxious lovebirds hadn't really been at the forefront of her thoughts.

'Maybe we should wait,' she said.

Heart's Sorrow sipped at his tea, darkly. 'Wait for what?'

'Well, it's hardly a nefarious thing?'

'You have doubts?'

'No.' Minh blushed. Well, she thought she didn't. She wanted the truth. She wanted to know how Quỳnh could be so conveniently there, so conveniently involved in everything Minh decided to try. But this seemed like a date between lovers, and she felt embarrassed to be breaching their privacy. 'But it feels wrong. They're having a private time.'

Heart's Sorrow glowered. 'You're very charitable.'

'You're not.' Minh sighed. 'Are you going to tell me what happened? You didn't used to be so suspicious of Quỳnh.'

'Then I inquired,' *Heart's Sorrow* said. 'You know when everything is too clean, too plausible, too ordered?'

Like Mother's life?

'Yes,' Minh said.

'That's Quỳnh's past. It's too ... plausible. Like she picked the probable answer for every question and gave it. I've never seen anyone's life align like this, or anyone's data.'

'And her mindship friend?'

'*Guts of Sea*? I can't find anything on *Guts of Sea*.'

'That seems worse,' Minh said.

'Mmm. Not necessarily. Many ships were ... less than eager to return to imperial service after the Ten Thousand Flags Uprising. Some of them have made new identities and are just trying to get back into society.' He sighed.

'You're worried,' Minh said. 'Have your mothers been talking about sending you away again?'

'I *know* I'm going away.' *Heart's Sorrow* sounded despondent. 'They want me to be a scholar, and that means a life beyond the Belt. I just need to do something good before I leave.'

Before he left. Before Minh left. Before their futures were sealed, and they found themselves on strange planets and habitats, serving their families' best interests. Serving their mothers' best interests. It was unfair. Why did she owe filial piety to someone like Mother?

'I don't want to lose you,' Minh said.

'I know.' His voice was quiet. 'We'll find each other. Anyway.' He stared at the compartment. 'Why would a celebrated scholar go all the way to the back end of nowhere?'

Minh opened her mouth to say it might be Hoà, but she knew it wasn't. Hoà had been following Quỳnh's lead, very clearly, and feeling anxious about it.

'She's hiding something.'

'Exactly. And I'm going to find out what.'

'Are you hoping that's going to get you into your mothers' good graces?' The words were out of Minh's mouth before she could stop them – exactly the kind of hurtful and nasty thing Mother might have said. 'I'm sorry.'

Heart's Sorrow said nothing, for a while. Then, listing slowly and carefully, in the way he usually did when thinking, 'No. Just that it's a problem I'd like to fix.'

He wasn't her. His world didn't revolve around his mothers. He'd accepted that they were going to govern the course of his life. He scared her, he angered her – because if he had bowed down to necessity, how could she escape the same? He was the future she'd wanted never to come to pass.

Why had she ever thought she could break free of Mother's hold on her?

A noise made her look up, at the entrance of the tea house: it was Quỳnh, talking briefly with the owner before walking straight to their table. Her sleeves billowed in an invisible wind; her face was creased in an ironic smile, as if she'd known exactly what they'd been arguing about.

'Children. What a delight to see you here.'

Her sharp gaze said otherwise, and suddenly Minh remembered how all the bandits had died, casually and with nothing more than a flick of Quỳnh's wrists. She was standing in front of someone who could casually kill, and who would not hesitate to kill her ... and then the moment passed, and the scholar's mask was back on Quỳnh's face, lightly pleasant.

A silence that neither Minh nor *Heart's Sorrow* knew how to fill. Quỳnh broke it as casually as she'd break the world into ten thousand pieces.

'You seem very interested in where I'm going and why. Why don't you come into the compound?'

What?

Minh looked at *Heart's Sorrow*, who looked back at her, equally nonplussed, his bots' gyration mirroring his own confused one.

'You want us to come in?'

'And witness my deepest, darkest secrets?' Quỳnh's face was

ironic. 'Yes. I can tell that you—' she was addressing *Heart's Sorrow*— 'don't trust me or where I'm coming from. The best measure of trust comes from a measure of trust, doesn't it?'

The word she used was peculiar: it was *measure*, but it was an archaic term to describe the size of a village and its fields in the far removed time of Old Earth. Minh asked her bots for a quick search; the last use of it had been in the moniker granted to the Measure of Bones Killer.

'And you ...' Quỳnh said to Minh. 'You don't know what to think.'

'You lied to me,' Minh said.

'When?'

'I don't know! I thought ...' She swallowed the burning taste in her mouth. 'I thought you were my friend. I thought you wanted to help me with ...' She made a gesture. 'I thought you *valued* me.'

Quỳnh cocked her head, watching her.

'I do,' she said. And it sounded utterly sincere, stripped of all the scholar pretence.

'Then what—'

'Why don't you come inside?'

'How do we know you're not intending to make us disappear?' Minh asked.

She didn't really believe that – and in fact, with Quỳnh standing in front of her, she really, really wanted to trust her again, to feel as though she understood her. For Quỳnh to be the person who'd rescued her from the bandits, who wanted to offer her sponsorship.

Quỳnh laughed. 'Disappear? I know these are the Outer Rings, but they're not Barbarian lands. It's not even the shipyards. You could send a signal to the imperial militia in less time than I could blink. And really—' her expression was matter-of-fact, her bots utterly still, gleaming like weapons on her shoulders '—if I wanted to kill you, I'd have done it before.'

Minh blinked. That ought to not have felt so reassuring, but it did. It felt so familiar, like something Mother or *Heart's Sorrow*'s mother Nhăng – the ex-enforcer – might have said.

'Let's go,' she said.

Heart's Sorrow looked as though he wanted to disagree, but he also followed Quỳnh – though Minh noticed that he ostentatiously left two of his bots behind in the tea house. Minh could have done that, too, but she watched Quỳnh instead, watching her back and the way she moved. She was tense and exhausted, and by turn, frightening and comforting. And no, she didn't know what to think, or what they'd find inside, at all.

It was a small compound furnished almost exclusively in virtual, the overlays and the furniture being of exquisite taste, carefully tailored to the space, which must have taken either a lot of time or a lot of money. As Minh followed Quỳnh through corridors and a courtyard that opened up, she remembered Quỳnh's compound, the courtyard where wind had ruffled the blades of grass. This was smaller and yet somehow by the same hand, the overlay of the courtyard a garden with a huge cracked planet hovering above them all – it looked like the Fire Palace near the boundaries of the Empire. And yet it felt more intimate. As though she was seeing something she shouldn't. She couldn't put her finger on why exactly.

Beside her, *Heart's Sorrow* was silent, the only noise the sharp clicks of his bots' legs. Minh felt her own bots riding in her hair, the ones on her hands like rings, the ones clinging to her belt – something about the place made everything about her body feel strange and alien.

Inside, it looked like a scholar's study, furnished with books and papers, and with bots clinging to every shelf, hiding beneath the overlay – *Heart's Sorrow* own bots pinpointed them one after the other.

'Are you trying to tell me something?' Minh asked.

And didn't get time to see his answer, because *someone* barrelled into her arms.

'Oh, visitors again! You didn't tell me there'd be more, Big Auntie! So cool!'

Minh struggled to keep her balance, flailed as whoever was in her arms – a young child by the weight of them – struggled and squirmed and tried to hold on tighter. Minh moved her bots to support her and avoid falling backwards – and finally relaxed as her feet stabilised on the floor.

She held a mindship: a small avatar with perception filters that mimicked a fraction of their weight.

'Hi, I'm *Moon*,' the mindship said, beaming. 'Who are you?'

'Minh,' she said, before she could think.

'You look nice.' *Moon* said. 'Do you want to see what I can draw?'

She reminded Minh of Vân, possibly younger – Minh only knew the one mindship.

'Sure.'

She let herself be half-pushed, half-dragged by the mindship in her arms and the bots that had sneaked behind her ankles – was sitting before she knew it, staring at swirls of colours on paper.

'It's like space.' *Moon* was smiling; Minh didn't even know her body language, or the quirks she'd have, as intimately as she knew *Heart's Sorrow*'s language, but she could feel it in the air. It was strong and so pure that it distorted everything around it, like a black hole of sheer enthusiasm and joy. 'Look, it's cold here, and then it gets noisy sometimes, around the stars.'

'That's the radiation.' *Heart's Sorrow*'s voice was subdued. He'd come by the table, too, his bots all scattered behind him.

'I know, silly!' *Moon* said. 'But that's not how I think about it, so that's not how I talk about it.'

'How old are you?' Minh asked, fascinated in spite of herself.

Moon was still in her arms, her weight steady and comforting. Minh had held Vân, but it was nothing like the odd feeling she had now: that utter contentment spreading from the core of her being, as though she'd always been meant to be there.

'Three!' *Moon* said.

'Mindship ages aren't quite the same as ours.' It was Quỳnh. She hadn't come to the table; she watched *Moon* with an odd expression in her eyes, neither threat nor sarcasm nor charm.

'We know,' *Heart's Sorrow* snapped.

'Not in front of the child.' Quỳnh's voice was sharp. She gestured to the three cups of tea on the table. 'These are for you, should you wish to talk.'

'Awww,' *Moon* said. 'That's unfair. I like them. Why can't they stay and play with me, Big Auntie?'

Quỳnh's face was soft – in a way that Minh had never seen it. It was extremely disconcerting. She didn't understand what was going on here. *Moon* was continuously wriggling in her arms and pointing to various items on the drawings, both verbally and on private channels that Minh wasn't really sure how she'd found, and Minh couldn't manage to hold on to one straight thought.

'We need to talk about adult things, and you need to get your evening builds sorted out, and go to bed.'

'I don't sleep!' *Moon* said, indignant. 'I'm a *mindship*! We never sleep.'

'You pause,' Quỳnh said firmly. 'If you don't pause, then the bots can't actually build anything inside you, and you're not going to be in full control of your body. You do want to turn those somersaults near the sun some day, don't you?'

'Mmm.' *Moon* pouted. 'I suppose ...'

'I believe your uncle also has a new story for you.'

'Oh, all right then.' *Moon* suddenly straightened in Minh's arms, throwing Minh off balance again. This time she couldn't quite control it and ended up on her knees, *Moon* giggling. 'Got you!'

'It's time to say goodnight,' Quỳnh said.

Moon made the same pose of children everywhere faced with bedtime, an unhappiness that seemed to fill the entire room.

'Fine. I'll see you another day, big sis and big bro,' she said to Minh. 'They can come again, right?'

'Maybe.' Quỳnh's face was stern. 'Bedtime.'

'Fine fine fine.'

Moon stretched – and Minh was held for a minute in an embrace that was larger than the avatar in her arms, something that could hold all of her in a cocoon of sheer enthusiasm, wild emotions and roller coaster mood changes. Her heart suddenly felt three sizes too large for her chest.

Heart's Sorrow didn't move as *Moon* rolled towards him, dragging an overlay from the table behind her – a carpet of wobbling stars with music snaking from them, which she maintained for perhaps a couple of blinks before it disappeared.

'Good night ...'

Moon moved towards him, mingling her avatar with his, before she disappeared like a popped soap bubble.

The room suddenly felt a great deal more silent – it was a relief, and yet it also felt markedly less joyful. *Heart's Sorrow* moved, in silence, his bots under his avatar, to the table. He hovered over one of the cups, sipping what looked to be a jasmine tea. Minh sat down, too; hers was Dragon Scales, a sweet and fruity brew that only grew on a handful of the Numbered Planets.

'Showing off?' she asked sharply, but then she looked at Quỳnh's face, and finally recognised the expression for what it was.

Quỳnh was trying very, very hard not to cry.

'She's not your niece, is she?' Minh asked, with that sinking feeling of a revelation. 'She's your daughter.'

Was this the secret?

'I don't understand,' *Heart's Sorrow* said. 'Why …?' He sounded bewildered. 'Plenty of people have mindship children.'

'Behave,' Minh said, privately.

If Quỳnh had gone through such lengths to hide *Moon* – even refusing to tell *Moon* her parentage – and if the always composed Quỳnh was struggling not to cry, then there was something painful behind it, and they weren't meant to pry.

'But …' *Heart's Sorrow* said. 'Why would you hide her? There's nothing wrong …'

Quỳnh said finally, 'One doesn't get to the imperial court without making enemies. Surely your mothers taught you that.' Her face was, once more, exquisitely composed.

'Yes, but—'

Minh said, 'You can't defend her, can you?'

'No.' Quỳnh sipped her tea, a move that was clearly for show. The bots on her shoulders were clinging too tensely to her clothes. 'I can't. Not against those who would harm her.'

And how many of those people were their parents? The question was on the tip of Minh's tongue, but it remained there. There was no good way to ask this – what would she do, in any case, if it turned out their families were doomed to be enemies?

'And that's it?' *Heart's Sorrow* sounded incredulous, and also more than a bit guilty. 'That's the secret you've been keeping?'

A shrug from Quỳnh, her bots leaping from her shoulders to the table. The peaches on the robes of her sleeves shimmered.

'I'm not sure what you want me to tell you.'

'You're not who you seem.'

'No.' Quỳnh sighed. 'Do you want me to tell you what you already know? Quỳnh isn't the name my parents gave me. The Alchemist of Streams and Hills doesn't really exist.'

'But—'

'I came from the shipyards,' Quỳnh said. 'You're both Serpents. You know what happens to those from the wrong backgrounds...' She spread her hands. 'I wanted more for my child than the chances we had, if we'd stayed.'

Heart's Sorrow watched Quỳnh, carefully. His bots would see the same vitals Minh saw: steady and clear, with just extreme exhaustion in her voice. The truth. The unvarnished truth.

'You wanted to be with the powerful?' Minh laughed bitterly.

Quỳnh said nothing, and when she finally spoke her voice was sour.

'The powerful make the world. They give people chances. The shadow of their blessings. Where else could I go?'

'Were you even in court?' *Heart's Sorrow* asked.

'Briefly,' Quỳnh said. 'Not as a treasured adviser to the Empress. But then I never pretended I had been. Both your first mothers read what they wanted to in what I said.'

What she'd led them to believe. What she'd sold them based on their own greed. And Minh wasn't even sure she felt angry about it.

'What now?' she asked.

Quỳnh sighed. 'I don't know. You're both reasonable people. You can see why I'd rather this remain a secret. What are you going to do?'

She trusted them. Even after they'd followed her and all but insulted her. Minh rubbed her arms, trying to feel *Moon*'s weight in them again.

Heart's Sorrow radiated guilt. 'Yes, I absolutely can see, and I'll keep quiet. Well, I think we should probably leave.' He moved away stiffly from his tea in overlay. It was untouched. 'My apologies for disturbing you. I guess ... I guess we'll see you around, then. I'm really sorry.'

'Yes,' Minh said, colouring. 'I'm sorry. It was all a misunderstanding. We'll just ... We won't say a word.'

'It's fine.' Quỳnh's face was neutral again – the scholar's face. 'You should go home. Your parents are probably worried about where you've been, and we wouldn't want them to think *Flowers at the Gates* is being fixed rather faster than she should be, would we?'

'No,' Minh said. 'I guess not.'

She rose, following *Heart's Sorrow*. Her bots felt heavy on her shoulders.

She was halfway through the door when Quỳnh said, in private, 'Child. I really meant it. You're talented, and you need to find a tutor who suits you. You, and not anyone else.'

'You mean, not letting my mother choose?' Minh asked sharply.

Quỳnh hadn't moved. The overlays were dimming, leaving the room beneath to emerge, shrouded in their remnants, like a ghost from times long past.

She said, 'I like you. But—'

'You don't like my mother,' Minh said.

'No.' Quỳnh's voice was quiet, whiplash sharp. 'Few of the scholars do.'

'Because she's unfair?'

'What would you do if I said yes?' Quỳnh sounded ... weary. Out of breath.

'Are you all right?'

Minh realised the way Quỳnh was sitting – ramrod straight, carefully positioned – was to mask her weakness. It was also the reason she hadn't risen from the table to walk them out of the compound.

A hollow laugh from Quỳnh. 'No. But thank you for asking. You really should leave now. I'll see you at the welcome ceremony for the Orca Censor.'

'But—' Minh said.

'Leave,' Quỳnh said, and it was an order.

Minh fled, unsure what to think about anything or anyone any more.

17

Threats

Hoà was on the shuttle home when someone pinged her. It was an auth-token she was unfamiliar with: a customer? She ignored it; she was preoccupied with what had just happened with Quỳnh – was she really all right? She'd never said outright that she was unwell, had she? Just that she could handle the situation.

What was she doing, questioning Quỳnh? She really shouldn't. They trusted each other, and paranoia wasn't going to help.

Whoever was pinging her pinged her again. Hoà blocked them with a curt 'will get back to you later.'

'I don't think so,' a voice said, just as the avatar of a mindship materialised into the shuttle.

Guts of Sea, Quỳnh's mindship friend and co-conspirator. Up close, she looked weird. It took Hoà a moment to realise it was because her hull had been patched in multiple places, and that the repairs repeatedly broke the line of the ship. She remembered what Quỳnh had said to her. That she'd fixed a mindship in another life, another time. It had to be *Guts of Sea*.

The unmistakable iridescence of a privacy screen materialised around Hoà and *Guts of Sea*. Hoà's heart sank. This was going to be a long and very unenjoyable conversation, and she didn't have the least desire to have it.

'I blocked you,' Hoà said.

'Yes. You did.' *Guts of Sea* didn't seem in the least bit concerned about respecting Hoà's wishes. 'So did Quỳnh. If you really think a few network blocks are going to stop me from doing what's right, you're mistaken.'

So she'd been the reason Quỳnh had got rid of Hoà. Hoà didn't like this at all. Maybe it was indeed more revenge stuff, but why the lack of transparency?

'"What's right",' Hoà said, flatly. 'Like respecting our consent?'

'I'm talking about something larger,' *Guts of Sea* said sharply.

'Revenge?' Hoà thought about *Guts of Sea*. 'Was the prefect responsible for breaking you? Or the general?'

Guts of Sea shifted, showing Hoà her broken hull, the glint of weapon-mouths, of sharp turrets.

'You misunderstand who I will take my revenge on.'

'Who, then?' There was really only one answer, wasn't there? Everyone. 'The Empire,' Hoà said, flatly. 'I don't want to be part of this. Any of this.'

'I know you don't.' *Guts of Sea*'s voice was mocking.

The shuttle had arrived at the Technologists' Docks. Hoà disembarked and headed towards the familiar streets – still full at this hour of the night, from food-hawkers to mechanics' street-stalls hurriedly fixing bots and appliances. *Guts of Sea* followed her, the privacy screen moving with them. The smell of grilled skewers and dipping sauce, sweet and salty and tangy all at once, wafted to her.

'Can't really stand for any of this, can you?' the mindship asked. 'Not even for her.'

Hoà's blood ran cold.

How dare she?

'You're the one who's hurting her and insulting her with every step.'

Hoà fought the wave of fear in her chest as *Guts of Sea* turned to look at her, looming larger and suddenly more threatening. Something twisted in the bubble around them and Hoà's own bots retreated out of their own volition, without her conscious control. She shouldn't have said that. The ship would destroy her as casually as she'd destroyed the lives of others. Hoà knew exactly what kind of person she was dealing with: one who had let pain distort everything in their lives, and whose only reason for living had become the inflicting of further pain on others. *Guts of Sea* didn't care about her, or even about Quỳnh, except as an instrument. Hoà tried to open her mouth to apologise, but something small and stubborn – one last vacuum-cold core of righteousness and self-respect – kept it closed.

'Oh, you grow bold, then. But will you say this to the prefect? To the Orca Censor?'

Hoà's stomach lurched. 'I'm not talking about them.'

'No.' *Guts of Sea* laughed, and it sounded malicious. 'You're not. Which is why, ultimately, you're unsuitable for her.'

Unsuitable.

As if she had the right to judge Hoà or Quỳnh for their choices, like a nightmarish kind of auntie. Hoà bit her lip not to protest.

'Why are you here? For a lecture?'

'Of sorts,' *Guts of Sea* said. 'A warning. You already know this. You're tangling with the powerful. The longer you stay with Quỳnh, the more you court their attention. And you know how this ends, don't you?'

Hoà thought of Thiên Hạnh – of the mob outside their house.

Of the splinters of metal in her hands that she'd held against the windows she'd just sealed, the weight of holding Thiên Dung against her, whispering it was all right, everything was all right, her ears full of Thiên Hạnh's screams.

Never stand out. It never ends well. Never.

'No,' she said, but it was a lie.

'As you wish. Quỳnh knows this better than you,' *Guts of Sea* said. 'That's why she lied to you and sent you away. For your own safety.'

'She didn't lie to me,' Hoà said sharply.

They'd had a deal. A promise. Honesty before all else, even the truth she didn't want to hear. But ... Quỳnh had behaved so uncharacteristically.

'She's having an attack right now.' *Guts of Sea*'s voice was conversational. 'Where you can't see it.'

There was an image, within the privacy screen: Quỳnh on her knees, pale and wheezing, hands to her throat, her chest swarmed over by *Guts of Sea*'s bots, and over it all, the avatar of the ship telling her to breathe again and again.

'She wouldn't,' Hoà said.

'You think I'm making this up?'

No, because it made horrible sense. Of course Quỳnh would push her away. And of course ... of course she would tell the truth, but not the entire truth. On the overlay, Quỳnh was pushing herself up again, shuddering.

Hoà turned. 'I'm going back,' she said.

'You'll never make it back in time. It'll be over by the time you arrive.'

Guts of Sea dropped the privacy screen nevertheless, and vanished, like a malevolent spirit that had done its work.

Hoà started running.

*

Hoà pinged Quỳnh, over and over, on the way back to the compound – on the shuttle, running through increasingly deserted streets, her bots ahead of her. There was no answer. Nothing. Not even the slightest acknowledgement.

Of course she was doing exactly what *Guts of Sea* expected her to do. But what did it matter? She couldn't let Quỳnh go through this alone with *Guts of Sea*'s toxic brand of support.

It was dark by the time she reached the compound, the habitat's lights dimmed, the tea house still doing brisk business in the dark. The double doors were closed, displaying an unfamiliar seal that Hoà didn't bother to read. She knocked on the doors instead – bots first, and then her hands, the sound of her fists making the structure shudder.

There was no answer.

She knocked, and still nothing.

'Big sis! I know you're here! Big sis!'

But she was locked out. By Quỳnh or *Guts of Sea*, or both.

Quỳnh would be collapsing again – that horrible attack she'd seen once already, going from upright to limp as if someone had liquefied all the bones in her body at the same time, lost in the grip of the traumatic past.

'Big sis! Big sis! I'm here!'

She knocked again, and again and again, weeping.

'Big sis.'

She was never going to gain entry. It was pointless. She knocked until her knuckles were raw and nothing budged.

Big sis. No.

At last – at long, long last – Hoà admitted defeat. She turned around, trying not to worry about Quỳnh – was she awake, was she even breathing? How much self-hatred had *Guts of Sea* poured into her ears?

She'd sent Hoà away. She'd ... not lied to her, because she'd never said a false word. But the promise they'd made wasn't a literal oath: it was a commitment to the truth, not a licence to dance around it.

She'd sent Hoà away.

How much could Hoà trust her, after that?

She was all the way home lost in her dark thoughts, paying little attention to anything, which was why she didn't see the militia barrage until one of them grabbed her arm – a small, lean woman with a bruising grip. Her bots climbed onto Hoà's back and gripped her clothes through all the overlays, their legs sharp enough to draw blood.

What . . . ?

As Hoà looked up, startled, spluttering, the militia woman pushed her towards the shop, grinning like a tiger who'd found some prey.

'Someone wants to talk to you, child.'

Inside the shop was a pale-faced Thiên Dung, hands laid on the table, her bots loosely scattered around her – not restrained in any physical way, but by the tension in them, she'd been there for a while. She stared at Hoà when Hoà stumbled in, the militia woman coming right behind her, shaking her face and mouthing a word Hoà couldn't hear.

The person who was examining the counter turned to look at Hoà, quizzically – and Hoà felt a sharp stab of fear in her stomach.

'Ah, child. Delighted to meet you at last.'

It was Prefect Đức.

Hoà sat, rigidly, in the chair next to Thiên Dung. It was difficult to do anything else – the air itself felt as though it had turned to tar, holding her upright in an uncomfortable position. Bots encircled them both, and everything had receded into featureless shadows, the familiar alcoves and counters – her only connection to something familiar – completely out of reach. Đức had overridden the perception filters, turning the shop into something alien and threatening, one step away from a prison or a lacerator chamber. There was a faint sound in the background, cycling back every few blinks – reminding Hoà of Quỳnh struggling to speak and making only that broken, mewling noise.

Đức sat down, smiling at them like a kindly grandmother – except that no grandmother had that sharp, glittering mass of silver in her hair, a thicket like broken metal. The kỳ lân and giải trãi, the animals of peace and justice, twined around the pins, their horns shining in the dim light. She poured the tea in a fluid gesture, and pushed two of the three plates with steamed bao towards them.

'Eat,' she said, and it was an order.

Hoà bit into the dough. It was salty and sharp, and it was like ashes in her mouth.

'As I said,' Prefect Đức said, smiling – except it went nowhere near her eyes, 'I'm delighted to meet you.' The pronoun she used wasn't plural: it was aimed at just one of them.

Hoà glanced at Thiên Dung. Even moving her eyes was hard, as if struggling against invisible bonds.

'Which one of us?' she said, finally.

Đức smiled even more widely. 'Why, you.'

Hoà's stomach plummeted. 'I can't imagine I'd matter much to someone as exalted as the prefect.'

'Don't you? You keep such interesting company.' Đức shifted. 'Sometimes it does take less than a hundred years of meditation for two heads to rest on the same pillow.'

Thiên Dung's head came up sharply. Hoà tried to tell her to keep quiet, but she couldn't access any of the private channels. Or her bots. She'd been stripped of everything.

'This is about Quỳnh, then.'

Quỳnh and her revenge. Quỳnh and the prefect. At least it

wasn't *Flowers at the Gates*. It *couldn't* be the ship, because otherwise Thiên Dung would have been targeted, too. And because the prefect wasn't involved in that ... not yet. Not ever, if Hoà had anything to say about it.

'Ah, yes. The Alchemist of Streams and Hills. Such an ... unusual person, with such unusual interests. I've had my eye on her for a while.'

Hoà tried to keep her face neutral. It was hard, because those bots were watching her. Because a cell without a trial, or a sham of a trial, or a lacerator, weren't far away. Because Đức would break her without a second thought if she believed it would hurt Quỳnh.

'She's very interesting,' Hoà said.

'Isn't she? So many people she's been talking to, asking questions, spreading rumours. So many scholars.'

Quỳnh, Quỳnh, Quỳnh. What did you do? What did you say?

She had no idea, and it was by design, but it wouldn't protect her.

Hoà said, with an effort, 'I'm really not sure why you're here talking to us.'

'It's always useful to know which ships fly in the heavens as one, or which branches grow planet-side as one.' Đức was quoting, not from scholars, but from common proverbs about friendships. She clearly thought that neither Hoà nor Thiên Dung would be able to understand the more obscure allusions Quỳnh's scholar persona dropped into her interactions so casually. 'Think of my presence here ... as a warning.'

It was all too clear what kind of warning it was.

I own the Belt – you can disappear any moment, and Quỳnh will not be able to protect you.

Hoà's heart was in her throat. Đức was right: there was nothing that they could do to prevent her from doing whatever what she wanted.

'I think you should be talking to Quỳnh,' she said, breathing hard.

Đức bent towards her above the untouched teacups. The invisible hold on Hoà's body tightened until she couldn't even move a single muscle on her face, no matter how much she struggled.

'You're insolent. Not even averting your gaze from your social superior,' she said sharply. 'Take care what you look at. It might be the last thing you see.'

Hoà tried to look away, but her eyes were held fast. This close, she could see Đức's face: the corpse-white of the ceruse, the blood-red of the lips, the sharp cheekbones. She tried to speak, but nothing came out but a strangled croak, mingling with that agonised sound of someone trying to speak in the background.

'I ...'

'I'm not sure what she sees in you. Nothing in particular to recommend you. Another technologist.' She spat out the term as if it meant *vermin*. Her face took on a musing look. 'You have no skills worth speaking of. Perhaps she does need to see the blind cat in her life.' She used the expression for a person of no skills. 'It would be fitting, wouldn't it?'

No. *No.*

Two bots unfolded from her topknot and leapt on to Hoà's own cheeks, legs creeping ever closer to Hoà's open eyes – every movement a sharp, bleeding puncture. Hoà tried to close her eyes, couldn't ... Tried to track them, couldn't ... Any moment now they'd reach her ...

Pain, searing and sharp, stabbed into her left eyeball – raking across it once, twice. Hoà tried to scream, but whatever held her wouldn't even allow her that, as if her mouth was filled with thick, viscous fluid. And then the hold on her disappeared, and she was out of the chair, screaming, the bots falling away from her – feeling as though something large and painful had been wedged into her left eye.

'It'll heal,' Đức said, above her. Her voice was casual. That was the worst of it. She wasn't taking any particular joy in it: it was part of the game she played as easily as she breathed. 'It's an abrasion. I'd advise not rubbing it.' Darkness was receding. Hoà had her head in her hands, struggling to not touch her eyes, to just hold still, to stay there until Đức had left. 'And in the meantime, you can take the Alchemist a message.'

'What message?'

It was Thiên Dung, and she sounded so far away – and so... subdued, so weary, all the usual anger leached out of her, as if what the prefect had done had just snuffed out the light within her.

'Oh, you are the message,' Đức said. Hoà felt more than saw her smile. 'There's a reception at my compound to honour the arrival of the Orca Censor on the habitat. You're both invited. It'll give me great pleasure to see you again.'

To toy with them. To enjoy their powerlessness. To know that she could harm Hoà at any time, and Quỳnh would not be able to do anything – not that it would matter, because Quỳnh was so very busy trying to shut Hoà out of her life. Hoà tried to breathe, but it hurt too much. Everything hurt, and she gave up and curled up against the surface of the table, gulping and crying and hating every moment of it.

Something grabbed her – Đức's bots, lifting her head up by the topknot, forcing her to look. Everything was blurry and ached, but she could see the prefect's satisfied, vicious smile.

'A blind cat.' Đức held Hoà that way for a few moments more, as tears streamed down Hoà's face and the pain from the position mingled with the pain from her eye. Đức's blurred face was that of a nightmare – a hungry ghost's, an essence-gulping demon's. 'Perfect.'

And then she let Hoà's head drop. It took Hoà an effort to prevent it from slamming into the table.

'I hope you enjoy my hospitality.'

She swept out, the militia behind her. Hoà tried to lift her head, and couldn't be bothered, and the pain in her eye was just too much, as though someone had poked an iron bar into it — and Thiên Dung was there, bots swarming over her.

'I'm here. Breathe. I'm here. I have you.'

Breathe. I have you.

But who had them?

18

Fallout

Quỳnh woke up, tried to breathe, and was surprised when it caused no pain.

She was in one of the guest rooms in *Moon*'s compound. It was late at night, and the room was deserted. Someone had left tea on the bedside table.

Where . . . ?

She had a vague memory of managing to send Minh and *Heart's Sorrow* out before the attack hit. It had been *bad*. She'd seen the faces of Đình Sơn and of her mother, of her teacher Thanh Khuê, of her friends on board *The Azure Serpent* – a string of people tumbling into deep spaces, washed over by swathes of ever-changing light, eyes shrivelled in their orbits, bodies stripped of their skin and muscle to become glimmering bones – and those bones compressed by gravity to become jade-like beads, held in the hand of someone who might have been the prefect, or might have been the general. She'd had time to direct her bots to inject the antidote, and then *Guts of Sea* had been there screaming at her, and she remembered being deeply resentful at the ship without knowing why.

Quỳnh ran a hand over her chest. She couldn't feel the needle holes, but she could see them: darker areas with a single speck of dried blood. Too many. No wonder she felt wrung out.

'You're awake, then.'

It was Băng Tâm, wearing a nightgown embroidered with sea-swallows and spaceships.

'Yes,' Quỳnh said.

'How are you feeling?'

'Like the King of Hell chewed me up and spat me right out.' Quỳnh rose, wincing, light-headed.

'Sit.' Băng Tâm's voice was stern. 'Eat something.'

There were a handful of round rice cakes with translucent outsides. Quỳnh bit into one, feeling the nutty taste of black sesame flood her mouth. She was so hungry. She ate one, then another, then another.

'Do you know what *Guts of Sea* is doing?' She remembered now: how *Guts of Sea* had been deeply unhappy she'd brought Hoà here, and been followed by *Heart's Sorrow* and Minh and endangered *Moon*.

And she'd driven them off with a lie.

No, not even that. Something that she'd have said neither of them deserved to have: something close to the truth. Her anxieties about *Moon* and her fears for her child's future. She … she should have blamed the prefect, given Minh the final nudge to turn away from her mother. But she'd been too tired and too stressed.

No. That wasn't true. She could have done it; except that when she'd seen Minh, frazzled and angry – when she'd heard Minh inquire about her health, seeing through all of Quỳnh's pretences – she'd been reluctant to hurt her again.

'No,' Băng Tâm said. '*Guts of Sea* isn't here.'

Quỳnh didn't want to talk to *Guts of Sea*, but she supposed she'd have to at some point.

'How are you?'

'Bedtime was complicated.' Băng Tâm grimaced. 'But it was good, all in all. She's growing very fast.'

'Yes.' Quỳnh wanted to weep and was unsure why. Because, in another life, she'd have brought Hoà to *Moon* and they'd have had another kind of talk? Because, in another life, she'd still have Đình Sơn? 'And here you are, with another child who can't sleep.'

'You're not a child.' Băng Tâm looked preoccupied. Quỳnh scanned her bots' readings of his vitals. He was deciding whether or not to tell her something.

'Whatever it is that you think I can't hear right now, I want to hear it,' she said.

He was too used to her perceptiveness to show anything more than mild surprise.

'You don't,' he said. 'You can't keep running this ragged. How are you ever going to bring anyone down on no sleep and no food?'

She stared at him. 'You think that?' The short sentence emphasised the pronoun she used for him: *child* — a reminder she was older than him by quite a few years, and they'd never been familiar. A low blow.

Băng Tâm sighed. 'You'll find out anyway. The prefect visited Hoà.'

She what?

'What happened?'

'She's fine,' Băng Tâm said, but Quỳnh had already grabbed two sesame buns and thrown up a privacy screen while she called Hoà.

Hoà picked up almost immediately, in spite of it being only a bi-hour before dawn.

'Yes?' she said.

She looked exhausted, and there was something off about her that Quỳnh couldn't immediately place.

Quỳnh's own head was spinning, and she was acutely aware she was in an even worse state than the last time she'd had a conversation with Hoà. Beside Hoà, Thiên Dung glowered, but there was something curiously subdued about her. Quỳnh pulled down the same overlay where she'd taught Hoà: the grassy plain with the white birds wheeling over them, a reminder of *The Azure Serpent*, long-dead, that had so shaped their lives. Hoà and Thiên Dung stood there, staring at her.

'I heard the prefect visited you.'

'Yes.' Hoà's voice was curt.

'And?'

Hoà held up something. It was an envelope with the personal seal of Prefect Đức.

'This is for you,' she said. 'An invitation for both of us to attend the reception in honour of the Censor.'

'There's no need—' Quỳnh spoke before she could think.

'I know there's no need!' Hoà said forcefully. 'But this is what she came here to deliver.'

'She threatened you.' Quỳnh's voice was flat. 'I'm sorry. I didn't think—'

'You didn't think she'd come here?'

Hoà raised her hand, pulled it down, and her face wavered. She'd been using an avatar to disguise it: the virtual overlay had hidden the black eyepatch on her left eye.

She'd been hurt. Quỳnh's blood boiled, her bots unfolding their legs with a sharp sound.

'What did she do?'

'It's *just* an abrasion.' Hoà's tone was too angry for the dismissal in the words. 'It'll heal in a few days. Unlike you.'

'I don't understand,' Quỳnh said.

'You lied to me,' Hoà said. 'Despite our promise.'

'Wait—'

'No word that wasn't true, but you were about to have a constriction attack, weren't you? And you still sent me away.'

'Are you reproaching me for sending you away? There was another promise – you didn't want to be involved in my revenge. I've kept you out.'

'Kept me out, with the prefect taking an interest in my life? How is that supposed to work out? How am I supposed to be safe?'

'You know I couldn't guarantee that. That's not something I promised you.'

'No, but you promised me honesty. And did you keep that promise?'

This was emphatically not the way Quỳnh had wanted the conversation to go.

'I'm sorry.'

'No,' Hoà said. Her bots were very still on her shoulders, her whole body language distant. 'I don't need "sorry". How does *sorry* fix anything?'

'I'm not sure what you want me to fix. I can't control the prefect.'

'No. I know you can't. That's not the point. The point is ...' She was shuddering, struggling to breathe. 'You thought I couldn't deal with it. You sent me away because you didn't want me to see you weak.'

'I sent you away because you didn't want to be there when I dealt with Minh and *Heart's Sorrow* and explained to them why we were with *Moon*! You're already running scared of a brief visit by the prefect. How were you going to deal with their suspicions?'

Hoà's face blazed. '*A brief visit?*'

Quỳnh spread her hands, her bots following her gesture. 'You're scared. I get that—'

'No, you don't! The prefect was in our compartment. In our shop. She held me motionless while she wounded my eye and talked about how utterly insignificant I was, about how she was going to show you. About how little I mattered.'

'You matter! Of course you matter.'

'Do I?' Hoà's lone eye glinted in the dim light of the overlay. The birds cooed mournfully above them. 'Do I matter enough for the truth, big sis? For trust?'

'I trust you.'

'Enough to make decisions for me?' Hoà's face was hard. 'I thought I was clear. I'd face danger for you. Anything. As long as it was my choice, freely given. As long as you left me space to choose. And if you don't – if you're not capable of understanding what matters most to me – then I don't know what we're doing together.'

She was losing Hoà. As she'd always known she would. She'd never deserved her, or the happiness she brought. Love was doomed to be lost to her past, to her revenge. Minh and *Heart's Sorrow* – and Đức – were taking it apart, but it was no more than had always happened. Everyone she loved always ended tumbling into space: executed; wasting away; killed in an entirely avoidable accident. Only *Moon* remained – but she'd sent *Moon* away for her own good.

Quỳnh stared at Hoà, feeling cold certainty rise in her.

'What we're doing together,' she said flatly.

'Give me something.' Hoà sounded as though she was about to weep. 'Anything, big sis. A hope that you see in the future. That you believe in us as equals. That I'm not just another pawn to be moved, another child to be sacrificed.'

Moon. She was talking about *Moon*.

'Don't,' Quỳnh said.

'I will! Do you think it's fair to her?'

'No! But there is no other choice.'

'Of course there is. There always is. You refuse to see it.'

Quỳnh was going to lose Hoà. Not just lose her because Hoà was pushing her away, but because Hoà was going to die. This time, it had been an eye, but the next time – and there would be a next time, because Quỳnh couldn't prevent it from happening, couldn't seem to protect those she cared about – it would be something worse. Then Quỳnh would feel that pain and that guilt and that grief all over again.

No.

Better end it now, before it could destroy Hoà. Before ... Better to be honest with herself – to end it now, so it would hurt her less. So that her hopes wouldn't get too high before being utterly destroyed.

'We're doing nothing together,' Quỳnh said coldly.

Hoà jerked as if she'd been struck. 'What—?'

'You're right,' Quỳnh said. 'I can't keep you out of my revenge. I can't protect you.' She laughed, and it was bitter. 'And *Guts of Sea* is right, isn't she? I'm not here to waste my time on this. I'm here for justice.'

'There's no justice!'

'Oh, but there is. Heaven's justice. The sword of a dragon prince. The cry of an owl striking down rebels. One last charge of doomed mindships.'

'They all died!' Hoà said. 'That's the whole point of those stories we're told as children, big sis. They *never* survive.'

'Precisely,' Quỳnh said. The word tasted like ashes in her mouth.

End it. Better now, before the pain. Before the loss. Before the grief. It's fairer to everyone.

'You can't—'

'I can.' Quỳnh brought down the overlay until it was just them, with a thin line between them, separating the shop and the bedroom where Quỳnh was standing. 'Or are you forcing me against my will?'

'You know I won't.' Hoà's face was hard. 'But you have a life, big sis. You matter. You should matter more than the dead!'

Quỳnh laughed, softly, bitterly. 'You don't understand, lil sis. I'm already dead. I've been dead for a long time.' For a moment she'd believed she wasn't. For a sweet, brittle, wounding moment she'd believed in the possibility of happiness. But *Guts of Sea* was right: she'd never been there for any of it. 'And it's time for me to bring all of my kin out of Hell, and back into the habitats. Goodbye, lil sis.'

'Wait!' Hoà said, but Quỳnh had already cut the comms.

Quỳnh sat down on the bed, dry-eyed and exhausted, and with a growing emptiness in her chest.

It was for the best. It was what she needed, what she deserved.

End it.

End it all. Bring it all crashing down – Tuyết, Đức, all those who kept hurting her, even years after Dã Lan's execution.

End it all.

It was time.

Minh and *Heart's Sorrow* walked together all the way to Minh's shuttle, in awkward silence.

'So,' she said, as they reached the docks. They were far enough away that she could barely make out the insignia of the militia.

'So.' *Heart's Sorrow* sighed.

'Are you going to say anything?'

Heart's Sorrow looked shocked. 'No. I gave my word I wouldn't. You?' He hesitated. 'You asked her for something, didn't you? Before we left.'

Minh thought of Quỳnh, sitting alone in the darkness.

Are you all right?

No. But thank you for asking.

'No,' Minh said. 'I didn't ask for anything. But she gave me some advice all the same.'

Heart's Sorrow hesitated. Then: 'Are you willing to tell me what it was?'

'Not now.' Minh still felt raw and vulnerable – and as though the entire world had shifted entirely too many times. 'What about Second Great-Aunt?'

'She's waking up, but it's going to take time,' *Heart's Sorrow* said. 'You can check the bots if you want.'

She had. There were small, incremental changes on the way to wakefulness.

'The welcome reception for the Orca Censor is in two days.'

'I know. I don't have an answer, and we said we were going to leave it alone. Not attract undue attention. The Orca Censor isn't going to get to work straight away after the reception.' He spun around thoughtfully, his bots following his shadow. 'There are still seven days until the thirteen-year delay expires.'

'Yes, but ...'

He was looking at her, kind and mildly concerned. How did she tell him that Mother was going to do whatever she thought was right for the stability of the Empire?

Minh said finally, 'What would you do if you found out your mother had committed crimes?'

A thoughtful listing. 'I wouldn't be terribly surprised.'

'And if you had the evidence?'

'Is this what this is about? Do you have the evidence?'

He was concerned. Not panicked, not judging her, and she couldn't deal with the unfamiliarity of it all. She couldn't deal with the quiet support when she wanted the familiar – the barely disguised anger, the disappointment at her lack of skills.

'You know what – never mind. You're right. I'm just exhausted. I need more sleep.'

Heart's Sorrow didn't look as though he believed a word of it, but he had the grace to look as though he did.

'I'll see you at the reception, then?'

They hugged – she felt the weight of him, metal and thrumming motors, through the perception filters – and then he was gone, and she was walking back home – back to Mother.

Minh's room was as she'd left it: a garish mess of books and empty teacups that no bots had picked up. She was only half-surprised; Mother wouldn't have wanted to take care of it.

'Child.' It was Stepmother, standing in the doorway. Minh half-expected her to raise boundary filters, but all she said was, 'Your mother is working late. She'll see you when she's home.'

Minh stared at her – manicured, perfect, the five-panel tunic an intricate series of folds of peach and orange, with dragon embroidery just short of recalling imperial family imagery. Something shifted within her.

'I've done nothing wrong.'

Stepmother raised an eyebrow. 'Leaving the house for an entire day? You understand how worried we were?' She didn't look worried.

'I was worried!' Vân said. She'd come right up behind Stepmother, holding one bot in one hand and struggling to balance the other two on a half-done topknot. 'You could have been eaten by void-monsters!'

'There are no—' Minh closed her mouth just as Vân came barrelling into the room, arms outstretched, and threw herself on Minh, toppling her on her bed.

'I missed you so much today!' Vân said, a flurry of limbs and arms and bots. Minh could have fought her, but she was too ragged from everything else – and it was simpler to just sink into the mattress and let Vân sit on her. 'Where were you?'

'I was visiting scholars,' Minh said.

Stepmother's head whipped up, sharply. 'Were you?'

'Yes,' Minh said. 'About my mentorship.'

Stepmother's burning gaze held her; and for a moment she was staring into an abyss that would swallow her whole, given half a chance.

'I should hope they were suitable people,' Stepmother said freezingly. 'You have a duty to uphold the family name and honour.'

'Oh, for Heaven's sake,' Minh said, too exhausted to be diplomatic. 'I don't have a duty to frequent only approved people!'

'Hmm. You can take that up with your mother.' Stepmother made it sound as though she was happy to wash her hands of Minh's failure. Minh was too tired to care. 'Come on, child,' she said to Vân.

'No!' Vân said. 'I want to show Minh my dance.'

Stepmother's face softened, but she still shook her head. 'Later. Minh needs to rest.'

'And be punished.' Vân pouted. 'It's not fair.'

'That's not your business,' Stepmother said, and Vân ran back to her. As she did so, she sent a message to Minh via a private channel.

'I don't think Mama is right,' she said. 'You're a very brave and nice person, and your friends would be nice, too. And here's my dance!'

'Come, child,' Stepmother said, clearly heedless of Vân sneaking comms under her nose.

And then they were gone. Minh watched Vân's dance: it was a blurry video obviously shot by one of the bots, while the other two and Vân moved through something like a lion dance, with a faint overlay of the lion's head over Vân's face, Vân making exaggerated faces and giggling. Vân finished it with a blown hug at Minh, and a message that said 'Welcome home!' – and then it was dark, and there was just Vân's voice.

'It's a home dance,' she said seriously. 'So you come back. To me. Because sometimes I'm worried you'll leave and never return.'

Minh sighed. 'You're growing up,' she said, her heart feeling three sizes too large for her chest.

'I'm all right,' she said to Vân. 'And I'm not leaving forever, promise.'

Vân's answer was blowing more kisses and hugs.

Minh cut off the communications, and stared at the battlefield of her room. Her bots had been cleaning the teacups: there was fresh Jade Spiral waiting for her on a hastily cleared desk, but to get it meant getting up. Getting up meant moving.

She didn't want to move. She was thinking of Second Great-Aunt, up there in the heavens, slowly putting herself back together. What would she think, if she realised that her family had tried to sabotage her? What would she think if she realised her own daughter was trying to depose her?

What would she make of her own great-niece? The heir, meant to carry forward the family fortune. To find a mentor, a post in the civil service. To continue the work her mother had done – to rise higher than her, unhampered by her origins on board *The Azure Serpent*.

The thought of that future – that well-worn path, traced by someone who'd hurt others for their own gain – made Minh sick.

You need to find a tutor who suits you. You, and not anyone else.

You don't like my mother.

No.

Because she's unfair?

Minh stared at her hands. Two bots, one on each. She wrapped them around her wrists like coiled bracelets, but all she could feel was *Moon*'s weight, *Moon*'s laughter, the way being with her had felt just right, like the unfolding of a solar sail.

What would you do if I said yes?

Quỳnh had looked so gaunt, so out of breath. So desperate and unhappy. What kind of life was that, to have to deny your own daughter in order to rise through the ranks of society?

The same kind of life, wasn't it, that caused one to manipulate one's own daughter to advance. That spoke of family honour and suitable connections.

Mother treated people as pawns to be manipulated to make the Empire safer. And Quỳnh ... Minh didn't really know what drove Quỳnh. It was more than just *Moon* — but what kind of life was that? Forever separated from a child who could only call her *big auntie*; having to perpetually swallow her own secrets.

Quỳnh was worse: she treated herself as a pawn in her own designs.

And Minh ...

Minh didn't want to be either of them.

Minh didn't want to be a scholar at all.

She thought of Vân; of the weight of *Moon*, of the laughter that lit up the whole room. That was what she wanted. A child. She wanted to be a mother. A mother to a mindship.

It would be more complicated than that. That dream was going to involve sleepless nights, and fights. But she wanted to be what Mother couldn't be, what Quỳnh had given up on: she wanted to have a child, and to be as good a parent as she could.

And there was absolutely no way in the Numbered Planets the family would let her do it.

Mother received Minh in her office. Which meant she was particularly unhappy, or particularly busy, or both.

When Minh came in, there were four other people in the room, and an overlay tracking the arcing trajectory of a large, glittering mindship, *The Goby in the Well*. Mother was speaking to Magistrate Toàn.

'... make sure everything is ready for the Orca Censor's arrival.' She glanced, briefly, at the overlay. 'She's landing in two bi-hours. Is her section of the compound ready?'

Bảo Toàn swallowed. 'The overlays are still being put together—'

'Put them together faster,' Mother said sharply. 'And show me the rooms when they're done. I'm sure they'll need retouching.'

The other people were the commander of the militia and two clerks. The commander was clearly having some kind of private conversation with Mother, eyes glazed and looking deeply harried. The clerks held a list that they kept trying to wave in front of her, who was so far ignoring them in favour of glaring at Bảo Toàn.

One of them finally said, 'Prefect?'

'Yes?'

'The list of guests for the reception. I understand there were several additions. Also, concerning those arrests you wanted in the dining room ...'

Mother wasn't listening. She looked up, and saw Minh. Minh froze: the full force of that gaze felt as though she was being skewered alive.

'Ah, child. Leave us.'

'The guests—'

'*Now*,' Mother said.

Another flurry of activity as the room emptied, the commander flashing a wry, sympathetic smile at Minh as she left.

'Sit,' Mother said.

Minh didn't move. This was Mother. This was the person who'd raised her, the one who'd always done what needed to be done. This was the magistrate and the prefect of the scholars' files, the one committing numerous injustices.

'I said *sit*. I should think you've caused trouble enough as it is, wouldn't you agree?'

Minh dragged her voice from where it had fled. 'Tell me.'

'Tell you what?'

'If I've caused trouble, then tell me what kind of trouble.'

'Why, inconveniencing me.' Mother gestured again to the chair in front of her desk. The overlay of the Orca Censor's ship didn't vanish, but almost everything else did, save Mother's figure. Her bots gleamed in the dim light. Minh found herself struggling to breathe. 'Worrying me. What if someone tried to kidnap you again?'

Minh sat down. The chair wasn't particularly large, but Mother had done something to it, and it felt hard and absurdly large. As though she was a child.

'No one tried to kidnap me.'

'That's beside the point.' Mother sighed. 'I'm told you've visited unsuitable scholars, too.'

Vĩnh Trinh. Mạt Ly. The printing house. A lifetime ago.

'They're not ...' Minh opened her mouth, closed it. 'How are they unsuitable?'

'Oh, child. You never pay attention. They're not good enough for you.'

'I ...' Minh swallowed. 'Maybe I get to decide what's good enough for me.' It cost her everything she had.

'Do you?' Mother laughed. It wasn't even malicious. 'You're

young, and you have no idea what you're getting into. Just like at the Tiger Games.'

Minh's face flushed. She tried to control the slight movement of her bots, but Mother had likely seen it.

'I can take care of myself.'

Mother's gaze was pitying. 'I don't think so. You'll understand, when you're my age.'

It was the same things – the same condescension, the same continuous stream of words that left Minh utterly wrung-out and nauseated. She put up the only defence she could think of.

'Will I understand what you've done then, too?'

A pause. Mother cocked her head, looking for all the world as though she was deciding whether to throw Minh in jail.

'What I've done?'

'Bạch Loan. Mỹ Thuần.' Minh added a few more names from the list. 'You gave them harsher sentences than they deserved. And the ship. Second Great-Aunt. You've been trying to sabotage her.'

Mother stared at her. Then she laughed.

'*Flowers at the Gates of the Lords?* She won't wake up, child. Your little project of fixing her ... *Heart's Sorrow*'s delusions – that's never going to materialise. You're *children*.'

Not any more. Minh clenched her fists.

'She will wake up,' she said. 'She will. You've got no right to take what's hers!'

A silence. Something was tightening in the room: the weight of Mother's anger, a feeling that Minh had truly overstepped the mark this time – the giải trãi and kỳ lân coming out of the darkness, light glinting on their horns and spines and fangs, their maws wide open under pitiless starlight.

'I see. Is that how it is, then? You question me. You ignore filial piety.'

'I am allowed to ask for an accounting.' Minh wanted it to

sound firm, but it just came out as a strangled squeak. 'Master Khổng said—'

'Master Khổng has no say in this house!' Mother's voice was the blow of a lacerator. And then, more kindly, 'You don't understand, do you? You're not old enough.'

'I'm old enough for explanations!'

A silence. The darkness receded, until it was just the familiar office.

'Oh, child ...' Mother rose, came to sit on her desk, closer to the chair Minh was facing, the beasts behind her receding into nothingness. Her avatar changed, too, away from the stern magistrate, the make-up fading until it was just a faint touch on her face, the robes becoming simpler and rougher. 'You really don't remember, do you? You were so young, and so little. Child against parent, sworn sibling against sworn sibling. Entire planets laid waste. *The Azure Serpent* and so many mining rigs fragmented into ten thousand pieces.' There was grief in her voice. 'We're just one step away from that happening again. It's been ten years since the death of The General who Pacified the Dragon's Tail, but the rebels are still here. They haven't forgotten. They're still hoping to depose the Empress.'

Minh said, 'I'm really not sure—'

'We're one step away from chaos overwhelming us all. I *have* to be firm. I *have* to be merciless.'

'You always said you were fair!' Minh started

Mother gave her a look. It was the same look she'd given her when she'd caught Minh trying to sneak out of the compound at seven years old – a look of pity given to a naive child.

'Fairness is in the defence of what holds us together. The three fundamental bonds, the five constant virtues. Harmony. Peace.' Mother sighed.

'But surely—'

'If I was lenient, people would believe their offences would be forgiven. They would think me lax. They would take liberties.'

'I thought you were cruel,' Minh said.

Mother made a small, huffing sound. 'You think I derive pleasure from it? I don't. I do what's necessary. Do you understand?'

No, Minh wanted to say. She didn't. Not in the way Mother wanted her to. But this had never happened before. Grief. Emotion. Something that was more than constant judgement.

She said finally, 'What if I don't want to become a scholar?'

A sharp look from Mother. 'Why?'

Minh spread her hands. Did she trust Mother? No – and the knowledge was a stone in her stomach – but what other solution did she have?

'I'm not made to be one. If I withdrew from the examinations—'

'Surely you can't be thinking about this.' Mother frowned. 'What else would you do?'

Minh's survival instincts kicked in: she closed her mouth on what she actually wanted to do.

Mother sighed, bending over the desk so that her face was almost level with Minh's – lined and weathered by time, her eyes two pits of darkness.

'I love you. You know this, don't you? I only want the best for you.'

Minh wanted to say she knew, but the words felt like ash in her mouth. Did Mother love? Did she understand what it meant?

'I want to choose. I want to raise a child . . .'

Scholar-officials – the greater partners in marriages – were never the ones who bore or raised children.

'You?' The sheer, simple disbelief in Mother's voice cut Minh to the core.

'Why not?'

'You'd be such a terrible mother,' Mother said. 'You're intelligent, but you don't know how to be practical.'

As she spoke, Minh saw herself as Mother saw her. Small. Inadequate. Unable to cope. She'd be lucky to get a posting after the examinations.

'I ...'

Mother shook her head. 'It's a good thing I'm here for you. But I can understand that you don't want to be posted far from the Belt. It's scary, having to fend for yourself, especially in your situation.' She smiled. 'I've given so much for you. But I guess I can give a little more. Because you're asking. A post not too far away from here, where I could guide you. What do you think?'

Minh tasted bile in her throat. She was meant to say yes, like she'd said yes to the dress, to Mother dragging her to scholar after scholar – to all of it.

'That's ...' She breathed in, bracing herself against what was going to happen, knowing that Mother was going to snap. 'That's not what I want.'

A silence.

'You'd disobey me? No one will ever love you for that, child. You know that, don't you? There's no love for those children who don't do as they're told.'

The darkness was back, and Minh cowered in the chair as the full force of Mother's anger filled the room.

No one would love her. Minh didn't deserve anything. She was unfilial, a failure and a shame to the family. And yet ...

She thought of Quỳnh, and Quỳnh's weary sadness – and how she really wasn't going to sacrifice her happiness for someone else's sake.

She sat very straight, and said nothing.

Disobedience.

A different path.

One of the kỳ lân had padded closer, its breath becoming warmer and warmer on Minh's face, the perception filter making it seem as though she was about to be burned to cinders. Like the murderers and the rioters, and the people threatening the harmony of the worlds.

'I sacrificed so much to ensure your place in society. Made so many efforts to ensure your pitiful talent found a space.' Mother snapped her fingers, and the commander of the militia was back in the room. 'Go back to your room. The commander will escort you. You can reflect on the importance of family until the Orca Censor arrives.'

19

Resolve

Quỳnh sat in her empty room, staring at the wall.

She'd slept badly. She'd woken up gasping, lungs crushed by a constriction attack, the room suddenly filled with echoes of the past – the plunge into deep spaces, the death of Dã Lan – and all her ghosts lined up watching her: Mother, Thanh Khuê, Đình Sơn. She'd screamed at herself to breathe, again and again, while her bots injected her with the medication – and finally she'd fallen back into sleep as uneasily as if she'd fallen into deep spaces.

'I thought I'd find you there,' *Guts of Sea* said.

Quỳnh raised a hand. Her bots clustered at the end of the bed.

'Don't,' she said. 'You're going to ask how I could be so stupid. You're going to tell me that this was going to happen all along and you knew it.'

Guts of Sea moved closer, her bots scuttling on the floor. She sighed, and hovered over the bed, becoming smaller.

'I'm not here to make you unhappy.'

'No. I do that myself, don't I?' Quỳnh laughed, bitterly. 'Never mind.'

'You broke up, didn't you?'

'Don't you dare say it's a good thing.'

She'd told herself that, over and over again. And maybe she'd believe it. Maybe she'd feel less miserable in the time she had left.

'For Hoà? Or for you?'

For Hoà. Always for Hoà.

'Tell me about the reception,' Quỳnh said.

Guts of Sea looked as though she was going to say something.

'Gia Kiệt's testimony has been going through the network of the scholars, passing from trusted person to trusted person. I expect the biggest vid channel to pick it up and make it public shortly before the general arrives at the reception.'

By which time it would be too late for her to turn around.

'And the prefect?'

'Gia Kiệt talked to her earlier.'

'And the rest? The children? The mindship?'

Guts of Sea hesitated. '*Flowers at the Gates* is fixing herself. She's also pulling from the network. My guess is when she comes back online, she'll be fully informed, and furious.'

But furious enough to take down the prefect? Quỳnh had hoped for more time. For the rest of the plan to unfold, for the prefect to be made vulnerable through Minh's public denunciation.

'I don't think it's going to be enough,' Quỳnh said. 'The Orca Censor will not transfer the head of lineage, but it's not going to materially affect the prefect.

Another hesitation.

'You're not going to like this.'

Quỳnh thinned her lips. 'Out with it.'

'This,' *Guts of Sea* said.

It was a message sent to both of them, lost in the morass of messages Quỳnh hadn't had the heart to touch yet. It was from

Quỳnh's allies at court, Minister Giai Khanh and Academy Chancellor Hàn Lâm Bình.

Or rather, former allies.

'They're pulling out,' Quỳnh said.

'Yes,' *Guts of Sea* said.

'Why?'

Her heart sank as she read it. It was because of Hoà – in a roundabout way. Because Đức had gone with a minimal escort into the Technologists' Ring and made a show of ruthlessness. Because the minister and the academy chancellor were both convinced that Đức would weather any unrest in the Belt.

'They're scared.'

'Cautious,' *Guts of Sea* said.

Too cautious. Which meant she didn't have court support, nothing to remove Đức.

'Do you think the scholars ...?'

Guts of Sea spun in a 'no' pattern. 'They hate her. They'd be glad to move against her. But they won't move against an imperial censor. Too much risk.'

She should have known. She really should have known that, in the end, she was going to lose everything – happiness, and her chance at revenge. She should have known that Đức was going to take from her again and again, and survive whatever could be thrown her way. It didn't leave many options. It didn't leave any options.

'Then I'll do it,' Quỳnh said.

'Do what?'

'Can you remove the prefect's protections?'

'Her bots? Her network access? Yes, only for a few blinks. But ...'

'Oh, spit it out.'

'But you're going to get caught.'

'Yes,' Quỳnh said. 'That's the plan. I'm going to get caught *after* I kill her.'

It would be more satisfying if Đức fell the same way Tuyết was going to – undone by her own sins and greed. But Đức was too careful, and too influential. She'd courted the powerful, corrupted the greedy, chosen her sides carefully in factional wars. She wasn't going to be taken down so easily.

'We have the evidence we gave Minh,' *Guts of Sea* said, 'and the scholars are spreading it. If we gave that to the censor—'

'You know that won't work,' Quỳnh said. 'She's been cruel, but is the Empire going to care? She stopped the rebellions. She put an end to the Ten Thousand Flags Uprising. All the people she mistreated had already committed treason. Besides, the censor will be like all the rest of them. Like Giai Khanh and Hàn Lâm Bình. There's no justice in the Empire. There's no forgiveness for treason.'

'Not all the people she arrested were guilty,' *Guts of Sea* said gently. 'You forget Dã Lan.'

The thought she'd have to argue her own case – to review the evidence, to call up the ghosts already haunting her nights, investigate the same cause that had already led her to be summarily tortured and thrown out of an airlock like so much trash – opened a pit of fear in her stomach.

'No,' Quỳnh said. 'Dã Lan didn't matter then. She won't matter now.'

Guts of Sea said, 'Are you sure?'

What point is there to living anyway?

'Absolutely sure,' Quỳnh said.

Her friend hesitated. Then she said, 'I don't want you to die.'

No anger, no resentment: but the fear of losing someone she cared for. The same thing that had led her to disapprove of Hoà; the insecurity that Quỳnh wasn't sure she'd ever be able to fill.

Quỳnh smiled. She held out her hands, hugged *Guts of Sea*, feeling the harshness of her hull, the rough lines of her repairs, that little hitch in the leftmost motor that ran through the avatar as well as the ship's body.

'It's all right,' she said. 'It's just a formality, and it's worth it.'

Hoà was in bed, simultaneously checking *Flowers at the Gates*' vitals – while steadily avoiding Quỳnh's messages in the group channel they'd set up – and watching the ceremonies marking the censor's arrival.

'Big sis?' Thiên Dung, from the lower floor. She'd been fixing some kind of large duct-maintenance machine, a huge spidery contraption with a dozen arms spread on the table like a metal flower. 'Auntie Vy and the others are going to watch the ceremonies from the tea house. You want to come?'

The light hurt. Hoà readjusted her eyepatch, wincing. It felt as though a large, sharp piece of metal was stuck in her left eye permanently, one that would fall out if only she scratched herself enough. She thought of having to be bright and cheerful; of Auntie Vy's casual, 'Oh, where is your friend, the nice lady with the bots?' It was like a core of ice in her stomach.

'No,' she said. 'I'll watch it from here. I can keep an eye on the ship.'

Thiên Dung made a face. They'd had a chat about being invited to the reception. Hoà had expected Thiên Dung, always the careful one, to advise going, but Thiên Dung had surprised her by shaking her head.

'She got what she wanted,' she'd said. 'She hurt you, and hurt Quỳnh.'

Hoà had winced. 'I'm not sure I need the reminder.'

'That's not the point. The point is, it doesn't matter if we go. And I'd rather not expose myself to Belt dignitaries. I feel we've had enough of them, and I'd rather not lose an eye.'

'Lil sis,' Hoà had said.

Thiên Dung had sighed. 'Trying to make it funny. Or at least bearable. But fine. Do you agree we're not going?'

Hoà had thought of the prefect and felt a deep, stabbing pain in her abraded eye. She didn't want to face Đức again.

'Let's stay home,' she'd said.

And now it was the time of the reception, and Thiên Dung was set on watching it happen. Hoà wasn't.

'Don't force me to march up here,' Thiên Dung said.

'I'm the eldest.'

'Yep, and it's the youngest's duty to correct you when you err against the teachings of the masters.' A sigh. 'It was a very short acquaintance, and sometimes these things burn brightly. And quickly.'

'I don't want to hear this,' Hoà said. 'Not this way. Please. I don't really have the energy for any of this. I love you, but—'

'Yeah, I know.' Thiên Dung looked uncertain, which was disquieting; she generally marched into problems, looking to solve them by sheer strength of will. 'Sorry, that was thoughtless. I want to say it's for the best, but ...' She took another deep breath. 'She made you really happy, didn't she?'

'Yeah.' The word seemed inadequate for the hole where Quỳnh had been. 'And really unhappy, too.'

We're doing nothing. She remembered how Quỳnh had looked when she said it – cold and distant, the same face she must show her enemies. The feeling of being punched in the gut – so, so much worse than the pain when Đức had scratched her eye.

Thiên Dung opened her mouth, closed it. 'I don't know what to say.'

At least it was honesty.

'Just leave me here. I'll be fine.'

Thiên Dung gave her a look that suggested she knew perfectly well that Hoà would not, in fact, be fine.

'You're always on priority comms, you know.'

Hoà made a gesture. 'I know.'

Thiên Dung vanished, and Hoà was alone in the shop. Not that it meant privacy, when Đức could come back at any time. Hoà didn't have to look downstairs to know that the invitation would still be there, a palpable weight in the house.

On the welcome ceremony overlay, the Orca Censor was disembarking from her ship, and Đức was walking up to meet her, standing by her side while the vids filmed and took stills that would be disseminated to every corner of the habitat.

The Orca Censor – Censor Tang Thuyền – was much younger than Đức. She couldn't have been much older than Hoà herself – perhaps thirty years of age – and the rejuv treatments made her look much younger. She was built like a wrestler, squat and broad-shouldered, and unostentatious in the physical and virtual: a mere patch of a lion roaring in virtual, and a few scattered sprigs of willow on her robes. Her topknot was similarly sober, neat, with titanium pins, an eminently practical metal. Her escort was similarly dressed in sober tones.

Đức, by contrast, was all sharp ostentation, her robes embroidered with giải trãi and kỳ lân, and the shadows of the beasts hovering at her shoulders – just short of being vulgar. She was smiling broadly as she embraced Censor Tang Thuyền, and the censor was smiling back, falling into what looked like casual conversation with her. So they knew each other.

Standing side by side on the docking platform, in the midst of an overlay saturated with vermilion, they looked like two old friends meeting up again. Of course. Quỳnh had been right: it was all an enclosed world with little space for the small people, or for anything like justice.

Quỳnh.

She was going to break herself bringing any of them down, and she knew it, and she didn't care. How could she have so little regard for herself?

None of Hoà's business. It was none of Hoà's business. Hoà was going to keep her head down. She was going to focus on *Flowers at the Gates* – at least, with all the fuss with the censor's coming and whatever Quỳnh was doing, no one except Hoà, Quỳnh, *Heart's Sorrow* and Minh was keeping an eye on what was supposed to be a dead, unfixable ship.

On the overlay, Đức and Tang Thuyền were walking side by side towards a shuttle decorated with apricot sprigs, headed to Đức's compound for the reception. Where was Quỳnh? What did she have in mind?

Hoà stopped herself halfway through pinging Quỳnh. No. They'd both made their choices and they'd both walked away, or been pushed away. They'd both reached the conclusion there was no future for them. There was nothing left to say.

She was spiralling in pointless recriminations, but she couldn't afford to be depressed when *Flowers at the Gates* was going to need her.

Hoà took a deep breath, and closed the overlay of the censor's arrival. Watching it just hurt her. But, even with it closed, it didn't change the nameless feeling in the pit of her stomach, the silence that dragged on and on, only broken by the click of her bots' legs on the floor.

'I miss you,' she said, into the silence. 'Demons take me, I miss you.'

And before she knew it, she was crying, in great heaving sobs that felt as though they were tearing her entire chest apart, one after the other in what felt like an endless hollowing of herself. She wanted Quỳnh to be there, to hold her, to kiss her and tell her they would find a way forward. That it might have been fraught and tangled and uneasy, but that they had each other.

She wanted so many things, and wouldn't get any of them.

The overlay opened again. She'd closed it, surely?

'Big sis?' It was Thiên Dung. 'You're going to want to see this.'

She didn't want to see an—

Oh.

It was a vid, and it was someone she didn't know: a scholar, except he was bloodied, skin gashed in multiple places – the thin, inflamed marks of a lacerator that had also torn his clothes. He'd been speaking for a while. Hoà's bots were reviewing the rest of the vid even as she listened to him, trying to piece together what he was saying.

'I was another person, back then.'

The first of her bots' feedback reached her, sentences in bits and pieces.

Murders.

'I haven't really slept since it was discovered ...'

It was easy, all I had to do was to lure them to my compound ...

Eighteen victims.

'I think we should all face punishment for the things we've done ...'

The general helped cover it up.

The vid cut abruptly; it was replaced by three scholars, talking acrimoniously.

'This can't be true. He's one of us.'

'The evidence is clear—'

Thiên Dung said, over their private channel, 'It's everywhere over the Technologists' Ring. Auntie Vy is pissed. There's going to be *riots* over this, big sis.'

'Yes, I know,' Hoà said. 'I'm sorry, I can't deal with it right now.'

'For sure. Just be careful. It's going to be wild out there.

Hoà muted Thiên Dung.

Tuyết. Murders. Complicity.

'This is your doing, isn't it?' Hoà said aloud to Quỳnh, not really expecting an answer.

Hoà checked on the ship: *Flowers at the Gates* was about a bi-hour from being functional enough to talk, and a few more bi-hours from having network connectivity. Hoà sent the bots on board the ship towards the cut network cables.

On the other overlay, the scholars were still talking.

'The general is at the reception ...'

'What response ...?'

Hoà dropped the privacy screens, and listened to the sounds outside the shop – the slow swelling of ten thousand voices, silenced for too long. She thought of Quỳnh and her fifteen years of unyielding patience; of *Flowers at the Gates'* thirteen years of unending pain; of Đức and the scratch in her eye. Within her, Thiên Hạnh's dormant mem-implants were stirring, whispering words in a language that might as well be from outside the Empire.

Hoà wasn't Quỳnh, and she couldn't say she was feeling particularly sorry about any of it. But there was only one response Đức could have – the arrogant, power-hungry prefect, obsessed by order and righteousness. As Quỳnh had said, there would be no forgiveness, no amnesty. Not on her watch.

Tuyết was doomed.

And it really shouldn't have been any of her business. Her responsibility was to *Flowers at the Gates*, and it stopped there, and she wasn't going to meddle any more than she should.

But ...

But Tuyết was *Heart's Sorrow*'s mother. And *Heart's Sorrow* – no matter how clumsily, how inappropriately – had genuinely cared, and genuinely tried to help Hoà.

Hoà took a deep breath, and sent a message to *Heart's Sorrow*.

'You probably have lots of people to talk to who know this better than I do. But if you want me, I'm here.'

Then she lay back on her bed, dry-eyed, exhausted, with the angry sounds of the crowd in the Technologists' Ring swelling on and on – and waited.

Minh used her time in her room to look up how to apply to bear a mindship.

It was surprisingly easy, and required little. Not even parental consent, since she was of age. She'd known she was, but it was the first time the consequences were manifest to her. It was disquieting.

It did require her to complete a pre-implantation examination prior to being able to sign a binding contract. Which was a little complicated, given that she was effectively grounded.

There was a centre in the Technologists' Ring, quite near where Hoà and Thiên Dung's shop was.

She thought for a while, letting the cold feeling of clarity wash over her – the tail end of that sense of resolution and rightness that had filled her when she'd first thought about doing this. Sneaking out the last time had ended up in an unmitigated disaster.

On the other hand, she wasn't heading into a riot this time.

Mother would be angry, and rage on and on and on, but Minh didn't believe Mother had her best interests at heart any more. Minh didn't believe Mother loved her. Had ever loved her. Was capable of love at all. And the thought was acid in her stomach, an emptiness that swallowed everything she'd thought about herself. A great wobbling of the people in her orbit that felt like a tearing of the universe.

Mother wasn't going to stop her, not this time.

She'd sneaked out the last time, and they hadn't patched any of the loopholes she and *Heart's Sorrow* had used to get into the safety system of the compound. No, she was being unfair. They'd made an attempt at patching things, but it was shoddy and inefficient.

Minh wasn't supposed to be plugged into the network, and certainly not this deep into its layers. But it was a simple matter to give herself privileged access again, and to make one of the shuttles appear to be down for maintenance.

She might get caught, still. Network security was abysmal, but physical security was higher, both because she'd done this once before, and because of the Orca Censor's visit, and the party that was in its opening stages. The first guests were already arriving – she'd caught a glimpse of the general's shuttle heading their way, probably with *Heart's Sorrow* on it.

She hadn't talked to *Heart's Sorrow* since she'd all but said no to Mother. She could have, but …

But she was afraid he would judge her, the way Mother had. To see her as small and pathetic, and with absolutely no capacity to be anything outside the path traced for her. Of course he wouldn't. But …

But she couldn't be sure. She knew that he was her friend, but she didn't *believe* it where it mattered – in her heart of hearts, in her guts.

Minh took a deep breath, and started applying her disguise again – the same avatar as last time, with the dragon's antlers and the showy bots. She touched up a few things – the galaxies were replaced by a dying, fractured sun, and she altered the colour of the clothes from peach to blue. She left the auth-token as that of a student.

She might get caught. And if she did … she'd probably not be able to sneak out a third time. That was a little too much to ask.

But she could do something about that.

Minh finished applying her disguise, and called up the

overlay again. She logged on to the imperial examination system, and stared, for a while, at her own profile. Her picture – pale and queasy, as though she'd been caught just coming out of deep spaces – stared back at her: that of a stranger from another time and space. There was an option for dropping out of consideration for this year's examinations. When she picked it, it asked if she was sure, given that such a decision couldn't be changed.

Yes. That was the point of it. That it couldn't be changed. That Mother – for all that she was the prefect, for all that she was well connected – couldn't reverse a decision that would have gone all the way to the First Planet, to the Empress herself.

Are you sure?

Yes.

The overlay fuzzed, and went black for a brief second, before Minh's style name, seal and picture were struck through.

Done.

It was done. She was free.

Why did she feel so scared? Why did she feel as though she couldn't breathe – that any moment now, something terrible was going to happen to her on account of the terrible thing she'd done?

She was of age. She was her own person. She could make her own choices.

She *was* going to make her own choices.

Minh took a deep breath, called her bots to her, and pushed the doors of her room open, striding outside towards the distant shuttle.

Everywhere Minh went in the compound, it was full of people and bots on their way somewhere else. Bots holding huge steamers full of food, human servers with trays of tea, militia people checking overlays against outside access – Minh had a brief pang of guilt for how badly done it all was, but it wasn't her problem any more.

No one thought there was anything amiss about her presence. Minh had turned off her disguise for the moment, and she simply looked as though she knew where she was going. It wasn't going to be a problem until she reached the outer reaches of the compound – and if she was lucky, the flow of guests moving the other way would be giving security a headache.

Wait.

The room ahead of her was just next to the main banquet room, which was being turned into a reconstruction of something Minh couldn't quite place: an old-fashioned compartment with windows opening on to a vast expanse of stars, except everything was larger than it should have been. And in the middle of it ... the commander of the militia, the woman who'd escorted Minh back to her room, was directing a couple of her people to do a final sweep.

The commander would *definitely* ask Minh why she was out of her room, and Minh definitely couldn't lie convincingly.

She pulled up her disguise; it wouldn't withstand close scrutiny, but hopefully it wouldn't have to. Then she took a deep breath and changed her posture and way of moving, as far away from possible from the confident daughter of the house, just looking like one of the servers on their way to the kitchens, or something else.

The overlay had perception filters that made the space much larger, and crossing it felt as though it took forever. Minh forced herself to breathe; to not look at the commander. She appeared to be berating one of the militia for some failure.

Ouch. Minh's knee had bumped into one of the tables. She caught the grunt of pain she wanted to let out, and forced herself to walk towards the door at the end of the space, which opened on a vast, spinning galaxy on the floor. She could do it. She . . .

One.

Two.

Three.

You can do it.

The commander's gaze turned to her – held her, brief and puzzled, before a flicker of recognition. She snapped her fingers, one of her bots scuttling up to her. But then one of her militia interrupted her, and she broke eye contact with Minh to deal with them – and then seemed to lose interest.

Phew.

Minh reached the door, slipped through it, barely daring to look.

'Ah, child.'

It was Stepmother. She was wearing a five-panel burgundy dress with carp slowly growing into serpentine shapes – just shy of turning into dragons, which were an imperial family prerogative – and a cape in the same pattern. Her topknot left her hair flowing loose, and in the darkness of it falling down her shoulder were glints like tens of thousands of pieces of silver. Her gaze raked Minh from head to toe, and she sniffed.

'I was looking for you.'

'Really?' Minh tried to sound casual. It didn't work, because her heart was hammering so hard in her throat it must have been heard all the way to the Outer Rings.

'Yes,' Stepmother said firmly. 'We need to talk.'

Before Minh could so much as open her mouth to protest, she swept away, her bots fastening themselves to Minh's legs, pushing her on.

There was no way Minh was going to get away from her.

Stepmother finally stopped in her own study: a room Minh

had only dim memories of, since she and Stepmother had carefully avoided dealing with each other ever since Mother had remarried. The physical layer was barely visible under the thick overlays: row upon row of alcoves for scrolls in the style of vintage libraries, a hint of a bamboo grove and stars on the ceiling. The low table in the middle of the room, the one Stepmother was sitting in front of, was displaying her personal seal, over the giải trãi insignia Mother so loved.

'What do you want to talk about?' Minh asked.

Calmer. She had to be calmer. Just get through whatever conversation Stepmother had in mind – a lecture, quite likely, on how Minh was a disgrace to the family.

Stepmother's bots were pouring tea into two cups. She gestured towards Minh, offering her the tea. Minh took the cup; stood, uncertainly, holding it, half-expecting Stepmother to demand she sit. But Stepmother didn't. She was merely looking at Minh with bright, curious eyes and a peculiar expression.

'Talk,' she said softly, and raised the cup to her lips, inhaling the steam.

She said nothing more. What could she want? How much had she guessed of what Minh was up to? Minh didn't know what to do. To keep herself from panicking, she drank the tea, wincing at the acrid taste. It had been left to brew too long, and it felt as though someone had thrown flecks of copper into it. Minh drained the cup, hoping the taste might go away. It didn't.

Stepmother was still looking at her, two bots on either side of her. There was ... something wrong with her smile.

'Let's talk about you,' she said.

'Me?' Minh said. 'Is this going to be about my visiting unsuitable scholars again? Mother's already punished me for this.'

'She did.' Stepmother sighed. She put down her cup, put

her arms up, elbows on the table, and her head on her joined hands. 'Just as she punished you for sneaking off to the Tiger Games. To little effect, it would seem.'

'That's ...' Minh breathed in, hard. It hurt. She'd been holding it too long. Too much stress.

'Still, I thought it was a teenager thing. That it would pass.'

Minh didn't say anything. She suddenly realised she wasn't really supposed to. Stepmother was lecturing her.

A pause. Stepmother didn't move. The moment stretched, on and on.

'Until today.'

'Today?' Minh was sweating.

'Your mother is busy. As she should be – this is the crowning achievement of everything she's worked for. An imperial censor here, to recognise her right to be head of the lineage, her daughter poised to become a scholar.'

'I told her I didn't want to.' Minh's voice sounded weak and tinny, as if she was putting up lead walls against an onslaught of radiation – too slowly, too inefficiently.

'What you want doesn't matter!' Stepmother's face became angry for a fraction of a second, then smoothed itself out. It wasn't just off. It was *scary*.

'Stepmother ...'

Stepmother gestured. In front of her was an overlay of the imperial examination interface, with Minh's name greyed out when she'd withdrawn.

'As I said, your mother is busy. She thought everything was under control. In so many places. In her own household.' She gestured again, and an image of *Flowers at the Gates* superimposed itself on the previous one. 'With her aunt.'

Minh stared at Stepmother. At the cup of tea still in her hand. She swallowed, the metallic taste in her mouth not going away.

'Cinnabar Clouds,' she said, slowly, carefully. '*You*'re the poisoner. Why ...?' she started, and then stopped. It was painful to speak. And pointless. Stepmother would gain from being the wife of the head of the lineage – from the increased status of the family. And she'd always been obsessed with the status, and she'd never liked Minh – who wasn't her own daughter.

Stepmother didn't move. Darkness deepened around her, and the overlay of the gardens behind her seemed to waver, all the features of the bamboo grove bleeding into one another.

'I'll tell Mother,' Minh said. 'I—'

'Your mother is busy,' Stepmother said. 'And you don't have time to reach her.'

Mother. Mother was ... Mother was many things, but she wasn't going to *harm* Minh. Not that way. Mother. *Mother*. Minh tried to speak, but it hurt – and the world was spinning and spinning, and she couldn't seem to hold on to anything. She tried to find her comms or her bots, but the interface kept slipping away from her.

Mother.

She fell, into feverish, choking darkness.

20

Unrest

Quỳnh arrived at the prefect's compound on one of *Guts of Sea*'s shuttles. She watched it grow larger and larger in overlay: an entire asteroid converted into an underground citadel, a place that was a house and a fortress and possibly a courtroom, too.

She rested her hand on the brocade of her clothes: a five-panel with the bare outline of giải trãi, hidden underneath the interlocked patterns of constellations and the centrepiece of the Fire Palace, the fractured planet on the edges of the Empire. The shuttle was navigating between smaller pieces of debris, veering to take its place in a queue of others.

'You're only going to have one chance,' *Guts of Sea* said.

'I know,' Quỳnh said.

She hadn't brought any sharp weapons: they wouldn't have let her keep them. But so many things that weren't intended to harm could be made to do so. She let her hand run over her hairpins: long and sharp and coated with a poison that would close up a throat in less than a heartbeat.

One wound. An artery, preferably.

It was going to be difficult: Đức was already suspicious of Quỳnh. She wasn't going to expect all her protections to fail, but it was still a chance ... one which Quỳnh was steadily trying to focus on, rather than think of what she'd done to Hoà.

'The news about the general just dropped,' *Guts of Sea* said. 'The network is alight with chatter.'

Quỳnh breathed. Darkness was creeping in on the edges of her field of vision: another of the constriction attacks she was having so much trouble keeping at bay. The past, catching up with her. She'd always known it would. She had the bots inject her with a touch of sedative.

'You have to keep sharp,' *Guts of Sea* said disapprovingly.

'Yes,' Quỳnh said. 'I have to stay alive. At least until it is over.'

The sedative was spreading through her, making everything a little less wounding, a little less fearsome. She could do this. She was ready. She was so close to getting everything she'd ever wanted, and yet everything was so far from the plan.

One chance.

One last spreading of the mạt chược tiles on the table.

If she could not have life and happiness – and she had known for a long time that she could not – then she was going to make sure neither of her tormentors had them, either.

The shuttle docked with an audible crunch. *Guts of Sea* turned off all the overlays, and turned to Quỳnh, spinning to take all of her in.

'It'll do,' she said. 'I'm ready.'

Quỳnh nodded. 'Let's do this.'

A bored-looking militia person searched Quỳnh, and examined *Guts of Sea*'s bots.

'You're good,' she said. 'Here.'

She'd imposed visitor's filters on them, with fairly stringent rules: no overlay access other than on their own bodies, no outside network comms, and an inability to turn off the local perception filters.

That was interesting.

'That's a lot of restrictions,' *Guts of Sea* said. Not that she cared, as she was going to sidestep them the moment she was out of sight.

The militia person shrugged. 'You're not the first to complain. Take it up with my superiors.'

So it applied generally, not just to them.

'It's fine.' Quỳnh moved forward to join the flow of guests heading from the docks to the reception.

Everyone who was anyone in the Belt was there: scholars, courtesans, data artists, a vast riot of avatars, elaborate clothes and scents ranging from the sharp, oily planet-side perfumes to the softer and more floral ones favoured by the Belt.

'Oh, younger sib, younger sister,' *Guts of Sea* said, moving closer to Vĩnh Trinh and Mạt Ly, the owners of the printing press.

'Elder sister,' Vĩnh Trinh said. They were wearing their hair long, with no topknot, falling in disarray over a robe with no patterns and no embroidery. Their partner Mạt Ly was more conventionally dressed, her multiple bots riding on her arms and in the braid down her back. 'Did you hear the news about the general? It's so shocking, isn't it?'

'Is she here?' Mạt Ly asked.

Of course she'd be here. Of course Tuyết would be want to be at the centre of things, always drawn to status as if it could guarantee her safety. Quỳnh tried to feel angry, or sad – or anything – but there was nothing.

'She's inside, I think,' *Guts of Sea* said smoothly. 'Do you know how it's playing out in the Outer Rings? There must be a lot of resentment ...'

Quỳnh couldn't stand still, or face the thought of small talk.

'Excuse me,' she said, forcing herself to smile, though her mouth felt full of glass shards. 'I'm going to wander down to the reception.'

As she walked away she felt something tear in the air around her. *Guts of Sea*'s presence shimmered close to her again. All the visitor's filters lifted — and she had network comms again, though it seemed to be flickering on and off.

'I'm working on the outside network,' *Guts of Sea* said. 'Their security on that is a bit higher. It's quite probable they're hoping to keep the general ignorant of what's going to happen. Don't wander too far.'

Quỳnh sighed. 'You're not my mother.'

'No,' *Guts of Sea* said. 'Your mother is dead because of them.'

'I don't need more motivation right now.'

I need . . .

She needed less stress, but that was impossible. She needed reassurance that all was going to be well, and she would never have that, either.

Quỳnh followed the corridors to the reception room — deftly disengaging herself from anyone who wanted to engage her in conversation. It was a huge expanse of darkness: the River of Heaven scattered at her feet, every constellation sharply outlined, stars moving under her feet alongside koi and miniature spaceships, and the unobtrusive household bots scattered among them. Tables were laid out on huge flat barges, under vermilion awnings — and over it all was the shape of the Belt and its most distinctive habitats, from the Lotus Vũ to the Apricot Hồ. The Belt dignitaries were on the largest barges — Quỳnh looked for Đức. She didn't know how much time she had before Đức got bored of toying with her. Censor Tang Thuyền's presence was going to keep Đức busy, but not for long.

Quỳnh couldn't see her, or the censor. *Heart's Sorrow* was on one of the smaller barges, in conversation with twin sisters that were vaguely familiar — oh, Oanh's children, from the merchant family. She made for him. Perhaps he would know where his mother was, or where Minh's mother was. She couldn't see Minh, either. She hoped Minh was all right. At least this didn't involve anything that would directly harm her, not any more.

At least it was just her now.

As Quỳnh moved towards *Heart's Sorrow* – stars wheeling beneath her feet, barges full of dignitaries slowly dancing around her – the atmosphere shifted and tightened, and *something* drew her gaze to the other end of the room.

There were Đức and Tang Thuyền, standing side by side on a large lacquered platform that only vaguely looked like a boat. Behind Đức was her wife, San, with a young child in her arms, wriggling to catch the fragments of asteroids that fell in overlay.

Đức raised her arms. 'Thank you all for coming,' she said, her voice booming over the room, and every face turned towards her. 'We are honoured to welcome Orca Censor Tang Thuyền.'

Quỳnh turned and saw that the barges behind her were moving, opening a straight path strewn with stars: on one side, the platform with Đức, and on the other, a path opening towards where Tuyết and her wife Nhăng stood, in the centre of a gradually widening ring. It wasn't just the people scattering: the fishes and the spaceships were leaving, too, and the bots were closing in.

Almost time, then.

Tuyết caught Quỳnh's eye, and moved on to stare at Đức, pale-faced and with fear in her eyes. But Nhăng held Quỳnh's gaze, burning and sharp, giving her a small, tight nod almost of camaraderie.

What? Why ...?

'However, before we can start celebrating, a little housekeeping is in order,' Đức said. 'It's been said that Heaven should not suffer any wrongdoers, and we all understand the importance of keeping a blue sky to live under, and a clean and orderly house, so that the bonds between parent and child, empress and subject, and greater spouse and lesser spouse, may be safeguarded.'

There was no one around Tuyết. She cast around as if hoping for someone – for anyone – to help her, but there was just the militia, closing in. Her mouth opened, but Nhăng squeezed her hand and she said nothing. Nhăng herself stood very straight, hands at her side, as if she was only moments away from picking up weapons and very deliberately didn't.

Finally.

Finally. The time had come.

'General Tuyết!' Đức called out. 'Her Majesty the Daughter of Heaven, the Radiant Prosperity Empress, does not suffer murderers in her realm. And those who were complicit are as guilty as those who committed the deeds. You and your wife are under arrest for the crime of Gia Kiệt's murders.'

It was done. Almost done. She needed to get to the prefect. Quỳnh turned to the dais, hoping to make her way there. There was no one in her path.

There . . .

'Ah, Alchemist.'

She hadn't even seen the prefect move. She stood next to Quỳnh – something she'd done through the overlays, or maybe she'd never been on the dais at all – but she was there at Quỳnh's side, not quite close enough to touch or stab, but blowing a perfume of grass and sandalwood into Quỳnh's nostrils, and smiling at her, the same way she'd smiled when Dã Lan had been brought before her. Quỳnh fought a wave of dizziness that made the entire world spin, trying to hold on to something – anything.

'Prefect,' she said, and her voice came up short and ragged.

'I'm so delighted to see you here,' Đức said. 'I was expecting to see your friend, too.'

Quỳnh said, 'Hoà? Hoà isn't my friend. Just someone I worked with for a time.'

Đức laughed, a sound that was too loud and pierced Quỳnh's eardrums, causing another wave of dizziness – the beginning of a constriction in her lungs. They were in the centre of a gradually widening ring, Quỳnh had noticed, and she suspected what was coming, but she didn't know what to do. She was back in that quiet room where she'd breathed in the smell of tea, and a younger Đức had opened the door, and the militia had filed in, and the long nightmare had started: the cells and the lacerator and the summary execution – and the loss of everyone she'd held dear.

'Yes, she doesn't matter, does she? And I would say you don't, either, but you've been keeping such intriguing company.'

'I don't see ...'

The hairpin.

Her hand crept up, into her hair – it was shaking, and even that gesture felt like lifting the heaviest of loads.

'Oh, spare me the lies,' Đức snapped.

The censor was waiting on the dais, unmoving and so far beyond Quỳnh's reach she might have been back in the Numbered Planets. The censor wasn't going to save her in any case – the Empire had given up on Quỳnh.

'You've been talking to the scholars, Alchemist. You and that mindship of yours. Sneaking about behind my back, as if I wouldn't know. Spreading rumours, collecting rumours. Sedition, Alchemist.'

Quỳnh's hand closed on the pin. It was cold, and the cold travelled up her arm like a shock, constricting her breath further. All she had to do was speak – signal *Guts of Sea*, reach out before it was too late.

'A scholars' debate. It's a common occurrence.'

'Sometimes debate goes entirely too far.'

'Sometimes the truth is hidden,' Quỳnh said, slowly, carefully.

There was nothing that would save her. There would never be anything, other than what she held in her hands.

'The truth is held in the hands of the Empress. The truth sits on the Dragon Throne. The truth is my province.'

Quỳnh opened the channel to signal *Guts of Sea*, tensing her arm to strike.

'Then tell me ... in which specific areas do you think I have erred?'

Đức laughed again, and stepped aside, out of Quỳnh's reach.

'Oh, Alchemist. The truth is that we'd all be much safer if you weren't around.'

Something rose, in the overlay behind her – the animals on her silver hairpins, detaching themselves to become large, horned silhouettes, just as the constriction seized up Quỳnh's lungs and sent her, gasping, to her knees, her bots so close and yet so completely out of her reach.

She was back in that room, on the carpet – back in the lacerator – back in space, drifting off and struggling for a breath that never came, eyes swelling up, everything burning and burning, and this time there would be no mindship to save her ... this time ...

'Sương Quỳnh, Alchemist of Streams and Hills.' Đức's voice was the lash of the lacerator. 'You are under arrest for breach of the peace, and sedition. And so is your friend.'

Friend. She meant *Guts of Sea*. She meant Hoà.

Đức knew about Hoà.

She needed to protect Hoà.

There was someone screaming and it was her, and it was *Guts of Sea*—

'Run! Warn Hoà!' Quỳnh screamed at her friend – and then

there was nothing but the militia closing in, and her useless hairpin falling to the floor.

Hoà woke up with a start.

Someone was pinging her insistently. *Heart's Sorrow*.

'Wait,' she said. 'One moment.'

She forced herself to sit up in bed, wincing at the way the light caught her damaged eye – her eyepatch had slid down again. She dimmed the lights, not feeling like dealing with anything that required a physical effort when she was busy motivating herself to get out of bed.

'Come in,' she said.

Heart's Sorrow's avatar materialised in the middle of the bedroom, spinning wildly out of control and pulsing in and out of focus.

Whoa.

'Slow down,' Hoà said. 'Slow down. Breathe. Can you breathe for me?'

He turned to her, front plate facing her, and then back again, as if he was expecting armed militia to burst out of the metal walls.

'Is it safe?'

Hoà threw a privacy filter over them both like she'd throw a comfy blanket.

'Breathe,' she said again, asking her bots to put together some tea in overlay. 'What's happening? I know the stuff that came out is a lot—'

'No,' *Heart's Sorrow* snapped. 'No, that's not it! You don't understand.'

Hoà spread out her hands. 'I'm not going to understand unless you explain.'

'Sorry. Sorry. I cut the comms before they could remember I was there, but they're probably on their way to me, too, it'll just take them a little longer. I'm moving my body out of the docks into the further asteroids ...' He stopped, voice hitching. 'My mothers are under arrest.'

'Oh. *Oh.*'

Of course. *Of course* that was the plan. Of course Đức wouldn't actually wait to make her move.

'At the party?' Hoà asked.

He gulped. 'Yes. They ... Everyone moved away from them like they had the plague. Like they were rebels. And I guess ... I guess no one really cares about a mindship and they'll get around to me later, which is why I need to move away from the Belt as fast as I can, though that's probably just gaining time ...' He stopped, then. 'Oh, lil sis, I'm sorry.'

That made no sense. Sorry for the arrest of the general?

'Sorry for what?'

'Prefect Đức arrested Quỳnh.'

'Why?'

'For sedition. And breach of the peace.'

Oh no. Oh no.

She'd always known this would happen, but it didn't make it any easier to bear.

'Those charges just mean whatever Đức is unhappy with,' Hoà said sharply.

Heart's Sorrow glared at her. 'I'm not here to judge you, or her.'

'You seemed happy to before.' Hoà realised as she said it that it was true, and summarily unkind. 'I'm sorry.'

'No, that's fair.' *Heart's Sorrow* sighed, sinking in front of the two cups of tea that had materialised in front of him. 'Minh and I have talked to Quỳnh already. I'm not here to judge her. Quite honestly, I want to curl into a ball and deny reality exists. I'm not going to blame anyone for wanting to change their name and escape their past.'

Hoà stared at him. It was very much besides the point, but ...

'You'd like to, wouldn't you?'

'Yes. But I can't.' He sighed. His bots were limp, manifesting despondency.

'Lil sis.'

Hoà started at the unfamiliar voice, just as *Guts of Sea* materialised next to them.

What in Heaven?

'Other people give a *warning*,' Hoà said sharply, trying to calm the beating of her heart. 'Besides, you're not welcome here.'

'I'm welcome wherever I want to be,' *Guts of Sea* said. 'And I won't stay long. I know what you think of me, and you know what I think of you. I'm just here to give you Quỳnh's message. She said to run.'

'Wait,' Hoà said. 'You weren't arrested?'

'Same as him,' *Guts of Sea* said. 'I'm not here physically. It's going to take the militia a little longer to get to me. And unlike him, they'll have to find me first.'

'Thanks,' *Heart's Sorrow* said darkly.

'Oh, sorry, I don't think you've been introduced. This is—'

'We've met.' *Heart's Sorrow* didn't sound happy about it.

'I don't understand why you're here,' Hoà said. 'You're the one—'

'Who disapproved of your relationship? Yes.' A sigh. 'Quỳnh fixed me, and I owe her. I'm here to tell you to run. And ...' She hesitated. 'If you need passage beyond the Belt, you and your family, I'll help you.'

'I thought you wanted to bring the Empire down.' Hoà was still angry at *Guts of Sea*, and she wasn't really masking that.

'Yes,' *Guts of Sea* said. 'That'll still happen. Just not now, not while we're in this position.'

'You're leaving her?' Hoà cried.

'Do you see any other way?'

'Of course there's no other way!' *Heart's Sorrow* said despondently. 'No one can stand against Đức. She holds all the reins of power in the habitats.'

'Minh could—' Hoà said.

A bitter laugh from *Heart's Sorrow*. 'For my mother? Minh has enough trouble doing anything for herself.' He sighed. 'She asked me ...' His voice trailed off. 'She asked me what I'd do if I found out my mother had committed crimes.'

'So she knew.' Hoà was quietly fascinated by how messed up this was.

'No! No, you don't understand. This was about her. She said ... she had evidence her mother had committed crimes. Not in so many words, but she sounded so distressed that I let her be.'

'Maybe it's time to call Minh,' Hoà said.

'I've tried,' *Heart's Sorrow* said. 'She's not answering. And you can't put her in that position.'

'Which position?'

'Of being unfilial.'

Hoà bit back a bark of bitter laughter. 'You worry about her being unfilial more than you worry about doing the right thing?'

But who wasn't doing the right thing, ultimately? It was them, running away.

'There is evidence,' *Guts of Sea* said. 'Multiple crimes. Multiple failures of justice. Starting with Dã Lan on *The Azure Serpent*.'

'How do you know?'

'Because I hung around in the scholar circles. It's public knowledge, you realise?'

'No, I don't!' *Heart's Sorrow* screamed. 'I didn't even know that my own mother was covering up murders for her lover! How am I supposed to know anything?'

He was crying, a low-pitched sound that bubbled, again and again, sounding hollow and metallic and altogether heart-wrenching.

'I'm sorry,' Hoà said.

'Look,' *Guts of Sea* said, her avatar shimmering in and out of existence. 'This is all well and good and I'm glad we're having this heart-to-heart talk. But we need to leave. And that means all of us. Whatever accommodations Minh and her mother reach, you have to realise nothing will change the outcome for Quỳnh. She knew that, going in.'

Because it was Quỳnh. Because she'd always believed she didn't matter. Because Dã Lan had died, and Quỳnh was unwilling to live on.

'You let her.' Hoà bit her lip. Her bots' touch on the skin on her wrists felt cold. 'We all let her.'

'There's nothing you can do,' *Guts of Sea* said. 'The sooner you realise this, the easier it's going to be for everyone.'

Doing the right thing.

Nothing you can do.

That wasn't quite true.

Officials who committed crimes were arrested by censors. This was what censors were for.

'That evidence,' Hoà said. 'Do you have it?'

'As I said—'

'So you do have it.'

Hoà drank her tea, testing the connection to her bots, feeling her heartbeat in every part of her body. *Guts of Sea* was right. She should warn Thiên Dung, and run. They'd saved *Flowers at the Gates*, and that was the best they could do. It was more than anyone had expected of them. And Quỳnh had left her, and there was no future for either of them.

Do not get noticed. Do not get seen. Do not interfere in the affairs of the powerful.

Hoà's eye ached. She could run. She could turn her back on Quỳnh, and not do the right thing, and die little by little having failed to defend what was right.

Quỳnh had thought there was no future. But Hoà believed otherwise. She believed it was worth fighting for.

'Send it to me,' Hoà said.

Guts of Sea turned to face her – the ship, misshapen with the lines of Quỳnh's repairs, the places she'd been broken. She'd said she hated the Empire, those who had left her to die. And Quỳnh had only known Đức and her unfairness. Of course, neither of them would see any other way to do this but to seek revenge.

'You cannot ...'

Hoà didn't move.

'You're going to die!'

Hoà didn't know if it was going to work. She didn't know if the censor was fair, the way they said she was. She didn't know if it was going to be enough. It hadn't been enough for Thiên Hạnh – and maybe it wouldn't be enough for her, either. But she understood now why her sister had done it: why she'd stepped outside; why she'd chosen to protect others. Because it was the only choice that didn't involve dying piece by piece while being unable to look at herself in the mirror.

There was hope. A tiny sliver of things that could be done differently. A chance to stop hiding. A chance at a future.

'Give me the evidence,' Hoà said grimly.

She dimmed the light so she stood in perfect darkness, in the shadow of Thiên Hạnh's grace, for a suspended moment before she threw herself bodily into the void.

21

Bitter Legacies

Minh woke up. She was lying on something hard, and everything hurt. Wincing, she tried to pull herself up, and the entire room wobbled.

Room.

This was Stepmother's room.

Wait ... How?

The poison.

She'd been poisoned. And Stepmother ...

The room was deathly silent. From outside, muffled by the perception filters, she could hear the sounds of revelry. The party to welcome the censor.

Everything was too hard to cling to. Her breath came in short, rapid gasps. The room, with its multiple overlays, kept wobbling in and out of focus; the chirp of crickets in the bamboo was like stabs in her ears. Minh crawled – every gesture seeming to come from a great distance – to the table, grabbing it with both hands. That set off a bout of wobbling that made darkness hover on the edges of her field of vision, and made her swallow metallic-tasting saliva.

Stand up.

She had to stand up, or she was going to die here. She called her bots, shivering, shaking – they felt so far away, but they came, steadying her as, bit by bit, she pulled herself upright.

When she was done, Minh clung, still shaking, to the table.

She looked up. Or tried to. The metallic taste overwhelmed her, and her stomach contracted, and it took all she had to not collapse on the floor again. She focused and pinged her bots, asking them to feed her the video of the room. Even that – the slow panning of their sensors, fed back to her own eyes – made her nauseous.

The room was empty. And the door was locked, but that was all right, because Minh had wanted to leave the house. She had bots. They could open the door.

She . . .

Mother.

Minh tried to find her comms, but they kept sliding like greased metal, just out of reach.

Minh moved, or fell, or spun, she wasn't sure.

Away.

She had to escape. She had to find . . .

Friends.

She had to find friends.

There were no friends inside this house.

Outside.

Step by step, leaning on the wall – her own heartbeat in her ears, deafening and too fast. Step by step, with that metallic taste in her mouth and the fear that this was it. That she was going to die here. Hoà had survived, but she wasn't Hoà.

Quỳnh.

She needed to find Quỳnh. She'd help her.

Outside, a wobbling and dark corridor with a faint overlay like lacquered screens, depicting the seasons on the First

Planet. There was no one there. Of course not. Stepmother wouldn't have wanted anyone to find her.

Minh was never going to make it. She needed her comms, but her comms kept sliding away from her.

Wait.

She had other bots, elsewhere. She couldn't remember, couldn't focus on anything, but perhaps, if she could reach them, if …

Abruptly, Minh was no longer alone, or even in the compound.

She was in a vast, growing darkness. She'd fallen again, on her knees, retching, the taste of metal unbearably sharp in her throat.

'Child,' something – someone – whispered in the darkness, and it was a voice she knew but couldn't place.

Light bloomed, and the glint of metal, and a hint of burned apricot flowers. It blinked and shifted, as if it were picking out the outline of someone huge, a being right in front of her – larger than the corridor, or even the compound, dwarfing her with their presence.

'Child, what's happening?'

Second Great-Aunt.

It was the ship, and she was awake. Minh tried to speak, but the metal in her mouth choked her.

'Child!'

A sense of great, rising fury as the presence connected to her – and through her,to the network of the compound as head of the lineage, shearing aside all of Đức's protections.

'Second Great-Aunt!'

The ship was gone now, and Minh was on her knees in the corridor, crying, because she was alone and she was going to die in the stupidest fashion possible …

Move.

She had to move. If she could find Quỳnh, or *Heart's Sorrow*, or anyone ...

'Child.'

Second Great-Aunt's voice was in her ears again – and something changed with the perception filters. Now Minh was standing in the middle of a halo of light. Beyond it, darkness was spreading, and ghostly, bloodied images – a sound like torn metal, like screaming bodies tumbling into the vacuum of space. Minh started to ask what was happening, but that wasn't the information she needed.

'Quỳnh,' she said. The words burned in her throat. 'Need ... Quỳnh.'

'Quỳnh.' Second Great-Aunt's voice was hard. 'Let's get you there, then.'

Something blossomed in her bots' overlay: a path she needed to follow.

'Can't ...' Minh said. It was too far, she was too tired, she didn't want to rise.

'You can,' Second Great-Aunt said. 'You *will*.' Something in her voice – the steel, the absolute belief that Minh was going to – was enough for Minh, wheezing, to pull herself up again, to toddle to one of the walls and cling to it, the darkness barely held at bay. Her heartbeat was so fast her chest hurt.

Breathe.

Breathe, except that it was hard, and every breath felt as though it was just making her heart beat faster.

Minh didn't know what was happening outside the small circle of light she was in, but it felt as though some vast predator had come to the compound, trailing wings of steel and darkness, and was now tearing each room apart, spreading chaos in its wake.

'*Go*,' Second Great-Aunt said.

Minh – fumbling, teetering, struggling to remain awake

– forced herself to put one foot in front of the other, clinging to a wall that felt as though it was spinning out of control, and moving towards the distant place where she could find Quỳnh.

'They'll have to wait,' the militia person said, eyes sharp in the oval of her face. The dock was empty behind her, looking oddly forlorn without the overlay, the smell of people's stale perfume drifting to Quỳnh's nostrils as she hung between two militia people, struggling to breathe – her consciousness drifting in and out and darkness threatening to swallow her whole. 'No secure shuttle ... riots ...'

The militia commander by Quỳnh's side sighed, from very far away.

'Put her with the others ...'

No.

She knew who the others were.

No.

But before Quỳnh could protest, she'd been shoved into a small, sparse holding room, and the door was slammed shut.

She lay where they had thrown her, drained of all energy. They'd won. The ghosts of her past, standing just where she couldn't see them, where she couldn't touch them – Mother, Thanh Khuê, Đình Sơn. The other ghosts, the other people in the room. Her victims.

Footsteps, and then someone kneeled by her, just outside her reach. Bots that weren't hers – hers had been deactivated by the soldiers – were crawling over her. She tried to bat them away, but couldn't. After a while they withdrew, and she could still feel the presence of the other person, watching her. The general, dispassionately watching her drown? Tuyết didn't care. She'd never cared.

Her lungs burned, and she was drifting off, swelling, her

fingers hardening and turning into stone and nacre in deep spaces. She was dying, piece by piece.

She was having another attack. Except she didn't have the bots, didn't have her sedatives. It could kill her, if she lost her hold on reality and stopped focusing on her breath.

Guts of Sea wasn't there any more, and her comms had been cut, but Quỳnh could imagine her, all the same – no, she could imagine Hoà, holding her, gently telling her to breathe.

Breathe, big sis. Breathe.

Breathe.

I can't, Quỳnh tried to say, and Hoà said, with the same anger she'd had, back then, *How long are you going to keep hurting yourself?*

I...

Breathe.

She breathed, clinging on to the memory of Hoà, a lifeline in the vacuum.

The constriction in her lungs receded. Neither the darkness, nor her ghosts, disappeared, but she could sit up, coughing – and then push herself to stand. Remembering, a fraction of a moment too late, that she needed to disguise how ill she was, because she only had enemies in the room.

'You're awake,' Nhăng said. Nhăng pulled herself up gracefully. She'd been kneeling on the floor. Her smile was wide and sardonic, and there wasn't a hair out of place on her topknot. Her bots skittered on the floor.

'You still have bots,' Quỳnh said. 'Your Highness.'

A shrug from Nhăng. 'I also still have a vacuum-knife. They searched us poorly. Not that it's going to help much. And drop the Highness, will you? I never liked it, and it's meaningless in our current situation.' She gestured to the room.

Quỳnh turned, briefly, and saw there was an overlay of featureless darkness that obscured everything – and that Tuyết stood, at the farthest end, her face glazed, seemingly unaware of either of them.

'What's wrong with her?' Quỳnh asked.

Laughter, from Nhăng. 'Shock. And a few chemicals. It'll wear off.'

'You—'

'She dosed herself.' Nhăng's voice was bitter. 'Easier to face than the truth. She was always a coward.'

'She's your wife.'

'Hmmm.' Nhăng stared at her, with the same disconcerting, sharp but not unkind gaze. 'And your former lover, isn't she?'

It was like a dash of cold water to Quỳnh's face.

'I don't understand what you mean.'

Nhăng laughed, and it was harsh. She shifted, leaning against the wall with her bots gathered to her, and abruptly she was no longer the harmless scholar, the general's wife, but the enforcer she'd been, distant and cold and always doing what needed to be done to keep order on board *The Azure Serpent*. The woman who'd overseen Quỳnh's execution.

'Dã Lan,' Nhăng said slowly, thoughtfully. 'It's been such a long time.'

Quỳnh weighed the possibility of lying, but it was late and she was at the end of her strength, and she was likely going to die anyway, and what would it change?

'How long have you known?'

'Since I first laid eyes on you at the banquet,' Nhăng said. 'You've changed, but not that much.'

And on some level, Quỳnh had always known or suspected, hadn't she? Always known that Nhăng was perceptive and observant with a long memory. But she'd always denied it to herself – because if she'd admitted that Nhăng had recognised her, she'd have had to abort her mission. To give up on revenge, and she couldn't bear to do that.

Quỳnh looked at Tuyết again – that familiar curve of the face she'd held between her hands, the shoulders she'd once wrapped her arms around, the lips she'd kissed.

'*She* didn't recognise me.'

An amused shrug. 'She never was very good at this.'

'I don't understand. Why would you ...?'

Nhăng's was a mask, her gaze hard – the enforcer's gaze – and Quỳnh was back being thrown out of the airlock, Nhăng watching her, making sure it happened properly. Laws being followed, justice being applied.

'Because it was your right,' she said. 'Tuyết told me what she'd done, you know. What ghosts haunted her when she couldn't sleep at night.'

'You know what I've done,' Quỳnh said. 'You know—'

'Whose hand struck the blow that led us here? Yes. I have eyes. I also know who I married. And why.'

Quỳnh looked from her to Tuyết. 'This isn't just about me, is it?'

'No.' Nhăng's bots moved closer to Tuyết. 'This is about eighteen people who shouldn't have died. Unless you tell me that the accusation isn't true – that their deaths were a lie you made up in the course of your revenge.'

Quỳnh opened her mouth, closed it. 'Would you like to hear that?'

'Not if it's a lie. Just ... We have no right to ask for this from you, but ...' Nhăng breathed in, shakily. 'Leave our son out of it.'

Heart's Sorrow. Ten thousand words pressed themselves against Quỳnh's lips, and the only thing that came out was hollow laughter.

'Does it look like I'm in a position to hurt him?'

'You have further plans, don't you?'

'Not any more.'

Quỳnh moved, slowly, carefully – darkness shifted, and the ghosts at the edge of her field of vision shifted with her, the burning in her lungs flaring up again – and she was leaning against a wall that was no different from the floor, her head against the bulwark. She groped for her bots, or her comms to *Guts of Sea*, and found nothing. No more masks. No more plans. No more secrets.

Except that wasn't quite true, was it?

Hoà.

Lil sis.

She needed Hoà to be safe. But that was more a hope than a plan.

'You have people you want to safeguard,' Nhăng said. Of course, she still had her bots, and she could read Quỳnh's vitals better than Quỳnh could. 'And so do I.'

'What are you talking about?' It was Tuyết, looking from Nhăng to Quỳnh. Her eyes were still fogged over, her movements slow and sleepy.

'Just sympathising over our situation,' Nhăng said.

'You're the Alchemist, aren't you? Sương ... Quỳnh?' Tuyết frowned. 'What's going on?'

'We're talking about your son,' Quỳnh said.

Tuyết stared at her. '*Heart's Sorrow*? Why?'

Nhăng's lips tightened in pain. 'Because they'll want to arrest him, too.'

'Oh. That's a shame.' Tuyết shook her head, and some of the fear Quỳnh had seen in the reception room crept back into her eyes. 'What's going to happen to me?'

'To you?' Nhăng's voice was soft, carefully devoid of emotion. 'You know, don't you?'

'There's got to be a way ...' Tuyết breathed, faster and faster. 'There's got to be something you can do ...'

She didn't seem to care. Not about *Heart's Sorrow*, and not about Nhăng. Something small and ugly twisted in Quỳnh's stomach.

'Ssh.'

Nhăng came up to Tuyết, gently running a hand through her hair. Quỳnh found her own hands clenching, remembering what it had felt like to run her fingers through Hoà's hair. A bot climbed up to Tuyết's neck, and there was the soft hiss of an injector. Tuyết's eyes fogged over again.

'You don't need to worry about it, not now.' Nhăng carefully lowered her to the floor, brushing her wife's hair back into her topknot. Then she looked up, at Quỳnh. 'Those we love,' she said.

'She can't love,' Quỳnh said, and the truth burned her. Because Tuyết hadn't changed.

'*I* love her. She could be so much more than what she is, if she wanted to.'

It was quiet and bitter, and Nhăng looked at the general, and Quỳnh saw fondness and love in her eyes and, underneath it all, a great pain that Tuyết wasn't the person that Nhăng wanted her to be – that she never would be; that it was a lie that made it bearable.

Pity grabbed Quỳnh's heart and squeezed until it felt as though her entire chest was filled with sharp, bloodied shards. No, Tuyết hadn't changed. And what had made Quỳnh believe that the general had been happy? That life had given her everything she'd wanted? What she'd seen in Tuyết's eyes, in Nhăng's eyes, in *Heart's Sorrow*'s demeanour, wasn't happiness. It was all a mask, just like Quỳnh's own. Masks that hid the profound desolation of their lives. The ghosts, the deaths, the lies they'd built them on, everything that prevented them from being true to each other, everything that hollowed them from the inside out – a loveless marriage with no intimacy, a life ringed with enemies, a son who was a status symbol but whom Tuyết couldn't even spare a thought for.

Quỳnh had wanted revenge, but life itself – the passage of time itself – had been its own revenge.

'I'm sorry,' she said.

Nhăng laughed, and opened her mouth to say something – some bitter, ironic pronouncement – when everything went dark for a blink.

What ...?

The lights came back, but they were strangely muted. The walls started shaking and twisting, as if some great hand had seized them and was pulling them apart like molten sugar. The sense of a great presence rose in the room: someone that waited just beyond them – someone huge and old and *angry*.

'What's going on?' Nhăng asked. 'Child?'

'Not me,' Quỳnh said.

Traceries of light slowly came together on the walls of the room – abstract patterns and characters that Quỳnh had seen somewhere before – and there was a voice, a distant voice like a child's.

> Where are you going, O white birds?
> Over which rice fields, which star nurseries?
> Where are you going, O white birds?

The Azure Serpent. It was impossible. *The Azure Serpent* was dead. Long, long gone, and unlike Quỳnh, he would not be coming back from the dead. But the birds were there, wheeling in the narrower and narrower space of the cell, which had started caving inwards, and from outside came the sound of running feet, the militia's panicked screams.

Quỳnh reached for her comms, which were still dead. The door, then. She moved towards it, forcing herself to walk through the pain. They needed to get out before they were crushed. Of course, it was just the perception filters, but if they died here it wouldn't be any less painful or less damaging.

'Someone's hacked the network,' she said. 'Move!'

A blink, and then Nhăng was at her side, pushing against the door, time and time again — as the birds wheeled in tighter and tighter circles, and the child's voice got louder and louder. It was so unfair; she'd thought she was going to die, but not like this, never like this ...

Abruptly, it all stopped.

'Quỳnh,' a deep and distant voice said. 'Apologies. It took me time to isolate this room from the rest of the compound.'

Guts of Sea? But that wasn't her voice.

'Who are you?'

'The ship,' the voice said.

'Which ship?'

'*Flowers at the Gates*.'

'Wait ... What?'

'Take care of her,' the voice said.

'Take care of who?'

The sense of vast presence vanished like a soap bubble popping. The door slid open — and Quỳnh found herself staring at Minh.

'Child?'

Minh was dishevelled and breathing hard, her pupils dilated until they covered almost all of her irises.

'I ...' She raised a hand, and it was shaking. 'Poison. Help me. Please.'

And then she fell, spasming, straight into Quỳnh's arms.

22
Dã Lan

Quỳnh stared at Minh. She was burning up – the same symptoms as Hoà, the fever and the too-fast heartbeat, a frantic thing she could feel even without having to take Minh's pulse. Her clothes – an odd mixture of cheap and expensive fabrics – were sodden with sweat.

Cinnabar Clouds.

Minh's eyes had rolled up, and her breath was frantic.

Help me. Please.

'Do you intend to do anything?' Nhăng asked, standing in the doorway.

From outside came distant screams, and a feeling of some huge storm.

'What's going on outside?' Quỳnh asked.

'I'm not sure,' Nhăng said. 'Sheer chaos. It looks like … the ship has seized control of the overlays, and she's twisting everything into some rather unpleasant settings.'

Of course she would. She was the head of the lineage, undeposed and awake. She'd have access to the entire compound, superseding Đức's own defences and privileges.

'It was a party to celebrate her upcoming legal death,' Quỳnh said, drily. 'I doubt she'd have been happy about it.'

Or Minh's poisoning. Which had to have been done by Minh's stepmother, the saboteur of the ship's repairs, though why she'd single Minh out was baffling.

Help me. Please.

Quỳnh stared at Minh, feeling her warmth — a fragile, tentative thing. She could let go. She could stand by. Đức might not care for Minh's wishes or happiness, but Minh was still hers, in the way that a bot or a ship was hers. No, more than that ... Minh was her hope for the future, the youth that Đức didn't have any more, the promise of a career unmarred by *The Azure Serpent* or the Ten Thousand Flags Uprising. She'd be devastated if Minh died.

Nhăng was still looking on.

'Are you just going to watch?' Quỳnh asked.

'I don't have the antidote,' Nhăng said. 'Besides ... I never liked the prefect, and I can't say the latest events have made me more sympathetic to her.'

She could let go. Watch as Nhăng was watching. Retribution. Revenge. It would be a poetic thing — the prefect's daughter dying, the same way Quỳnh's mother had died.

Quỳnh thought of Minh asking, hesitantly, if she was all right. Of the lies she'd told Minh, and how Minh had blossomed listening to them, like planet-side earth too parched to make a difference between water and molten metal. Of Đức, and the way she'd treated everyone in her orbit, even her own daughter.

Quỳnh was struggling for resolve and strength, and all that was left was honesty, or at least some measure of it. And some sense of responsibility: if she'd warned Minh that her stepmother was a real danger, perhaps Minh wouldn't have been poisoned.

Guts of Sea would tell her to let Minh die, without a second thought. To let the accursed line come to its end – let the poison that Đức had allowed to fester in her own compound swallow her family whole. Quỳnh … . Quỳnh was too weak for that.

Help me. Please.

'I will,' she said – and searched within her sleeves for a small vial of antidote.

Minh woke up, and everything hurt.

'Gently,' Quỳnh said, her voice coming from a great distance. 'You've had a shock.'

Minh tried to speak. Her tongue wouldn't move – nor would anything else.

Elder aunt.

The words wouldn't come out.

Quỳnh was speaking to someone else, someone Minh couldn't quite see.

'Will you keep an eye on her?'

'Until we can find a shuttle.' The other person sounded bleak. 'We can't afford to stay here.'

'A few moments is all she needs.' Quỳnh kneeled, staring at Minh, though her gaze was distant, and something in its intensity made Minh uncomfortable. 'Child, I don't think we'll see each other again. Not this time. So … go where you will. Take care of yourself. You should leave this house.'

Minh wanted to laugh hysterically.

'I tried,' she said, the words feeling like metal in her mouth.

Something crossed Quỳnh's face. Surprise? Fondness?

'Good,' she said.

Minh tried to speak again, but it hurt and her head lolled back on the floor.

'Where are you going?' the other person asked.

She finally came into focus for Minh: it was Nhăng, *Heart's Sorrow*'s Second Mother, looking like a soldier about to make a last stand.

'To finish what I have started.' Quỳnh picked up something from the floor: a gun discarded by the militia. 'There will never be such disarray in the prefect's compound again.'

A silence.

Nhăng said, 'I really shouldn't, but ... you know it's not going to be that easy.'

'I know,' Quỳnh said. 'But what other future do I have?'

Silence, from Nhăng. Minh lay on the floor, shivering, trying to pull herself together.

'Dã Lan—' Nhăng finally said slowly.

'Dã Lan is dead,' Quỳnh said sharply, and not looking back as she stepped through the door.

What?

Wait, Minh wanted to say. *Dã Lan? Quỳnh is Dã Lan? The first person Mother had betrayed and unjustly sentenced?*

Wait!

But by the time she managed to pull herself up – shaking and leaning on Nhăng's arm – Quỳnh was gone, and it was just her and Nhăng, with the unconscious general in a corner of a darkened room.

In the end, Hoà flew on one of *Heart's Sorrow*'s shuttles, the mindship's avatar by her side, silent and still. It was just the two of them: *Guts of Sea* still thought it was a doomed and foolish quest, and Hoà had forbidden Thiên Dung to come. Thiên Dung had glowered, but said nothing. Hoà half-expected one of them to show up, regardless.

She walked to the docks through deserted streets, listening to the distant sound of the riots – half-expecting them to affect her, half-surprised when they didn't. The docks, too, were deserted, not even the usual skewer-sellers or bots-handlers overseeing the cleaning of the floors. Hoà boarded the shuttle waiting for her in utter silence.

As they lifted off, away from the habitat and towards Đức's compound, *Heart's Sorrow* showed her, in overlay, the images from the Technologists' Ring.

'It's really bad,' he said.

A mass of people pushing against the militia. Weapons, the sound of bodies crumbling. A great roar like a wounded beast. Large gashes on the walls, burn marks and fires – all things that would endanger them, that would end them. The habitats couldn't burn, or be torn apart; it would expose everyone within to the cold vacuum of space.

'I don't have an answer,' Hoà said.

She held her arms against her chest, bots gathered in her embrace, as if she could turn the evidence that *Guts of Sea* had given her into a flimsy defence against the censor, against Đức. As if she could make Quỳnh care about herself. They'd repress it in blood, the way they always did, because technologists didn't matter.

It was only when *Heart's Sorrow* fell silent she realised she'd said those words aloud.

'I'm sorry,' she said.

She saw him spin and tense, ready to tell her not to be so servile.

Instead she said, 'You don't need this worrying you, in your current situation. And you didn't have to come back with me.'

Heart's Sorrow said, 'You matter. And ...' A deep, shaking breath. 'I'm not going in with you. You know that.'

And Hoà didn't blame him. 'I do,' she said. 'Your mothers—'

'I don't know.'

Hoà wanted to tell him, then. Who Quỳnh was, what it meant to him. But it would have been unkind, and achieved nothing.

The shuttle docked with a crunch. Hoà's bots sought to connect to the comms network, but there was ... Nothing, she'd have said, but then she realised it *wasn't* nothing. It was a storm of swirling data, so dense and compact she had no hold on it. She slid the shuttle door open. Instead of the docks, there was darkness. At first she thought it was the vacuum of space, but as she peered into it, it moved: minute swathes of light that felt like reflections on something large and hostile, hidden just out of view. A transport brimming with soldiers: a secret weapon – a war spaceship.

And Quỳnh was in there somewhere.

'What is going on?'

Heart's Sorrow spun, radiating confusion. 'I don't know. I don't have comms either. But I can't let you go into that.'

'You're not the master of me.'

Hoà stared at the darkness. It looked ... It looked as though someone had thrown a vast overlay over this part of the compound, thick enough that she couldn't see anything through it. Her eye itched. She readjusted the patch on it, wincing at the now familiar pain that felt out of proportion to the scratch.

'Big sis!'

But Hoà was already stepping off the shuttle.

The moment her feet made contact with the darkness of the floor, she felt it, through her body and through her bots' sensors – a presence in the whirling maelstrom – rage and sadness and grief all mingled together, and she knew who it was. She'd felt it before.

'*Flowers at the Gates*?' she said.

A silence. A swirling in the darkness – and this time it wasn't images or feelings or bots, but words from a voice that resonated in her chest.

'Child,' the voice said. The darkness receded until Hoà was standing in the middle of a lighter circle: metal beneath her feet, and the suggestion of an overlay of running water over the stars. 'What are you doing here?' It asked.

Flowers at the Gates was awake. She was there. In spite of everything, Hoà felt a burst of pure pride. They'd done it. They had fixed her. But ... 'What are *you* doing here?' Hoà asked.

'You're questioning me?' A sense of anger from the ship, barely leashed. The circle fracturing. That same coiled power Hoà had felt on board *Flowers at the Gates*, except this was in the middle of the habitats, where the ship seemed to be in complete control of the overlays, and unbalanced. That wasn't good. That really wasn't good.

Hoà almost took a step back, but there was nowhere to go.

'I'm here for Quỳnh,' Hoà said. 'And the censor.'

Laughter, from the ship. 'The censor and my niece have retreated to the reception room. They're still holding that, but not for long. Quỳnh is on her way there now.'

'And the other guests? The militia? The servants?'

'Most have fled.' *Flowers at the Gates*' voice was vicious. 'Some are wandering around in a daze. Except in the reception room. My niece has some elaborate safeguards I haven't managed to breach yet.'

Wandering around in a daze. Going mad in the corridors, with only darkness and those faint suggestions of large, angry things. That was horrible.

Hoà breathed, slowly, carefully. The fragile resolve she'd gathered, which had propelled her all the way here, was in danger of disintegrating. She looked back, where *Heart's Sorrow* was patiently waiting – taut and fearful. She knew he'd wanted to turn and run the moment she left, but he hadn't. He'd said he'd wait for her. For ... whatever came of this.

She knew why *Flowers at the Gates* was doing this, of course. Her motivation was not so different from Quỳnh's – anger and rage and the desire for revenge after being wronged for so long. She wanted to say something; she wanted to reason with the ship, whose psyche looked on the edge of fragmenting, but she didn't have the energy or mental capacity to spare. She couldn't help everyone. No, not even that: she'd blasted Quỳnh for not respecting her capacity to make choices, and she wasn't going to take away *Flowers at the Gates*' choices.

'Can you help me go there?' she said.

A twist in the darkness around her, as if the entire ship were lilting. 'You won't be helping my niece.'

Hoà rubbed her eyepatch, heedless of the pain it caused her.

'No. It's time Đức faced the consequences of what she's done.' Hoà wished she felt as confident as her tone.

Laughter, from the ship. 'Revenge, then.'

Hoà wasn't Quỳnh. The whole point was that she wasn't Quỳnh – that she was going to fight for what Quỳnh had given up on. For the future. Hoà balled her hands into fists, feeling her bots cluster behind her in the corridor.

'Justice,' she said.

More laughter, more traceries of light in the darkness, in some alphabet Hoà couldn't decipher.

'Call it what you will, it will do. Come, child.'

Hoà was worried about Quỳnh. But the truth was, Quỳnh could probably take care of herself. Except in the immediate vicinity of Đức, which was what Hoà was here for. Nevertheless, she wished they were together. She wished they could laugh at the futility of it all – hold each other, heedless of the future they didn't have. A luxury she'd lost – they'd both lost.

Could she salvage something from all this?

Time to see.

The compound was darkness, and fire, and distant screams that didn't sound as though they belonged to people. Bots skittered in the shadows. Hoà felt an escort of them at her back, like being pushed by the emanation of a tiger, or a hungry ghost. Or an angry, unstable warship with grudges to settle. There was music, too – that same Serpent song she'd heard with Quỳnh, the one about white birds. The voices were children's, but Hoà heard Thiên Hạnh in her head instead, and the ghosts of her own past.

Only Thiên Hạnh was dead, and she was with Hoà – in the fragmentary mem-implants that were like a warmth in her thoughts, in the circle of light from *Flowers at the Gates*. Only Thiên Hạnh's memory, the thought of Quỳnh and her careless giving on behalf of others, her stubborn refusal to stand up for herself ... Even combined, it wasn't enough to keep the fear at bay.

'Here.'

It was a door in the middle of the darkness. A perfect circle with the vermilion seal of the Dragon Throne, where the shadows stopped. As Hoà walked up to it, her bots clustering around her, the circle of light she'd been in disappeared, and so did the darkness. This was solid, physical, with only a faint hint of the overlays on either side, a clear demarcation line.

'What's inside?' she asked.

The ship laughed, and the laughter twisted in Hoà's lungs.

'I don't know. I can't go there.'

Because she wasn't physically present.

'Your bots—'

'They're the compound's bots. I lose control of them beyond this line, but I'll find a way in. With time.'

And when she did, it would be chaos.

Hoà stared at the door. At the seals. This was it. No more excuses, no more delays. She fished into her sleeves for the overlay invitation Đức had left her when she'd hurt Hoà's eye.

'I'm invited.' She wished she sounded more certain.

A silence. A feeling of being watched. And then something shook itself loose, and the door opened a fraction, its panels beneath the vermilion unlocking.

The message was clear. She could come in, but she'd have to work for it.

Hoà took a deep breath, and pushed the door open.

Noise hit her in the face like a punch: the babble of distant conversations, barely muffled by overlays. A huge expanse of stars underneath her, constellations sharply outlined – fish, spaceships, dragons; household bots unobtrusively scattered across tables. Barges under vermilion awnings, in the shadow of the most distinctive habitats in the Belt. People in rich, layered outfits, physical and virtual, laughing and talking to one another as they picked up slivers of fish and rice from translucent bowls, from plates where calligraphed characters appeared and faded, delicate and elusive. Scholars. Merchants. Soldiers. The elite of the Belt, feasting, and heedless of what was happening outside.

Hoà walked past them. They had to see her: the technologist with shabby clothes and the utilitarian bots, standing out like a scared mouse in a circle of hungry tigers. They had to see her, but they all looked past her. All looked at one another. She was invisible. And yet, she could feel the tension, palpable in the air. The conversations that were taut and on the verge of turning sour. They were in their fortress, surrounded, and they didn't know what would happen when it fell.

Barge after barge. Table after table. No one even registered her presence. Bots served food; it looked as though the servants had fled. Hoà kept her gaze straight ahead, towards the middle of the room, where Đức and Tang Thuyền sat side by side, looking over the banquet as if they owned everyone in the room.

We don't matter.

Hoà's eye ached. A blind cat, Đức had said. Inconsequential. Insignificant. So easily scared out of her wits.

It was only when Hoà reached the foot of the dais that the first member of the militia moved to bar her way: a commander with a grey-haired topknot, and bots on each finger. Hoà felt her own bots' legs dig into her shoulders.

Breathe. You have to breathe.

'What are you doing here?'

Breathe.

Hoà said, simply, with all of the self-possession she vaguely remembered from Thiên Hạnh's lessons, 'I'm invited.'

The commander stared at her. At the invitation she was holding, eyes raking her. grabbed her, pinning her wrists together. Her bots dug into Hoà's skin, and pain flared up.

'And where did a lowlife like you get this?'

'From the prefect,' Hoà said.

'Did you now?' The commander turned briefly, and called up to the dais. 'Prefect, there's a technologist here to see you.'

Đức's gaze turned to Hoà – saw her, all of her – and Hoà saw the malice and satisfaction that crossed her face. The temptation to inflict pain, even greater now that the prefect's power was being challenged.

'What a delightful surprise,' she said. 'Let her come up.'

The commander escorted Hoà to the top of the dais, and firmly pushed her, hinting she should kneel. Hoà bowed deeply, forehead touching the floor, the gesture of respect for high officials, her bots' legs clicking as they moved out of the way.' They hadn't bothered deactivating them, and why would they? The overlays were under Đức's control. Some of them wouldn't survive. *Hoà* wouldn't survive. That's what had happened to Thiên Hạnh. That was the ending she knew she was walking towards.

'You may stand.'

It wasn't Đức's voice; it was the censor's, low and cultured and a bit puzzled. When Hoà pulled herself up, she was in front of their table – kneeling while they sat cross-legged, looking at her.

She felt so vulnerable. They knew who she was now, and they were going to swat her like the smallest of ships, taking her apart, killing her piece by piece. They knew her and they knew Thiên Dung and everyone else, and no one but her would ever have thought it a good idea to come here.

'Who is the lady, Mama?' a child's voice. Đức's child. Hoà couldn't remember her name. She was about six years old, with expensive clothes and large, unwieldy bots that perched on the table.

Her mother – San, the one who'd sought to poison Hoà and Thiên Dung – put her hand on the child's hand.

'Ssh, child.'

The child pouted. 'It would be more fun if Minh was here.'

'Your sister,' Đức said, without so much as moving her head, 'needs to reflect on her behaviour. I'm sure she'll stop sulking and come out of her room eventually.'

'Prefect,' Tang Thuyền said, with a hint of impatience, 'can we deal with whatever this woman wants?'

This close, Tang Thuyền didn't look like the prefect. Her diction was cultured, but there was a hint of a twang in it – something that suggested she had been raised outside the wealthy families. She was irritated by Hoà's interruption, and worried – and who wouldn't be worried by a mindship raging out of control beyond the room?

'Quỳnh's little blind cat,' Đức said. 'Are you here because you found your wits, or because you found your courage?'

She extended a hand and a bot came to rest on its tip, even as something seized Hoà and held her immobile in front of them. Nausea welled up, harsh and unforgiving. Hoà couldn't do this. Đức had left her mouth untouched – because it was more fun if she screamed, wasn't it? She couldn't—

But then Hoà saw the beads of sweat on Đức's face, the ceruse-powdered cheeks hollowed by the effort. She was smiling at Hoà, anticipating the scene that would follow, but there was an edge to it – to her, to this whole surreal scene. Hoà pushed on her bots – they were held immobile, too, behind the same bonds – and beyond the comms network of the room, she could feel the pressure of *Flowers at the Gates*' attack.

'I'm here for Quỳnh,' Hoà said.

She looked, not at Đức, but at Tang Thuyền. At the Empire. At the highest official in the room – who was looking at her, mildly curious and mildly disapproving at the same time. She needed to catch Tang Thuyền's attention, because otherwise Đức was going to silence Hoà before she could make her accusation.

'Sương Quỳnh?' Đức laughed. 'I think you'll find you're too late.'

Hoà swallowed. 'I have evidence to present,' she said.

Đức shifted, and a privacy filter came up – something separating Hoà from the censor and the rest of the room, a perfectly transparent wall that nevertheless swallowed up every sound Hoà uttered. And now she could speak all she wanted, but the censor wouldn't hear her.

Đức smiled. 'You can present it to me, and her case will be reviewed by the tribunal. That's hardly worth disturbing us for, is it? But I can understand your panic for a beloved one, and of course as a technologist you can hardly be expected to understand the intricacies of power work, can you?'

She made Hoà feel small, and worthless. And powerless. And of course Hoà should have known that coming here, kneeling before the censor, wouldn't make a difference, because the censor couldn't hear her, even here, and she wouldn't intervene. She'd let Đức handle this, because she trusted the prefect, and why should she not? And Đức would simply make all of the evidence vanish.

Hoà should have known this was a doomed attempt. Standing up meant nothing. Đức waved her hand, and the bot on her hand left it, and scuttled closer to Hoà. Her control of the overlays forced Hoà's eyes open – the eyepatch flying off, the light of the room raw and painful, too bright, too sharp. It was going to be the same again: Hoà, held motionless and powerless, hurt just because Đức could. Just because she'd been noticed, and wasn't that the way it always went?

'You could use a reminder of who holds the power here, little cat,' Đức said.

Her bots had come out of her sleeves, sharp and elegant, except that unlike Quỳnh's they looked as though they'd been designed to impress and hurt. Like hooked knives.

Tang Thuyên's mouth was pursed in mild distaste, but she didn't intervene. She was never going to.

I'm sorry, Hoà said to Quỳnh in her thoughts. *I tried. I really did.*

Quỳnh looked at her – and in Hoà's thoughts she was as she'd been on *Flowers at the Gates*, floating in the darkness with her bots a halo around her, asking what Hoà needed, what Hoà wanted. Deferring to it. Leaving her space to be herself and make her own decisions, with nothing less than absolute faith in her and what she could do.

Hoà didn't have power, not the way Đức did, and never would have. But she didn't need it. She needed the smallest of spaces, the smallest of leverages. It was the technologist's view of things: where to pry them apart in order to fix them.

Đức's hold on everything – on Hoà, on the room – was tenuous. All Hoà needed was a moment of distraction.

'You can't hold it against her, can you? This room.'

A flash of anger in Đức's eyes; one bot moving a fraction closer to Hoà, as it had done when scratching Hoà's eye.

'*Flowers at the Gates* will be dealt with.'

'But you won't become head of the lineage.'

Hoà could see – from the corner of a gaze she couldn't move, blurring and aching because of the strain – Đức's wife, her face darkening with anger. She'd poisoned and schemed to avoid this.

'You misstep.' Đức's voice was a lash.

The bot was crawling up Hoà's hands now. Hoà flexed, testing the bindings in overlay. It was an effort to hold her there, and a larger effort to hold the room against *Flowers at the Gates*.

Time to stop being nice.

'Ask your wife,' Hoà said. 'Ask her why the ship is so angry with you.'

She saw San flinch, her elegant jade-coloured bots quivering for a moment. More importantly, Đức saw that flinch and turned towards San, her hold on the room wavering. The flicker was of little importance, but her hold on Hoà, and the privacy screen, dropped for the briefest of moments. And in that moment Hoà pushed. Not to get up, but to speak, pulling up the contents of her bots' memories and having them displayed in a circle around her.

'I have evidence of miscarriages of justice in the Belt and on *The Azure Serpent*,' she said. 'All under the direct jurisdiction of Prefect Đức.'

The last such case – Bạch Loan, the data artist arrested for the Tiger Games incident and condemned to the slow death – bloomed around Hoà in overlay, even as Hoà looked up, holding Tang Thuyền's gaze, fighting a wave of nausea and fear.

'Lies.' Đức's voice was steady and calm. She regained control, and the privacy screen *slammed* back into Hoà – not just holding her immobile but squeezing, wringing her limbs like wet rags, a twisting pain shooting up her fingers and wrists and arms. 'Let me handle this, elder aunt.'

Tang Thuyền hadn't moved. Neither had Hoà; it took all of her will to stare back at the censor, her heart beating madly in her throat. At length the censor looked from Hoà to Đức, and said mildly, 'I'd like to hear this evidence.'

'Surely, this is beneath you.'

A hint of anger in Tang Thuyền's face, her broad shoulders bunching up under the brocade, the bots around her wrists tightening their legs.

'This is a serious accusation, and what I can see of it is entirely plausible. Perhaps it is indeed nothing, but I'll be the judge of that.'

The pressure on Hoà vanished. She fell on all fours, struggling to breathe and not merely flop like a dislocated puppet. When she looked up again, Tang Thuyền was staring at Đức, and the entire dais was under a privacy screen. Hoà reached for her bots, feeling the tremendous pressure of *Flowers at the Gates* through them: the ship pushing again and again, relentlessly looking for a weakness in Đức's control.

Tang Thuyền held out her hand across the banquet table; within it, shimmering, was a personal contact channel. The food wobbled, the sweet and sour sauce in the porcelain dish spilling on the metal table.

'The evidence, child.'

This is for you, big sis. I hope it helps.

Hoà transferred what *Guts of Sea* had given her. It went more slowly than it could have – and all the while the table was shaking harder and harder, and on the floor beneath the dais the stars were darkening out of existence. Đức was losing control. San sat rigidly, and the small child on her lap would have leapt away if San hadn't had a bruising grip on her.

After a long, long silence, Tang Thuyền said, 'You mentioned you were here for a friend. Sương Quỳnh. I see her name nowhere in this.'

Hoà breathed in, feeling the fear harden within her stomach. But if she said nothing, then this was just revenge, the same thing Quỳnh was doing. Taking down Đức, but not remedying the injustices that she'd committed. Quỳnh needed to be pardoned.

'That's because her birth name isn't Quỳnh. It's Dã Lan, from *The Azure Serpent*.'

'Dã Lan.' Tang Thuyền's voice was thoughtful. She chewed on the words as she might have chewed on rice noodles, or a particularly tricky mouthful of pork.

'Dã Lan is *dead*,' Đức said, and this time there was real fear and anger in her voice.

Hoà opened her mouth to answer her, and as she did so, everything burst apart.

The pressure that had been building up behind her bots abruptly vanished, leaving Hoà out of breath, struggling to recover her hold on them. Darkness stole across the room, extinguishing all the stars and the koi and the spaceships on the floor, taking apart the banquet tables – and in the darkness were traceries of light, and the shadows of larger, fanged things.

'Finally,' the deep, booming voice of *Flowers at the Gates* said.

Someone screamed, and then someone else. People were moving, scrambling to get away from the tables, the tension finally collapsing into the muddle of a crowd stampeding for the exits – and finding that the huge banquet they'd been in had become a small, cramped room with barely enough space to breathe or elbow one another aside.

Good. They'd feasted while people rioted. They deserve this.

In the darkness, the ship coalesced.

She hung, huge and pitted, damaged by the weapon-strikes that had wounded her. In overlay, she was at once monstrously close and far enough away that Hoà could take all of her in, hanging, weapon-like, over the dais. She wasn't physically there, but she didn't need to be: her utter control over the overlays and the bots meant she could kill them whenever she felt like it.

Tang Thuyền stood up, frowning – dismissing what she was looking at with a brush of her long sleeves.

'This is the Empire, not the shipyards or the lawless planets,' she said, sternly. Her bots leapt from her sleeves, forming a circle on the floor around her. 'If you want justice, you'll stand down.'

'I don't need to,' *Flowers at the Gates* said. The entire room was shaking with the sound of her damaged motors – a stuttering vibration that merged with the madly beating heart in Hoà's chest. 'I'm head of the lineage, and this is my house. My overlays. My descendants.'

A slight noise, to Hoà's left. Đức must have realised she'd lost, because she and San were both scrambling down the dais, with the child on San's shoulders. A small light tracked them as they made their way – not towards the mob of scholars and dignitaries fighting for the door, but towards the opposite side of the room, where another circular door was slowly coalescing into sight. The ship knew where they were, but didn't care. Of course, it didn't make any difference where they ran.

As Hoà was about to turn back to the censor, she saw the door open. Her gaze, inexorably drawn to it as if to the bright, blooming light of a wounded ship exploding, made out the silhouette on the threshold.

Quỳnh.

She looked ... wrong. Dishevelled and pale, topknot undone and long hair streaming down her back, with no overlay to hide the grey flecked throughout it. Hoà's bots picked out the fast, unnatural rhythm of Quỳnh's breathing, the whistling in her lungs. She was having a constriction attack, and she was having it in full view of Đức.

Oh, big sis. What's happened to you?

Hoà didn't think. She ran down the dais, her bots behind her, feet skidding on the wine stains of the reception's worst excesses, struggling to stay upright even as the light stabbed into her wounded eye. She ran, screaming 'Stop!' – and she wasn't sure who she was screaming at, whether it was Đức, or *Flowers at the Gates*, or Quỳnh.

But Quỳnh looked up, saw Hoà and smiled, heartbreakingly happy and vulnerable – a fraction of a blink before her face hardened and she pointed a gun straight at the ruling prefect of the Belt. An act of sedition was happening in full view of witnesses, already too late to be taken back.

23

In the Name of Ghosts

'I don't understand,' Minh said.

Nhăng was kneeling by Tuyết's side. 'What's there to understand?'

'Dã Lan is dead,' Minh said.

Nhăng turned to look at Minh. They were still in the room, with Quỳnh gone, an odd space of stillness amid the storm outside. Minh could feel the network pressing on her bots, but it was a distant thing, like someone had put up a screen and isolated her.

Second Great-Aunt.

Nhăng's gaze was ... It wasn't *Heart's Sorrow's* mother, the one who fussed and seemed to be caring for her son in the absence of any care from Tuyết, but someone older and harsher – a stranger.

The same way Quỳnh was turning out to be a stranger.

'I knew Dã Lan,' Nhăng said. 'I executed her.' Her voice was matter-of-fact.

'But she's alive.' Minh clung to that fact, because nothing else made sense and she was still reeling from having been poisoned and healed, and she didn't know what to do any more. 'And—'

'And she healed you. Yes.'

Nhăng didn't volunteer any more information. She'd already briefly confirmed that *Heart's Sorrow* wasn't with them – that he'd escaped, that he was safe.

Which just left Minh with her and her friend's parents to worry about.

Minh rose, and walked to the door. Outside was still roiling darkness, and a song that felt too familiar – not that Mother had ever been one for singing, but she must have heard it elsewhere, as a child. It was ... It ought to have been comforting, barbed and known, like the party with the scholars where Mother had confiscated the offer of mentorship from her. But it wasn't. It felt alien, and wrong, and jarring.

Minh knew where Quỳnh – where Dã Lan – was going. Of course. To Mother. To finish it all – or rather, to die trying.

And the wisest thing, really, would be to leave them to each other. Pawns. Anger. Cruelty. Revenge.

Mother had manipulated Minh her entire life, and Quỳnh had done the same, even if she'd stepped back from it in the end.

Leave, Quỳnh had said.

Did that count for something, that caring at the end? Minh wasn't sure. She was ... bereft and exhausted and angry, and that was even without considering Stepmother, and Second Great-Aunt, and the poisoning – and everything that was rotten within their family.

She thought of standing in the belly of *Flowers at the Gates*, that feeling of tightness and shame in her whole body as she looked up name after name after name, and found nothing but cruelty. Nothing but a mask of fairness over the gaping black hole of Mother's hunger for control and power. And the woman Mother had married – not Minh's long-dead first mother, but Stepmother: like drawn to like.

And, really, yes, she should have left them to it, but what would happen to Vân if she did? What would happen to the habitats?

And ...

It was childish, and utterly unbefitting the daughter of a prefect, but she wanted to stand before Mother and yell at her that she'd never be the child Mother wanted, that she'd escaped and would never come back.

It wasn't really about Quỳnh, but about herself and those she loved.

'I'm going,' Minh said. She gathered her bots to her, trying to feel some confidence. 'Can you ...?'

'We'll get out.'

Nhăng stared at Minh, from her place on the floor, bots clustering on her hands where the overlay made pearlescent patches shimmer. The look she gave Minh was disturbing.

'If you see ... *Heart's Sorrow*, will you tell him ...?' Her heart was in her throat, resonating in every one of her bots' legs. They wouldn't see each other again. As the son of a murderer, he'd become a fugitive from the Numbered Planets. His best chance lay in the shipyards, or in the systems beyond that. 'Will you tell him goodbye from me, and good luck?'

Nhăng inclined her head. 'Of course. Goodbye, child.'

Minh was halfway down the corridor, still walking in that odd patch of light *Flowers at the Gates* had deployed around her, when she realised what had been so disturbing about Nhăng's gaze.

It hadn't been that of a mother to a child, but of an equal to an equal – one enforcer to another – secure in the knowledge that they'd both do what needed to be done. It made Minh feel as though she stood at the end of an open airlock without a tether or glider, ready to leap into the void.

Quỳnh walked with the gun in her hand, and in the darkness she heard children sing the songs of *The Azure Serpent*.

> Where are you going, O white birds?
> Over which rice fields, which star nurseries?
> Where are you going, O white birds?

White birds, in the shadows of the corridors. Stars blinking in and out of existence. *The Azure Serpent* alive, in the days before it died, before Dã Lan died.

She'd never missed it, not so much as she'd missed her old life, before the Empire turned her into a fugitive. As she walked, she saw them in the shimmering darkness – the ghosts of those who'd died: Mother, small and diminished, as if prefiguring the solitude and hunger and grief that would kill her; her teacher Thanh Khuê, with that sigh of annoyance whenever Dã Lan was too clever for her own good; Đình Sơn, with his arms outstretched, the memory of his touch on her belly, of the fear in his eyes when he'd learned who she was, what the Empire would do to her.

She remembered tumbling into the vacuum of space – how the cold had seized her, lungs expanding, vision going, everything spasming and that feeling that she couldn't breathe, would never be able to breathe again ...

Quỳnh was in the darkness, and in the dark there was a ship – not *Guts of Sea*, because she'd lost *Guts of Sea* – but another ship, a presence that was all of the compound and all of its overlays and bots, buoying her. Someone who knew what it felt like to be betrayed by Đức, someone who knew what it was like to be believed dead, to be dismissed, to be taken apart piece by piece while she was still alive. Someone whose anger and rage and desire to watch them all burn was palpable in the air.

I know you, Quỳnh whispered. There was barely any breath in her lungs but it didn't matter, because the ship was holding her as she walked. *I know you.*

And I you, the ship whispered, like great beating wings at her back, sharpened steel with the sheen of deep spaces. And Quỳnh was walking, not in the corridors of the compound with the ruins of elegant overlays around her and the distant sounds of people crowding on the docks, but in the ruined corridors of *Flowers at the Gates*, shearing down alien bots one after the other – not a task she was revelling in, but something that needed to be done.

So close.

She was so close.

It was like a warmth in her belly, a flame she dared not hold too close to her chest, a piece of eggshell celadon that might shatter if she looked at it. Tuyết was disgraced, her own son a criminal by blood, and now Đức was weak. There would never be a better time.

Ahead was a door, a circle with an âm dương dual-teardrop shape, black and starkly white. As she pushed it, she heard the ship cry 'Finally!' – and a cold wind blew her into the room.

Finally.

It was and wasn't the banquet room. Quỳnh caught a glimpse of fragments of paper, of huge barges on a River of Heaven – a blink before the wind swept them all away, and darkness rushed in to pool around the dais at the centre of the room. And then it lifted, and the shape of *Flowers at the Gates* – pitted, charred, burned, overwhelming – hung over them, crushing them all into insignificance.

She saw Đức, a handspan away from her, heading her way.

She couldn't breathe; she could barely stand, with the ship's presence focused away from her.

'Move.' Đức's voice was cold. 'You're in the way.'

Quỳnh stared at her. At Đức's wife San, the small child in her arms.

'No,' she said.

'Stop!' It was a scream from the dais – Hoà.

What is Hoà doing here?

She couldn't let Hoà be drawn into this. Quỳnh raised the gun, unsteadily pointing it at Đức.

'No,' Quỳnh said, shaking. 'I won't move. It ends, now.'

Quỳnh could barely hold the gun up. It took all of her effort to keep it steady. She had no air, and everything felt too tight and too distant, and her ghosts were congregating by her side, hard to tell from the people in the room. Just this one thing, and she'd be done. She'd be avenged. They would be avenged. Just this one act, and it wouldn't matter if she survived.

'Dã Lan,' Đức breathed, and she *saw* Quỳnh – not as the Alchemist, not as the bothersome scholar she'd ordered put away – but as the terrified woman she'd manipulated and then executed. Quỳnh's mouth burned with the spent taste of grassy tea, the sharp one of blood from the lacerator. She tried to stand straight, but she couldn't seem to.

'*Stop!*' It was Hoà's scream, and Hoà's bots scuttling towards her. 'Stop, please. I beg you, big sis. Stop. Put it down.'

Đức only had eyes for Quỳnh. 'You survived. No matter. That is a problem soon remedied.'

But Quỳnh heard the fear in her voice, the fear that hadn't been there before. The dead weren't meant to come back, not holding a gun trained on one's chest.

'Dã Lan is dead,' Quỳnh said. And, with all the strength she could muster, she raised the gun, finger tensed to shoot. 'And this is sedition.'

A bot seized her wrist, held it – followed a blink later by Hoà's hand, her touch like a shock travelling all the way into Quỳnh's chest.

'I don't care about sedition!' Hoà yelled. And, to Quỳnh, 'Put it down.' Hoà's eyes were wide, and she was shaking, blood smeared between her nose and her lips. 'Please. I gave the censor the evidence.'

'What evidence?'

'Everything from *Guts of Sea*. Everything the prefect has done. Please, big sis.'

Tang Thuyền was still on the dais, but she was turning towards them. From this far away – struggling to hold on to consciousness – Quỳnh could barely see her face. But she heard the voice of *Flowers at the Gates*, echoing all around her.

'I didn't come here for bloodless revenge, and neither did Quỳnh.'

No, that doesn't ring true. I came here ... I came here because ...

Quỳnh stared at the gun in her hands, trying to find the air that didn't want to come. Where was *Guts of Sea*? Where was safety? Where was ...?

'She's a rebel,' Đức said. 'A sympathiser of the Dragon's Tail general.'

'I told you already.' Tang Thuyền's voice was distant and cold. 'This is the Empire, not the lawless planets. The Ten Thousand Flags Uprising has been over for more than a decade. Dã Lan. *Flowers at the Gates*. Some anger is understandable, but I will ask you to stand down. If you don't, I'll have to assume that you're not willing to repent, and treat you accordingly.'

'I need more time,' Hoà said, somewhere far away. 'Please.'

'I won't repeat myself,' Tang Thuyền said. 'She stands down now, or faces arrest.'

Quỳnh tried to breathe again, and slowly slid down to her

knees, the gun dangling from her fingers. Someone snatched it, or tried to, but Quỳnh held firm. She needed the gun. She needed to ... She ... It needed to be ended.

'Prefect Đức!' It was the censor's voice, and then *Flowers at the Gates* was howling in pain, just as footsteps ran past Quỳnh, and a child's voice said, 'Mama, where are we going?'

'The prefect – she's getting away,' Quỳnh said. 'Please ...'

Hoà's grip on the gun didn't falter. 'No. This isn't about the prefect.'

'Then what is it about?'

'This is about *you*. You didn't come here for revenge.' Hoà's voice was quiet and filled with such raw sadness that it twisted in her. 'You came here to die.'

No. That ... That isn't true.

'I didn't—' Quỳnh started, and then Hoà's finger was on her lips, gently pressing down like a prelude to a kiss.

'No lies,' she whispered.

It had never mattered if she survived. That was the bleak, honest truth, the one Hoà had seen, the one she'd told Nhăng: there was no future for her. Đức wouldn't be dying to atone for the death of Dã Lan, but for stealing her future. She'd made life – let alone happiness – such an unthinkable, unattainable goal.

'She stole my life,' Quỳnh said. She tried to scream, but she was back in the vacuum of space and there was no one to help her – no ship, no last moment rescue, nothing.

'Big sis.' Hoà's voice was insistent and urgent. 'The censor has your case. Dã Lan's case.'

Bitter laughter welled out of Quỳnh . Everything was fuzzing, growing more and more distant. She'd lost Đức again. Thrown away her chance of revenge.

'You trust in fairness?'

Hoà said, 'I trust in Thiên Hạnh's choice to stand up for

those who can't. Will it work? Maybe not. But I trust more in the chance of a better future than in murder and lies. Did it make you happy – any of it, big sis?'

Quỳnh thought of Tuyết and Nhăng, and the cold, uncomfortable realisation that none of what had happened to Dã Lan had brought them contentment.

'Of course not, but it wasn't supposed to!'

Hoà still held her, her bots on Quỳnh's wrist aiding her grip. Quỳnh could feel her heartbeat now, the constriction in her lungs slowly easing, leaving her wrung out and with nothing left but raw vulnerability. Quỳnh breathed, feeling only hollowness and pain in her chest. She'd let go of the gun.

'Then why are you doing it?' Hoà asked.

For my ghosts. Because I almost died. Because I don't have a future.

'Because I have nothing else left! Because ...'

She stopped, then. Hoà was sitting cross-legged, supporting Quỳnh's head in her lap, her bots in Quỳnh's hair.

'You have me,' she said simply.

'I sent you away.'

'You did,' Hoà said. 'And I left, and that's on me.'

'I took away your choices. I lied to you.'

'You did.' Hoà was crying. 'And I didn't stand by you when I should have. I got scared and didn't do the right thing. I'm here, big sis. I'm here now. I'm holding you. Will you trust me? Will you trust *us*?'

Trust.

No, not trust.

Hope.

I can't. I don't deserve it. Not any of it.

Quỳnh was falling away in the darkness. She was desperately fixing *Guts of Sea*, with only rage and bitterness to fuel her. She was learning about Thanh Khuê's death, about Mother's death, about the fall of *The Azure Serpent*, running to the edges of the Empire. She was holding Đình Sơn's corpse. She was listening to *Moon* calling her Big Auntie and *knowing* that the only brightest future for her child lay in her not being part of it. She was holding Hoà's face in her hands like the most fragile of celadon cups, breathing in a happiness she didn't deserve and couldn't hold on to. Again and again, she had lost everything and everyone, because that was the way the world worked.

She remembered Hoà – Hoà, who saw so clearly, asking her, *How long are you going to keep hurting yourself?*

Did it make you happy, any of it?

Of course not. Of course it hadn't: it hadn't been meant to. Of course things would never change.

And yet ... She thought of Nhăng and her disillusioned, one-sided love, expecting something Tuyết wasn't capable of giving him; of Minh, and how she'd tried to leave her mother's orbit instead of shrivelling in the prefect's wake; of *Heart's Sorrow*, resigned to his fate but trying to build something that wouldn't belong to his parents; of Hoà and Thiên Dung, making a new life in the shadow of Thanh Khuê's death. Of being with *Moon* and Hoà and wishing things were different.

Wishes had never brought her anything – and the only differences she could control were the ones they made.

Trust.

Hope. A deep-seated desire for things to be different. An outstretched hand.

I trust more in the chance of a better future than in murder and lies.

She wanted to, so desperately.

'I'm scared,' she whispered.

'I know.' Hoà laughed, and Quỳnh felt the tremor of that laugh in her bones; felt the unsteadiness in Hoà's entire body. 'You want a secret? So am I.'

Quỳnh stared at the gun still clenched in her hands. It had stopped being a threat some time ago, but this hadn't been about Đức for a while, either – but about whether she chose to live. To think of herself and Hoà, rather than of her ghosts. Quỳnh took a deep, shaking breath – forced herself to unclench her hand, finger by finger.

'Together,' she said, and she felt the small hitch of relief in Hoà's breath.

'Together.'

Trust. Hope. Fragile, intangible things that might break at any time. The gun had cut grooves in her palm. Quỳnh held out her hand to Hoà, and felt Hoà's hand slip into hers as if it had always belonged there.

24

Mother and Daughter

The corridors were deserted, but there was a rumbling in them — a distant howling of pain that shook the compound, once, and then nothing else but an uncomfortable silence spreading to cover it all.

'Second Great-Aunt?' Minh asked.

The ship didn't answer her. Minh felt her, distant and focused on something entirely different.

Abruptly, she spoke. 'Child, don't—'

But it was too late, because Minh turned a corner of a corridor, and came face to face with Mother and Stepmother.

They were running — from what? And then Minh saw the other end of the corridor — what seemed like weird textures and shapes until she realised she'd seen them before. It was a fragment of a huge gash on a hull, a faded painting of apricot flowers, the sheen of metal in deep spaces — all preceded by a flood of bots, so numerous that they seemed a sea of shivering metal.

Flowers at the Gates.

'Second Great-Aunt?'

'Child. Leave, now.'

'What are you doing here?' Mother asked.

Mother looked ... wrong, and Minh realised it was because her topknot was slightly less than impeccable, her make-up infinitesimally smudged.

'Big sis!' Vân, in Stepmother's arms, bent towards Minh. 'Look, Mama, Big sis is here.'

Stepmother looked less than thrilled, and no wonder.

'Come,' Mother said. 'We're leaving. You can explain yourself later.'

Minh stared at the mass of bots blocking the corridor. They weren't moving, and she thought she knew why. Because she was there. Because Second Great-Aunt didn't want to hurt her.

'I want to know what's going on,' Minh said.

Mother grabbed her, gently and firmly.

'This is no time for selfishness,' she said. 'I thought you'd have learned your lesson, child.'

Minh never seemed to learn that lesson.

Minh breathed in, trying to remember the cold certainty she'd felt when she'd resigned from the civil service. 'What lesson was that? The value of family?'

'Respect,' Stepmother said sharply.

That was more than Minh could take.

'Tell me about family,' she said to Stepmother. 'Tell me why you thought poisoning me, and poisoning the ship, was a good idea.'

Mother's face turned, sharply, to Stepmother.

'The girl said something similar,' she said. Minh knew that face. It was the predator's face, the one that sensed a weakness. 'What is this about?'

'Did you know Minh withdrew from the state examinations?' Stepmother snapped.

'So you poisoned her?'

Mother's face was oddly still. Minh braced herself for something – unsure what – and realised it hadn't come.

'Move away, child,' *Flowers at the Gates* said to Minh on a private channel. 'It ends now. It has to end.'

'What are you going to do?'

A silence.

Then, 'You know.'

Blood for blood. A life for a life. Minh stared at Vân.

'No. My sister is here.'

'A sister your stepmother killed for.'

'She's a *child*,' Minh said. 'Your child. I get that you're angry.' She was buzzing with it herself – the rage she'd repressed for years and years, the one she could barely express in words. 'Don't do this. You can't be the matriarch if you commit murder. Whether it's Vân, or Mother.'

'You're trying to tell me what to do?'

Minh had forgotten how bad it was. How much hatred there was between Mother and Second Great-Aunt. That the person she remembered – the ship who'd laughed with her – was perhaps a lie, or in any case, since long gone.

'No. I can only tell you what I think. You know I can't prevent you from doing anything.'

She cut the comms, and came back to Mother and Stepmother arguing.

'You should have told me!' Mother said.

'You were busy,' Stepmother said. 'And they were children. It was easy enough to stop them.'

Them. *Heart's Sorrow*, Oanh's children, Minh. *Children*.

Mother's face still had that odd stillness about it.

'You had no right,' she said. 'I don't condone any of this, lil sis. It is unacceptable. I'm a prefect of the Belt, and there can be no poisoners in this house.'

Minh slowly, cautiously opened a comms channel – not

towards any of them or *Flowers at the Gates* — whose impatience she could feel mounting — but towards Vân.

'Hey, lil sis. Come down.'

Vân made a face. 'Mama says it's not safe.'

'It's safe here,' Minh said. 'Come on.'

Come on, come on.

Vân threw herself down, followed by her three bots — Stepmother tried to grab her, but Vân was too fast. Minh extended her arms ... but Mother was the one who scooped her up instead.

No.

Minh bit her lip. Somehow she had managed to make the situation worse.

'A creditable idea,' Mother said. She was still looking at Stepmother.

'Big sis,' Stepmother said, 'I did it for you.' She was almost pleading. 'Think of all you could have done, with the lineage. All you ever wanted. I love you.'

And maybe she did, but Mother ... Mother didn't really love. Minh looked at Mother, and at Vân who was trying to wriggle down, but Mother had her in an iron grip. She looked at Stepmother, and Minh could feel the fury rising in the air. Even weakened and diminished, and challenged by Second Great-Aunt, she could still make them all feel she was passing sentence.

'There is no place in this family for poisoners.'

'Big sis—' Stepmother said.

'You can throw yourself on the censor's mercy when she finally musters the troops to pursue us. She may be more generous than I am.' Mother turned to look at Minh. 'And you ... weak and clumsy child. You know you're ill suited to navigate the avenues of power. You know you need me.'

And it might have been true. No, it *was* true. Minh had

withdrawn from the civil service, and she didn't even have the skills to keep Second Great-Aunt at bay. She would never be as ruthless, as charming, as successful as Mother. Her little spate of rebellion had run its course – what was she thinking, imagining she could change something? As if she could change anything. Mother had shaped her and would continue to shape her.

Shaped. Her.

Not just her.

Minh looked at Stepmother ... at Mother ... at Second Great-Aunt. She laughed.

'What's so funny?'

'Nothing,' Minh said. Laughter hurt. 'It's your house. Your compound. Your rules.'

'I'm so glad to see you acknowledge this. We might finally make something of you.'

'You made people small. Insignificant. Unworthy of being in your orbit. You made them crave recognition. Your recognition.'

Mother raised an eyebrow. 'Of course.'

'You taught us all.' Minh raised her hands, and the data she'd found – the data Vĩnh Trinh and Mặt Ly had given her – shimmered into existence in overlay, a bare blink before Mother wrenched it from her. 'You taught us that anything was worth doing for power. That bending the law didn't matter if it got you noticed. You taught us to be *cruel*. You think Stepmother crossed the line, but *you're* the one who made the line seem worthless. You're the one who taught us that no matter what crimes we committed, what laws we bent, it was all worth it, for the family's sake. For your sake.'

'Child!' Mother's face was ... annoyed.

Minh braced herself for anger, but then she saw it for what it was: Mother was badly rattled, and trying not to show it, and it felt as though the universe was shifting on a huge axis Minh didn't even know it had.

'We're the house you built, and it's rotten, Mother. There's no justice in the Belt. There's no justice in this family. And you think you can stop it short of murder? You're the reason I was poisoned.' Minh stared at the bots, at all of them, massed to take over. 'And you ... You'd harm a child just because you're angry? You'd throw away your chance to be accepted as the matriarch of this family for that? Nothing in the teachings of Master Khổng or his successors makes that acceptable, and you know it.'

'Filial piety ...' *Flowers at the Gates* whispered.

Minh was done with the lot of them. Filial piety was earned, not owed.

And, to Mother, 'Put my little sister down. Now.'

Mother stared at her. 'You don't know what you're doing, child.'

Her gaze was the one which made Minh feel small and unworthy – the one that made her back down, the way she'd backed down over the blue dress. And then she'd be forgiven, even though Mother knew she'd err again and again. Because Minh couldn't take care of herself. Because she was *weak*.

Nothing about that was true, unless Minh believed it to be true.

'Put her down,' Minh said.

She didn't move. Just crossed her arms over her chest and stared – and Mother stared back at her and something shifted in her gaze. She let go of Vân and stood up again, brushing dust from the bots on her arms.

'I always knew you were going to fail.' Mother's voice was dripping with disappointment. 'You're going to be eaten alive by the censor. One day you'll realise I was right about everything.'

Minh cringed, but Vân was already running towards her.

'Big sis!'

Minh lifted her, hugging her, breathing in the warmth and solidity of her – no matter that her arms were shaking with weakness.

Bots flowed forward, encircling Mother and Stepmother; Second Great-Aunt's anger trembled in the air. Mother lifted her chin, staring at them. She wasn't going to give anyone the satisfaction of hearing her beg. Of course not.

Minh kneeled, putting Vân on the floor but not letting go of her.

'Do you want to live in the house your niece has built?' she said, to *Flowers at the Gates*. 'The one built on cruelty and ruthlessness. The one where the only thing of worth is what you can grab for yourself? The one where you murder a child to get the power you think you deserve, and call it justice?'

The ship was all around them, her breath flowing in and out of the corridors, shaking the entire compound.

'I'm not her. I'm not.'

A silence.

Minh hugged Vân, and – spent, exhausted – said nothing. She wasn't in control of other people's decisions. All she could do was take care of herself, and it was already hard enough.

'Fine,' Second Great-Aunt said. A spike of something like ill humour ran through the metal floor. The bots bristled, but didn't move. 'You're not worth the effort, anyway.'

Minh let out the breath she'd been holding. 'Thank you,' she said.

'Hmmf,' Second Great-Aunt said.

Minh looked at Mother, and at Stepmother – the way Mother's make-up had smudged, the way Stepmother shook. The disappointment in Mother's face that should have hurt her like a stab to the heart – but it didn't. It was just a sad and small thing, one last barb that didn't have the power to wound any more.

I'm done, she thought, hugging Vân and focusing only on her slow, steady heartbeat – on herself: the deep-seated tiredness in her bones, the weary satisfaction as the adrenaline from the confrontation wore off.

It's over.

I'm free.

25

Hope

Hoà had expected the summons. Not just awaited it, but braced herself for it.

It was to the court room, not to the former prefect's compound – which was still in ruins from the party, after *Flowers at the Gates*' takeover, and the combination of panicking guests and fleeing militia trampling through corridors.

She hadn't expected it to be for both her and Quỳnh – and even less to be shown, when they arrived, into some kind of private office overlooking a garden overlay, where Tang Thuyền was having tea with an unfamiliar mindship.

'Children,' Tang Thuyền said.

The ship's avatar – fist-sized, so small as to be almost invisible – shifted, and Hoà saw that it was *Flowers at the Gates*, a much smaller and less threatening version than the monstrous avatar that had loomed over the reception room.

'Your Excellency. Elder aunt,' Hoà said.

The censor was staring straight at her. Seeing her. Knowing who she was. Hoà lowered her gaze, unsure of the mass of feelings roiling within her.

Quỳnh said nothing. She just bowed – elegant and graceful,

in spite of the fact she was standing and walking slowly and with the assistance of her bots, clustered on her legs and lining her hips, spine and shoulders.

Tang Thuyền watched them for a while. Then she sighed.

'You understand there won't be a trial,' she said.

'I didn't come to the compound for a trial,' Hoà said, squeezing Quỳnh's hand and feeling – through her own bots on Quỳnh's shoulders – Quỳnh's heartbeat accelerate.

'No,' Tang Thuyền said. 'You came for amnesty.'

'Amnesty implies she did something wrong,' Hoà said.

She raised her hand to touch her eye, half-expecting it to hurt again. It didn't, and it was oddly and subtly wrong. And she'd expected to be afraid of being noticed, of speaking up like this, and the fear was there, but it was just a ghost of what it had once been, like Thiên Hạnh's ghost in her thoughts.

'Lil sis!' Quỳnh said, scandalised.

'Quite the firebrand you're turning out to be.' Tang Thuyền sounded amused. 'The power structure of the Belt is in tatters, with both the prefect and the general disgraced for corruption and murder. I don't really know how we came to this juncture. Nor am I interested in looking in to it. We have far better things to do than inquire in to how a pair of corrupt officials were toppled.'

Flowers at the Gates radiated smugness.

'I can't rewrite the past,' Tang Thuyền said. 'But I can offer you the future you were denied.'

'Why?' Quỳnh asked. 'It's never mattered to anyone before.'

Hoà wasn't sure whether anyone else heard the anguish in her voice.

Hoà closed her eyes, trying not to cry.

'Consider it . . . a mark of gratitude,' Tang Thuyền said. 'For exposing what was going on. As I said – I'm not going to inquire too closely.'

She knew. She knew exactly what Quỳnh had done, and she was going to let it go.

'It's the riots, isn't it?' Hoà asked. 'You can't afford another one.'

It had taken days for order to be restored in the wake of Tuyết and her wife's flight. The Technologists' Ring was quiescent, and what had once been a military administration was swiftly replaced by a civilian one. Thiên Dung doubted it'd change anything. Hoà hoped it would.

Tang Thuyền frowned, but said nothing.

Flowers at the Gates said, 'I have a lot to take care of within my lineage. May I be excused?'

'Not yet,' Tang Thuyền said. And, in a conversational tone, 'You're also here because if either of you – or any of your friends – attempt anything like this ever again, I'll personally ship the people responsible to the First Planet for execution, and it will not be a merciful or a fast death. Are we clear?'

Her gaze raked from Hoà to Quỳnh, pinning them in place – as if she knew exactly where to find all of them, and in a way she did.

Hoà swallowed. She thought of *Guts of Sea* – who'd left on her quest to take down the Empire – and nodded. Tang Thuyền held her gaze, as if she knew exactly what Hoà was thinking.

'Good.' Tang Thuyền smiled, and it didn't quite reach her eyes.

Hoà said, 'Can I ask a question?'

'Yes?'

'About *The Fruit of Heart's Sorrow*. And Minh.'

'Ah.'

'They're the relatives of ... condemned officials.'

'Yes.' Tang Thuyền was silent for a while. 'The charge isn't one of sedition. It doesn't carry an order of extinction of the family line. Prefect Đức overreached.'

That was the first time Hoà truly believed that Dức was disgraced and all but gone: the simple and bald admission that she'd erred made by another official.

'I see,' she said. She thought of what it meant to lose their parents, and she didn't have a good answer.

'If you have no other questions, then allow me to offer my congratulations.'

It was a dismissal, and they took it as such.

Outside the tribunal, Quỳnh took Hoà's hand, feeling its warmth in hers. The realness of it. The thrum of the station in her belly, resonating through her bots, the smell of the skewers from the nearby food-seller's cart. She brought up her messages: the auth-token in them was her own, in Dã Lan's name.

'How does it feel?' Hoà asked.

Like wearing new clothes, ill-fitting and strange. Like a new breath after a constriction attack, burning her lungs.

'I'm not sure I can put it into words.'

Hoà squeezed her hand. 'It's all right. You don't have to.'

Quỳnh stared at the station. In overlay, she could see the censor's militia clearing out the debris in the Technologists' Ring. There had been few arrests, and a general cautious quiet descending over everything.

'Is she going to be fair, you think?'

'No,' Hoà said. 'But it'll be better than it was. That's the whole point, isn't it?'

'I guess.'

They walked back to the shop, where Thiên Dung was waiting for them.

'Thank you.' Quỳnh thought back to lying on the floor of the reception room, curled in on herself and struggling to breathe. 'Thank you for believing in me.'

Hoà smiled, and it was luminous. 'Oh, I have a very good idea of how you can express your gratitude, if you're agreeable.' She leaned over and kissed Quỳnh. For a moment Quỳnh forgot about the Belt, and everything that needed to be dealt with, and simply hung, weightless, breathing in Hoà's presence around her. Hoà withdrew, but remained a thumb-width's away from Quỳnh. 'And it involves quite a bit more than a kiss.'

'Don't fret,' Thiên Dung said.

Quỳnh grimaced. 'These pins are really annoying.'

She took a shaking breath. Her whole body felt stiff and out of sync, and she was very much aware that if not for the bots, she wouldn't be upright. Everywhere they held her – back, hips, spine – she felt ... not pain, but a sense of multiple pinpricks boxing her in.

'It's traditional.' Hoà frowned. 'There. The ceremony is about to start.'

'It's not *about to start*,' Thiên Dung said, picking up the golden dragon pins and putting them away in a box. She gave Hoà – who was wearing the matching phoenix ones, a scattering of bots in red and gold, and a red and gold five-panel dress – a critical look. 'You're late, but I suppose the guests can wait. It's not like the ceremony can proceed without the brides.'

'Elder aunt?' Minh was in the doorway, dressed in bridesmaid's finery of red and gold. 'What should we do with your ancestral altar? It's in your bedroom. Usually, for the presentation ...'

It should have been in the courtyard. Quỳnh thought of her dead, of how fragile the thread was between her and them. Of bringing them into the midst of a fraught ceremony.

'No. Keep it there. Hoà and I will visit it later.' She stared at Minh. 'Thank you for coming. And for agreeing to be my bridesmaid. I ...'

Minh laughed, and it had an edge. A privacy screen shimmered, encasing them.

'It's all right. It's going to take us a while to be honest with each other, isn't it?'

The fate of Minh's mother – currently in jail awaiting the Imperial Court's judgement – hung in the air between them. Minh broke the silence.

'She deserved it. Mother did.'

'But you didn't deserve to be used as a pawn,' Quỳnh said.

Minh bit her lip. Her bots quivered on her shoulders. 'No. But you were hardly the first.'

'I'm sorry,' Quỳnh said.

'And I'm sorry about what my family did to you and your family.' Minh said. 'Is this going to change anything, this exchange of apologies?'

Quỳnh bit her lip. Was it? Perhaps everything had already been said. She was about to say she didn't know, but she did. Trust. Hope. A future.

'Maybe it will. Maybe it won't. It's up to us, isn't it? To figure out what we want to do with the rest of our lives.'

'I don't know what I want to do with the rest of my life.' Minh rubbed the curve of her belly, in a gesture Quỳnh knew all too well. 'It's going to depend on what happens with this, isn't it?'

A grand gesture. One that broke with everything her mother and Quỳnh had been doing to her. Quỳnh appreciated the magnitude of it.

'It's not my place to judge or approve.'

'No.' Minh laughed. 'I did well, though.'

It wasn't a question. Quỳnh inclined her head, acknowledging it, as Minh dropped the privacy screen and left the room.

Since she was dealing with unfinished business ... Quỳnh brought up her messages again, stared at the comms-request she hadn't taken.

'Can you give me a moment?' she asked Thiên Dung and Hoà.

'Are you all right?' Hoà asked on a private channel.

Quỳnh sighed. 'Yes. But there's something I need to take care of.'

Hoà gave her a look. 'Don't kill anyone.'

It was a joke, but one with an edge.

Quỳnh shrugged.

'I'll go and keep *Moon* company.' Hoà gave her a quick peck on the cheeks. 'Don't be too long.'

Inside the tightest privacy screen she could devise, Quỳnh finally answered her comms.

It was *Guts of Sea*. The ship was on a background that was clearly fabricated: space, but the constellations were too regularly laid out in the sky, and the River of Stars too close and too well defined. Only on Old Earth would that kind of view make sense.

'Big sis,' Quỳnh said.

Guts of Sea inclined her body. 'It's good to see you.'

A silence, as they stared at each other.

Quỳnh said finally, 'You're going on, aren't you?'

Guts of Sea said finally, 'Remember when I told you we had something?'

Duyên. A bond between them.

'Yes,' Quỳnh said. 'We can still have that.'

Low, bitter laughter from *Guts of Sea*. 'We can't.'

'Because of what I did? Because I no longer want revenge on the Empire, and you still do?'

'That, and ...' A silence, from the mindship. 'And because of what I did. Because I hurt Hoà. Because I hurt you.'

Ah.

Quỳnh thought for a while.

'You sent Hoà back to me. In the prefect's compound.'

'Oh, lil sis.' The ship sounded ... not angry, which would have been easy to deal with. But sad. 'I know what I am. I'm bitterness and revenge, and I want to bring it all down. The officials and the army and the court. As you said – you're not me.'

'I'm not.' Quỳnh braced herself for something – she wasn't sure what. Anger, disappointment, reproaches.

But instead, *Guts of Sea* slowly spun in a pattern that was sadness and bitterness, and missed opportunities.

'Sometimes oaths of sworn sisterhood break apart, and it's just the way it is.'

Quỳnh felt something squeeze her chest. She fought an urge to give her reasons, to explain herself. She wasn't here for her own defence.

'I know it sounds trite, but sometimes it is for the best.'

Duyên. So entwined with each other, feeding off each other's anger and desire for revenge. *Guts of Sea* genuinely cared about Quỳnh, except that she'd also tried to mould Quỳnh into something she wasn't, and to drive her and Hoà apart. In the end, it hadn't been the best of relationships for either of them.

Another silence from *Guts of Sea*.

'Sometimes ...' she said finally. 'Sometimes we just end up believing in different things.'

Quỳnh said, 'I guess this is goodbye, then.'

Guts of Sea said, 'I don't blame you. We always said that you were getting your revenge, and you did. And we always knew that it might cost your life, and that it wasn't going to be enough for me. And it's not.' Her voice was carefully controlled, her entire body still, from fins to exhaust ports. 'So, yes, this is goodbye.' And, carefully, 'And my best wishes for the future.'

Quỳnh stared at herself. At the red dress with the gold embroidery, the boxes of gifts arrayed in the courtyard. She thought of Hoà, and Hoà's touch, and having tea in a pavilion – and growing old together.

'Yes.' She was surprised to feel not a sense of failure, but a deep sadness. 'Goodbye, my friend.'

She closed the comms, slowly and carefully, and rose, wincing at the pain in her chest.

Goodbye.

Just outside Quỳnh's compound there were two lines of people: Hoà, Thiên Dung, Aunt Vy, *Heart's Sorrow*, holding the trays of traditional gifts, covered in red cloth embossed with a double happiness symbol. And, on the side of Quỳnh's friends and family, Băng Tâm, Minh and her half-sister Vân, and *Moon*, the toddler vibrating with enthusiasm.

Quỳnh stood on the steps, overlooking them all.

'She's here! Big Auntie is here!'

'She's not your auntie,' Băng Tâm said patiently. 'We've been over this before.'

Moon spun. 'Mommy?' she said, slowly and carefully. Quỳnh's heart suddenly felt as though it was too small and too fragile for her chest.

'Let's get this moving,' Thiên Dung said, ignoring the stern look Aunt Vy gave her for failing to respect elder precedence. 'We're here bearing gifts for the bride's family. May we come in?'

'You've already come in,' Aunt Vy said.

Thiên Dung sighed. 'Yes, yes. We've talked about this. It's a small ceremony, and the bride doesn't have a whole lot of family. Please, elder aunt.'

Aunt Vy sighed. 'All right.'

Băng Tâm bowed. 'Come in,' he said. 'The bride is ready.'

The trays of gifts changed hands from Hoà's bridesmaids to Quỳnh's bridesmaids. Hoà climbed the steps, coming to hold Quỳnh's hand.

'Let's go,' she said, and Quỳnh had never heard sweeter words.

They walked into the compound side by side. It was no longer empty: Băng Tâm and *Moon* had decked it with red and gold, in vast sweeps of colour. The courtyard was a garden with a pavilion beneath the sweep of the smaller asteroids of the Belt – an overlay that rained peach flowers on them, swirling in an invisible breeze. In Quỳnh's bedroom, the altar was waiting – for Hoà to be formally introduced as her bride, just as she'd introduced herself earlier to Hoà's ancestors. To Thanh Khuê, at her forgotten grave.

The bots laid the gifts on the table, and the cloths were removed. Areca nuts and betel leaves, spouse's cake, pearls from deep spaces, tea, fruit of every kind from mango to rambutan to dragon fruit and star fruit ...

Family introductions were going on, spearheaded by Thiên Dung, and then by Băng Tâm. Quỳnh barely heard them. She was clinging to Hoà's hand, feeling Hoà's breath on the nape of her neck.

'It's real,' Hoà said. There was laughter in her voice.

It was. It wasn't going to go away. It wasn't going to break or be snatched from her. And yet ... And yet ...

Someone large and heavy butted against Quỳnh's legs.

'Mommy?' *Moon* said. 'Can I?'

Quỳnh stared at her. This relationship, too, was going to require time. She felt buoyed and fragile and at the mercy of things she couldn't control: things she'd desperately wished for and never had; things she didn't deserve.

'You deserve them all,' Hoà said, her lips gently nuzzling Quỳnh's neck.

'Mommy! Mommy!' *Moon* rubbed against Quỳnh's legs again.

'Of course.'

Quỳnh wasn't sure whether she was answering *Moon* or Hoà. She swept *Moon* up in her arms, feeling the heaviness of her in the perception filters, the solidity of Hoà's presence by her side, her own heartbeat getting faster and faster, warmth spreading through her entire body until she felt alight and buoyed by an unfamiliar feeling of happiness.

Much later — after the tea had been served, after they had pledged themselves to each other, after the meal — Hoà followed Quỳnh into the bedroom. Laughter drifted in from outside: Aunt Vy, recounting a particularly salacious anecdote to Băng Tâm, *Moon* giggling as she chased Vân's bots around the courtyard.

'Look what I can do with my bots,' Vân said.

'Pff, that's nothing. I can do an overlay, look ...'

Vân laughed, and *Moon* laughed with her, and that was the last Hoà heard before Quỳnh raised a privacy screen, with a raised eyebrow.

'Are we going to do something the children would disapprove of?'

'Not yet,' Quỳnh said, and she was smiling. 'Come.'

The bedroom remained stark, with no furniture but the bed, and the altar that was little more than an unadorned table.

Quỳnh knelt in front of it, and Hoà followed suit.

'Mother,' Quỳnh said. 'Teacher. Husband. Here is my bride, Thiên Hoà.'

Names shimmered, above the table. Hoà felt Thiên Hạnh's mem-implants stir within her, a ghost within her own mind.

'I'm honoured,' Hoà said, bowing.

She waited, for a while longer, thinking of the dead, and how they were always with them – of ancestors taken from them too soon, of war and its wake.

They rose, slowly, facing each other. Quỳnh tipped Hoà's chin up.

'Lil sis.' Her eyes were dark and glistening.

Hoà reached out, running a hand along the side of Quỳnh's face.

'Big sis,' she breathed, her bots moving from her fingers to Quỳnh's cheeks and neck. 'It's done.'

She thought of the future. Of moving between vastly different worlds, among the scholars and the technologists both. Of being Quỳnh's wife, *Moon*'s mother. The woman who'd gone to face Censor Tang Thuyền and brought down Prefect Đức.

She'd done the right thing: she'd stood up and taken a side. And she was still here. Still alive. Staring at the future she'd helped secure, and knowing that it was theirs.

'I see you,' Quỳnh whispered, and bent to kiss Hoà. 'I see you, lil sis.'

Yes. *Yes.*

'I'm standing with you always,' Hoà breathed, and bent to kiss Quỳnh, again and again.

Minh found *Heart's Sorrow* on the first floor of the compound, staring down from the gallery that ran around the entire courtyard. It was late, and the celebration was winding down.

'Your younger sister?' *Heart's Sorrow* asked.

Vân had fallen asleep in one of the chairs, while protesting she didn't want to. *Moon*, Quỳnh's daughter, had gone quiet as well.

'All taken care of.' Minh sat, feeling something within her shift, like ten thousand bubbles in her womb. 'How are you?'

A spin that was a shrug, his bots mimicking the movement.

'As well as can be. I hadn't really expected to become the head of the family quite so soon. On the positive side, I'm not going anywhere anytime soon.' He laughed. 'You?'

Minh sighed. 'Second Great-Aunt isn't happy.'

Heart's Sorrow pointed at Minh's womb. 'About the mindship?'

'About most things,' Minh said. But after Mother, standing up to Second Great-Aunt had felt almost anticlimactic. 'Your mothers?'

Heart's Sorrow sighed. 'Second Mother left me a message. She's resourceful. I expect they'll evade the militia and hole up somewhere.'

'How do you feel about that?'

'I don't know. What do they deserve?' He spun disconsolately. 'What do *we* deserve, after what our families did?'

Min said, gently, carefully, 'Sometimes we don't get what we deserve. That's not always a bad thing. And you've been through hell.'

'Not as much as you have.'

'It's not a competition.' Minh breathed out. It felt odd, to be pregnant. Her entire body was starting to shift out of balance, her spine curving to bear the weight that was still mostly invisible. Minh watched Quỳnh and Hoà, kissing each other at the entrance to the bedroom. 'What do you think?'

'About the wedding? That's hardly my place to comment.'

'You came.'

'Yes. So did you.' His voice was sharp.

Minh thought of the conversation she'd had with Quỳnh.

'Yes. Because ...' She gestured towards the overlay of the Belt above them. 'Because everything has to start somewhere, I guess. Even forgiveness.' She wasn't sure whether she meant forgiving Quỳnh, or forgiving herself, or both. 'I'm glad you're staying.'

'I'm glad you are, too.' *Heart's Sorrow* laughed. 'At least we won't have to sneak out for the Tiger Games, but it's going to be a boring year if we have to spend it in the dignitaries' booths.'

Minh grinned. 'You say we won't have to. Doesn't mean we can't.'

'I'm surprised you're even suggesting it.'

'It's changed,' Minh said, with a confidence she was surprised to feel. She rubbed her belly again – more bubbles, the mindship within shifting and tumbling. 'Everything has changed.' She looked at the Belt spread out above and below them.

'Hope,' *Heart's Sorrow* said. 'That's what we have, isn't it? Hope for a different future than the one mapped out for us.'

'Hope.' Minh turned the word over and over in her mouth, feeling the texture of it. 'Yes, you're right.'

The unfolding of possibilities, of choices, the bitter cost of gaining control of their own lives. The weight of the mindship in her womb.

'Hope,' she whispered, and the word was uncertain and welcome at the same time.

Acknowledgements

Many thanks to my editor Gillian Redfearn and everyone at Gollancz who worked on this book, my agent John Berlyne, and my cover artist Alyssa Winans.

To my friends for their help with this book, and their support: Stephanie Burgis, Max Gladstone, Sheila Perry, Marissa Lingen, Dario Ciriello, Fran Wilde, Kate Elliott, Likhain, Dev Agarwal, Zen Cho, Vida Cruz, D Franklin, Kayden Johnson, Liz Bourke, Charlotte Cuffe, Claire Blandin-Goulard, Jean-Michel Deruty, Florie Fauché.

To my kids, for being delightful and supportive.

I would also like to thank Dr Nguyễn Tô Lan for her very kind help with Sino-Vietnamese.

Credits

Aliette de Bodard and Gollancz would like to thank everyone at Orion who worked on the publication of A *Fire Born of Exile*.

Agent
John Berlyne

Editorial
Gillian Redfearn
Bethan Morgan
Claire Ormsby-Potter

Copy-editor
Steve O'Gorman

Proofreader
Andy Ryan

Audio
Paul Stark
Jake Alderson
Georgina Cutler

Editorial Management
Jane Hughes
Charlie Panayiotou
Tamara Morriss
Claire Boyle

Contracts
Dan Heron
Ellie Bowker

Design
Nick Shah
Tómas Almeida
Joanna Ridley
Helen Ewing
Rachael Lancaster

Finance
Nick Gibson
Jasdip Nandra
Elizabeth Beaumont
Ibukun Ademefun

Inventory
Jo Jacobs
Dan Stevens

Marketing
Lucy Cameron

Production
Paul Hussey

Publicity
Jenna Petts

Sales
Jen Wilson
Victoria Laws
Esther Waters
Frances Doyle
Ben Goddard
Jack Hallam
Anna Egelstaff

Operations
Sharon Willis
Jo Jacobs

Rights
Flora McMichael
Ayesha Kinley
Nathan Kehel